Lucky
Chance
Cowboy

TERI ANNE STANLEY

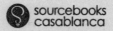

sourcebooks
casablanca

Published by Sourcebooks Casablanca, an imprint of Sourcebooks
P.O. Box 4410, Naperville, Illinois 60567-4410
(630) 961-3900
sourcebooks.com

Printed and bound in the United States of America.
OPM 10 9 8 7 6 5 4 3 2 1

For Homer, the best boy dog we ever had.

Prologue

Early last summer

"THIS IS GONNA HAVE TO BE GOOD ENOUGH," MARCUS Talbott said as he gently slid his 1980 Camaro into the shade between a dumpster and an ancient tree out behind the Big Chance Dairy Queen.

"Are we...hiding?" Jake Williams looked around at the nearly deserted parking lot.

"Of course not. We're just making sure my baby doesn't get scratched by any tumbleweeds rolling down Main Street."

"They don't have...um...rolling woods..." Jake rubbed the still-pink scar that peeked from beneath his short hair as he searched for the right words. "I mean...damn."

"Tumbleweeds," Marcus supplied. "I don't know if they have 'em here or not. I'm just messin' with you. I wanted to park in the shade so we don't bake when we get back in."

Jake rolled his eyes. "It's...June. It's...Texas."

"I know. These seats are genuine Detroit pleather. They're not built to withstand this kind of abuse. I'm gonna protect 'em as much as I can." He gestured to the side. "Be careful when you open the door, you don't hit that tree."

It took Jake a few moments to unfold his long legs from the front seat and bring himself to his full height, and it took Marcus even longer to unkink his rebuilt spine and convince his legs to support him for the fifty-foot walk around to the front of the restaurant.

A huge, undulating part of him wanted to stay in the car and just drive the last fifteen minutes to their destination, but Marcus knew if he didn't walk around now and get some stretching in, he'd look like an invalid when they got to Adam's.

"You coming?" Jake was already at the side of the building by the time Marcus convinced his right leg to move in the right direction.

"Hold your horses, Slick," Marcus said. "They won't run out of ice cream."

Just as Marcus was used to helping Jake find the words that had been shaken out of his brain by that bomb blast in Afghanistan last year, Jake was used to seeing Marcus force himself to unwind from the twisted wreck his body had become after being blown to high heaven.

Adam, the friend they'd followed into a hellhole nest of insurgents, the soldier in charge of clearing the room and keeping them safe, didn't need to see the effects of the improvised explosive device his dog had missed. What Adam needed to see was how well Marcus and Jake were recovering from a bloody *accident*.

And they *were* recovering. Would Jake ever see the inside of a Humvee again? No freaking way. His wires were too scrambled from his traumatic brain injury. He got confused easily and had trouble finding his way around, but he was steadier by the day, and his language skills were coming back. Marcus, however, had every intention of returning to his unit, to redeploy as soon as his docs cleared him.

In the meantime, he'd finish rehabbing himself in the

lush paradise of Big Chance, Texas. Starting with a foot-long chili dog and a Butterfinger Blizzard. Once he had something in his stomach, he could take his next dose of Percocet and start to feel more human.

He followed Jake into the semi-air-conditioned restaurant, and they studied the menu board while they waited for the teenager behind the counter to look up from his cell phone. The front door chimed as someone else came in.

The kid continued to ignore his customers.

"What kind of bull hockey is this?" A thin, gravelly voice rose behind Marcus. "This ain't no way to run a food joint. We oughta grab one of them ice cream cakes and run."

"And you think I'll bail you out after Sheriff Chance comes to arrest you?"

Marcus turned to see a woman with hair as multicolored as the tattoos that covered her arms smiling as the older man scowled. A smattering of piercings—ears, eyebrow, nose—accentuated her fine features, and the oversize *Big Chance Feed and Seed* T-shirt didn't disguise some appealing curves. She shot Marcus a glance, and her shining blue eyes widened as she took him in, lingering over his shoulders and chest.

He tried not to flex, but was glad that he'd kept up with all that strength training as part of his back rehab.

"Kids these days don't respect their elders," the older man grumbled to Marcus.

"Well, then you shouldn't share your ice-cream heist plans out loud," Marcus said, smiling at the woman. "Sets a bad example."

She twisted an earring and blushed, looking away. "What are you going to get, Granddad?"

"Heartburn, probably," he answered as another voice interrupted, impatient and nasal.

"Can I *help* you?" The teenager stood behind the counter with his hands on his hips as though he'd been waiting *ages* for someone to come in for food.

When it was her turn to order, Emma Collins-Stern couldn't focus on the menu to save her life. Between Granddad grumbling and the cute guy, there wasn't much room for food on her mental horizon. Who was he? She was pretty sure she'd never seen him, or his friend, in town before.

"Come on, girl. Tell 'em what you want," Granddad urged. "I'm not getting any younger here."

"I'll have the same thing," she told the kid at the register, figuring she could eat just about anything at the moment.

The two men, who'd taken seats at a booth by the front door, were a study in contrasts. The one who'd spoken to Granddad—the hot one—was about her age, she thought—close to thirty. He was Black, his thick hair tightly twisted into coils that would someday become dreadlocks.

His friend was White, younger and thinner, and seemed fragile, though both men had seemingly effortless perfect posture—a military bearing. Her guy—*her guy, sheesh*—was almost solicitous of the thin man, standing back and holding his drink while he waited for him to choose a side. Were they a couple?

That would be disappointing. Wait. *Where did that come from? You see a good-looking guy in a Dairy Queen and fall in love in ten seconds?* Well, she'd fallen for Todd in Dairy Queen, hadn't she? And Todd had been gone for a long time. Maybe—

"Emma." Granddad's impatient voice cut through her reverie. She refocused to see the cashier scratching his chin in puzzlement.

"Oh for Chrissakes," Granddad muttered. "I told him I'd have whatever you're getting. You told him you'd have what I'm having. One of us needs to pick something."

"Oh. Umm... I'll have a cheeseburger and onion rings. And a Coke. And a butterscotch sundae."

"You're buying," Granddad said.

"I kinda figured," she told him. She always bought—especially since she'd taken over Granddad's day-to-day finances a few years ago. Once it became clear he wasn't going to remember whether he'd paid the electric bill once, twice, or not at all, he'd given her his checkbook for good.

"I want hot fudge instead of butterscotch," he told the cashier, who nodded.

Emma fished her debit card from her pocket, but the teenager waved it away, saying, "That guy paid for your lunch."

"Oh." So maybe they weren't a couple. She turned, expecting to see him looking at her with some sort of expectant leer. Instead, he was scooting over to permit Granddad to sit next to him.

Well, heck. Any guy who could welcome her cranky, absentminded grandfather into his world was okay with her. Emma loved Granddad, owed him everything, and was determined to take care of him for the rest of his life, but *whew*. Dementia was exhausting.

As she filled her drink cup and got one ready for Granddad, it occurred to her that this was the first time since Todd died that she'd come into Dairy Queen and not felt the weight of her failures. Certainly it couldn't be all due to having a cute guy flirt with her, but something suggested that maybe, just maybe, it was time to move on.

She approached the table, prepared to sit next to the thinner guy, since Granddad was buddied up to her guy, holding him hostage with some sort of long, complicated story. Her guy was listening and fumbling with something in his lap.

"Thanks for buying our lunch," she said.

He looked up with a welcoming smile and said, "Hey, join us?" indicating the empty spot next to his friend with a flourish.

She was about to sit when an amber prescription bottle fell from her guy's pocket and rolled to a stop next to her foot.

She picked it up, unable to avoid reading the label. It was one she'd seen before, many times. Acetaminophen and oxycodone. Generic Percocet. A warning screamed inside her head.

"No thanks. We need to get our food to go."

Chapter 1

Late summer

"WHERE ARE WE GOING?" GRANDDAD ASKED EMMA FOR the fourth time in five minutes.

Emma rolled her eyes at the heat waves rising from the asphalt ahead of them. "We're going to the ranch."

"Why would we want to go there?"

"Damned if I know," she muttered, twisting an earring with the hand that wasn't on the steering wheel of her dusty Honda. She had a sock drawer she could be organizing. Instead, she was running blindfolded into a herd of cats— clueless about how she was supposed to help and about to trip over a few tails.

"What did you say?"

"I've got to go to a board of directors meeting," she said louder.

"Huh?"

"Board of—"

"I know what you said. What are you directing?" he asked.

"I'm not directing anything. Adam is. Remember? He's starting a group to rehabilitate rescued dogs."

"Why would he want to do that? You and your brother sure have some goofy ideas."

"You might be right," she said half-sincerely. She *did*

believe it was a great idea for her brother to work with dogs. It was a less great idea to think she had any business sitting on the board of directors of a nonprofit organization. She knew exactly bupkes about how charity groups were supposed to work, and between her job and caring for Granddad, she was hardly in a position to provide life support to the barely breathing Big Chance Dog Rescue.

"What's Adam gonna do with a bunch of dogs nobody else wants?" Granddad asked.

Emma eased the death grip she had on her earring and transferred her hand back to the steering wheel. "Assistance dogs. You know, service animals."

"Like Seeing Eye dogs?"

"Yes. Except not so much for the visually impaired."

"Why you can't just say 'blind' is beyond me," Granddad grumbled. "Gotta use four words when one would do. And trying to *rehabilitate* an old dog is too complicated. Seems like it'd be easier to get Labs or shepherds from breeders than to fix some rejected mutt." Granddad was qualified to suggest the best dogs as he'd spent most of his life training police dogs. But there was more to Adam's project than training dogs.

"The end result isn't the whole point. The dogs are going to people who think *they're* rejects. He's going to help other veterans who are having trouble since getting out of the military. If they can work with a dog who was once abandoned and considered useless, they can form a team and be better together."

Granddad snorted. "Pass the Kleenex and cue the shivering mutt. You sound like a damned late-night TV commercial."

Emma grinned. That was the response she'd expected.

Not an ounce of sentimentality in his body—at least none he'd admit to. Except she remembered all the times he'd listened to her pour out her teenaged heartbreak over what this girl said or what that boy did, wiped her tears, then offered to feed the offender to the dogs, even though it might give them indigestion. He cared; he just didn't say it in so many words.

"That's like your brother, charging off to save the world without asking for help from someone who knows what they're talking about," Granddad complained. "I don't remember being consulted about this."

Emma smiled. Granddad might complain and grumble the whole time, but his gruff exterior hid a generous heart, which was what had made Archelaus Collins the best K-9 breeder-trainer in Texas, back in the day. Law enforcement entities from all over the state—even out of state—came to him for dogs, and there were rumors that he'd done secret training with the military.

"I'm sure your help would be appreciated. Adam's been really busy getting things off the ground." *And he's talked to you about it a dozen times; you just don't remember.*

Granddad's memory was getting worse by the day, and he was confused by the simplest things, causing him immense frustration. The doctor had suggested Emma and Adam might want to start looking for long-term care, but Emma was determined to keep him living with her for as long as possible. It was the right thing to do, especially after she'd screwed up so much in her life, but the time was fast approaching, no matter how hard she tried to ignore it.

Granddad was following the conversation for the time being and asked, "What's your job gonna be?"

"I'm not sure yet." There wasn't much she had time for, between her regular job and looking after Granddad. Adam had asked her to participate, though, and she couldn't say no, especially since he'd helped her stay afloat when Todd was still alive and they were drowning in debt. If only Adam's money had been enough. Except it wasn't the money. If *Emma* had been enough...

She shook her head. Today was about the future, doing better—*being* better—and anything she could do to help Adam get his dream off the ground.

"You gonna bring a dog home tonight?" Granddad asked.

"Nope."

"Why not? You're the one who knows the most about training dogs to behave and do tricks. Adam can get 'em to behave and find bombs and bad guys, but you're better at the fancy stuff. When you show Adam's friends what you can teach a dog, they'll all be eating out of your hand."

Emma's heart stuttered at the thought of bringing home a dog to train—she still wasn't ready to be responsible for a dog again—and at the thought of doing anything in front of Adam's friends—one friend in particular. "I don't think we can handle a dog right now, Granddad. It takes a lot of time to housebreak a new dog."

"So?"

"So, I work at the Feed and Seed almost constantly. It wouldn't be fair to the dog to stay caged up all the time."

"Hogwash. You might be too busy, but I've got nothing to do but take it outside and let it back in."

He was right. Even if he wasn't available to take a dog out regularly, she worked about ten feet from her own front door, so she could do it. It was more about her heart not being ready for a dog. Not just yet. To end the argument, she said, "We'll have to find the right dog. Be patient."

"*Hmph.* Why do you keep fiddling with your ear?" Granddad asked now. "You nervous about being a fancyschmancy board director for the Heroes of Has-Been Hounds?"

Emma jerked her hand back to the steering wheel so fast she nearly de-lobed herself. "I'm not nervous."

There was no reason to be keyed up just because she'd soon see Marcus Talbott. She barely even knew the man. He was just another soldier, and even though Adam seemed to trust him, Marcus's good looks, sense of humor, and friendliness were more like warning flags than positive attributes. Ever since she'd first run into him in that Dairy Queen the day he'd rolled into town, she'd known this one was trouble and tried to avoid him as much as possible.

Todd's been gone a long time, her hormones pointed out. *And this Marcus guy isn't Todd.*

Don't go there today, she told her hormones. *There's too much to do in the* now *to be mucking through the past.* "Hey, we're here." Adam's newly painted mailbox gleamed white, in contrast to the dying, brown late-summer foliage. A small sign hanging below the mailbox read "Welcome to Big Chance Dog Rescue."

"I remember this place!" Granddad announced, a happy surprise in his voice as the lane opened into the farmyard. "Your grandma and I are thinking about moving here when we get married."

"Oh." Emma was caught off guard by the shift in Granddad's reality. He usually knew Emma was his granddaughter, but didn't always remember that Grandma had been gone since before Emma was born.

Emma parked next to the small barn they'd always called the horse shed—even though it had never held a horse— which was slowly being converted into a bunkhouse. Granddad was out of the car before she had the key out of the ignition. She grabbed her bag from the back seat and got out, then bent to check herself out in the side-view mirror.

What was she doing? She didn't give a crap if her hair looked like...crap. It was supposed to be a mess anyway. The tinted lip balm she ran across her mouth was only to keep the Texas sun from frying off a layer of skin (and to give her non-purse-carrying hand something to do besides twist her earring while she didn't look to see if Marcus was anywhere nearby).

"You look fine," Lizzie said, making Emma jump.

"Don't creep up on me like that!" Emma laughed around her surprise.

"Who're you?" Granddad asked.

"I'm Lizzie, remember? Emma's friend from school. And I'm Adam's girlfriend."

"Don't try to pull that shit on me. Adam's in the war." Granddad turned to Emma, his forehead creased. "I want to go home." He turned and tried to reopen the car door.

"Come on, Granddad, we're here for a meeting," Emma coaxed. "It won't take long."

"I don't care. I'm not staying out here. Too many bad memories."

Oh no.

Lizzie shot Emma a worried glance, moving around to Granddad's side of the car. Not only did he have time shifts, but sometimes he got scared or worried about random things, and often there was no way to help him settle down.

"Do you want to go inside and watch *Jeopardy* on Adam's big TV while we have the meeting?" Lizzie asked, giving him a tug to try to get him moving.

"No." But then he looked up toward the house and his demeanor changed. "Well, lookie there!" He almost cooed and shuffled toward the house.

Lizzie's rescued pit bull, Loretta, sat on the top step of the front porch, four of her half-grown pups lined up politely next to her. "Aren't you sweet little things." Granddad reached to pat one on the head. The pup—Emma thought its name might be Reba—leaned her head into the caress, licking Granddad's wrist to urge him to continue.

"I'll take this one. She can sleep with me," he said, lifting the young dog into his arms with surprising vigor since Loretta's pups were not tiny.

"Why don't you take her inside with you to watch TV?" Emma suggested, holding the front door and ushering Granddad inside. Hopefully, he'd forget that he wanted a puppy before they had to leave for home.

"I'll go tell Adam you're here and get Mr. Collins a drink," Lizzie said as they entered the living room. She disappeared down the hall.

What appeared to be a giant, black seat cushion in the recliner morphed into a lot of dog panting a long-tongued welcome to the newcomers.

"You. Get down," Emma said.

D-Day, Adam's oversize Great Dane/woolly mammoth mix, tilted his head as though he didn't quite understand what Emma was telling him, but then lumbered down and padded off in search of ear scratches. Emma was so distracted by Granddad—getting him and the dog settled, finding *Jeopardy*—that she almost forgot to be nervous.

At least until she heard a deep, rich voice behind her say, "Well, if it isn't the world-famous Mr. Collins! How you doin', sir?"

Emma's stomach flipped as she straightened and turned to see that while Marcus's words might be addressed to her grandfather, his gaze had been squarely fixed on the vicinity of her backside. And he wasn't even sorry, because when she glared at him, he grinned, toothpaste-ad smile gleaming in his chiseled, deep brown face.

Granddad, oblivious to Emma's discomfort, said, "Are you that Mark fella that Adam wrote home about? What are you doing here? You're not AWOL, are you?"

Without missing a beat, Marcus said, "Yep, I'm Marcus, and no, I'm not AWOL. I got hurt a few months back. I guess Adam didn't remember to let you know about that, huh."

"No, I guess not. He's busy fighting them terrorists, you know."

"He's good at that," Marcus said, nodding.

Emma was always amazed at how smoothly Marcus dealt with Granddad. Even she fell out of step when Granddad had an obvious time slip, and she was with him more than anyone. Marcus, however, just rode the conversational wave with him, as though it was all smooth sailing.

"What happened to ya?" Granddad asked.

"I had a run-in with a bomb. No big deal, but a few of my vertebrae got knocked out of whack, so they want me to lay up here for a few more months. It's a free vacation, so I figured, why not?"

Emma felt her lips compress and eyed him skeptically. The man had no shame. He was in perfect shape. Any injury he'd suffered had to have long since healed. As far as she was concerned, he was taking advantage of the army's medical leave and prescription pain medication with his "vacation." She shifted uncomfortably. Granted, it had been a while since she'd seen him with that pill bottle in the Dairy Queen. And yeah, given what had happened with Todd, she was paranoid. Adam really liked Marcus, and their friend Jake seemed to count on him for a lot of support. She didn't know for sure whether Marcus was still using opiates.

"When are you going back, then?" Granddad asked.

Marcus nodded. "A few more weeks. I can't leave the rest of my guys alone out in that desert—no telling what problems they'll cause without me to keep 'em in line."

"You'll have to cut your hair, you know," Granddad said, wagging a finger.

Marcus tugged at his tiny locs and smiled. "That'll be a shame, won't it? The ladies love them." He turned his attention and raised an eyebrow. "Hey there, Emma. How *you* doin'?"

"I'm fine," she answered, hoping to inject chilly disinterest into her voice. Maybe if she could convince him she was a frosty ice queen, he'd stop being so flirty. Then she could convince herself she didn't like the way he made her insides warm up when he smiled at her.

"I'm good, too." Marcus took a step in her direction, one hand around the harness attached to Patton, his mobility support dog-in-training. In spite of his obvious physical perfection—nearly six feet, two-hundred pounds of muscle—Marcus was doing a decent job of leaning on the dog to reinforce Patton's purpose.

"Hiya, Patton," Emma said to the big golden retriever, squatting down to the dog's level.

Patton glanced at Marcus, then—ears lowered and eyes averted as though he already knew he was in trouble—broke ranks and stepped forward to nuzzle Emma's pocket for the treats he knew she always carried. Oops—not good to tempt the service dog. With a guilty wince, she looked up to see Marcus teeter slightly. A slight tightening of the skin around his eyes was all she saw before he simultaneously caught himself from falling and firmly corrected the dog.

"I'm sorry, Patton," Emma told the dog, who looked both ashamed of his lapse and desperate for her attention. She rose, digging in her pocket. "You can have this later." Without thinking, she held the treats out for Marcus to take. It was too late to pull her hand away before he cupped his palm around her fingers, and she couldn't help giving him a shocked glance at the hot tingle the contact sent through her. In that moment, she couldn't have released that Milk-Bone for anything.

"Oh good. You're here," Adam said, coming into the room and breaking the spell. "We need to get started. There's a lot to talk about."

Marcus shoved a fist full of dog biscuits into his pocket, hopefully camouflaging the effect Emma had on his anatomy.

How freaking inappropriate was he, sporting wood over one little square inch of skin-to-skin contact with a woman who seemed determined to dislike him? She didn't even look his way when she passed by, arms held tight to her sides. He let her pass, then turned to follow her to the kitchen.

He gasped as a muscle spasm gripped his lower spine. Emma turned to glare at him, and he winked so she wouldn't see the truth of his agony, but he probably needn't have worried. She no doubt thought he was watching her perfect backside sway in front of him.

And honestly, the view *did* distract him, at least a little. Emma Collins, with her spiky blue hair and creamy skin, intricate watercolor tattoos and chunky piercings, was an intriguing mix of delicate and dangerous. She was slender and strong—inside and out.

And completely off-limits. If Adam had any idea what Marcus was thinking about his little sister, Marcus would be homeless in Houston before he knew what hit him.

"You comin', Talbott?" Adam's head appeared around the kitchen doorway. "Beer?"

"Yeah, thanks." Marcus accepted the bottle, then gritted his teeth and took another few steps. Maybe he shouldn't have pushed himself to try dead lifts yet. But Christ—it was only a hundred pounds. His grandma could do that.

With Patton's help, Marcus made it into the kitchen, where he took up position against a wall. Between the dog's support and the drywall, he could fake being well long enough for the Percocet he'd dug from his pocket to take effect.

He slid two tablets into his mouth and swallowed before realizing he was chasing drugs with beer, then mentally shrugged, knowing he'd be okay if he switched to water after this one drink.

"Sit down and have some chili?" Adam indicated the pot simmering on the stove.

"Not right now," Marcus said, needing to stand until his meds kicked in.

The tiny kitchen was filled to the brim as everyone else filed past to load their bowls and find a seat at the scarred oak table.

A couple of minutes later, everyone else was settled, and Marcus instructed Patton to sit and eased into the seat next to Adam. Adam was one of his two best friends in the world. They'd somehow survived long enough to find themselves on the same elite insurgent-sweeping team in Afghanistan. Marcus had been the lead enlisted member of the team. Adam had been the dog handler—not technically in charge but always out front, taking responsibility for everyone's safety. On the other side of Marcus was Jake Williams, the young West Point-educated lieutenant, with both a heart and a brain the size of Texas.

One night, a bomb had dismantled the entire team. Nearly everyone had been hurt, some worse than others. Two team members, one human and Adam's dog, had died. Jake had suffered a traumatic brain injury, leaving him in a coma for weeks. He'd made huge strides in his recovery, though he still suffered memory loss, headaches, and confusion at times.

Adam had lost not only his dog but his self-respect. It was only by coming home to Big Chance and reconnecting with Lizzie Vanhook that he'd been able to let go of his guilt and find a new purpose in life—helping other veterans help themselves through rescuing and rehabilitating abandoned and abused dogs.

Lizzie sat on Adam's left, smiling as she watched her man shuffle papers nervously.

And there was Emma, across from Marcus, doing her damnedest not to look in his direction but laughing at a comment Adam made. Marcus felt a pang, missing his own family in Kentucky.

Someone slid a folder into Marcus's hands. He opened it. "Wow. An agenda?"

Adam hooked a thumb at Lizzie. "Her idea, since I don't know what I'm doing here."

Lizzie rolled her eyes. "Yes you do. I'm just here to help you stay on task."

"Thank God you've done this stuff before," Emma said. "We're clueless."

"Well." Lizzie clicked a pen and slid a piece of paper from the pile in front of her. "I don't know much about animal rescue groups, but I do know how to set up a nonprofit. I volunteered to help you get started, but after that, you're on your own."

"Thank you, Lizzie," Jake said between bites of chili. He was highly focused on his food but also polite as hell, in spite of his reluctance to interact with most people.

"I guess we'll call this meeting of Big Chance Dog Rescue to order," Adam said.

Lizzie whispered, "Don't forget to have someone keep minutes."

Adam sighed and looked around the table.

Emma exhaled dramatically. "I suppose I get to be secretary."

"Since you offered," Adam said, passing her a pad of paper. When she raised it as though to thwack him upside the head, he added, "Because you're the only one with legible handwriting."

"Okay, give me a minute to get the basics down here…" She held up a slender hand and bit her bottom lip, concentrating while she wrote on the pad. For someone with such an edgy vibe, she was clearly determined to get everything organized and right—careful. Marcus could have sat there watching her all night.

Adam cleared his throat before speaking. "Here's the rundown. Financially, we're…" He waggled his hand in a so-so gesture. "We're gonna need money, but we've got enough to feed the dogs right now. Still, there's a lot to do to get this party rolling, and I need as much help as I can get."

He took a deep breath. "And we need to get our facilities in better shape. We're almost functional now. The barn has enough kennel area and training space, and the horse shed will function as a bunkhouse, but none of it's pretty. Jake, I'm nominating you director of facilities management, and all of us are here to lend a hand."

Jake nodded. Without looking up from the chili he scraped up, he said, "My dad will be…p-proud of his janitor son."

"That's not—" Adam started to protest, but then Jake looked up, wearing that crooked grin he so rarely put on these days.

Marcus smiled, too. If Jake found pleasure in the idea of sticking it to his parents, then more power to him.

There was bad blood between Jake and his family. If Marcus's own parents were high achievers, Jake's were sitting on top of the mountain, pushing off everyone else who came close. Jake's parents had been thrilled when their son entered West Point and then graduated with honors. They were less supportive now. His brain injury seemed to have made him an embarrassment and an exile. Jake took it all in stride, however.

"I'll second your nomination to muckety-muck of muck," Marcus offered.

Everyone did the "aye" thing, and Adam went on. "Then we've got to let people know we exist. That means a web presence, social media, networking with other dog rescue and training groups, and so on. Emma, I'm nominating you to be in charge of communications."

"Well, since I've already got the pen and paper, I guess I'll be executive board secretary *and* vice president of communications? My résumé runneth over."

Adam's head came up. "You job hunting?"

If Marcus hadn't spent so much time watching Emma these last few weeks, he might not have recognized the regret passing through her eyes, especially since she masked it so quickly and said, "Are you kidding? I love my job. I'll probably still be slinging nails at the Feed and Seed when I'm ninety."

Adam only *hmphed*. "I've got a schedule for our first group of dogs. We've got Patton there to be our poster boy"—Adam hitched a thumb at the dog sitting next to Marcus—"but we need to hit the ground running and show the public what we can do so we can build on this. We can't just sit here hoping the perfect dogs show up on our doorstep. To this end, I'll be going out to shelters in the nearby counties over the next few weeks and checking out likely candidates. Meanwhile, let's keep working with Patton, Loretta and her kids, and D-Day."

Hearing his name, Patton shifted but held his position. Thank God. For a minute back there, when Emma confronted him with a dog biscuit, Marcus thought he was going to fall on his ass. After tweaking whatever muscle he'd pulled working out yesterday, that would have likely set him back on his plans to return to action.

The doctors said he had a chance, and Marcus was determined to take it—where there was a will, there was a way, and he had will by the bucketful—which was why he refused to admit any doubts.

"Loretta's doing really well," Lizzie said. "She comes with me to work most days and even comes out from under the desk to greet people sometimes."

This was frankly amazing. After the abuse—followed by neglect—that Loretta had suffered at the hands of a dog-fighting scumbag, it was a wonder she trusted anyone at all.

"Now we just have to get her kids to behave," Lizzie added, raising an eyebrow at Adam, who, in turn, stared at Emma.

She raised her hands and shook her head. "I can't. Not now."

Adam started to speak, then apparently saw the same thing Marcus did—a tinge of desperation.

Weird. She was so good with everyone's dogs. Why didn't she have her own?

"Well, we sure appreciate all the help you can give us," Adam finally said before moving on.

There was some discussion of basic training for new dogs and continuing education for the dogs already at the ranch, and then Adam said, "Anyone need anything else?"

Yeah. A job. Marcus cleared his throat to ask what he could do until he went back to active duty, but Emma beat him into the space with her own question. "Are you bringing in veterans soon?"

Adam shook his head. "Not for a few months yet. We've got a few applicants already, but—"

Marcus half listened, because he wouldn't be here long enough to become involved. And hell, he wasn't much help at the moment anyway. Although his back was almost completely healed, he was kind of afraid to swing a hammer or anything else not strictly part of his rehab routine, in case he strained anything. His medical review board was only a few weeks away, and he couldn't jeopardize his chances of getting back to combat. *Still.* Being idle—and useless— rankled. He shifted, grateful to feel his meds kicking in.

A crash sounded from the living room, and everyone's head swiveled in that direction. Emma was out of her seat and sprinting out of the kitchen before Marcus's brain caught up. The front door slammed as everyone else sped after her. Everyone but Marcus, whose first few steps were slow and stiff. By the time his slow ass made it to the front porch, everything was over but the shouting. Unfortunately, the shouting was pretty ugly.

"Listen, you control freak," Granddad hollered at Emma, who stood with arms outstretched toward the dog Granddad clasped against his bent frame. "You don't get to tell me what I can and can't have."

"But, Granddad, we don't have a yard. We can't take care of a puppy right now…" Her voice trailed off when she realized she had an audience, and she scanned the group for support.

Adam stepped up. "Granddad, you can come out here anytime you want to hang with the dogs."

"Bull hockey," he spat out. "You wouldn't come to town to get me unless the world was on fire." He pointed a gnarled finger at Emma. "She's too busy at that dead-end job to bring me here. Hell, she's got me in adult day care, for Chrissakes."

"Bright Days is an adult day *club*," Emma said, though the way her nose wrinkled suggested she knew that was a bullshit response.

"I don't care what you call it, and I want a dog. It'll keep me company at that lame old folks *club*."

"Granddad..."

Since the pain meds were kicking in, Marcus's brain had detached from his mouth, which opened. "I have an idea. What if I bring the puppies to town to visit you at the day club?" The flash of gratitude that flitted over Emma's face was worth a million times the healthy dose of skepticism that followed.

Chapter 2

BOOM! ANOTHER DEAD ZOMBIE, A LUCKY SHOT. DARK *hallway...footsteps...* Marcus squinted, trying to find the next attacker before it found him.

"Okay, I'm off."

"Huh?" Marcus looked up, startled by the voice coming from behind him.

Adam said, "I'm heading toward Austin to check out some shelter dogs. Do you need anythi—Never mind, I forgot you're going into town."

He was? He needed to get a prescription refilled, but couldn't do that until tomorrow, so...no. "I'm good. Thanks anyway. Have a good trip."

"Okay. Jake's behind the kennels, working on that obstacle course. He'll probably be there until dinner if you don't remind him to have lunch, all right?"

"Yep." Marcus waved Adam off and switched the TV from video game to CNN. He was getting his ass kicked anyway.

After what could have been five minutes or five hours later, Marcus turned off the TV and sat up. He hadn't registered anything the newscasters had been saying.

Dogs barked in the distance, where the kennels had runs behind the barns. Jake was already out there, right? The man had trouble remembering which way to turn to get from the kitchen to the living room, but he found his way to those dogs and worked his ass off with them. Marcus would have gone to watch, but it seemed like a hella long way to walk just to stand around doing nothing.

Like the high-pitched hum from a newly awakened housefly, the ache that lived in Marcus's hip buzzed up his back and into his shoulders. He stretched his neck, wondering if he was coming down with something. The sustained warm weather here in Texas seemed to encourage a hell of a lot of cold germs to take up residence in his system.

Marcus shook his head. He didn't begrudge Jake his physical health. They'd both been blown to bits on that last deployment. It was just that Jake's blown-up bits slowed down his brain, while Marcus's mobility was the problem. Marcus's body would get better, but some of Jake's cognitive issues might be permanent. Still, it rankled that Jake contributed to the upkeep of the ranch, while Marcus was little more than a lawn ornament most days.

His phone vibrated with an incoming call, which he sent to voicemail. It was his sister's best friend, Maya, and he couldn't deal with her drama at the moment. Last time he'd been home, there had been a lot of wine and some stupidity, and Maya just didn't get that Marcus might be an okay choice for a twenty-four-hour hookup, but his long-term prospects included lengthy deployments and no followthrough. He'd thought Maya understood the score when he told her he couldn't get with her again, but the way she kept calling had him doubting himself.

Emma came to mind, with the vulnerability she tried to hide behind snark and distance. Yeah, it wasn't just his body that needed some rehab, it was his libido, because he needed to stay the hell away from his sister's friends and friends' sisters. He should get out his virtual little black book and see who else was in the greater boondocks area.

Problem was, Emma was the only one he thought about these days.

A twinge along his spine reminded him it was med time.

"Come on, Patton," Marcus said to the big golden retriever.

Patton popped to his feet and stood still until Marcus grabbed the harness handle. The dog braced to help Marcus to his feet.

He dragged his useless ass to the foot of the staircase in the old farmhouse, berating himself for taking the upstairs bedroom and leaving the couch for Jake, but with every step he forced himself to take, his battered body was a little bit closer to full rehabilitation. He'd been placed on the TDRL— temporary disability retirement list—and he'd been working his ass off to get in shape. When he was green-lighted by the medical evaluation board—and he *would* be approved, that was the only option—he'd get back to his Ranger unit, back to the men who'd stayed to fight when the rest of them were shipped to Germany on a medical transport.

After he was released from the hospital, Marcus had tried to stay at work for a while, at a desk job. It had been okay for a few weeks, because he was able to stay near Jake, who'd needed someone to give a damn about him while he was still in the hospital. But Marcus wasn't quite focused enough to hang with the office crew. He couldn't stay on his feet long enough to go back to combat and couldn't sit still in a chair long enough to do desk work. The army gave him the option to medically retire or go on the TDRL. No way would he retire—he was only twenty-nine.

Although right now he felt about ninety-two.

That pill container in his top dresser drawer seemed sixty miles away, but he wasn't going to get there by wishing, and there was no one else here to get it for him.

"Okay."

Patton glanced up, then apparently convinced Marcus was ready, started to climb the stairs.

Marcus followed, muttering curses the entire way. He was stronger—he knew he was. He'd worked the muscles around his once-broken bones until he collapsed, then gotten up and done it again. The nerves and blood vessels, however, were slower to cooperate.

In the meantime, he needed his pain meds so he could get on with his day.

He had the nagging feeling he was supposed to be doing something, but that restless discontent often came on days after an especially hard workout. He'd really busted his ass yesterday and was still tired and groggy today. Probably should tweak his post-workout protein drink a little.

Once he'd taken his meds, he'd chill for a while and then figure out what was next. He opened the drawer, took out the compartment labeled "Tuesday," and shook out today's chemical relief.

Marcus stared at the pair of tablets in his palm. He should have four more for today—two for this morning, two for before bed.

He must have miscounted. *Oh well.* He'd be fine later, he told himself, just needed to get through the now. He grabbed for his water bottle, knocking over the nearly empty beer can he'd brought up last night. *Crap.* He pulled off his T-shirt and used it to mop up the dregs of alcohol.

He tossed the pills into his mouth, chasing them down with a long gulp of cool water.

It would take a while for the meds to kick in, so he lay down to wait for the magic to happen. He liked to pretend he didn't enjoy the tendrils of warmth that seeped through his veins as the oxycodone dissolved into his bloodstream, sending soothing messages to his brain, easing his fears and making most everything seem doable. *Who was he kidding?* He loved the feeling, the floating.

The clock radio, a throwback to 1982, clicked as the minute tab flipped over. Fourteen hundred hours. Wasn't he supposed to do something this afternoon?

Wait. Fourteen hundred? Didn't Adam just leave? Wasn't it still early morning? Crap. He blinked. Were those pills his morning pills, or his evening ones?

Well, it was too late now. Might as well enjoy the ride. Maybe he'd sleep through until tomorrow. He could tough it out until then, if the meds wore off. Or not. He was due for a refill tomorrow anyway.

Whatever. He'd figure it out later. No big deal. It wasn't like he was hanging around at the convenience store down near the railroad tracks looking to score.

Patton jumped onto the bed and rested his big yellow head on his paws. He'd stay there until Marcus was ready to get moving again. He was a good dog. Marcus would miss him when the dog was passed on to a more deserving veteran, one whose damage was irreversible.

All the way down in Marcus's pants pocket, his cell phone vibrated. He ignored it.

"Dad-burned puppies are going to be as old as we are before they get here." Ms. Lucy Chance, retired bank president and matriarch of Big Chance, thumped her cane imperiously on the Bright Days Activity Center floor. "Today's dog day. You said there would be dogs."

"That was the plan," Emma agreed. "I'm really sor—"

"Well, you might want to rethink that plan," Ms. Lucy snapped.

Emma searched for a response that wouldn't get her banned from the center, but Granddad, in his own special way, beat her to it.

"Just 'cause you're old and dried up don't give you the right to act like a donkey's wingle-wangle," he snarled.

"Oh, bite me, you old coot," Ms. Lucy said, mandarin-orange lips pursed.

As a war of colorful insults broke out among the members of the Big Chance Senior Day Club, Emma checked her phone. *Nothing.* Damn that Marcus Talbott and his earnest eyes. And pretty smile. And big, shiny muscles. All joining forces to convince her that he'd bring those dogs into town on time, just like he'd said he would.

Well, she'd been covering for other people's screw-ups her whole life, so no reason to stop now. "I may have gotten the day confused. Could y'all excuse me for a moment?" She pulled up Marcus's number and slipped outside to the courtyard.

Straight to voicemail. The deep, rich voice on the message said, "Heyyyyy, this is Marcus. I'm otherwise occupied at the moment..." There was a pause, then a throaty chuckle. "You know what to do after the beep."

What Emma wanted to do after the beep was reach

through the phone and rip his irresponsible ass a new you-know-what. She should have known better than to count on him. She *did* know better. This was as much her own stupid fault as his. Instead of screaming, she used her big-girl voice and said, "Marcus, I hope everything's okay, and you're on your way to town with those puppies. The senior citizens are really excited." *Restless. Grumpy. Impatient.* "Please call me when you get this." She disconnected.

Maybe he was on his way, which would explain why he didn't answer. There were dead spots between the town of Big Chance and the ranch. A more likely reason she hadn't seen puppies today was because Marcus was up to his ears in bicep curls or on a zombie-killing Xbox rampage. Or curled up with a pain pill. She thought she'd seen him take something last night before the board meeting, but he'd seemed lucid enough, so maybe she was mistaken.

Unless he was lying bleeding and unconscious in a ditch between the ranch and here.

She was 99 percent certain Marcus, of the gotta-love-me smile and gotta-want-me muscles, had simply forgotten his promise. However, there was a 1 percent chance something bad had happened to him, as Emma's own nightmares regularly reminded her.

On the other side of the glass door, Ms. Lucy waved her arms and beckoned. Emma held up a finger—and not the one she wanted to put up—to ask for another minute. Then she dialed her brother's number.

This call went straight to voicemail, too. "You've reached Adam Collins at the Big Chance Rescue Ranch. Please leave a message."

"Adam, it's me. Where are you? Call me back. Please."

She considered calling Lizzie. But if Adam was with Lizzie and he'd ignored her call for a good reason, he'd think there was an emergency if she called them both.

Despite her best attempts to keep her imagination from going into hyperdrive, the nugget of dread, the one that had been living inside her gut for as long as she could remember, woke from a restless nap and told her to get to the ranch.

"I'm sorry," she said as she slid open the door and reentered the room. "I'm going to have to reschedule for next week."

"I knew it," Ms. Chance grumbled. "Young people are so unreliable."

"Not this one," Emma said between gritted teeth. "I'll have puppies here next week, come hell or high water."

"Famous last words."

"Shut it, you old flama-lama-ding-dong," Granddad said.

In spite of her growing unease, Emma smiled. One bright spot in Granddad's increasing dementia was the way he filled the blank spots in his vocabulary.

"I love you, Granddad," she said, kissing him on the cheek and gathering her purse.

"I love you, too, girl with funny hair," he said.

"I'll be back by five," Emma told Pam, the staff member at the front desk.

"No problem," the woman said. "We're here until six."

Emma jogged to her car because she had to satisfy the compulsive little bastard in her stomach that insisted she check anytime someone she cared about was AWOL.

And it really annoyed her that no matter how much good sense suggested otherwise, Marcus Talbott was one of those people.

Chapter 3

EMMA SLAMMED HER CAR DOOR, THE RESOUNDING ECHO bouncing around the deserted barnyard.

A few barks sounded from the other side of the barn, which was normal. Loretta's half-grown pups constantly stirred up things with the other dogs, but there were no humans in sight.

Adam, she remembered now, had gone to visit a couple of rescue shelters. Lizzie would be overseeing construction on her community park project at Mill Creek Farm, which was conveniently just over the hill, sharing a back fence with the ranch.

The pounding of a hammer told her Jake was working on the agility course near the kennels. It wouldn't be Marcus, she knew. The man rarely lifted a finger, much less lumber. She knew Marcus had been injured in the bomb blast that had killed Adam's dog and given Jake the traumatic brain injury, but he said he was healed now. Considering how much he worked out, he was more than healed. Maybe she should see if he was over there helping Jake, which would explain why he wasn't answering his phone. She didn't hear any voices that way, however, and she didn't imagine Marcus ever stopped yammering.

Eh. The house was closer. She stepped onto the front porch and knocked on the door of her childhood home. It was also the house where she'd spent her marriage, and where she'd fled from memories of the final few months with Todd. Still, other than the outlines, the house was barely recognizable as the place where she and Adam had done homework in the evenings after dog chores were done.

Adam had done a lot with the house when he'd first returned home, adding fresh paint and new shutters, and reconfiguring the porch. Jake had helped a lot, too. He didn't talk much, but he did like to work.

She wasn't sure what Marcus contributed, other than aesthetics. He was willing to pretend to need the mobility dog he was sort of helping to train, but Jake did most of the dog-care chores. Heaven forbid Marcus lift anything not specifically designed to increase the circumference of his biceps.

That they were exceptionally fine biceps annoyed the hell out of her, but then she'd always gone for the big strong guys.

Todd had been, as his friends described him, a fricking *beast*, and Emma had crushed on him from the moment Adam introduced her to his science-project partner a few days after they started school in Big Chance.

Emma had been a nerdy, shy kid. In elementary school, she chewed her cuticles raw and tried to pretend it didn't matter that Lizzie Vanhook was the only person in town who ever invited her to a birthday party. As a teenager, she hid her insecurity behind dyed-black hair and a smartass attitude. Somehow Todd, captain of the football team and homecoming king, had seen through Emma's mask and fallen in love with her.

Of course, Todd had worn two personalities, too—at least after he came home from the army. The good-natured man-about-town was available at a moment's notice to go out and party, but few people other than Emma saw the angry, distant, scared veteran who hid under a fog of drugs and alcohol.

So what was Marcus's facade covering? She told herself she had no interest in finding out.

And unless he was really back there helping Jake with construction, she wouldn't see him today, because no one had come to the door while she woolgathered.

Marcus's ridiculous vintage muscle car was parked in its usual spot next to the barn, but he could have gone with Adam.

She thought about calling again, but what would she say? "Hey, I stopped out at the ranch to make sure you weren't being held hostage by terrorists, but you're not here"?

No thank you.

She decided she'd say hi to Jake, then head home and fume until it was time to fetch Granddad from day care. Day *Club*.

A quick movement from the other side of the frosted glass next to the door made her pause. She saw it again…a flash of something light passing by.

And then she heard it. A light thump, followed by more movement. One of the dogs was inside, jumping up and down by the window.

"Hey, who's that?" Emma asked, squatting to look.

Another thump, and the flash—this time she realized it was a big, light-colored dog.

Adam's D-Day was black. Lizzie's dog, Loretta, was white, but would be in the kennels with her pups anyway. The only other option was Patton, Marcus's big golden retriever, who never barked. Like, ever.

He was also trained to never leave Marcus's side unless

he were dismissed—or if Marcus was injured and in need of help.

All the paranoid fantasies she'd ever had about bad things happening to her family squeezed Emma's heart and lungs.

"Marcus?" she called, pushing open the unlocked door and stepping into the dim interior of the house.

The dog stood panting and wagging at Emma.

There was no obnoxious eighties hair-band music blasting from the kitchen, no explosions and screams coming from the giant television and game console in the living room. No creaks and groans from an old house giving clues to the whereabouts of its inhabitants.

Patton wagged and nudged her with his head, so she petted him. "Good boy. What's going on? Where's Marcus?"

He turned and padded toward the stairs, stopping to make sure she paid attention. Was Marcus upstairs, somehow injured? The band around her chest tightened another notch. She followed Patton, but by the time she reached the top step, a thought occurred to her. What if Marcus wasn't alone? What if he'd exiled Patton because he had company?

It was quiet in the house, but maybe Marcus and his guest were snuggled down, enjoying some postcoital z's while everyone else was working their asses off.

Well, she was outside his door now, and she had to be sure he was safe.

On Patton's heels, she pushed open the door to her childhood bedroom and saw Marcus laid out flat on his back, feet crossed at the ankles, hands folded neatly on his hard stomach, eyes closed. He was sacked out so hard he didn't seem to be breathing.

But Marcus wasn't dead. He was living, breathing, and very warm, which she knew because she'd somehow made her way to his side.

The room smelled of spicy man and something she couldn't quite put her finger on…something dangerous.

Since he was sleeping and not winking, smiling, or flirting with her, she gave herself a moment to study him. He was beyond beautiful. His thick, black hair was twisted into little corkscrews that normally bounced and bobbed like an outward extension of his personality. Russet brown skin, large nose, square jaw, and soft-looking, sensual lips that seemed to smile, even in sleep.

Before she knew it, she'd reached out toward him, then stopped, feeling like a creeper.

"Hi."

"Oh crap!" She jerked her hand back, but not before Marcus took her slim wrist in his big hand.

"It's okay. I don't bite," he murmured, his gaze hooded. "Unless you ask me to."

A pool of heat formed low in Emma's belly, chasing away her reason for being there. "I didn't mean to wake you," she said, though she didn't even convince herself.

"I'm glad you did," he said softly, slowly tugging the hand he held. She didn't pull away, intoxicated by his scent, the heat in his eyes. When he tugged her hand again, she toppled onto his chest. To escape those half-mast eyes, she looked down at his full, luscious lips, which opened to say, "You can kiss me if you want."

She wanted. Oh, how she wanted as his hands spanned her waist, then traveled to her hips. There was something unreal about this moment that made her believe she *could* kiss him, that it would be a good, good thing to kiss this man.

No. That was not why she was here. As a matter of fact, she was supposed to be angry. The regretful sigh she let out as she righted herself was a little disturbing.

Gathering her wits, she said, "You blew me off. You were supposed to bring the puppies to town."

He didn't respond, and as she glanced back over at him, he let out a gusty snore.

Of all the—"Marcus, damn it, wake up!" That's when she saw the empty amber-colored prescription bottle on the nightstand, right next to a Bud Light can. That scent wasn't danger; it was beer.

Anger and fear chased each other through her body as she used both hands to jostle him awake.

Nothing but another snore. He was just talking to her. How much had he taken?

The pill bottle was empty, and so was the beer can. He was alive at the moment, but he might not be for long if she didn't get him some help.

She pulled her phone from her pocket and hit 9-1-1.

Busy.

Busy? What was wrong with this county?

She ran to the window, threw up the sash, and screamed for Jake, grateful he could finally find his way around the ranch without getting lost.

Then she tried Adam, praying hard to get a connection.

Chapter 4

"I'm not a drug addict, and I didn't OD." Marcus hoped he didn't sound as...*pleady* to everyone else as he did to himself. He was still a little fuzzy around the edges and not entirely certain his mask of confidence was in place. "Emma overreacted."

"I didn't say you're an addict or that you OD'd," the doctor said. "But you've got a problem if you can't remember how much medicine you've taken."

"Yeah, I could see how that could freak you out a little," Marcus agreed, trying a laugh that wasn't reciprocated by the doctor—or Adam or Jake, who were stone-faced sentries on opposite sides of the exam-room door.

"I'm sorry we busted in at the end of your workday, and I appreciate that you're seeing me unofficially, but it was a one-off mistake. I got distracted, forgot the time, and took my afternoon meds twice."

"Is that the first time you've done this?" the doctor asked.

"Definitely." *Damn*, did his nose just grow?

Adam narrowed his eyes, but mercifully, neither he nor Jake offered any commentary, even when Dr.—something Chance, naturally—glanced at each man with raised, questioning eyebrows.

"And I'll set up an alarm on my phone so it doesn't happen again," Marcus offered, though he suspected he should stop talking, lest he condemn himself further.

Dr. Chance's phone buzzed, and he looked down to see the message. He looked up and fixed his gaze on Marcus. "I'd like you to go to the hospital in Fredericksburg and talk to a friend of mine who works in behavioral health—"

"But—"

The doctor raised one hand to cut him off as his phone buzzed with another incoming message. "Hold that thought. I'll be right back."

The white coat disappeared, and the men were left in a small pocket of silence amid the beeps, footsteps, and muted conversations of the Big Chance Emergency Clinic.

"I don't need to check in anywhere," Marcus practically begged his friends. "I'll never get past the medical board if the army thinks I have a problem."

"*Do* you have a problem?" Adam asked, one eyebrow raised as though he already knew the answer and had passed judgment—not in Marcus's favor.

God, he wished he was sure about what had really happened and what was a crazy dream: sweet, sexy Emma turning into a panicked wreck, Jake's closed expression as he dragged Marcus to his feet and marched him to the car, this moment right now…all because he hadn't paid attention to his meds. *Again.*

"This is *not* a problem." *Not anymore.* He was serious about setting alarms, making charts, and color-coding the calendar if he had to. He'd track his meds until he didn't need them anymore.

"Listen," Adam said, running a hand through his hair, "I'm here to help. We all are." He waved to indicate Jake, but Marcus knew he was talking about everyone else who'd passed through the Big Chance Rescue Ranch in the past couple of months.

Adam had practically become the ambassador for veteran transition to civilization recently.

Marcus didn't need his help, though, because he was only a temporary civilian.

"Listen," Marcus said, "I appreciate your concern, but it would take a lot more than a couple extra Percocets to do me in."

"You still might...kill yourself."

Adam and Marcus both turned to look at Jake. The third member of their trio didn't talk much—his brain injury made it necessary to search harder for words when he wanted to communicate—but when he did say something, it was unfiltered.

"You saved me," Jake said, referring to the day Marcus helped Jake check out of the hospital before his parents could have him declared incompetent and sentence him to a life of monitored institutionalization. "I don't know if I can save you."

"I appreciate that, man," Marcus said, honestly touched. "But I'm good. I am."

He shifted uncomfortably on the bed, wanting to make a break for freedom—but unless he tucked his tail between his legs and went home to Kentucky, he had nowhere to go but back to the ranch.

Dr. Chance returned with a handful of papers. "Like I said. I think you should go to the hospital, but you're an adult. I can't force you to do anything."

Wow, these civilian doctors are different from the army docs. Chance continued, "I believe you're *dependent* on opiates. That's technically different than addiction, but dependency still means your body and brain need this drug. The line between is very fine and fragile."

He handed Marcus a couple of pamphlets and a sheet of paper with names of rehab clinics.

"Thank you, but I don't need these," Marcus said, though he took them to be polite.

"Like I said, you're an adult. But this shit is serious and sneaky, and addiction's middle name is denial."

"I hear you," he said, deciding then and there this was not going to be an issue ever again.

Following Adam and Jake out of the clinic, Marcus folded the "Am I an Addict?" pamphlet in with the rest of the papers and shoved them into a recycling can as they walked by.

"What are you doing, man?" Adam stopped at the can.

Before he could dig the papers out of the trash, Marcus raised a hand and said, "I'm done. I don't need it anymore."

"What do you mean?" Jake asked.

"I mean I quit. I'm out of pills anyway, I just won't get any more."

"But you're still having a lot of pain, aren't you?" Adam asked.

Marcus shook his head, anxious that Adam not have any reason to fall back into blaming himself for Marcus's problems. "Some days are a little rough, but I can get by with over-the-counter stuff from here on out." Besides, maybe if he had a clearer head, he'd be able to find some useful way to contribute to the ranch while he finished his physical rehab.

"The doc said you're dependent. You'll get sick if you quit cold turkey," Adam warned.

"It's not like I've been injecting heroin regularly. I'll be fine."

The text from Adam came as Emma arrived at Bright Days to fetch Granddad home for supper.

Adam: All okay, leaving clinic now.

Marcus was still alive and kicking.

A knot of tension she didn't know she was holding onto released and relief spread through her body.

She told herself her concern had been for the well-being of a fellow human, and for one of her brother's best friends, not because she personally cared that much about Marcus.

She couldn't. Marcus was too much like Todd for her comfort—another soldier, back from war with a bottle of pills—and history had shown her that she wasn't equipped to deal with that. She couldn't fix him, and she shouldn't try. She'd just screw it up. If she was stuck being attracted to guys who were charming, gung ho, and messed up? Well, too bad for her, even if it meant staying celibate and alone for the rest of her life.

Well, alone except for Granddad.

What would she do then? Become a crazy cat lady? She was really more of a dog person, but crazy dog ladying wasn't going to happen. No more men, no more dogs.

Pushing open the front door of the center, she spied Granddad in a nearby chair and walked over to him. "I'm back. Are you ready to go home and make dinner?"

Granddad ignored her and stared through the window at the empty street beyond.

She tapped his shoulder. "Granddad?" He continued to ignore her, somewhere else completely.

Now that she wasn't worried about Marcus, she was awash with fatigue. She almost envied Granddad's ability to disappear from the here and now.

Pam, who had been working on a jigsaw puzzle with another guest, rose and beckoned to Emma. "We have to talk."

Emma regarded the day-care coordinator with dismay. Those four words were never good. "What happened?" she asked, glancing at Granddad again.

"Come on over here." Pam led Emma to her desk, which was out of earshot but still in view of the guests.

Emma sorted through the possibilities and her stockpile of excuses and explanations.

"We had an...incident a few minutes ago. I would have called, but I knew you'd be here soon, and it didn't seem like something to discuss over the phone."

Emma's stomach knotted. This couldn't be good. "What happened?" she repeated.

"Your grandfather had an altercation with Mr. Brown, and it got physical."

The sorrowful yet resolute set to Pam's mouth told Emma that Granddad was the one who did the getting physical. "Is Mr. Brown okay?"

"Just a bruised ego, I think," Pam said. "I'm not sure what started it. They were watching *The Price is Right*, and all of a sudden your grandfather stood up and shoved Mr. Brown out of his chair."

"Oh my God." Emma twisted her earring, imagining how easily Mr. Brown, who was ninety and toothpick-thin, could have ended up with a broken hip, or worse. "I—I don't know what to say."

Pam patted Emma's other hand in a way that was supposed to be sympathetic, but felt condescending. "You know I love Archie, but I have a responsibility to the rest of the guests. I'm so sorry, but I'm afraid you're going to have to make other arrangements for him."

Emma's mind spun into panic. She wanted to argue, to rail at Pam, to convince her to give him another chance. He wasn't that bad. He had some really good days when he was his normal, crotchety self, helping everyone else with whatever they were doing. She was tempted say this was the first time Granddad tried to hurt someone, that she'd take him to see Dr. Chance and ask if a change of medication might settle him down. But this *wasn't* the first time Granddad had caused problems. He'd walked out more than once and gotten lost. He'd taken off his clothes and refused to put them back on one day when the first graders from Josiah Chance Elementary had come to make cookies with the guests.

This wasn't his third strike; it was more like his fifty-third. The fact was, she'd been afraid this was going to happen and already had a plan in place. *Sort of.*

She'd figure this out somehow. "I'm really sorry this happened," she told Pam. "Coming here was good for Granddad, but I understand."

"There's a new Alzheimer's unit opening at Golden Gardens over in Fredericksburg," Pam said, sliding a shiny brochure across the desk.

"I've heard about it. My brother brought it up, but it's expensive…and I really… I can take care of him better than some stranger." He hadn't let her and Adam be carted off to foster care; he'd taken them in. She owed him.

Pam didn't argue, but said, "They offer respite care. You could give it a trial run."

Tears pressed at the backs of Emma's eyes, and she fought them down, along with panic at the idea of abandoning this man who'd loved her so much, who'd taken in two kids when their parents died and raised them to the best of his ability, even while she struggled to imagine how she'd be able to take care of him if she couldn't bring him here while she worked.

"The folks at Golden Gardens know how to help people with dementia, to keep them comfortable and engaged as much as possible for as long as possible," Pam added.

"Thank you." Emma forced a smile and got to her feet. "Come on, Granddad," she said. "We need to get a move on if we're going to have supper before *Jeopardy* comes on."

The community center was only a block from the house Emma shared with her granddad, but it took longer than usual to get home. Granddad kept stopping to tell Emma a story about the people who'd lived in each house they passed.

These stories never failed to delight Emma. She adored the history that anchored Big Chance here in south central Texas and the connections between the residents and Granddad—and by extension, Emma and Adam. Even though they'd lived here since she was a kid, she still felt like an outsider at times.

Sometimes that was because she'd been a shy kid who

was, if not exactly bullied, then ignored by most of the other kids at school.

Except for Lizzie. Lizzie had been a loyal friend to Emma since she'd been assigned to show Emma around school her first week in Big Chance. Sometimes she'd wondered if she wasn't a burden to the more bubbly and popular Lizzie, but to her credit, Lizzie had never made Emma feel like she didn't want her around. Fortunately, as an adult, Emma was on more solid footing and trusted the friendship they had now that Lizzie was back in Big Chance for good.

"And here's where that couple from New York live," Granddad said, pointing at Emma's in-laws' modest home, which backed up to the little cottage where Emma and Granddad lived. "They run the Feed and Seed, you know," Granddad continued.

"You don't say." She knew this perfectly well. She'd been their employee since high school—first at the Dairy Queen, then at the Feed and Seed, even before she'd started dating their son.

"I was surprised they wanted to come out here and run a hardware store," Granddad went on.

"I heard Mr. Stern's uncle owns the Feed and Seed Company and wanted Mr. Stern to learn the ropes from the ground up. They came out here to run the franchise and liked the town so much they stayed," Emma said, reminding him of the story from almost thirty years ago.

Granddad harrumphed. "Too many troublemaking outsiders coming this way for my liking," he said. "Your brother's got a bunch of them out there on the ranch, that's for sure."

Emma was nearly dizzy from the speed with which Granddad buzzed through time. One minute he was somewhere fifty years ago, and then he was in the here and now.

"Why do you think Adam's friends are trouble?" she asked.

"Oh, you know." Granddad waved his hands around as though she should understand. "That quiet one... He makes me nervous."

"Why's that?" Emma asked. Jake was hardly what anyone would describe as trouble. He didn't talk much, that was for sure, though when he did, he usually spoke truths that no one else was ready to say. But trouble? Hardly.

"He's got some secrets he's keeping," Granddad said, nodding. "Now that other guy—what's his name? Martin?"

"Marcus."

"Yeah. He's okay, I guess."

Hardly, Emma thought, remembering the way she'd found him earlier that day. The memory of his hands on her sent an involuntary shiver down her spine.

"You should invite 'im over for dinner," Granddad said as they finally reached their own front porch.

"Granddad, I don't think all those guys will fit in our kitchen." She opened the door and looked in at the tiny two-maybe-three-person kitchen table.

"Hogwash," Granddad said. "I only mean that Marvin kid. You should call him right now. Invite him on over."

Oh sure. Invite a drug-addicted playboy over for dinner with her and her time-slipping granddad who had no filter. That's all she needed.

Emma helped Granddad settle into his recliner and turned on the television, then handed him the remote. "You're all the entertainment I can handle right now, Granddad."

Chapter 5

"WHAT DO YOU MEAN, YOU'VE GOT IT HANDLED?" ADAM was in the next room, but to Marcus, it felt as if he was standing a foot away with a bullhorn.

Marcus winced. He'd give Adam a you're-being-rude death-glare, a come-back-to-the-couch-and-play-this-video-game-with-me-and-Jake glare. Yep, he really would—as soon as the muscles in his neck decided to cooperate. *Damn.* He'd have to watch his form next time he did bench presses and stretch better afterward. Especially since, to make everyone happy, he'd flushed his drugs. Or rather, the prescription for his next refill, since he'd taken the last of his actual pills.

Or had he? Did he have a few left for emergencies in his shaving kit?

He didn't need them right this minute, but he *was* feeling pretty rough. He'd need relief soon. It wasn't that I-might-be-getting-a-muscle-spasm kind of pain that had gotten him in trouble, but *actual* pain, the kind the drugs were supposed to be for.

Yeah, you want to get yourself a piece of the Brooklyn Bridge while you're selling that bull? No more pills. A wave of nausea tried to take him under, and he breathed in slowly and deeply, and out—slowly and deeply.

"What's wrong?" Jake put his game controller down and stared at Marcus. "Are you going to barf again?"

"No." Puke avoidance was mind over matter. He'd learned that during high school football practice and carried it through boot camp and beyond—into weeks of physical therapy. "I ate something bad last night, but I think it's out of my system now."

Jake didn't have to say anything because Volume One of the *look* he gave Marcus said no one else was having trouble with last night's pizza.

And Marcus had only had one piece before he fell onto his bed and stared at the ceiling until his intestines revolted. He tried to convince Jake anyway. "I'm surprised you guys aren't sick, too."

Jake's *look*, Volume Two, said Marcus might want to think about why he *really* felt like shit today.

But he wasn't an addict, damn it, so he *wasn't* going through withdrawal. If he didn't have food poisoning, it was a touch of the flu.

"Just…go kill zombies," he told Jake, who shrugged— and the sonofabitch's shrugs had their own unspoken opinions. *Judgmental bastard.*

Adam's voice rose again, his words clanging inside Marcus's head. "Okay, but listen, Emma—" What was up with that? Adam idolized his sister. What could they be arguing about? "We're going to work it out. I promise." He walked into the living room and rubbed between his eyebrows with his thumb. "Okay. Let me know." He put the phone down and sighed.

"What's wrong?" Jake asked. Well, if he had to ask the same question, at least he was asking someone else.

"Granddad got kicked out of that day-care thing he was going to."

"Why?" Marcus asked, praying it wasn't because of his screw-up about forgetting to bring the puppies.

Adam frowned. "He pushed someone."

Marcus knew the old guy was a handful and wandered off sometimes, but he didn't mean any harm. "So they kicked him out?" That was bullshit.

"It's not the first time, and if he hurts someone…" Adam shook his head.

"So what's Emma gonna do while she's at work? Bring him out here? Hire someone to stay with him?"

"I can look after him in a pinch," Adam said, "but he can't be out here every day while we're all working. He'd get hurt. And we've kind of run out of people to stay with him. I think it's time for him to move into an Alzheimer's unit."

Marcus nodded. "That makes sense."

"To everyone except my sister. She still wants to keep him at home. She says she'll watch him while she's at work over video monitor. Apparently she's got the house rigged up with cameras and alarms set to go off if he tries to get out."

"But what if he tries to get out while she's mixing paint or something?"

"Oh, she's got some sort of GPS thing she'll hang on him, too, so she can't lose him." Adam's dry tone suggested he believed it would work about as much as he trusted Marcus in a room full of OxyContin.

Marcus smiled in spite of the pain twisting his insides. He did admire the woman and her take-charge ways. She probably had a contingency plan for everything.

"Granddad…is gonna get hit by a car," Jake offered.

"Dude. That's not helpful," Marcus told him.

"Sorry."

But Adam nodded. "You're right, Jake. She can't be everywhere at once. Granddad needs full-time care."

Marcus thought about offering to stay with Granddad himself—it wasn't like he was busy at the moment—but that would only be a temporary solution, and too many disruptions wouldn't be good for the old guy. "Why doesn't Emma want to get him in a nice nursing home?" Marcus asked.

"She says it costs too much."

"I thought you were okay after you sold Mill Creek Farm to the county for Lizzie's park."

Adam hesitated, then admitted, "It looks like it's gonna take more than I budgeted to get things up and running here."

Marcus felt a small measure of energy at Adam's words, because this might be something he could help with. "You know, I haven't been spending much since I've been here. I could definitely chip in."

Adam was already shaking his head before Jake added, "I've got money, too."

"No. I'm not taking your money."

"Don't be such a blockhead," Marcus said. "We can—"

"Who's a blockhead?" Lizzie walked in, tying her hair back as she spoke.

"Me. These clowns," Adam said, leaning to kiss her, even though they'd woken up together not an hour ago.

"I love you whatever shape your head is," she said, smiling. She turned to Jake. "Are you ready to walk dogs?" Jake nodded and rose. He and Lizzie walked all the dogs every morning before anyone started working with them. Not only did they need to get the dogs some exercise to burn off a little energy, but their regular trips around the ranch seemed to be helping Jake, who struggled to find his way around since his TBI.

Good, Marcus thought. Jake wouldn't be here to stare at him while he retched. Maybe Adam would go with Lizzie and Jake. Then Marcus could curl up in a ball on the couch until he felt better—or drag himself upstairs to search for that elusive last pain pill.

The gods knew better than to give him a break, however.

As soon as Lizzie and Jake were gone, Adam sat on the chair across from the couch and stared at Marcus.

Well, damn, son. Marcus had learned this game of wills at his parents' kitchen table. He stared back at Adam until it became clear he wouldn't buckle under the pressure of silence and beg for forgiveness, or whatever was expected. Instead, he said, "This is getting awkward. Either kiss me, or move along."

Adam cracked first, the side of his mouth twitching right before he laughed and looked away. But then he pinned Marcus with that master sergeant stare again and said, "What are you going to do with yourself?"

"Right now? I thought I'd work out a little, then get a shower."

Adam muttered a curse under his breath. "What are your plans? For the future?"

The weight of his family's disapproval rose from the past and tried to push Marcus into a defensive posture, but he said, "I'm going to keep rehabbing for the next couple weeks, then I'm going back to work."

"What if they don't find you fit?"

"They will." Marcus was positive. He'd held that belief in

his heart with each push-up every single day. Going back to his team was the only option, and if he let doubt get in and mess with him, he was screwed. "Listen, if I'm in your way, I'll take off."

"And go where?" Adam asked. "You know you're welcome to stay here as long as you want. As long as you're not going to overdose on me."

That again. Marcus's blood pressure rose. "It wasn't an overdose. And I told you—it was an accident. It's not going to happen again, because there are no more pills here. No more drugs. You can search my room."

"I'm not gonna do that." Adam rolled his eyes. "And you don't have to cut yourself off cold turkey. If you're in so much pain you need the stuff, use it."

"I don't," Marcus said, though his resolve was as weak as the half cup of coffee he'd managed to get down this morning.

"Your call. In the meantime…"

"In the meantime…sitting around here, looking pretty all day is getting to me," Marcus admitted.

"Do you need a change of scenery?"

Marcus worked to keep the disappointment from his face. In spite of his offer to leave, he didn't want to. He felt like deadweight here, but at home, he'd feel like moldering, festering, deadweight. "I—"

"I'm not going to kick you out," Adam said. "Just asking if being *here* is part of the problem."

Marcus wasn't big on true confessions, but he owed it to Adam to be honest. "I want to earn my keep," he said. "I need something to do. I'm getting stronger every day. Not sure I can bale hay yet, though."

Adam laughed, because the ranch didn't grow hay. "You're not a burden, but I *could* use your help."

Thank God. Old, medicated Marcus had wanted to contribute since he'd gotten to Big Chance, but always chickened out. New, drug-free Marcus was ready to be a fully functioning individual. "Whatever you need. Light yard work, cleaning kennels, painting..." It'd be good for his recovery to put his muscles to some gentle, practical use.

"I was thinking about something else. Jake's feelings might get hurt if I let anyone else cut the grass," Adam said. "He's already worried we're going to ship him off with Granddad."

"I won't fight about getting to do yard work," Marcus conceded.

"Yeah, and I worry this stuff with Granddad is going to be a trigger for him."

"He'll be all right." Marcus hoped his power of positive thinking was as effective for Jake as it was for himself. "In the meantime, what are you going to do about your grandfather?"

"I don't know," Adam said. "This is killing Emma. If anyone needs a change of scenery, it's her. I keep thinking she's ready to move on, but then..."

Marcus was missing something. "Moving on from your granddad?"

"I think Granddad's just an excuse. She's holding on to him because she lost Todd."

"Ah. The mysterious late husband." Of whom Marcus was suddenly, irrationally jealous.

"Not so mysterious. He was my best friend, back in high school," Adam said. "And he was a great guy. I was glad when he found Emma, and it sucked like hell when he died. I miss him, too. But he's been gone longer than they were together."

"So she's still grieving. That sucks." Now Marcus had more reason to keep his hands off the woman he couldn't stop thinking about.

"I can't fix Emma right now. What I can do is give you a job."

"Yeah? Let's hear it."

"We probably have to make this formal at a damned board meeting, but as self-appointed chairman of my own board, I nominate and second and say 'Aye.' You are now the Big Chance Rescue Ranch's vice president of bookkeeping and other computer shit."

Ah, hell. Anything but desk work. *Anything.* "Are you sure you don't need someone to shovel dog shit?"

"Hi, Emma, how's it going?" Linda Stern asked, bustling through the back door of the Feed and Seed and spilling an armful of grocery bags across the paint counter.

"Hey, Mrs. Stern," Emma said, smiling at her mother-in-law.

"When are you going to call me 'Linda'?" she asked.

"When you're not my boss, I guess." Emma just couldn't bring herself to call the woman by her given name. It wasn't that she didn't feel comfortable with her, it was just... Well, she was Emma's boss way before she'd become her mother-in-law, and she'd stayed her boss, while...

Mrs. Stern shook her head, knowing it was a lost cause, and asked, "What's new?"

"Not a darn thing." Emma was relieved that it was more or less true. The screen of her laptop assured her that Granddad was still watching his shows. He'd been restless the past few days, and she was beginning to think her brilliant plan to keep him at home might not work out. She looked at her mother-in-law's mountain of bags and asked, "Whatcha got there?"

"Decorations for Veterans Day." Mrs. Stern glanced up at the dozens of photos gracing the walls of the Big Chance Feed and Seed. They were all pictures of Todd and shared space with sports awards and commendations, a shrine to a dead son and lost love.

Between waiting on customers of the Feed and Seed, and now looking in on Granddad every five or ten minutes, added to working on media for the Big Chance Dog Rescue, Emma was busy enough that she hadn't looked up a lot lately. She did so now, fixing on High School Senior Todd and accepting the familiar surge of sadness and guilt.

"I think I'll put these streamers between his photos." Mrs. Stern held up a roll of blue and red crepe paper. "I think he'd like that, don't you?"

"I'm sure he would," Emma assured her mother-in-law, though she was almost certain Todd would have laughed and told his mom to find a hobby.

"Oh, and look at this!" Mrs. Stern unrolled a poster of a malicious-looking eagle holding a bedraggled poppy. "It looks just like your tattoo."

Emma glanced down at the unfinished tat sleeve partially covering her right arm. "You're right, it does."

"When are you going to get it finished?"

"One of these days."

"That's suitably vague." Mrs. Stern raised an eyebrow.

"I've just been busy lately." She'd been more than busy lately, actually. She was on the verge of overwhelmed, but wouldn't let the Sterns hear her complain about work.

And really—it was a great job. They paid her well enough and gave her free room and board in the little cottage she shared out back with Granddad. This job had not only sustained her physically, it forced her to develop people skills. Okay, so maybe not *skills*. More like, asking people what color paint they wanted without making a fool of herself skills. Granddad—when he was lucid—told her she was wasting her life here, but she had no intentions of leaving.

Anyway, if Mrs. Stern had said it once, she'd said a million times that she didn't know what she'd do without Emma. No way would Emma be able to sleep at night if she abandoned her in-laws, even if working in a shrine to her dead husband was less than ideal. She ran a hand over the unfinished tattoo. She couldn't get it finished, not yet. That would be like taking down Todd's photos—relegating him to the past.

Emma's right hand slid to the gold band on her left hand. The diamond engagement ring, the one Todd's grandmother had worn, was long gone. "Lost." At least that's what they'd told Todd's mom when she'd noticed it was missing. Emma had let Todd take it when their finances were bad, but had kept her wedding ring—it was only gold-plated and not worth pawning. Hot shame filled Emma at the memory. She could have fought to keep the engagement ring, told Todd's parents what was going on. They'd have stepped in, but she'd let pride and fear rule her actions.

"Oh darn," Mrs. Stern said, bringing Emma back to the present. "I've got a frame at home I want to use for this poster. I'm going to run over and grab it."

Emma waved goodbye as her phone rang. "Hi, Adam." She glanced at Granddad over CCTV.

"Hey. Did you get those hinges ordered?"

"Oh yeah," she said. "I've got them right here."

"Great. Someone will pick them up soon." Adam wouldn't do it himself, not if he could get someone else to come. His PTSD symptoms were better these days, but he still preferred to avoid town if at all possible.

"They're under the counter in a bag with your name on it," she said, wondering why he'd really called.

"Great." He paused, and the empty air seemed to be a great sucking void, which made sense when he said, "So, I've got some news."

Emma's heart stuttered. Anytime information was prefaced with "I've got some news," there was usually a "bad" in there somewhere.

"I've made arrangements for Granddad to get a week of respite care at Golden Gardens next week."

A mixture of unidentifiable feelings rendered Emma mute.

"Emma? You there?"

She sorted through her thoughts and found annoyance. How could he just up and make that kind of a decision? But she also recognized a dose of interest. She knew she should have already been looking into this place. And there was also a bit of shame—shame, because the biggest chunk of emotion was relief. Relief that someone else would take a turn with Granddad.

"Emma?" Adam repeated.

Finally, she choked out, "We can't afford it."

"I can pay for it, Emma," Adam said in a voice that reminded her he'd said it before.

"I don't want you to use ranch money for this," she insisted for the umpteenth time.

"We'll manage," Adam reassured her. "Marcus ran the numbers this morning, and we're in decent shape."

"Marcus. Ran the numbers."

"I hear a little skepticism there, Emma."

"Maybe a lot? Adam, you remember I found him barely breathing from an overdose a few days ago, right?"

"You're overstating things a little. Besides, he quit all that," Adam said with positive finality.

"Adam—" She stopped herself. She could explain that addicts promised a lot of things they might actually intend to follow through on, but then she'd have to tell him how she knew so much, and she couldn't do that. "I wish I had more to contribute."

If she hadn't allowed her own finances to get in such bad shape when Todd was alive, they might not be having this conversation.

There was a beat of silence, then Adam added a new line to their never-ending discussion. "If you wanted to make some extra money, you could take on some private dog training clients. I'm getting phone calls from the public."

The spark of pain that never quite faded focused a little sharper at Adam's words.

"I don't know," she said.

"You're good at it. You love dogs," Adam reminded her. "I still don't understand why you won't take one of the ranch dogs home with you."

Because I'm not ready. I might never be ready. "I don't know," she repeated. "I don't think a couple of private dog-training clients would bring enough."

"You could do a group class and make a lot more."

Emma was already shaking her head. "I don't think I can do that."

"Why not?"

"I don't do well with...people staring at me."

"Since when? You work in a hardware store. You're with people all the time."

"That's different. I'm not standing in front of them trying to make them believe I know what I'm talking about." *Or to convince them that their local war hero who died tragically was a lily-white angel.*

He laughed. "All you gotta do is *act* like you know what you're doing and remember you know more than they do."

"I don't know," she hedged.

"Well, think about it," he said. "In the meantime, we've got some possible funding opportunities."

"Like what?"

"There's a veterans' services convention in Houston next week. There are a few groups going that give out grants, and Lizzie thinks we're good candidates."

"That's great," Emma said, fearing where this conversation was heading.

"Since you'll be at loose ends next week without Granddad, I wonder if you'd like to get away for a few days and go to Houston?"

Chapter 6

Marcus hit the enter key, and waited for the last of his cost projections to appear in the spreadsheet he'd been filling.

Instead of a satisfying swoosh sound followed by a prompt to save his work, he got a flashing "Unexpected Error #87091020384755."

"Damn it!" He yanked at his hair. His locs had gotten fairly useful in his new job, because the pain from pulling them distracted him from the agony of sitting in this *stupid* chair at this *goddamned* desk, trying to enter Adam's chicken scrawls into this *fucking* computer program. He hit Control/alt/delete to see if a reboot would help.

"You okay?" Adam appeared in the doorway, a pile of papers in one hand.

Marcus thought about being honest, to admit he hated, hated, *hated* computer work, but knew he couldn't do anything else useful right now, like dig postholes or help their occasional part-time handyman Clint hang drywall in the horse shed-slash-bunkhouse. It had been four days since Marcus had ditched his pain meds, and every muscle in his body prickled with anguish. Whoever called this *getting clean* was batshit crazy. He felt like he was being burned alive. Instead of whining, he dug the crumpled list of dog-food prices from the trash, flattened it on the desk, and said, "I'm fine."

Adam raised a disbelieving eyebrow, but the chime of an incoming email saved Marcus from further questioning. Adam read his phone screen, typed a response, sent it off with a swoosh. "That Golden Gardens place has a spot for Granddad for a couple of weeks."

"What did Emma say?" Marcus asked.

"The usual. We can't afford it."

Jake walked in. "Are we broke?"

"Not quite," Adam assured him, but Marcus had seen the bills, had squeezed together enough money to cover Granddad's "vacation" to Golden Gardens, and he knew that they weren't quite teetering on the edge of collapse, but they were definitely wobbling on the outskirts of hard times.

"Something good will happen," Marcus said. "We just gotta keep putting one foot in front of the other."

"Thank you, Mr. Sunshine," Adam said, but his eye-roll held a smile.

The computer beeped, alerting Marcus that it had restarted, so he turned back to face it. "I'm going to smash this thing if it doesn't cooperate this time," Marcus told Patton, who ignored him, shifting with a sigh.

Adam's dog, D-Day, flopped down and started chewing on Patton's tail, which was tolerated with a half-assed sniff. A moment later, one of Loretta's puppies began to bark, and both big dogs raised their heads with interest.

Soon Loretta's whole pack was yapping at the window. Patton practically vibrated with the need to see what was happening.

Jake went to the front door. "Someone's here."

Adam, Marcus, Patton, D-Day, and Loretta's Country

Dog Jamboree joined Jake on the porch to watch a battered green SUV with Louisiana plates pull to a stop a few yards from the porch.

The sun glinted off the windshield and made it tough to tell exactly, but it looked like the driver and passenger were arguing, based on the gestures flying through the air.

A moment later, a middle-age woman got out of the driver's side, her round, pink face hopeful as she gazed up at the men on the porch. "Is this here the Last Chance rescue place?"

Adam hesitated. "Uh…"

"I'm Maureen Beauchamp," the lady said. "My boy Tanner's in the car. He don't want to get out, but I heard you could help him. He got burned real bad in Afghanistan, and between the pain and the way he looks…" She shook her head.

Adam glanced at Marcus and Jake, then said, "Well, ma'am, I'm not sure—"

"Listen. He came home and his fiancée dumped him, and he's afraid to talk to anyone else. Tanner's a good boy, but he won't hardly leave our mobile home unless I make him. I don't know what else to do." Tears spilled over her cheeks. "Can't you give him one of those dogs that's supposed to help? He don't have anything else to live for right now."

The Rescue Ranch was barely a real thing, but already the news had spread that there was a combat veteran living on the outskirts of Big Chance who trained dogs for other veterans. Adam's phone never stopped ringing, but this was the first time some desperate soul had shown up unannounced.

"Ma'am…" Adam's spine stiffened and he cleared his

throat. "I'd really like to help, but our dogs aren't ready to be service animals yet. I'll be glad to take your information and get your son on our waiting list..."

One of the pit bull pups—Marcus thought it might be Garth—clambered over the gate at the top of the porch stairs and went to sniff around the car. It was a sign of how discomfited Adam was that he didn't give a correction and make the half-grown dog get back in line with his siblings.

"Mama—" The young man in question had gotten out of the car and stood next to it. His face was shadowed by a ball cap, but the hand with which he held onto the top of the car was gnarled and shiny. Then he looked up. When Marcus saw the extent of the damage to the kid's face, his heart squeezed painfully. The kid regarded Marcus, then turned his stiff, scarred face to Adam. "I'm sorry sir. We shouldn't have come. We were, uh, out this way and got to talking, and—" He shook his head. "Sorry to disturb you."

Adam shot a desperate look at Marcus and Jake.

This, Marcus thought. This was what the ranch and these dogs were here to do. To help one another out. The absence of some mythical *readiness* was no excuse for turning away a man in need.

"Hey, kid," Marcus called, and the young man halted his return to the car. "You know anything about spreadsheets, and if not, are you willing to learn?"

"Kinda," Tanner said with a shrug that belied the spark of hope firing behind his eyes.

"Well, come on then." Marcus pointed his thumb over his shoulder at the house. "We've got a job for you."

"What did you just do?" Adam asked a few minutes later, shaking his head with a laugh.

"I think I fired myself and hired my replacement in the same breath," Marcus said.

"Well, that's probably okay," Adam told him, pulling a brochure from his pocket. "I've got something here you and that silver tongue might be better at than data entry."

"Thank God for small favors," Marcus muttered, then asked, "Does this new job come with a fancy title?"

"Yep. It's also gonna require a little travel."

Probably a good idea to get him out of Big Chance, Marcus thought. Before he invited *another* mouth they couldn't afford to feed to stay at the ranch.

Chapter 7

"Come on, Patton, I bet we can stir up a whole pot of trouble here," Marcus told his companion as they approached the Big Chance Feed and Seed. Patton didn't answer, but wagged agreeably and padded beside his trainer.

With a few more steps and a whoosh of automatic doors, the blazing Texas sun was replaced with dusty, cool air and the scent of paint thinner, corn, and leather. Marcus paused to blink and scan his surroundings, then proceeded carefully toward his objective. Why Adam thought he was the man for this mission was beyond him.

The store was bursting at the seams with everything from screws to Christmas decorations, but the thing that always struck him most was the number of images staring down from the walls, seeming to take Marcus's measure.

"I'll be right with you," Emma said, not looking up from her laptop.

Emma's late husband, Todd, however, *was* looking at him. Marcus knew who it was because he'd been here a couple of times over the past few months, but had the man always looked so…judgmental? Todd had been an all-American boy, a ginger-haired giant—here a football photo, there a basic training graduation picture, all meaning business. There was one with a smile—a damned wedding portrait. Was that really Emma in a long, white dress with flowers in her hair? She looked out from the past with a shy grin, so much more innocent than she seemed now.

Marcus preferred the now version of her, with the take-no-shit attitude that he was certain camouflaged a delicate, sensitive soul. He smiled as he watched her for a long moment while she tapped away on her keyboard and muttered under her breath. Whoever was on the other end of this heated argument should probably count their lucky stars that this was an imaginary battle of wits, because the woman looked *pissed*.

"Just another second," she said, still focused on her work.

He didn't mind waiting, since it gave him a chance to admire this week's hair—gradations of blue and green, short and silky smooth instead of choppy and spiky as usual. "Take your time."

She looked up. "Oh." The *It's you* was left unsaid. Then, "Hi, Patton," she said in a sweet doggy-talking voice.

The dog shifted anxiously, more than happy to get to the woman who always had a treat in her pocket and was willing to scratch where it itched. Patton was learning and managed to stay put, though he shot Marcus a look filled with reproach for not taking off his service vest before they came inside.

When Patton didn't break ranks and step toward her, Emma gave Marcus a grudging nod of approval.

"We're getting there," Marcus said, stroking Patton's ears. "I bet by the time I'm cleared to return to duty, he'll be set to take on a disabled vet full-time."

Emma's one be-ringed eyebrow raise was enough to suggest that she had her doubts—probably more about the trainer than the dog.

"He's still pretty distractible," Marcus went on. "So it's great you like to entice him so much. You're good practice."

Her eyes narrowed, and she almost rose to the bait before rolling her eyes and asking, warily, "What do you need, Marcus?"

"Hinges. Adam said he called."

"Oh yeah." She reached beneath the counter and fetched a bag, which she slid toward him.

"What did you think I wanted?" He smiled, waiting… and *yes*. There it was. That blush that no tattoos or piercings could hide.

The blush that suggested maybe there was a slight possibility that she didn't hate him as much as she tried to make him think. Which would be a good thing, considering what he was supposed to be convincing her to do.

"They're already paid for," Emma said.

"What?" Marcus asked.

"The hinges?" she said, eyeing the bag in his hand. "Adam paid with a credit card when he ordered them."

"Oh. Yeah." He shook his head, trying to focus on the conversation and not the way her slim fingers tapped the counter impatiently, and how it would feel to have those fingers running over his chest.

A moment of déjà vu unbalanced him, a flash of his hands on Emma's hips as she lowered her face to his, to… Patton shifted, leaning into Marcus's suddenly wobbly knees. He glanced up and caught a glimpse of Todd Stern in his dress uniform, glaring at him from near the ceiling.

"Did you drive here?" she asked.

"Yeah, why?"

"Does Adam know you drove here?" she asked, peering at him closely.

"Yeah, why?" he repeated, but then he understood. The last time they'd seen each other, he'd been loaded on two-too-many pain pills. She didn't know if he was sober.

He put his injured pride aside for the moment—no use adding failure to carry out his mission to the indignity of having other people believe he was a drug addict.

Emma leaned in a fraction as though to hear better. "Is there anything else I can do for you?"

Oh, honey. Is there ever. There was that vision again, of Emma in his bedroom. He cleared his throat. Fantasizing about his assignment was *not* why he was here.

"Did you hear about my promotion?"

Emma didn't quite snort, but her raised eyebrow spoke volumes. "Really. A promotion?"

"Yeah. I'm the Big Chance Rescue Ranch's new director of development."

"What was your title before that?"

"Head of accounting. Before that, I was chief remote control holder and vice president of beer cooler emptying."

Ooh…*nope.* He thought he saw a twitch, but he must have imagined it, because she was *that* good at the stone-faced thing.

"Well, that's lovely for you, I'm sure," she said drily.

"Yeah," he said. "The thing is, I'm in charge of making sure you've asked your boss here for vacation time next week."

The tension in Emma's already tight shoulders ratcheted up about a dozen notches. "I don't need to take vacation time."

"Didn't Adam talk to you about the convention in Houston?"

"Yes. As a matter of fact, he did. But I told him I didn't want to go."

"Ah. Too much to do here, huh?" He scanned the deserted hardware store.

She folded her arms over her chest and lowered her brow in his general direction. "I'm not going," she said.

"Your grandfather's gonna be cool at Golden Gardens, and if anything happens, Adam's a phone call away."

Her quick glance at the computer screen told him he'd hit on at least one major objection.

Marcus sighed and put his teasing aside. "Listen. I understand," he said. "It's not really my thing, either. But I promised Adam I'd go and schmooze with the donor types. He wants me to be the example of what our group does. Put Patton through his paces, that sort of thing. I can do all that. But you know more about what's involved in the day-to-day training and what it's likely to take to get things up and running."

"Wait a minute," she said, holding up her left hand, rings glinting on slender fingers, including a gold band on the third. "Adam wants you to go, too? *You*'re going to meet with the rich donor types?"

"Yeah," he said, trying not to feel defensive.

"And Adam's *not* going."

"Right. He can't bail on the new dogs he's bringing from that shelter in Comanche."

Emma stared at Marcus until he wanted to squirm.

Finally she rolled her eyes, shook her head, and said, "Fine. When do we leave?"

What had she just done? Emma felt a little shell-shocked after dropping that bomb on herself. Apparently she'd surprised Marcus, too, because he was quiet for a change, blinking at her. But then he recovered, and his wide mouth curved in a smile.

"Great! The conference starts Thursday night at the Hilton with a cocktail deal."

Great. Emma, Marcus, and alcohol in a hotel. Why did her mind immediately go to long, slow kisses fading into morning-after regrets? That was not why she'd agreed to go on this trip. She was only going to keep Marcus from using that big mouth to promise the moon to a million people, *not* to have him use it on her.

She glanced at the computer screen to check on Granddad and tried to think. There was something… *Oh yeah.* Could she leave the Sterns in the lurch? "I've got to clear it with Mrs. Stern first."

"Clear what, dear?" Mrs. Stern entered the room, bringing with her the scents of honeysuckle and cookies. She eyed Marcus curiously. "Hello."

"Mrs. Stern, have you met Marcus Talbott? He's a friend of Adam's."

"You've been in here before, right? And I've seen you around town with the dogs. It's lovely to be officially introduced," Mrs. Stern said, reaching her plump, freckled hand across the counter to shake Marcus's.

"Nice to meet you, too, ma'am," Marcus said. "We were talking about a conference Adam wants Emma to go to next week. A veterans' event in Houston, where we're hoping to share Adam's plans for the Big Chance Rescue Ranch. The more people who know about it, the more likely we are to find the resources to help more vets."

Mrs. Stern's expression softened and she said, "Absolutely. We'll do anything we can to support this cause. I think what you're doing out there is wonderful. I only wish it had been available when Todd…" She paused, as she did any time Todd's name was mentioned, and glanced at one of the dozens of photos hanging around the store. "Well, Emma, if you can help, then you should go."

Emma pushed away the thought that perhaps she was helping a few years too late and said, "Are you sure? I don't want to leave you shorthanded."

Mrs. Stern glanced around the still-deserted store and laughed softly. "I think we can handle things for a few days. Besides, when was the last time you asked for time off?"

Emma started to open her mouth, but Mrs. Stern shook her head. "I mean for something other than one of your grandfather's doctor appointments." The woman frowned meaningfully, and Emma laughed.

Mrs. Stern was the closest person to a mother in her life, and that pursed mouth was powerful.

"Okay. I'll only be gone a couple of days. I don't want to leave Granddad for too long."

"Oh, pshaw," Mrs. Stern said, waving a hand at her. "He's going to be fine at Golden Gardens. You should let someone else take a turn with him. Stay more than a couple days. Stay a few. Several. Many, even. Enjoy yourself. Go out on the town."

"That's not necessary," Emma rushed to assure her. "I don't want—"

"That's a great idea," Marcus interjected. "The Texans have a home game. I'll see if we can get tickets."

"Don't do that," Emma said, glancing to see if Mrs. Stern caught the *we* in Marcus's statement. From the interested tilt of the older woman's head, Emma deduced that she had.

"You're going, too?" Mrs. Stern glanced between Emma and Marcus.

"This is for work," Emma emphasized. "We don't have time to mess around." She cringed. Why had she said "mess around"? Now she might have put the wrong idea in Todd's mom's head, and that was the last thing she wanted—to have her mother-in-law worried that Emma was planning to get busy with a man who wasn't Todd.

Nope, just going to babysit my brother's second-in-command. No matter how strongly Adam insisted that Marcus wasn't taking any more pain pills, Emma knew those drugs were stronger than most people's willpower.

"It's business, but there's always time for pleasure," Marcus said, apparently oblivious to—or just not caring about—Emma's distress. She tried to shoot him a warning glare, but he was looking at the computer, where—

"Oh no," all three said at once, just as the front door bell jangled announcing a customer.

They stared at the computer screen, where Granddad was standing next to his chair. His back was turned to the camera, pants around his knees, and he appeared to be peeing on the floor. "Not again," Emma moaned.

"I got this," Marcus said, laughing. "Come on, Patton." He moved toward the back door, which opened to provide access across the parking lot to Emma's little house.

"No, I'll go—" Emma started to untie her apron, but Marcus shook his head.

"This is guy stuff. You've got a customer."

"He's right," Mrs. Stern told her, a hand on her arm as she nodded a greeting to Mr. Harper, who stood near the paint chips. "Let someone else take responsibility for a change. This can be practice for when your grandfather goes to Golden Gardens."

But Granddad was Emma's responsibility, and she should be taking care of him. Except that Marcus was already out the door. Then, while Mrs. Stern waited on Mr. Harper, Emma had to watch helplessly—and with reluctant gratitude—while Marcus arrived and, smiling and laughing, got Granddad back into his drawers with no fuss. Granddad *never* cooperated with Emma like that. If she didn't know what a mess he was, she might think Marcus was some sort of miracle worker.

And then—to top it off—he found the mop and bucket, and cleaned her floor.

Chapter 8

"WHAT ELSE DO YOU NEED FOR YOUR TRIP?" ADAM ASKED Marcus for the ninety-ninth time in three days.

"A big, juicy expense account?"

"I only wish." Adam shook his head.

"Just kidding, man." Hell, the table fee for this gig was more than they could afford, and Marcus had already decided to pay his own way on this trip, whether Adam liked it or not.

"You've got your Big Chance shirts, right?"

"Your overpriced swag, you mean," Tanner said from his darkened corner of the dining room, a.k.a. office.

The kid had taken to his job—and then some. He'd become the self-appointed financial control freak and fashion critic.

"What's wrong with the shirts?" Adam asked.

"They're blue," Tanner said, *duh* implied. "Kentucky Wildcat blue."

"Which is a very nice shade of blue," Marcus said primly. They'd already had a couple of good-natured knockdown battles of wits over which SEC team was better—LSU or Kentucky.

"Whatever." Tanner waved dismissively.

Marcus rolled his eyes and said, "I like these shirts." Would Emma like them? Would she look good in the T-shirt? *Of course.* She'd look good in a muumuu.

Oblivious to Marcus's inappropriate musings, Adam added, "We need to look legit if we're going to make a go of this."

"If we *are* legit, then we shouldn't have to worry about *looking* like it," Tanner said.

Adam shook his head and said, "We're a new organization, and it's important to be extraprofessional."

They were outside before Tanner had a chance to argue, where Jake was slamming the trunk of Marcus's Camaro.

"You sure you don't want to take him with you?" Adam asked once they'd cleared the door.

"He'll warm up to you," Marcus assured Adam. At least he hoped so. "He's scared and in pain." Something Marcus understood only too well. Maybe that's why he was extra patient with Tanner when the young man didn't exactly go out of his way to endear himself to the others.

A twinge of guilt reminded Marcus that he'd invited Tanner to stay, which meant he was responsible for getting the kid's attitude in order, as well as finding a way to feed the extra mouth.

Which was his reason for heading out on this trip. He was going to convince anyone and everyone to contribute to the Big Chance Rescue Ranch. All the shirts, banners, business cards, and dog-themed stuff might show that they were more than a slap-a-magnetic-sign-on-the-side-of-the-truck-and-call-it-a-real-roofing-company operation, but it was up to Marcus and Emma to deliver the goods. Come hell or high water, he was going to do it, because he had to find a way to earn his keep with his brothers here—and to repay Adam for his hospitality over these long months.

"Seriously, man," Adam said, oblivious to Marcus's inner

basket-case. "We're not rolling in dough, but we've got enough funds to look like a professional organization. You don't have to pack a sack lunch to take to the conference. Just turn in your receipts when you get back."

As if. Marcus owed Adam more than he could ever repay, so covering himself and Emma on this trip would go a short way toward easing his conscience over how much oxygen he'd consumed while everyone else out here worked their asses off to make the ranch a go.

"I've got all of Patton's stuff in the back of your car," Jake said, stooping to inspect the fastenings of the dog's new vest.

Patton sat up straighter, clearly proud to be sporting his new vest with the pretty, shiny logo of the Big Chance Rescue Ranch Support Dogs.

Marcus ignored him and reached for the duffel he'd put out here earlier, but Adam beat him to it.

"I got it. You bring your dog."

Yeah, like Patton wasn't the one bringing him. It galled Marcus to have someone else fetch and carry for him, but the truth was, his back had been zinging him all day and he didn't want to push it before he had to—like after he'd spent far too many hours in the slouchy seat of his car. Marcus followed Adam off the porch into the burning Texas sun. Hot as hell, even in October.

He paused for a moment, leaning his head back and soaking in the heat. Damn, but he loved the weather here. Relentlessly hot as fuck. Everyone else had pissed and moaned about it when they were in Ranger School at Fort Benning in equally hot Georgia, but this was the kind of weather that Marcus lived for, especially after his injury. The only thing that sucked was that winter was coming, and even here between nowhere and nowhere else, it got chilly sometimes.

Patton shifted next to him, and Marcus pulled himself out of his weather trance and went to his beloved car where Adam was—*Oh, for crying out loud*—checking his oil.

"Seriously, *Dad*?" Marcus groused. Adam could not stop mother-henning him.

Adam shrugged, unaffected by Marcus's sarcasm, and shut the hood of the car. "I don't want you breaking down in the middle of nowhere with my sister in the car."

Marcus smiled at the thought. "I have a feeling that would send our sweet Emma over the edge."

"*Sweet* Emma? My sister? We talking about the same girl?"

"It's in there. You know it."

"Yeah, *I* know it. I've known her since she was two days old. But I don't think *you're* ever going to see it." Which was probably why Adam wasn't giving Marcus the don't-you-think-about-touching-my-sister stare at the moment.

"I'm a preacher's son. I have faith," Marcus reminded him.

"Yeah, well, you're gonna need divine intervention to get her to loosen up." Adam shook his head. "Seriously. I didn't think she was ever going to leave Granddad at Golden Gardens last night."

"She's protective of the people she loves, man," Marcus said, and wanted to ask what had happened to make her so afraid to let people in, but knew it wasn't his business.

Adam nodded. "It's gonna take some major artillery to break through those bunker walls, though."

Marcus raised his eyebrows. "Wow, Sar'nt. Being in loooove has brought out your inner poet, hasn't it?"

"Kiss my ass," Adam said, punching Marcus on the shoulder. He looked at his watch and said, "I wanted to stick around to see her before you leave, but if we don't get these dogs gathered up, we're going to miss our vet appointment."

"I'll give her a kiss for you," Marcus said.

"Do that at your own peril," Adam said, though it wasn't clear whether the danger would come from Emma or Adam. "But seriously—she could use a good time, even if it's a week at a veterans' expo with your useless ass."

"Hey. I may be useless for most things, but I do know how to show a girl a good time."

"Jesus. That's my sister you're talking about."

"I remember. I'll be gentle."

Adam opened his mouth, and Marcus expected a warning but instead heard, "Thanks. Be careful."

"Always."

Adam cleared his throat and stared off into the distance. "I worry about her." He shot Marcus a sideways glance and went on. "I think the last year they were together—before Todd died—was pretty bad. She won't talk to me about any of it, but I get little hints here and there that she's messed up over it. Keep an eye on her."

"Absolutely." Marcus wasn't sure what else to say.

"I better get going before Doc Chance gives our appointment to someone else." He waved and headed into the barn, where he was greeted by a cacophony of barks.

"Come on, Patton," Marcus said, "I wanna get a shower before we go."

He let the dog help him up the stairs, wondering if it would be possible for Emma to have a good time on this trip. Marcus had no intention of becoming the next love of her life, but he could certainly do his part to provide some entertainment in the form of…himself.

"This is going to be a train wreck," Emma griped to Lizzie as she shouldered her cell phone and made the turn from Main Street to Wild Wager Road.

"It'll be fine," Lizzie soothed. "Between your incredible organization and Marcus's way with people, you'll have everyone in Texas lining up to give you money."

"What I'm afraid of is that he's going to promise people things we can't deliver."

"Why do you think that?" Lizzie asked, sounding truly puzzled.

Lizzie knew about Marcus's drug use, but Emma suspected her friend was fairly naive about how addicts operated. She wanted to enlighten Lizzie, to explain how easily an addict could lie and ruin your world, but then she'd have to air her own bad history. Even shining a light on the locked door made the beast extend its claws through the cracks. "Never mind. I'm going, I'll keep an eye on him, er…things. It'll be fine." Please, God, let it be.

"It *will* be fine," Lizzie repeated. "You're going to have a great time in Houston. I hear the convention hotel is practically a resort. Get a massage, eat good food. Go dancing."

"Dancing? Why would I want to do that?" Emma suppressed the shiver that tried to overtake her at the idea of being cradled in Marcus's big, strong arms and swaying to the velvet tones of some seventies pop crooner.

"Welllll…" The way Lizzie dragged out the word made

the suggestion unmistakable. "Marcus is a fine-looking guy, and you could do worse than spend a night on the town doing the…I don't know…the Cupid Shuffle with him."

Now Emma really did snort. The idea of herself tripping over everyone during a line dance was as funny as the idea of Marcus twirling her into a deep dip was…hot. "I better go. I'm almost here," Emma said, though the driveway to the ranch was still three miles off. She rationalized the fib because she was about to hit one of the notorious cell-phone dead spots that littered Chance County.

"Seriously," Lizzie said before she hung up. "Marcus is a good guy, and you should give him a chance. You deserve a good time."

"For God's sake," Emma said, "are you sending me off on a business trip or a blind date?"

"Well…" There was noise in the background, someone coming into Lizzie's makeshift office trailer at her construction site. "I'm sorry, I've got to go," she told Emma.

"I'll talk to you when I get back," Emma said, laughing as she hung up. That was ridiculous. Lizzie might have romance in her heart, now that she was all happily-ever-aftering with Adam, but Emma knew her brother wouldn't send her into that kind of lion's den. Although she did believe that part of his motive was to distract her from Granddad's stay at Golden Gardens.

Dropping him off had been harder than Emma had expected, though when she'd stopped in to visit this morning, he'd been happily cutting fruit for salad with his new best friends.

Granddad might not want to come home with her when she got back from Houston, and what if they weren't able to secure funding for the ranch? She couldn't dip into Adam's savings to keep Granddad in long-term care, no matter how much her brother swore that's what the money was for. With Emma's luck, she and Marcus would come back to Big Chance with the nonprofit deeper in the hole than when they'd left.

Her wedding ring glinted in the sunlight when she hit her turn signal before the lane. She'd almost left it at home today, telling herself she didn't want people to think she and Marcus were married. Had even slipped it off, but there was a groove in her finger where it had been, a little paler than the rest of her skin, and she realized she might look like a married woman stepping out on her husband, rather than a woman with her husband. Who wasn't her husband.

Which was irrelevant. Emma was going on this trip to keep an eye on Marcus. That was all.

A minute—and a million paranoid fantasies later about all the crazy things Marcus might do while they were at this conference, she pulled in front of the ranch house. Getting out of the car, she hoped that her attraction to Marcus wouldn't get in the way of protecting her brother from the misdeeds of a smooth-talking addict.

She knocked before turning the front doorknob, despite having gotten a lecture from Adam about how she should still consider the place her home—even though she'd sold her share to Adam years ago—but she didn't just walk in, in case Marcus the Magnificent was pumping iron in the living room, wearing nothing but a…a…jockstrap.

Aaaand she didn't need to perv on that visual, thank you very much.

The door opened to reveal not her brother or a sexy,

scantily clad man, but a complete stranger. This must be the new guy she'd heard about.

"Hi," she said.

At first glance, he seemed young—early twenties, with sandy-brown hair and a jaw so smooth that she doubted he had enough stubble to shave more than once a month. But then he moved, and Emma had to stifle a gasp.

The entire left side of his face was a meshwork of scar tissue, stiff and unmoving. His eye on that side watered, the lid didn't seem to close, and his lower lip was almost completely gone.

She did her best to control her features. She couldn't pretend she hadn't noticed his disfigurement, but on the other hand, she didn't want to make him feel any more self-conscious than he probably already did.

"Jesus," he said, scanning her from head to toe, taking in her tattoos, blue hair, and piercings. "What happened to your face? You should be more careful." He pointed at her and touched his own eyebrow, indicating the pair of silver rings she wore there. "Did you fall and get your ears smooshed around to your forehead?"

She blinked and then saw the slight quirk of his mouth. She could play *this* game. "Well, at least I know better than to try to roast marshmallows with my teeth."

He blinked in surprise, then smiled and nodded. As he stood back to admit her, he asked, "You're the sar'nt's sister?"

"I'm Emma," she said, holding out a hand.

He hesitated, then held out his own, stiff and unmoving fingers awkward in hers. "Tanner," he told her with a shrug. "I know, it should have been Bernie, but…"

She rolled her eyes at that one. "So you're the new guy."

"I guess so," he said. "I said I'd do the bookkeeping in exchange for a few weeks in the lap of luxury." He waved his undamaged hand to indicate the ranch house, which currently bore witness to its number of residents, both human and furry, in the form of discarded shoes, chew toys, and various items of clothing scattered about the entry.

And dumbbells. The owner of which padded into the room—long, brown feet; long, brown legs bare to the knee. Shiny red basketball shorts covered him from knee to just below his belly button, which rested in the middle of the hardest, most ripped stomach she'd ever seen in her life. Which was good for it, because the chest above that belly? She could barely breathe. It was second only to the arms and towel-draped shoulders—

"Hey, Emma," Marcus said.

Her eyes shot to his face, and yep, he bore enough of a smirk to let her know that he'd seen her checking him out. Water droplets glistened in his hair, which he blotted with the towel.

"I see you're ready to go," she said drily.

"I didn't want you to get tired from mentally undressing me all the way to Houston, but I can't go totally commando. My car has vinyl seats." He tugged at the waistband of his gym shorts. "I had to compromise."

Emma felt her face heat, so she rolled her eyes, hoping he'd think she was grossed out at the idea of smooth skin slipping on slick vinyl. She noted that his eyes were clear and he spoke clearly. So he at least *seemed* sober. That was something, but she reminded herself not to trust appearances.

"I see you've met our new team member," he said, indicating Tanner.

"Yes, we met," she said, smiling at Tanner.

Tanner nodded, then said, "It was nice to meet you, Emma," over his shoulder as he left the room.

"He seems nice," she said.

Marcus nodded, then said in an undertone, "To most of us."

Emma matched her volume to his. "He's not to everyone?"

Marcus shrugged. "He hasn't warmed up to Adam or Jake yet. Barely speaks to them."

"But he likes you."

Marcus grinned, then said in a normal voice, "Everybody likes me."

"Everyone?"

"Yep."

She snorted.

"Oh, darlin', you like me, too. You just won't let yourself enjoy the wonder that is me." He pulled a T-shirt from the pile of laundry on the couch. Emma slid her phone from her pocket to avoid staring directly at the way his muscles knotted and released while he stretched the fabric over those hard muscles.

"Right." She tapped her screen. "We've got to get going if we want to get checked in before the cocktail thing starts."

Marcus made a sound, a sort of a sigh that, if she weren't wiser and more experienced, might have sounded like frustration that she wasn't responding to his flirtation.

But she *was* experienced with bullshit artists, and she wasn't going to get taken in on this ride.

Chapter 9

MARCUS SQUIRMED UNCOMFORTABLY—PROBABLY BE-cause he was in the *passenger* seat of his own car. Emma managed to hit every bump and pothole on the road, and he tensed tighter with each one.

She shot him a glance. "Would you relax? You're making me nervous."

"You're making *me* nervous. This is my baby." He reached to stroke the dashboard. "It's okay, sweetie," he told the car. "I'll keep an eye on her." He was only half-kidding.

"I've never had an accident. Not even a fender bender. I've never even run over one of those concrete things in a parking lot. But if you keep flinching every time I pass someone, I'm gonna blindfold you for the rest of the trip."

"You're killing me," he muttered, but fell silent. Why had he handed over his keys, again?

At first, Emma had insisted they take her ridiculous little subcompact. Marcus played the service-dog card. Even though his Camaro had barely enough room for Patton to stretch across the back seat, Emma's was smaller. She then launched an interrogation, asking him a bunch of random questions, like what he'd had for breakfast. "I had two eggs, a protein shake, and four Advil," he finally said.

She'd crossed her arms, stared at him, and shaken her head. "I get carsick," she told him. "I have to drive."

"The hell you do," he said, moving toward the driver's side door. "Nobody but me drives this car."

"Then I'll drive myself. You can follow me."

He had no idea how it happened—the idea of spending the next three hours looking at the back of Emma's head from two car-lengths away disappointed him so much, he must have said "Fine," because the next thing he knew, she was buckling the seat belt and adjusting the seat behind *his* steering wheel.

Now, as she hit the blinker to signal that she wanted to pass a slow semi, Marcus had a momentary flash of desire for one of his pain pills, triggering a wave of self-loathing. He hated that he wanted drugs, because he wasn't in massive physical pain at the moment. Psychological pain from allowing someone else drive his car almost qualified, but he reminded himself he was not an addict, so he didn't need anything.

He *did* need a distraction. "What do you want to listen to?" He reached back, grabbed the case containing his tunes, and opened it on his lap. "The antenna broke off, so radio's patchy at best. We'll have to go with prerecorded jams. What's your pleasure?"

"Oh my God," she said, shooting a glance at the tapes and then at the console on the dash. "Are you serious? Eight-track?"

He smiled at her reaction. "Only the best of my parents' seventies collection, baby." He ran a finger over the backs of the cartridges. "Kool & the Gang, Bee Gees, O'Jays, Thelma Houston, Aretha Franklin, the Carpenters…"

"The Carpenters?"

"Well, yeah. My parents had to have a little something to take the edge off their cool."

"Play it."

Of course *that* would be the one she chose.

He popped it into the tape deck and turned up the volume. As Karen Carpenter's low, velvety voice filled the tight interior of the car, Emma began to sing along.

Dayum. The girl had pipes. She harmonized right in there with Karen and Richard, singing about rainy days and Mondays, and if Marcus had been able to reach his phone without being obvious, he'd have recorded her so he could take her out and listen to her again anytime he felt down.

Even Patton was impressed. He'd been stretched out, snoozing in the back seat, but now stood with his chin on Emma's shoulder.

As the last notes of the song faded away, she seemed to realize she had an audience and shrugged, dislodging Patton, who lay back down with a sigh. "It was my mom's favorite song."

"You have a great voice," he told her in the understatement of the century.

She snorted. "Whatever."

"Seriously. Don't you know that? Weren't you in the choir or anything in high school?"

She shook her head but didn't answer.

"That song. Did she sing it to you a lot?"

After a second, Emma said, "I guess so. I know she had it on a record, and when we were little, she let us play with the 'big CDs' on her old stereo."

"That's cool. My granny made me learn how to play the piano, but *nobody* wants to hear me sing," he told her.

"You play piano? Did you have recitals and stuff?" She was paying attention to him now, playing the getting-to-know-you game, so he gave in to a little humiliation to keep her talking.

"I only had one where I was alone. It was right after my dad took over as pastor of our church. Gran was so proud and wanted her sisters to see how great her family was. I was supposed to play at church on Easter Sunday. But I was really nervous because I hadn't practiced, and I threw up right after I got up there."

"Oh no!" She was laughing now, husky and low, the sound stroking his entire body in a way that distracted him from the memory of how ashamed he'd been for letting his family down.

"Yeah, it wasn't my best moment. But it worked out for Gran. I felt so guilty for not practicing and for throwing up in front of the whole congregation that I forced myself to learn to read music and to play almost every damned hymn in that book."

"No kidding." She said it as a statement, not a question, as though the information was something she needed to file away in the mental locker labeled *Things I know about Marcus Talbott*.

"Yeah. So now when I go home to visit, I have to play."

"Is your dad still preaching?"

"Oh yes. Remember that scene from the *Blues Brothers*, when the guys go into James Brown's church?"

"Yeah…"

"It's not like that."

She giggled, and he felt like he'd won another point or two. "So what's it like?"

"It's a little Methodist church in the middle of nowhere, Kentucky. All the Black people in the area—there aren't many—and about ten White people go there every week, religiously."

"Ha. Ha." She was quiet a moment, then asked, "Did you join the army right out of high school?"

"Maybe I should have," he said. "Could have cut to the chase."

"What does that mean?"

He hadn't meant to say that, but since he had, he told her, "I had a partial football scholarship to the University of Kentucky. I didn't make it past my freshman year."

"Did you get cut?"

The pain from that summer after his try at college still throbbed, but it was a dull ache, his father's disappointment when he had to admit he'd flunked out wasn't as sharp now. "Did I get cut from the team? No. I... Academics aren't my thing. I'm more of an action man."

Before she could ask anything else, he leaned forward and ejected the Carpenters in favor of another tape. "How do you feel about the Ohio Players?"

By the time they got to Houston, Marcus was a little twitchy. Emma could have believed his shifting and fussing had been from nervousness about her driving, not because he was jonesing for drugs—but her benefit of the doubt elapsed once they reached the hotel.

"Why don't I drop you and the stuff off here? I'll park the car and join you in the lobby in a minute?" Marcus suggested as she turned into the drive.

She eyed the crowd jockeying for position in the valet

area and decided she'd rather tough it out. "I'll go with you. We can manage from the garage. I don't see any of those luggage-cart things anyway."

He hesitated a moment, as though preparing a counterargument, but was interrupted as an attendant spoke through the open driver's side window. "Are you using valet parking, ma'am?"

"No, we're self-parking," she told him.

"Then please move along." The man stepped back and motioned for them to continue past the drop-off point.

A minute and a couple of narrow underground turns later, she eased the Camaro between two enormous pickup trucks, turned off the ignition, and pulled the emergency brake.

Emma opened her door and hopped out with her backpack. Marcus did not. He said, "There're a lot of people here already. If you go get our room keys and leave me here to get the stuff, that just means we can get in faster."

With a jolt, Emma realized he wanted her to leave him alone at the car, and she didn't have to think too hard to figure out why, *damn it.*

He'd done the same thing when they'd stopped to get gas and have a bathroom break an hour ago, she realized. Told her to go ahead and go inside, he had a phone call to make, then he'd get out and pump the gas. Maybe he kept his stash under the seat or something and didn't want her to see it. Was he already loaded now? He hadn't seemed fuzzy, but sometimes Todd had seemed fine and later she'd learn he didn't remember anything for long stretches of time.

Disappointment flooded her.

Somewhere between Austin and Houston she'd begun

to let go of her suspicions. He'd started telling stories about his childhood in Kentucky—peeling off a little bit of his smooth operator gloss—and damned if that didn't just add to the effect of his sexy smile and twinkly eyes.

Not good. She'd actually been thinking that if she wasn't careful, she'd be saying, "Faster, Marc, faster" before this trip was over.

Not. Happening. Not getting busy with the man, and not giving him any extra time or space to do his drugs. She stuck her head back into the car. "Pop the trunk. I need to grab those shirts."

"Sure." His answer was quick, but he still wasn't getting out.

She heard the latch let go and eased the trunk lid up, then pulled out her little travel bag, keeping one eye on Marcus around the edge. He'd opened the door and had one leg out, but was coaxing Patton to climb from the back seat over the center console, across his lap, and out.

"Hey, you're supposed to get out first, and when you're standing, then you tell him it's okay to get out." She came around to the side of the car and put her hands on her hips, in full dog-trainer mode. Just because she wasn't working at the ranch didn't mean she'd stowed all of her experience in her mental attic.

"Yeah, I know," Marcus said, pulling a harness from the back seat and buckling it on the dog, who waited patiently. "I'm supposed to pretend to use the car to balance myself on before I move to the dog, but we're working on teaching him how to pull someone up if they need a little help out of their seat."

Was he already too high to stand up on his own? She

narrowed her eyes, considering his ridiculous vintage muscle car. "That's great, but don't you think someone with actual permanent challenges would drive something a little easier to get in and out of?"

He didn't comment, just grabbed the handle of the harness and gave a command. The dog stepped forward, leaning into the move while Marcus held onto the handle, accepting the extra tug to get his large self out of the low bucket seat. He sounded perfectly fine, though, once he was on his feet and telling Patton he was a good boy. He wasn't slurring, not the way Todd did when he was using. The edges of his words were a little soft, the way they always were—the dropped consonant at the end of "good" making "good boy, Patton," sound like a long, smooth stroke of affection.

Oh for Chrissakes. Emma shook her head.

Sweet words didn't mean a man was sober; they just meant she'd have to stay close any time they were in public, or he'd start making promises of instant dogification to every sad-eyed veteran they met—promises that the Big Chance Dog Rescue wasn't ready to keep.

Marcus stayed in the open car door for a long moment, holding the dog's harness with one hand, the doorframe with the other. He smiled at her, but lines that didn't belong on that perfect face had formed at the corners of his eyes and mouth. Lines that came from deep pain.

As he finally shut the car door behind him, any trace of discomfort disappeared. She'd probably been mistaken. It had been a long drive, and anyone over the age of fifteen would have a few kinks to stretch out before their body was ready to walk normally. A trick of the light. This guy was fine.

She grabbed a canvas bag filled with Big Chance Rescue Ranch shirts and stuff, and looked up to find Marcus within touching distance.

Damn. Even after hours shut up in a car with him, out here in the exhaust-and-concrete dust-scented parking garage, she wanted to lean into his spicy scent. She was turning into a damned German shepherd, she thought. Nose so sensitive she could pick one Marcus molecule out of a jillion others.

He reached into the trunk without leaning down and grasped his enormous travel suitcase. He extended the handle before thunking the thing down and held it with his non-Patton hand.

"Wow, Ahhnold," she said, doing her best Schwarzenegger impression. "Did you bring your entire home gym with you there?"

He eyed her small backpack and the bag she'd slung over her shoulder. "I brought a couple of changes of clothes. And dog supplies."

"Oh yeah." She'd been working with dogs her whole life, give or take the last couple of years, but had never actually traveled with a service dog. "Sometimes I forget he's even here."

Marcus broke the "Don't pet me, I'm working" protocol and stroked the dog's ears. "Patton's working hard so he'll be ready when another vet actually needs him full-time. Come on." He stepped past her toward the elevators.

As she noticed the very slight hitch in his step, she scurried to catch up and said, "Here. Give me your suitcase. You've got the dog."

He paused, looked like he was about to argue, but then let her take the handle.

Chapter 10

THE ELEVATOR FINALLY PINGED ON THE NINETEENTH floor, and Emma breathed a sigh of relief as the doors slid open to air that didn't screw with her sanity because it wasn't yet saturated with Marcus pheromones. He'd barely spoken between the registration desk and here, but she was as aware of him as her own body—more so, if possible.

"Oh, hey," he said, as she let go of the handle of his suitcase in front of 1914 and proceeded to 1915. "We're next-door neighbors, not across the hall."

"Oh, yay." With her luck, their beds would share a wall and she'd be able to hear every move he made, all night long. She slid her card into the slot in the door, waited for the little light to turn green, then turned the handle, pushing her way toward solitude.

"So, wait," Marcus called.

She leaned back, stuck her head into the hallway, and looked at him, keeping the rest of herself inside, in what she hoped was I-want-to-be-alone body language.

He quirked his lips, clearly on to her, but didn't let her off the hook. "The meet and greet for presenters and organizers starts at seven. Do you want to get dinner before we go?"

No. She needed to be away from him. But an hour was long enough for him to get really drugged up, and the last thing they needed was a woozy first impression. She had to keep an eye on him, she realized. She sighed and straightened—but blocked her door open with her body. "It's six now. Do you think there's time to go to a restaurant?"

"Good point," he said. "Why don't you change, and I'll figure something out. Fifteen minutes enough for you?" He was gone before she could answer.

Fifteen whole minutes, huh? But what did she expect? That he'd suggest she take a long, hot bath while he picked up foie gras and a nice bottle of Cabernet?

Todd had done that once, she remembered, only it had been Cheetos and Miller Lite. It was shortly after he returned from his first deployment. They'd been spoiling the hell out of each other—newlyweds still, since he'd been gone for most of their first year of marriage. He'd still been striving for *normal*. Maybe didn't even realize yet that he wasn't.

She threw her backpack onto the bed. Why hadn't she brought any more luggage than this, she wondered, unzipping it. If she'd at least brought a real suitcase, she'd have something to throw down hard on the floor, instead of this flimsy-assed backpack that offered absolutely nothing satisfying in the way of damageables—except her laptop, and there was no way she'd brutalize that.

Throwing things wasn't all that helpful for stress relief anyway. Todd had proved that with most of their dishes. Emma wished—not for the first time—she could have helped him find an alternative. It would have been great if Adam had been around then, to be his friend, to have the brotherhood he'd developed with Marcus and Jake at the ranch. Or to witness her humiliation as she let her marriage and her husband fall apart completely.

Ugh!

How had she gone from thinking about dinner to wanting to murder luggage and revisiting the past?

She glared at the door separating her room from Marcus's. Who's idea had *that* been, she wondered. Knowing Marcus, he'd called ahead and asked them to set that up, just so he could torment her sex-starved brain with the knowledge that he was barely dressed—or maybe completely naked—and only a flimsy panel of drywall away.

A panel he'd walk through in a moment from his room. Another room with a bed.

Double *ugh*. It had been years since she'd had sex, which hadn't been a problem for most of that time. It was only in the last few weeks—weeks that included the arrival of Marcus Talbott in Big Chance—that she'd noticed a reawakening of her lady bits.

Dwelling on orgasm deficits wouldn't help things, so she went to the window and yanked the curtains aside to look out at the brilliant blue sky and fluffy white clouds sprinkled over the Houston skyline. Did it have to be so *pretty* here?

Her stomach growled. It had been since… Oh, great. She hadn't even had breakfast today and had a nervous stomach at lunchtime. Probably if her blood sugar was back in a healthy range, her mood wouldn't be so bleak.

She grabbed the handful of toiletries that she'd dumped on the bed and carried them into the bathroom. She might as well use some of the stupid cosmetics she'd brought. She couldn't be paler if she lived in a cave and only went outside at night.

Usually the pasty thing worked for her. She'd begun to adopt a modified goth look in high school as a way to separate herself from the other kids. In case they planned to bully or tease her, she could at least *look* like she didn't give a damn. Granddad threw a fit when she tried to pierce her nose and grounded her from the library when he caught her with black lipstick. So instead, she was stuck with emo-hick. Only Lizzie had ignored Emma's self-protective angry look and treated her like a friend. But then Lizzie went away to college, and Emma turned eighteen—and Granddad could only sigh when she threaded rings through her face and spent every spare cent putting colorful ink on her skin.

And then Todd—cute, funny, preppy Todd—had asked her out, and continued to ask her out. By the time they were married, she'd ditched most of the weird makeup and bought clothes to wear that had a little color and even— *gasp*—patterns! After he died, she regressed a little and started coloring her hair, but now here she was, putting on normal eyeliner and lip gloss just *because*.

Well, yeah, because she was going to a professional event and wanted to look at least somewhat approachable. To the other attendees. Not to the big lug in the next room.

At least, that's what she told herself, until there was a knock at the door that separated her bedroom from his. That was when her stomach lurched and she shoved both hands into her hair, desperately trying to get it to either stand up or lie down—none of this weird bedhead halfway thing it was doing after a day in the car.

"I'm coming, I'm coming," she muttered, straightening her new Big Chance shirt. *Weird*. Whoever had done the ordering had gotten her a small instead of a medium. She normally hated tight-fitting clothes, but as she caught sight of herself in the mirror over the dresser, she decided she didn't look too terrible.

"Hey," she said, opening the door and admitting Marcus,

who looked even *less* half-bad, of course, because his biceps—and pecs and trapeziuses and abs—were being lovingly caressed by 100 percent made-in-the-USA cotton.

"Hey." He led a vest-free Patton into the room and checked her out from head to toe, smiling.

She tried to tell herself she didn't like the warm feeling that hit her when he did that.

"We got supper," he said and handed her one of two bags from the hotel gift shop.

"Oh." She took the bag, not sure what else to say, and pulled the wad of tissue paper from the first, heavier one, to reveal…two bottles of Coke, two protein bars, and two packages of potato chips.

"Kettle-cooked," he said.

"Fancy."

Emma thought he looked a little embarrassed—almost shy—as he said, "Well, you know, nothing but the best." He handed her the second bag.

Her smile snuck out in spite of her attempts to keep it in. "What's in here?" she asked, hoisting the smaller bag.

"Dessert. But only if you eat all of your supper."

She looked inside to see a small package of Oreos and another of Nutter Butters.

Damn.

How was she supposed to keep her hands off this man for another three days?

"They're Shit Poos," said the traumatic-brain-injury expert as Marcus tried to focus on the three little fuzz balls on the cell phone screen shoved in front of him. What the hell kind of dog was that? And how was he supposed to think of something nice to say about them while Emma distracted him, tugging at the hem of her T-shirt for the ninety-ninth time in as many minutes?

It was good he'd convinced Adam to splurge on the better grade of fabric, because it would probably hold its shape a little better than the cheap stuff.

He should never have told her how nicely it fit her and made her self-conscious. Emma wasn't big on top, but the baggy shirts she usually wore gave the impression that she was trying to hide some gross imperfection—and he knew that she had none.

He knew that because he'd had his hands on her when... *Oh yeah*. When he'd been barely conscious from a near-overdose of narcotics. The more time that passed since the incident, the more ashamed he was of about how much he'd relied on drugs to blunt his pain. And now, even though he was clean, he still had moments where he missed them like crazy.

Like tonight, after he'd been in a car for hours, followed by more hours on his feet, smiling and schmoozing with guys like TBI Guy, who was now sharing his dog pics with Emma.

"They look like a lot of fun," she said.

"They keep me on my toes." The guy handed Emma his card. "Can I have yours? I'll stop by your booth tomorrow when I get a break."

"Um, sure," she said and blinked at Marcus as though puzzled about why the guy was asking for *her* card instead of one from the man with the dog.

Duh, Marcus wanted to say, *I'm a six-foot bag of testosterone, not an edgy little sex goddess with a sugar-sweet smile.* He *didn't* say that, though. Instead, he smiled and said, "I look forward to hearing your talk tomorrow. We have a friend with TBI, and he'll be interested to know about your research."

"Definitely," Emma added. "I've read some about virtual reality therapy. It sounds really cool."

They both let out a breath as soon as he was out of earshot. The preconvention cocktail party meet and greet was finally beginning to fizzle, thank God. Marcus had about run out of the energy to stand up straight. Perfect timing.

"You ready to head back upstairs?" he asked. Sensing an opportunity, Patton shifted against his leg. The dog had been a trouper, sitting patiently, letting Marcus lean on him, just a little, every chance he got.

"Sure."

They said goodbye to the organizers and accepted their complimentary goody bags, filled with flyers from every group present.

"Wow," she said, digging through the bag. "I had no idea there were so many people out there doing so many different things for vets."

"Yeah, it's pretty incredible," Marcus agreed, pushing the elevator call button. There were no fewer than four other service-dog organizations in attendance. In addition to big veterans' groups like Wounded Warriors, there were dozens of smaller grassroots teams who did everything from employment assistance to home adaptation to family therapy.

The elevator arrived, and they got on.

Emma said, "And still there are so many people who

need services and don't get them." A muscle in her jaw ticked. "You'd think with the internet and social media and everything else that people who are struggling could push a couple of buttons and find exactly what they need."

Marcus thought of his friend Max Zimmerman, who'd come to the ranch a few weeks ago, devastated because he was losing his family and on the verge of suicide. "It's hard for most people to ask for help."

A soft ding announced their floor, and Marcus stood back to let her exit into the hallway first before he went on. "You have to remember that you're dealing with military people here, guys—and girls—who learned very clearly that you don't whine if things aren't going your way. You suck it up and soldier on, no matter how miserable you are."

"Don't I know it," she muttered, looking down and twisting the ring she still wore on the third finger of her left hand.

She must miss Todd like crazy. Marcus felt a flash of guilt for lusting after another man's wife so much—although the guy had been gone for a couple of years. He wanted to ask her about him, but didn't want to hear how much she loved him. He was selfish…he wanted to find out if she had any interest in easing her pain the good old-fashioned way—with a roll around the sheets with a rebound guy.

She pulled herself out of her sad moment without his help, however, and stopped outside of her door. "So I guess we should get some sleep now, right?"

"I guess so," Marcus said, though it was only 9:00 p.m.

"I don't know about you, but I'm about half-dead. Aren't you tired?"

"Sure." Not likely. He'd keep the TV down low, if she was worried about him keeping her up listening to sports.

"We should meet at eight fifteen to get the flyers and table stuff ready before people start coming in."

She was cheerier, but she'd drawn away. He wanted to drag her back to him, so he asked, "Do you want to have breakfast together first?" *Maybe after you've come apart in my arms a half-dozen times tonight?*

"That's a good idea, but we'll have to get up earlier. Is that okay with you?"

"Yes…" *Probably.* If he got up early enough to take a few ibuprofen, warm up a little, stretch, make an offering to the gods of pain management…

She shoved her key card into the slot and turned the handle when it unlocked. He followed her into her room.

"What are you doing?" She didn't try to shut him out, but she was definitely surprised to see him in her space.

"I'm getting Patton's bowls." He'd had his dinner at the same time they had.

"Oh. Of course." Flustered, she turned and gathered the bowls from the floor outside the lavatory.

"We've still got dessert," he said, spying the gift-shop bag he'd brought her earlier.

"I didn't have room after our fancy supper," she said, smiling. "But I could go for a bite now. Want some?" She didn't look directly at him, instead sorted through the bag. "I really want the Oreos, though. I hope you like Nutter Butters."

"I do." Hell, even if he didn't, he'd force himself to eat them, just to have an excuse to sit with her for a little longer. "Hey, Patton, let's get that vest and harness off." He leaned over and stifled a groan when his back sent a jet of fire through his body. Not a good sign. He carefully smoothed the dog's fur and took his time sitting in one of the chairs in the corner. Patton looked at Marcus, who said, "Okay. You're done." The dog gave a big shake, emphatically glad to be off the clock, then jumped into the middle of Emma's bed and curled into a giant hair ball. *Dude.*

Marcus shifted, trying to find a comfortable position.

Emma must have heard him grunt, because she shot him a glance. "Are you okay?"

"Sure," he lied, accepting the pack of cookies she handed him.

"Really? All that stuff that was wrong with your back doesn't bother you anymore?"

"Nope. I'm right as rain. Just killing time until I get in to see the docs," he said, when really he wanted to say *Yes! It's fucking killing me, and I'm terrified I'll never get better.* But that was giving in to the negative voices, and he wasn't going to do that. "Nothing more wrong with me than the wear and tear of old age."

"Oh yeah, Grandpa. You're so ancient."

He *felt* old. He hadn't done all of his stretches today and was paying the price—but it was worth it to be sitting here with Emma now. "How old do you think I am?" he asked. He knew she was two years younger than Adam.

She looked at him closely, squinting at the crow's-feet he knew he had accumulated from too long in the dusty desert. He liked that she stood so close, her scent wafting around him, near enough that he could lean forward and pull her onto his lap. Except then she'd clock him with a hard uppercut.

"I think," she said finally, "that you're somewhere between twenty-two and forty."

"That's right," he deadpanned. "Wow, you're amazing!"

"Yeah. I know." She cocked one hand on her hip. "If the Feed and Seed thing doesn't work out, I'm gonna go on the county-fair circuit." She sat in the other chair and plucked at the plastic around her Oreos. Once it lay flat, she inspected each cookie and stacked them up.

"What are you doing?" he asked, tearing open his Nutter Butters and dumping half into his hand. He shoved two into his mouth.

"I'm sorting them." The look she sent him added the *duh*.

He crunched and swallowed. "They're all the same. How can you sort them?"

"They are *not* all the same." She held up the top one and showed him where one of the cookie pieces had broken off. "I eat the most broken ones first and save the perfect ones for last."

"There's a metaphor in there somewhere," Marcus said.

"Probably. Or some slight, undiagnosed OCD." She pulled the broken side off the Oreo and set it aside, then used her teeth to scrape the white icing from the other piece. He couldn't help but imagine her running her teeth over his skin and then licking, which she now did to get the remnants she'd missed.

Interesting to note the shards of glass sticking into his spine at the moment didn't impair his erectability. He dumped the remaining Nutter Butters into his mouth before he said something stupid, while Emma began to dissect the next cookie. *Ooh.* Okay, *that* twinge took the edge off Mr. Happy's glee. Time to go home. Where five minutes ago, he'd have given his left nut to sit in here for a few more minutes and flirt, he needed to get back to his side of the wall and surrender to the pain. If he could get down to the floor, he could probably stretch out and catch a little sleep so he was relatively functional tomorrow.

Please, God, I'm sorry about spending my offering money on candy when I was ten, and I'll double down next time I'm in church, but please don't let this go full-fledged spasm attack on me. I've got work to do.

"I should get back to my room," he said, trying to figure out which configuration of legs, hand supports, and muscle contractions would get him upright with the least amount of pain.

Emma finished the cookie she was making love to and stood. "Are you sure you're okay?" Her forehead wrinkled in concern when he moved slower than slow to get up.

"Yep. Just too long in the car after I overdid it with the free weights yesterday." Better she think him a vain idiot than a helpless fool.

"Hmm."

He got to the adjoining door and opened it, clucking for Patton to follow him through. "Enjoy the rest of your Oreos," he said, looking down at her.

"I will. Thanks again." She was close. So close he could see speckles of green and gray in her mostly blue irises. She stared back up at him. And then she looked at his lips.

So of course he had to look at *her* mouth, and imagine it coming close to his, breathing sweet chocolate into his peanut butter. He might have even begun to lean forward—then she stepped back and said, "Good night."

He couldn't resist one little tease before she shut herself away from him. "I'll leave my side unlocked tonight.

You know, in case you get scared and need to crawl into bed with me."

Her eyes rolled, but he was pretty sure he detected a blush, and maybe even a little smile. That was cool. He felt like he'd definitely made some headway today. Except now he was going to have to lie in that bed on his side of the wall, trying not to give in to the need to jack off to the fantasy of her naked body, because seriously, those walls were thin, and he knew he'd be moaning her name.

Chapter 11

EMMA WATCHED MARCUS WORK THE ROOM LIKE A PRO, reluctantly admitting—only to herself—that he knew what he was doing when it came to getting people to stop, take one of their flyers, and listen to his spiel about the Big Chance Rescue Ranch. Veterans responded to him, probably because he clearly understood their issues and cared—he listened more than he talked. All he needed Emma for was restocking the stack of flyers and collecting email addresses for the mailing list she'd decided they should have. Her fears he'd get wasted and start making unattainable promises were unfounded.

At the moment, Marcus stood in front of the table, talking to a young couple with two kids—a toddler in a stroller and a smaller one in a carrier on his dad's front.

"Doggy! Doggy!" the toddler whined, thrashing and arching in the stroller. Her mother tried to shush her, but was smacked away by a chubby little hand. The husband leaned in to hear what Marcus said over the din.

Patton, in his vest and harness, held his ground next to Marcus but sent furtive, longing glances at the small, noisy creature a few feet away.

"Hey, Marcus," Emma said, though she was loath to interrupt his discussion. Each and every veteran who stopped by their table left smiling and thoughtful, and she didn't want to ruin Marcus's record. But still: Screaming kid. Anxious dog. "Would you mind if Patton takes a short break to meet the little one?"

A flash of uncertainty crossed his face, but he nodded and released the dog, reaching behind himself for the table.

She thought about his hesitation at getting out of the car yesterday in the garage. And probably at the gas station, when he'd sent her in ahead of him. Could it be that when he insisted she leave him alone, it wasn't about drugs, but because he didn't want her to think he actually needed help? But he'd told her last night he was perfectly fine.

It was like he was lying to her either way—though it didn't matter, right? She already knew better than to trust him, and she wasn't getting involved with him. Right?

Now was not the time to follow that train of thought. Instead, she motioned for the young mother to come around the end of the table with the stroller, while Emma unfastened Patton's working uniform. The mother glanced at her husband—to check that he was good with the baby, Emma supposed—then nodded.

"Hey there." Emma led Patton closer to the stroller. "Do you want to meet Patton?"

"Doggy," the toddler said, tears immediately cut off.

"I don't like to give in when she's acting like this," the young mother said. "But I don't want to make Davis leave."

"That's fine," Emma said. "Under normal circumstances, we wouldn't do this, but it looks like your husband and Marcus were having trouble hearing each other, and we couldn't let her pet Patton while he's wearing his vest." To the little one, she said, "This is Patton. What's your name?"

"I'm Nicole," the mother said, "and this monster is Jenna. This is real nice, what you and your husband are doing."

Patton carefully approached the girl, eagerly wagging his tail and lowering his head. Jenna immediately grabbed an ear with each hand.

"Easy!" Nicole said at the same time Emma said, "My husband... Oh. No. Marcus is a...a coworker. My brother's actually in charge, but he's swamped right now, so we're here to represent the group."

Nicole glanced at the rings on Emma's left hand and shrugged. "Well, y'all look pretty good together."

Emma automatically twirled her wedding ring, wondering again if she should have left it in her jewelry box. Except she never took it off. It wasn't that she needed it to be a talisman against Marcus and his smooth moves or anything. She cleared her throat and changed the subject, turning it back on Nicole. "How long have you been married?"

"Almost five years," she said, looking over at her husband again. "Davis and I went to high school together, and we got married after he was in the marines for a couple of years. But right after our wedding, he got deployed. It was right at the beginning of his second tour—a couple of weeks after we found out that we were expecting Jenna—when he got hurt."

"What happened?"

"IED. The usual." Again, a turn to look at her husband.

"I'm sorry. It was bad?"

Nicole winced. "He lost a foot."

Emma couldn't help but glance under the table where she could see the men's lower extremities.

Nicole must have caught her look. "Oh, he's got a new foot. It doesn't look weird when he's got long pants on. But he walks funny, and that makes him mad."

"That sucks."

"I know. I tell him he should be proud of his foot, but he's just not happy, and he can't seem to get over it. It's messing up everything else in our lives. I'm not even sure how we managed to conceive Dustin." She waved in the direction of the baby happily cartwheeling his arms and legs through the air. "He says the reason he can't get a job is because no one believes he can do everything a normal guy can do, but I think that's *his* fear, not anyone else's. Self-sabotage, you know?"

And depression. And PTSD. Emma nodded. She had no business counseling anyone else—look at how badly she'd fucked up with her own veteran—but she could certainly relate. Maybe that's why this woman was suddenly spilling her guts.

"I talked him into coming here today so maybe he could meet someone who could help him find a job. I know he can do stuff, and maybe he'd try harder if there were other vets there."

"That's a great idea. There are some recruiters here whose whole purpose is to hire veterans to work for some great companies."

"We were on our way to that booth, but he got side-tracked by your man—I mean your *friend*—there." She smiled as though she recognized that Emma might not think of Marcus as a friend.

And that was true. He wasn't her *friend*; he was her albatross. Her sexy, funny, likable in-spite-of-herself albatross.

"Phew." Marcus fought a grimace and lowered himself into a chair behind the table. "I'm glad we went for the volume discount on pamphlets. Do we have any for tomorrow?"

Emma checked the box she'd stowed beneath the table. "We should be okay. It's cool that we got a spot right next to the entrance. Lots of people stopped."

"I think having a dog with us makes people notice, but they're not weird about it. They actually meet your eyes. They don't look away because they're so uncomfortable to see a disabled person." He gave Patton a stroke. "I want to tell everyone, 'Hey, look, he's in training. I'm not really disabled.'"

Did Marcus even realize how much he relied on the dog? "You were leaning on him a lot," she pointed out.

"Hey, you were sitting back here collecting email addresses. I was the one standing all day, working my charm."

"Uh-huh. I don't think you get to call it hard work if it's something you do in your spare time anyway."

There was that devastating smile again. "You think I'm charming?"

Oops. She plastered on what she hoped was a conde-scending smile. "I know you think so, anyway."

He didn't respond because he had to reach into his pants pocket for his phone. "Oh, hey. This is a text from that guy with the two kids and the fake foot."

"Really? You gave him your personal phone number?"

He gave her a funny look. "Yeah, why not?"

"Because it seems…dangerous. I mean, yeah, he seemed like a nice enough guy, but his wife says he's having a hard time getting reintegrated into life, and you never know when someone's going to turn into a stalker."

Marcus shook his head as though she'd disappointed him. "That's exactly why I gave him my number—not the stalker part, you're totally overreacting there—because he's in bad shape. He's standing there, holding his kid... Did you see those kids? Damn, they were cute."

Yes. She'd noticed how cute the kids were. Cute enough to make her ovaries jump around and threaten to pop.

"He's standing there with his kid in his arms, telling me about how often he gets his gun out, trying to decide where he should do himself in so he'd make the least mess for his wife to clean up."

Oh God. Emma's heart fell into her stomach, and she covered her mouth with her hand.

"Hey. Hey, Em—" Marcus was standing now, too. He pulled her into his arms, and her eyes immediately began to leak. "Don't cry, sweetheart. Please don't cry."

She couldn't help it. The guy reminded her so much of Todd. He even had the same color hair, same build. When she'd seen those kids, they'd seemed familiar, and she realized that she might have been looking at the kids she and Todd might have had. Could have had.

"I think he's going to be okay." Marcus was still talking to her, murmuring into her hair, stroking her back.

It felt so good. So...safe, as if he were going to keep her isolated from all the horror of the real world. She realized she'd put her arms around his waist and held on for dear life.

No. Not a good idea. She took a deep breath, gathering her wits and pushing away from him, only to see his deep-brown eyes examining her with concern.

"I'm okay. Sorry."

"It's okay. There were a few times today I felt like crying, too." He put a hand on Patton's head. "But that always makes the dog nervous, so I try not to do it often." He laughed.

Was he serious? Did he ever cry into the dog's fur at night when the nightmares got too bad?

"Let me answer this text, and then we should go get some dinner, yeah? And I bet ol' Patton would like to use the facilities, wouldn't you, buddy?" The dog panted happily, not really caring what was next on the list as long as he got to go along.

"So what did the guy want? The guy with the cute kids?" She couldn't help but ask.

"Just to thank me for the information. To tell me he wants to find out about getting a support dog, and if it's possible to train one himself."

"That's ambitious," Emma said.

"Yeah," he agreed. "With a houseful of babies who are going to want to play with it all the time, separating work from fun would be challenging." And then some. "That little girl screamed and cried for Patton the moment you put his work vest and harness back on him."

"Maybe an 'emotional support' animal would be more appropriate," she said. "And that would be basically a pet."

"Good idea. When I was talking to him, he said he was struggling to connect with his kids, and his wife was constantly terrified he'd lose his shit in front of them and scare them."

"That's awful. I did notice she was pretty attentive to him the whole time she was sitting back there talking to me." Just like Emma had watched Todd, never knowing if he was having a good day or a bad one.

"Yeah. So maybe a dog could bridge the gap. He'd have

someone to take care of and to help him practice acting like a dad, kind of. And the kids could play with the dog as much as they wanted."

That wasn't a bad idea, she mused. There were a few dogs that would never pass muster as a service animal, but who *could* be adopted and loved. "Maybe he should come stay at the ranch for a couple of weeks and work with some dogs before he took one home," she suggested.

Marcus's smile was devastating, as usual. "I had the same great idea. We just have to convince your brother that it's brilliant, too. And find a few more bucks to house more guests."

Emma thought about that while she gathered her backpack from below the table and looked around to make sure they weren't leaving behind anything that might get stolen. She also thought about Marcus, and how, no matter how hard she tried to convince herself otherwise, he wasn't the anti-Christ. He cared for people. *Doggone it.*

"Hey there. Dog man."

An older man, probably sixty or so, paunchy and with white hair and mustache, stood on the other side of the table, smiling broadly at Marcus.

"Hello," Marcus said.

"I want to talk to you about your business."

"Okay. What can we do for you?"

"It's not what you can do for me; it's what I can do for you. Not that there's nothing in it for me, you understand," the man said, winking.

Chapter 12

"I'll have the prime rib, extra bloody," Dale Thornhill told the server. "And another double of Pappy."

Marcus shrugged slightly at the wide-eyed stare Emma sent him. It seemed their would-be donor had not just champagne tastes, but *Holy Crap* tastes. Pappy Van Winkle bourbon was like fifty dollars a shot for the younger stuff, and this guy had ordered the twenty-five-year-old.

"You sure you don't want one?" Dale asked Marcus.

"No, thanks. I'll stick to beer." He sipped from his mug. He noticed Thornhill hadn't asked Emma if she wanted any, but an eyebrow-raised nonverbal exchange with Emma told him to ignore the slight. Which he would do—for now.

"What are you gonna have?" their host asked Marcus.

"I... Emma, why don't you go first."

She blinked. "I think I'll try the half rack of baby back ribs. And a side salad with ranch."

Thornhill shook his head. "The prime rib is mighty good," he told Marcus.

Marcus looked at the menu again. He couldn't quite wrap his head around an entree that cost eighty-five dollars. Hell, an entire meal for three people at eighty-five dollars was almost outside his realm of comprehension. He cleared his throat and said, "That sounds great, but I think I'm in the mood for the grouper. Blackened, please, with blue cheese on the salad." At sixty-dollars a plate, that was too damned much, but unless he ordered mashed potatoes and nothing else, he didn't see an alternative.

"Lovely," the server said and disappeared without tripping over Patton, who lay patiently next to Marcus's chair.

"You don't know what you're missing," Thornhill said. "I'll have to take you to N'Awlins one of these days. There's a little place there with the best damned crawfish étouffée you've ever tasted. So spicy it'll make your balls twitch."

"Wow," Emma said. "I'll definitely have to try that."

Marcus suppressed a laugh, but Thornhill didn't seem to get the joke. Who *was* this guy? And why on earth would he think he would ever have any reason to take Marcus and Emma anywhere besides this dinner, right now? They still hadn't learned what this was about.

"I'm sure you're anxious to hear what I'd like to do for you," Thornhill said.

"Well, yes, actually," Emma said, poking an ice cube around in her Diet Coke.

"It's like this," Thornhill said. "I'm an attorney here in Houston, and I've done well. My fees are astronomical, and I have more cash than I know what to do with."

"What kind of lawyer?" Emma asked.

"Corporate merger-and-acquisition stuff. I get in the middle when one company wants to buy another, that sort of thing."

Clearly it was too complicated for her to worry her pretty little head about, and Emma shot Marcus a look that said *Your turn. You and your penis can take over from here.*

"Okay," Marcus said. "You're rich."

Thornhill laughed, more heartily than was necessary, but hey—he was buying dinner. He could laugh as artificially as he liked. Marcus might be leery of the overpriced food, but he wasn't too proud to be bought.

"I am, indeed, rich. And I've got to do something with some of this money before the IRS comes knocking on my door, if you know what I mean."

Not really. Marcus was doing okay financially right now, but mostly because he was freeloading at the ranch.

Thornhill went on. "I need to donate a significant chunk of change into a charitable organization by the end of the year, or I'll have to pay way more in taxes than I think Uncle Sam deserves. I saw your dog there, read your flyer, and thought, 'Dale, old buddy, these are your people.' I love dogs. I love people who love dogs. If it was up to me, I'd have thirty of the summbiches myself. The wife, though… She's a cat person. She's got a few of them white ones with the squinched-up faces." He shuddered. "Can't stand the nasty things myself. Women, right?"

"Uh…"

Thornhill didn't need an answer before he turned to Emma. "What about you, miss?"

Emma blinked and said, "I'm mostly a dog person, I guess, but cats are okay, too."

"How many dogs do you have?" he demanded.

"Ah…none right now."

"*Hmph.*" Thornhill shook his head. "Seems like everyone with a dog business should have a few dogs."

"I… It's not the right time," she said.

"Dogs can get expensive, can't they?" Thornhill asked. "You gotta feed 'em and take 'em to the vet, and there's all that other stuff you're looking to do."

"Yes, sir," Marcus said, trying not to drool on the

tablecloth over the thought of delivering a huge amount of money to the ranch in time to do a hell of a lot of good. "We have a decent nest egg, but we're operating on a shoestring right now, and that string's a little frayed in spots. We could certainly use all the financial support we can get to keep our facilities operational and hopefully expand."

"Yes, yes, I can see how that could be." Thornhill chuckled. "Well, let me tell you. I've got fifty thousand dollars with your name on it—and possibly more after that—but I need to see your business plan and confirm some details before I cut you a check. Think you can get that information together for me and reserve a board room by the time that awards ceremony ends tomorrow? I have a couple of friends I'd like to bring by. Nothin' fancy, just an introduction."

"You bet." Marcus began to hope that Dale Thornhill wasn't so much an obnoxious show-off as he was a slightly insensitive, quirky benefactor. Marcus had no idea if they had a *business plan* or not, but he'd stay up all night until he got one done. Surely there were YouTube video tutorials. He looked at Emma, saw the gleam in her eye, and knew she'd stay right up with him until they were sure they could convince wealthy Mr. Thornhill that they were worth his money.

The next hour consisted of Emma smiling and nodding or shaking her head, while Marcus said, "No shit?" or "That's crazy!" in response to the increasingly ridiculous stories Mr. Thornhill told about his exploits. It was like listening to a script reading of *Indiana Thornhill and the Temple of Bullshit.*

Finally the meal ended, and they said good night at the entrance to the hotel. They shook Thornhill's hand and promised a thorough presentation of the Big Chance Rescue Ranch business plan the following afternoon. "I'm counting on you, buckaroo!" Mr. Thornhill said with a spine-realigning slap to Marcus's upper back before he marched to the valet stand and demanded a taxi. "Not one-a those oober things, either."

Emma and Marcus were silent while they waited for Patton to have some personal time in the patch of grass near the front door and as they walked across the lobby. It wasn't until they were alone in the elevator, the doors closed, the floor number button pushed that Emma spoke. "Did he seriously just call you 'buckaroo'?"

"I'm still recovering from how hard he smacked me on the back. I'll be creeped out about the 'buckaroo' thing later. At least he knew *I* was there."

"Right?" Emma tugged at her spiky blue hair and frowned. "It's like my vagina produced a cloak of invisibility or something."

Marcus snorted. "You did not just say that."

She grinned. "I totally just said that."

He opened his mouth, then shut it again. Finally, he said, "I'm speechless."

"Wow!" she said, leading the way into the hall when the doors opened on their floor. "It really is a magic vadge."

They were both still laughing when they reached her door. She had her key card in her hand, but turned to meet his eyes before she unlocked the door.

She was always pretty—not in spite of her unconventional looks, but more like…her perfect pointed chin and high cheekbones, perfect bow lips and sparkling eyes made the hair, makeup, and jewelry look like they belonged on her. But *now*—now that she was smiling *at him*, she was so fucking beautiful his breath caught.

"What?"

He shook his head. If he tried to tell her, she'd laugh and slam the door in his face.

She said, "Well, Mr. Thornhill might be a Class A jerk, but if he wants to give us money to do good things, I'm all about listening to his pitch."

Her excitement was infectious, and Marcus let it push any misgivings he was feeling aside. They weren't signing any paperwork; they were only going to make a proposal. No one was getting married. "It would be pretty cool to come home with a big, fat check, wouldn't it?"

"Oh. My. God," Emma said, hugging herself and wiggling with happiness. "I'm so psyched to tell Adam about this I could just—just—" She unhugged herself, threw herself into Marcus's more-than-welcoming arms, and kissed him. Her perfect red lips landed on his mouth, and he thought he might die of ecstasy.

Emma felt her knees weaken as Marcus took her happy-grateful-excited celebratory kiss and turned it do-me-right-now sexy. His mouth—those soft lips, tentative for a microsecond before taking command, moved over hers, stroking, savoring, *consuming* her before he even introduced his tongue, and *then*—holy ma-freaking-loly. His tongue slid over her lips, her teeth, exploring, tasting, making her desperate to feel everything of his against everything of hers. He held her in his arms, crushed against him. The pressure from his erection against her body made her squirm with need.

She had to have him. All of him. Every hard, sexy—

Something squeaked, reminding her they were in a public hallway.

She came up for air, gasping as Marcus tried to follow her mouth, but he released her, deep-brown eyes probing hers. "Are you okay?"

No, I almost lost my mind and invited you to boink me against the wall. Emma pushed at Marcus's big, solid chest, and her wedding ring reflected the wall sconce like a lighthouse beacon. Something—a cross between sexual frustration and despair—began to bubble up in her gut. "I'm okay. Just…back up."

A flash of concern crossed his face before he dropped his arms and stepped away.

She drew a deep breath, dismayed that the air was filled with him, with his scent, and that her body was still pulsing with the need to pull him back against her and then inside the room, and then down on the bed…

Down the hall, the elevator dinged, and a young college-aged couple got off. "Oh, look! A dog!" the woman said, scurrying toward them. "Can I pet your pooch?" Without waiting for permission, she squatted, took Patton's head in her hands, and began rubbing his ears. She made kissy noises and began to coo. "Oh, you're so sweet, you big lug of puppy!"

Patton glanced up at Emma and Marcus, as though to ask for help.

The woman's inconsiderate behavior on top of Emma's thwarted libido were too much. "Ma'am," she said through gritted teeth, then louder when the woman didn't respond, "Ma'am!"

"Hi!" The woman looked up as though she'd just realized the dog had humans.

"Please take your hands off of my friend's *service animal*."

The woman's brows drew together in confusion.

"Now, please."

"Well!" the woman said, straightening to glare at Emma. "I was just saying hello."

"This is a service dog, as it clearly says on his vest." Emma pointed at the patch on Patton's vest. "Right there. In big, yellow letters. Never, ever, *ever* touch a service animal unless you are invited to do so." Emma had a brief flash of fear that she was going way overboard at the moment, but was too far gone to stop herself.

"But I was just being friendly. He's not taking you anywhere, he's just standing there!" The woman pursed her gooey pink lips in annoyance.

"Heather, come on," her companion said, taking her arm.

Heather all but stomped her foot. "Why can't I say hello to your dog if it's not doing anything?"

"How do you know he's not doing anything?" Emma shot back. "Do you know if this dog is supposed to be sensing chemicals that would let us know if Marcus was about to have a seizure?"

Heather's eyes rounded as she backed up a step. "I—"

"Or maybe he's going to warn us that Marcus's blood sugar is dropping," she went on.

"I'm really sorry."

Heather seemed to get it now, but Emma was determined to drive home the point. "And in case you didn't notice, there's a veterans' convention in this hotel this week. If Marcus had PTSD and felt like you were threatening his support dog? He might be triggered, and there might be an incident. Do you want to be responsible for that?"

"Emma—" Marcus put a gentle hand on her shoulder, not yanking her arm like dog-molester Barbie's guy was doing, but as a friend offering support. Emma stopped ranting and took a deep breath. She clutched her earring, twisting it as she realized she'd just made a complete ass of herself. All of the fear and anger that had motivated her rant hemorrhaged onto the hall carpet, leaving her weak and on the verge of tears.

"I really am sorry," the woman repeated, letting herself be led away.

"It's not that big of a deal." Emma tried to keep the quaver from her voice, but her change in tone made the couple look back at her with confusion. So she made it worse. "Have a great night. Maybe we'll see you tomorrow." God, what was *that*?

There was a beat of silence as the couple let their hotel room door slide shut behind them.

Emma released her tormented earlobe and waved at her face, trying to cool the hot flush that burned her cheeks.

"That was... Wow," Marcus said, mouth compressed in a stifled grin. He scanned her key card and ushered her into her room, sending Patton to lie down near the foot of the bed. How had he gotten her key? "That was quite an eruption."

"Well, you know," Emma quipped, trying to make light of her fit, "they call me Miss Vesuvius. You never know when I'm going to erupt in a fit of passion."

Marcus's eyebrows rose, and she thought about what she'd said. And then about what they'd done before her tirade.

Please don't mention that kiss. "I mean...passionate

about service dogs. And how people act around them. It's not like they're a new invention, you know? Even little kids usually know how to behave around a dog wearing a vest. At the very least, wait for permission before—" She threw her hands up and waved them back and forth, mimicking the way that girl had molested Patton's head.

"Miss Vesuvius. I'll have to remember that." Miraculously, Marcus was laughing instead of backing away from her slowly. His smile sent warm wisps of something better ignored through her. "But while we wait for your next eruption, what do you say we call Adam and find out what he's got in the way of a business plan that we can remodel into a world-class proposal?"

Thank God he wasn't going to talk about the kiss. She couldn't deal with that right now. "Sure," she said, deliberately moving to the door that joined their rooms and opening it. "Can I have ten minutes to change clothes and scrub off this makeup?"

"Sure," he said, sauntering to the door and nodding for Patton to follow. "But there's not much makeup left. I think I might have kissed it all off you."

"Oh God," she muttered, slamming the door behind him with more force than necessary.

Chapter 13

MARCUS WAITED A FULL FIFTEEN MINUTES BEFORE knocking on Emma's door. He had no idea how to play it when he saw her again, because he suspected she'd be prickly after that kiss comment as he was leaving her room. He should have saved the Oreos. She'd really liked the cookies.

He glanced in the mirror and rearranged a couple twisted locks that were out of place. He'd have to get them cut off before he reported for the medical board, but he wasn't going to do it too soon, afraid he'd jinx himself. Even thinking about doing something to make the board think he wasn't up to snuff was a bad idea, so he banished the thought and knocked on the door that separated his body from Emma's.

She opened it before he had his hand back at his side, but turned away without meeting his eyes. "I texted Adam and told him to gather everyone for an emergency phone call. He should be calling any minute now. He wanted to wait for Lizzie to get there so he could get her input."

Made sense. Lizzie was all up in her own charitable organization, so she'd have some ideas about what donors were looking for and how best to court them.

He entered the room, ushering Patton along and signaling to the dog to follow. "Do you want to talk about—"

"No!" She raised both hands, palms out, to ward him off. "I do not. Let's just work on—"

"You *don't* want to talk about things we need to know so we can make a list?" he finished, trying not to smile.

With an exasperated sigh—and a flaming blush—she hopped onto the bed and started banging away on her laptop. She ignored him while he made himself comfortable in one of the two chairs in the room. Patton leapt onto the bed and curled up.

Emma was so uncomfortable about the kiss that if he hadn't been there, been on the other end of it, he might think she was disgusted with him. But no, he'd felt her breasts press into his body, her hips move under his hands, tasted her coffee-and-mint-flavored lips, felt her sigh.

She was attracted to him. He'd sensed that the first several times he'd met her, when he and Jake had shown up to infiltrate Adam's hermit compound. They'd had some nice talks and shared a little in the way of long, lingering glances—in between her cold-shoulder moments, which had become more and more frequent.

She acted like she wanted nothing to do with him, but then he'd catch her staring at him. He wasn't going to go where he wasn't wanted, but damn it, he liked her quirky self, so he'd made sure to talk to her every chance he got and to be as indispensable as he could be. He'd even volunteered to take puppies to her grandfather's day-care place. Wait. He *had* offered, he was sure of it. And had plans to go. So why hadn't he—

Emma's phone rang, interrupting his musing. She answered, saying, "Let me put you on speaker."

A moment later, Adam said, "Okay, what's this big news?"

"Who's there with you?" Emma asked instead.

"Jake, Lizzie, and Tanner."

"Okay, Marcus is here with me." She took a breath, shot Marcus a smile, then said, "We had dinner tonight with a man who wants to donate fifty thousand dollars to the Big Chance Rescue Ranch."

There was silence on the other end, then a flurry of voices, none of which came through clearly until Adam said, "Okay, you guys, shut the hell up!" After things settled down, he asked, "What's the catch?"

"Catch?" Emma looked at Marcus. "There's no catch."

"There's got to be a catch. No one just walks in off the street and gives away free money."

He had a point. The wining and dining were a little over-the-top, but Marcus had chalked that up to the man's overblown ego, not ulterior motives. "I don't know, dude. The guy's just rich as shit and came to this gig looking for a charity to donate to. Says he needs to do it for tax purposes. If it looks like we're going to be a successful organization, he'll give us more."

"Who is this guy?" Lizzie asked.

"Dale Thornhill. A lawyer."

"I'll see if I can find out anything about him," Lizzie said.

Someone, probably Tanner, said, "And he's just going to give us a bunch of money."

"Well, not *just* like that," Emma told the rest of the crew. "He wants us to present a proposal to him tomorrow afternoon. To show him our business plan, what we've done so far and what we plan to do in the future."

The conversation got complicated after that. Everyone had ideas, and while fifty grand was a huge amount of money for a struggling charity, it wasn't enough to keep them afloat for long.

After Adam promised to send a file with copies of all the charitable organization forms and permits and so forth, which Emma would organize into a tidy summary, they finalized their wish list.

"We've already got dogs. Using rescue animals is great, even if it does complicate matters sometimes," Lizzie said. "The rescue angle works for a lot of people, and they're even more sympathetic."

"We're squeezing by with dog food and, thanks to Doc Chance, cut-rate veterinary services," Adam said. "What we need most now is some more indoor space to work with the dogs. Winter's coming, and barn space is tight, with all the kennels, runs, and stuff stored in there. I'd love to have some more room."

"We also need some more beds," Marcus said. "The house is getting a little crowded."

"Thanks for the warm welcome." That remark was Tanner for sure.

"Okay, so let's make a list of immediate needs and wants, and then prioritize," Lizzie said. "I'll write up the list and send it to you guys in Houston. You can add whatever you think you should to it and include it in the proposal. Let's aim for the stars, but give him something closer to the moon that he can deliver."

After another hour of conversation about where else they should look for funding—big and small—Emma said, "We've got a lot to work with and my battery's about to die, so let's end this call."

"Plug it in," Adam told her.

"Bite me," she said back.

"Oh boy. I forgot to say 'please,' didn't I?"

"Goodbye, Dipwad." Emma rolled her eyes.

"Goodbye, Buttface."

Emma grinned and disconnected. Marcus couldn't imagine having a conversation like that with his siblings. He was surprised sometimes they didn't want him to address them as "Doctor" and "Your Honor."

The next two hours flew by in a flurry of brainstorming, and typing, and rehearsing so they'd be ready for anything when they met with Mr. Thornhill.

"I think we're almost there," Emma finally said, setting her laptop aside and yawning. She rubbed the point where her neck met her shoulder. "I don't think I've typed that much since high school."

"Let me do that," Marcus said, brushing her hand out of the way.

When he began to knead the tight muscles, she groaned. He moved from her shoulders to her upper arms, unable to ignore the contrast between his dark skin and the colorful swishes of ink running over her pale flesh. How would they look entwined together in bed? And how colorful was the skin beneath her clothes? Did she have tattoos on her stomach? A belly-button ring?

"Thank you," she said, and he realized his hands had slowed from massage land and into caress territory.

He cleared his throat and shifted away. "I'm always here, anytime you need a massage," he said.

She snorted and said, "You can't fool me with the old back-rub trick. Todd tried that a few times before I wised up."

That was the first time Emma had mentioned her late husband. Before Marcus had time to cypher out a question so he could learn more, she toppled over on the bed, cradled her head in her arms, and asked, "Do you care if I shut my eyes for fifteen minutes before we start working again?"

Before he could answer, she let out a gentle snore.

Marcus dimmed the lights, then settled back in his seat and propped his feet on the end of the bed. He pulled out his own phone to check for messages. One from his sister's friend Maya, asking him to give her a call. *Delete.* The fact that he always thought of her as his sister's friend before *lover* was a clear indication he shouldn't talk to her if he didn't have to.

There was already something from Tanner—a couple of documents with current operating costs and projections for the next two years with various scenarios—if they continued with their current goal of training six dogs this year, what if they doubled that, and so on.

The kid was good. He seemed determined to keep everyone at arm's length, but he knew what he was doing on the computer. It seemed to give him an escape from pain that wasn't just physical, from the horrendous damage he'd sustained. Tanner didn't think he had a place in the world anymore.

That was a feeling Marcus identified with, which was why he'd spoken up and offered him the job. Marcus was already a big lug of uselessness at the ranch. Maybe not completely useless, he reminded himself. He was going to get Thornhill to donate a butt load of money for the ranch because he was a master schmoozer.

He'd even gotten Emma to thaw toward him. A little.

He looked at the woman curled on her side in the middle of the bed, the blankets pulled up around her like a cocoon. He was going to have to talk to her about things, because that one kiss earlier hadn't been nearly enough, and before he tried again, he had to make sure he wasn't going to screw up.

Chapter 14

EMMA RECOGNIZED SOMETHING DIFFERENT FROM YESTER-
day morning before she even opened her eyes. For one thing,
she was wearing her least-comfortable bra and the jeans that
rode down a *little* too low in the back every time she bent over.
Distracting her from the discomfort of her clothes, however,
was a delicious spicy scent, both familiar and exotic.

Marcus.

Her lids popped up and there he was in the chair next to
the bed, feet propped on the mini-fridge, arms crossed over
his chest. His head tilted forward slightly, but she could still
see his face well enough—and that normally present teasing smirk of his was nowhere to be seen. Those lips were
even sexier now, if that was possible, making her wonder if
the kiss last night had been an anomaly, or if a repeat would
send her libido into orbit.

Marcus's lips and tongue had taken her mouth like tasting her was the only way to survive. And that was a first kiss.
Would future kisses be even hotter?

Probably not. It was just that Emma hadn't had many
other first kisses to compare it to.

Her first kiss from Todd, spring break during her senior
year of high school, had been one degree removed from a
medical emergency. He'd drawn the short straw—or so
Emma had believed at the time—and driven her home after
she'd worked a late shift at Dairy Queen.

Todd was days from getting on the bus to basic training for the army. Adam had gone the day after he graduated, but Todd hadn't turned eighteen until late the summer before, so he had only enlisted recently. He'd taken a few college courses online in the meantime, but mostly he'd been at loose ends, working at his parents' Feed and Seed or hanging out at the Dairy Queen, where Emma worked the counter.

Emma knew Todd missed Adam, because he asked her every day if she'd heard from him, even though he knew Adam was unlikely to call or write, even if he was allowed to.

But then Todd—larger than life and almost as funny— drove her home that warm spring night, telling her about his plans, actually asking her about hers, talking to her as though she were *his* friend, not just Adam's weird little sister.

Of course, she'd always had a crush on the big, goofy offensive lineman who had been teasing her since the first time Adam brought him home from school, shortly after they'd moved in with Granddad. Todd had starred in all of her teen fantasies, but on that spring night, it was almost as though he saw past the dyed-black hair, the black fingernails, the eyeliner, and noticed she was a woman.

When he pulled up in the quiet barnyard at the ranch, he'd turned to her. Instead of speaking, he'd looked at her for a long, serious minute before saying, "I'm gonna miss you."

It had been Emma's turn to make a joke then, to try to lighten the intensity that had filled the car. She didn't remember what she'd said, something like, "Well, yeah, who else will put extra sprinkles on your butterscotch sundae?"

Instead of responding, he'd closed his eyes for a moment as though making a decision, then opened them again, leaned in, and kissed her.

Emma was surprised, and her gasp was mistaken as an invitation for tongue, which surprised her even more, but after a few seconds, she managed to appreciate the effort. She'd just begun to recover, to slide her arms around Todd's neck and enjoy the experience, when a jolt bounced Emma so much that she almost bit his tongue. The pair leapt apart to realize that, in his enthusiasm, Todd had forgotten to put the car in Park, taken his foot off the brake and let the car roll into the back of Granddad's truck.

Fortunately, they got better at kissing and eventually said "I do," during one of Todd's leaves.

Odd that waking up with one man—one very sexy, appealing man—made her think of Todd, of *good* times with Todd, when usually she only remembered the end. Casually, trying not to think about it too much, and pretending to herself she didn't even realize what she was doing, she slid her wedding band from her finger and put it in her pocket.

Marcus shifted, bringing Emma's attention back to the present, to the man who was here now. There were tight lines at the corners of his eyes, and as she watched, his fists clenched. What was he dreaming about?

During daylight hours, the man never seemed to get angry, or worried, or anything else negative. And it wasn't just his flirty nature—he'd worked hard yesterday, talking to veterans and their families, and she saw that underneath his superchill exterior was a man who cared deeply and wanted to help people.

So what was bothering him now? Did his demons only come out while he slept? Did he manage to keep them suppressed under a thick coating of opioids? He honestly hadn't seemed drugged up at any point so far on this trip, so maybe Adam was right and he'd quit.

Of course she *could* simply ask him about it.

Yeah. That had always worked so well with Todd. As in, not at all. As in, she asked if he was taking anything, and he either protested too much, or not enough.

Hopefully, if Adam was right and Marcus was clean, he'd dealt with whatever demons haunted him. Otherwise, the bad stuff was still there and would visit again, and again, no matter how hard he tried to avoid it.

She was overcome with the urge to go to him and wrap herself around him, to try to ease whatever concerned him. Tell him he didn't have to kill himself with drugs to get by. But it was pointless. She'd already failed to save an addict and would never put herself through that again.

She reminded herself they were heading home later that afternoon, where she could escape the man who was so good at making her question her rules, partially because he was also good at kissing.

Marcus woke to the sensation of dull spears nudging his lower spine, probably because he was in an overstuffed but uncomfortable chair, and his feet had both gone to sleep. *Remember what that yoga rehab doc said. Breathe through it. In...out...move a little. In...out...move a little.* Eventually he'd ease into a better sitting position. Once the blood started flowing to the right areas, he could stand up.

Problem was, he had to take a leak, pronto.

He blinked, rubbing the sleep from his eyes, and found

Emma on the bed next to him, curled on her side, staring at him as though he were a strange foreign specimen.

"What time is it?" he asked to buy himself some time and hopefully distract her so he could move without an audience.

When she reached for the phone, he managed to get one foot on the floor before she looked back at him. "Six thirty."

"We're going to be late!" He sat up abruptly. Bad, bad idea. Pain streaked from his tailbone and fanned along the muscles of his lower back, seizing and holding him hostage. He had no idea how he managed to keep in the dozens of f-bombs desperate to escape his throat, but he must have, because Emma only furrowed her brow when she looked at him.

"We're okay on time," she said, mercifully oblivious to his distress and focused on her phone.

Patton raised his head and immediately got to his feet, moving next to Marcus, holding his harness in his mouth, ready and willing to get to work. "Good boy." Marcus patted the dog, grateful that he didn't have to pretend with him, except he needed more than the dog at the moment. This was likely to be bad. Really bad.

He'd been doing well lately. He'd made it through the week without meds, and he hadn't woken with this kind of pain in a while. But this one—this one felt like a setback. Normally, when the morning started like this, he'd be immobile by noon.

Not exactly how he planned to wow the world of veterans' services and leave the Big Chance Rescue Ranch financially secure when he returned to active duty.

Emma said, "Go get a shower, and I'll get a shower, and then we'll have breakfast and go over the presentation one more time. You're going to blow this away." The way she smiled, he almost believed her. Maybe a nice, long shower would loosen him up. A strong cup of coffee, and he'd be the self he wanted to be in no time.

But fifteen minutes and a few hundred gallons of hot water later, he wasn't sure he could ever be Functional Marcus. Getting pants on was practice for hell, his muscles protesting every attempt to lift his right leg and aim his foot in the right direction. He finally wound up lying back on the mattress where he could fold his leg up and hold the waistband of the pants, get his foot in the right hole, and tug the pants up far enough for him to rock forward and pull them up. He managed to stand and get the fly fastened before collapsing backward, sweating, onto the bed.

"Knock-knock," Emma said at the open door between their rooms, pausing when she saw his position. "Are you okay?" Her eyes traveled over him, from head to toe, and maybe lingering at the midway point.

His pain was nearly forgotten as he responded to her invisible touch. Her cheeks colored as she focused on his face, pressing her lips together, but he caught the brief appearance of her tongue when it crept out to lick her lips. What he wouldn't give to see her cross the room and climb over him, straddling him, bending over to kiss—no. He engaged his abs and managed to sit up before he punched out the front of his khakis, and he barely even whimpered from the pain in his back.

He shook his head on a deep inhale. "Just a little muscle spasm from sleeping in that chair." *And a groin spasm from looking at you in that snug tank top.*

"Oh." Her eyes narrowed momentarily, then she gave a fairly bland smile. "Shall we get breakfast?"

He slowly released the breath he'd just taken and nodded. "Sure. Hotel coffee shop okay?" He could do this; it was only a few dozen yards across the lobby. He *would* do this, damn it. He'd worked his ass off to keep the muscles in his body strong enough to protect the crap that was weaker, and he wasn't about to let a few hours in a hotel chair throw him off his course.

Emma yawned and stretched like a cat, distracting Marcus from his back pain because the blood all rushed somewhere else. "Wow, considering I slept in a pile in the middle of the bed, I feel pretty well rested," she said. That made one of them.

He allowed Patton to pull him to a standing position and offered his arm. "Shall we?"

After the briefest of hesitations, she put her hand on the crook of his elbow and allowed him to lead her to the door.

The walk to the elevator was relatively painless. The ride down to the lobby slightly less painless, as the car was filled with other conventioneers and Marcus found himself pressed against the back wall, with Emma's ass pressed into his lap. Just the smell of her hair was enough to make him tingle, but her scent combined with the feel of her body against his sent him from zero to rock hard in less time than it took to push the lobby button. He stood stock-still, hoping against hope that she wouldn't notice she was being probed. Should he say something? Apologize? Tell her he had a zucchini in his pocket?

The car stopped on every single floor, and each time, at least one more person got on. And Emma was pressed more and more firmly against him.

Patton, folded up against Marcus's right leg, let out a

whimper when someone stepped on his foot. The dog shifted, throwing Marcus slightly off-balance, and he grabbed the first solid thing his leashless hand came across, which was Emma. Emma's hip, in particular. And he could swear he heard her breath stutter slightly when she put her own hand over his and turned her head to ask him if he was all right. Again, that little move where she tried not to lick her lips when she looked at him. He was face-to-face with the woman he'd been fantasizing about for months, and his body was clamoring for more. He leaned forward. Emma's eyes widened a fraction.

A flash of pain in his lower back yanked him back from the edge of insanity. With a sharp breath, he straightened away from her just as the elevator pinged. No way could he come on to her with a body that wouldn't even let him put his pants on like a man. He covered his near-miss with an "Oh, hey, here we are." Like she'd be fooled that he wasn't about to kiss her in a crowded elevator?

They were the last to exit the car, and Marcus followed Emma to a stop near a potted fern, looking between the coffee shop and the front doors. "Do you want to take Patton out to do his thing before we eat?" she asked.

The dog looked up at Marcus expectantly. "Okay," Marcus said. "I guess we should get moving." But when he told his right leg to lead the way, it refused to cooperate.

He flashed hot and cold with the possibility that all the physical therapy and strength training in the world didn't always stop this shit from happening. It was bad enough when he couldn't hide these little relapses from himself. Knowing Emma would see what a damned weakling he was made it a million times worse.

Chapter 15

EMMA WAS HALFWAY ACROSS THE LOBBY BEFORE SHE realized Marcus wasn't with her. When she turned, he was standing next to a big ceramic planter, staring at nothing with brows furrowed and lips tight. His shoulders were slumped until she caught his eye, then he straightened, Patton patiently shifting to take his weight. In an instant, the frustrated, dejected look was gone, replaced with the cocky smile she both adored and mistrusted.

"Are you coming?" she asked, walking back toward him.

"Sure. I was just"—he waved vaguely at an older couple a few yards away—"trying not to run over people."

Okayyyy… Those people hadn't been within five yards of them a moment ago, had they? What was going on here? His skin shone with a haze of sweat. He was *sick*. How many times had she seen Todd looking this way? Right before he made some sort of lousy excuse and—

"I need to stop in the men's room," Marcus said. "Do you mind taking Patton outside?"

Right. *Damn* it. "Sure. Come on, buddy," she said to the dog, taking the leash without another word and moving quickly to the exit. She didn't look back until she'd made it through the sliding glass doors. She expected to see Marcus disappearing into the men's room, but he was right where she'd left him, eyes focused in the middle of nowhere. Eventually he pulled something out of his pocket and popped it into his mouth, dry-swallowing his drugs. And *then* he turned and walked stiffly toward the restroom.

As a lump of disappointment swelled in her gut, Emma cursed herself for letting her guard down. She followed Patton to the pet relief station. She'd begun to let herself believe Marcus was different than Todd. *And in many ways, he is,* the foolish, hopeful part of her brain pointed out.

Marcus wasn't completely locked into himself and the inner misery that drove him to overmedicate. He was involved in the goings-on at the ranch and made an effort to reach out to people to help and get to know them, not just to find out what they had to help him escape his demons. She'd never seen him lash out or throw anything in anger, either.

And Adam trusted him. Was Adam a good judge of character, or was he under the delusion that the intense band-of-brothers friendship he'd developed with Marcus under fire was still in play? Even though Emma had never picked up an M4 rifle, she knew as well as any soldier that things were different in the civilian world.

She blew out a frustrated breath, distracting Patton from the potpourri of wonderful scents he'd found next to a small tree. She wasn't letting Todd ruin her life anymore, she reminded herself. But was she still trying to fix him? After the fact? Because here she was, attracted to another man who popped pills. And this one was doing it only a few hours before he was supposed to present their proposal to Thornhill.

She'd come here to keep him out of trouble, and it looked like she'd merrily fallen into her old habits. "Damn," she muttered. She had to confront him, and it wasn't going to be pleasant. Patton finally finished his business, so she told him what a good boy he was and took him back inside.

Marcus waited right inside the door, and the way his eyes lit up—along with the welcoming smile he gave her—sent warm tendrils to wrap around the rock in Emma's stomach, trying to hug it into disappearing. Lines of tension marred his perfect complexion, but his pupils seemed normal.

Confusion paralyzed her tongue. She didn't want to cause a scene, but she had to be sure—

"There's a breakfast buffet and a guy making omelets in there," he said. "I might have to have one of everything."

She didn't respond.

"What's wrong?" Marcus asked, a concerned hand on her upper arm.

"I need to know if—"

"Are you bringing a dog in here?" a middle-aged woman in a pink polo shirt asked from a nearby table.

"Here we go again," Marcus murmured. "Did you bring your Service Dog Superwoman cape down with you?"

Emma was so surprised at the way the conversation shifted from what was in her brain that she snort-laughed, which probably didn't help when she turned to speak to the complaining woman. "I'm sorry, is there a problem?"

"You've got to be breaking all kinds of health codes by bringing a *dog* into a *restaurant*," the woman said slowly, as though Emma and Marcus might not understand.

"We can bring him just about everywhere," Emma said, promising herself she wouldn't overreact like she had with the woman in the hall the other night. "Patton's a service dog-in-training."

"Well, isn't that something!"

Emma pulled a flyer for the Big Chance Dog Rescue from the folder she carried and said, "Here's some information about service dogs and our program, run by veterans for veterans."

"How interesting." The woman's gaze cut to Emma's arms, to the tattoos that covered her skin, before she looked at Marcus, then shrugged. "Huh."

"Have a lovely day, ma'am," Marcus told her, steering Emma and Patton to the other side of the room.

"For God's sake," Emma whispered when they were out of earshot. "What was that 'Huh' about? Did you see her give me the hairy eyeball? Was that some sort of judgment?"

"I don't know," he said, peering back over his shoulder. "But she's still looking at us." And he leaned down then and planted a very big, make-no-mistake kiss on her lips.

Marcus heard Emma's sharp intake of breath and smiled against her lips. He did love keeping her off-balance. But damn it, he hated it when anyone else messed with her peace of mind.

With a tiny nip at Emma's bottom lip, he raised his head and pulled out the chair for her. "Is she still looking?" he asked.

Emma rolled her eyes and tugged at her shirtsleeves, as though to pull them farther down over her tattoos. "Yes."

"Good."

"What was that about?" She waved her hand back and forth between them, referring to the kiss.

He got Patton settled beneath the table and carefully lowered himself into the hard chair before answering. "I couldn't tell what she was being judgy about. Your body art, or your Black boyfriend."

Her eyes flashed. "You are *not* my boyfriend," she hissed.

"Then why did you let me kiss you?"

"I didn't let—" She broke off to smile at the waitress who approached with a coffeepot.

"Can I get you a menu?" the server asked.

Emma glanced at Marcus, and said, "Can you give us a minute?"

"I didn't *let* you kiss me," she said as soon as the server was out of earshot.

"You're right. You totally met me halfway," he countered.

"Because you surprised me! I didn't *mean* it," she sputtered.

"Oh. So then what was that little bit of tongue action for?"

Her mouth opened, and he could tell she was revisiting the moment in her mind. "I…" She paused, then closed her mouth again, blushing furiously. Then she took a deep breath, let it out, and nodded. She'd obviously just made some sort of decision, and he was afraid it wasn't going to be in his favor.

"What is it?"

"Marcus, I have to ask what's going on with you."

"What's going—"

She held up a hand. "It's not really any of my business, except it kinda is, because it's my *brother's* business."

Marcus wasn't sure what made him look up, but between trying to puzzle out Emma's words and the throbbing in his back, it took a second to register. There was a kid, a few feet away, squirming to break free of his mother's hand.

And here he came. Right. Toward. Patton. Time slowed

down, and the kid barreled along the collision course. Marcus stood and tried to step in front of Patton to protect him.

The kid bounced off Marcus's legs, laughing and giggling as his mother swooped him up and left behind a quick apology.

"No problem," Marcus told her. And it wouldn't have been, except when he tried to sit back down, his body put him on lockdown. A clutching fist of pain twisted the muscles in the lower half of his body.

Oh Jesus, and no, Mama, I am not taking the Lord's name in vain. This is a real prayer for mercy.

Before he could take a breath, Emma was on her feet, taking his plate. She put his food on the table and her hands on her hips. "What's the matter?"

"Something didn't agree with me." His voice sounded slurred as he tried not to gasp when he semi-lied. Hey, it was movement that didn't agree with him, not food, as he implied.

Her jaw tightened and she nodded. "How *sick* are you about to be?"

He took a long moment to evaluate his pain level and decide if he'd be able to get through the next couple of hours at this conference without selling his soul for a morphine pump. There was no way.

If only he'd kept a few of those pain pills for a day like this, he'd be able to get through that talk. Today was definitely a day to use them. *Yeah.* Like he'd have had any left for emergencies at this point. He sighed and said, "I need to go back to the room. You—you're going to have to deal with things today, okay?"

She nodded. "This is what I came for."

"What?"

"I expected this to happen." Her lips firmed into a thin line.

She'd known his body was going to betray him? "I don't understand—"

She shook her head to cut him off. "Not now. I've got to prepare to see Mr. Thornhill."

She was pale, and Marcus could see the whites of her eyes. But then Patton rose from the floor and nudged her hand—which he'd done for Marcus a time or two when the heebie-jeebies got to him, and which D-Day did when Adam was having an anxiety attack.

She was pissed. He didn't blame her; he hated himself right now.

She glared at him for a long moment, then looked down at herself, indicating the snug Big Chance Ranch polo tucked into khakis, but then tugged at her hair, which was as choppy as usual, though not as spiky as always. She twisted one of her earrings and said, "I don't exactly look professional." Okay, so she was mad, but she was also scared.

"I'm sorry. And you're perfect," he told her, meaning it. From the top of her silky head to the tips of her combat-booted feet, she was everything he could ever want. He had to get upstairs and lie down before the pain made him deliriously announce his undying love. "Seriously," he told her, when she rolled her eyes at his compliment. "You're fine."

She seemed to come to some conclusion and took a big, deep breath. "Okay. We don't have time to deal with your shit right now. I'll do this, and I'll do my best, but when I get done, we're going to have a long, serious discussion about your situation."

"Okay. Anything you want." Or not. The last thing he wanted was to have to look into Emma's eyes and see her pity when he told her how much he was hurting. She'd feel sorry for him, and he'd be tempted to wallow. Giving in to that sympathy would set him back more than another bomb blast. It was that much worse because he already felt like a freeloader and was likely to continue to be a drain on the Big Chance group for a while longer. Snagging the big donation from Mr. Thornhill would have eased his conscience, but now it looked like that wasn't going to be in his plus column, but hers. Hopefully.

Marcus started to consider his options as he shuffled toward the bank of elevators, tightly gripping Patton's harness. Maybe there was something he could do in the way of civil service. Like be the dude behind the counter at the post office. Or a greeter at Walmart. If they'd let him sit down while he did it.

He fought the urge to curse, reminded himself to chill. It would all work out somehow. All he needed to do was get to his room, take another couple Aleve—he knew he was over the dosage, but not by much—and try to lie still.

Chapter 16

EMMA WATCHED MARCUS SHUFFLE ACROSS THE LOBBY, Patton patiently matching his pace. As though he knew she was watching, Marcus straightened his enormous shoulders and slid a hand over the dog's head before they disappeared behind the elevator doors.

How was she going to do this? She hated trying to sell anything. Granddad had had to buy all of her candy bars when she had to sell them for school, she didn't even *try* to be a Girl Scout, and her ears still burned from the way her classmates laughed when she tried to give a speech about why a dog would be a better classroom pet than a gerbil.

She *would* do this, though. This was why she'd come, to make sure Marcus didn't screw things up for Adam. No way was she letting a high Marcus get in the way of a donor—*if* he was high. Anger at his behavior warred with concern: what if he was in withdrawal from going off his meds, like Adam said, or in pain? Well, she could find out and be forgiving later.

It wouldn't matter, she tried to tell herself. He was still bailing on her.

And she was confused! She was starting to like the guy—a lot.

Her traitorous body flushed, thinking about Marcus and what had happened in the elevator on the way to breakfast. Right in the middle of all those people, she'd been pressed back against him and his hard, hot body. She'd felt not only safe, but wanted. Not just because of the erection pressed against her backside, but his grip on her hip. The gleam in his eye when she'd turned to look at him. Her body was responding to him big time, but so was her heart. The self-absorbed pretty boy was turning out to be more than she'd given him credit for.

He cared. He took great care of Patton. He'd spent long hours with those veterans yesterday, worked late with her to make sure the ranch could stay solvent. And he'd brought her cookies. Damn it, she had to keep her feet on the ground, because no amount of sexy times or mushy feelings would overcome an addiction—for either of them. She remembered what Adam had said, that Marcus was off those drugs, but she knew better than to believe, no matter what her emotions wanted.

This was bad. Really bad. If she wasn't careful, she was going to love Marcus right into an early grave. She returned to her seat in the cafe and signaled the waitress for a fresh cup of coffee. Before she stood in front of Mr. Thornhill to beg for money, she needed her A game.

Her phone buzzed.

Adam: Good luck this morning.

She sent back a simple "Thanks," because she didn't want to wreck his hopes with the news that she was on her own at the moment, that his golden boy had bailed on them.

But then another text came in:

Adam: You'll do fine.

Aaand another one:

Jake: The dogs are counting on you.

This came with a photo of half a dozen ranch dogs, all lined up and looking longingly into the camera.

They knew she was going it alone. Marcus must have already called the ranch and confessed his defection.

Lizzie: You've got this.

While she appreciated her cheering section, she was beginning to wonder if they weren't protesting in her favor a little too much to be believed. Would she get a participation medal, even if her team didn't win the league championship?

She sent thank-you's, put her phone down, and opened the folder containing their notes. She double-checked her pocket for the flash drive with the presentation. She had a little while before she would meet Mr. Thornhill in the board room. Signing her name and room number to the breakfast bill, she made her way to the ballroom where the keynote address would be held and found a seat near the back.

The coffee she'd drunk turned to battery acid in her stomach, and the few bites of muffin threatened to make a reappearance as the speaker, someone from the Veterans Administration, was introduced. *Just concentrate on the facts,* she reminded herself. *You know why a group of veterans helping veterans to train assistance dogs is a great project. You know why the Big Chance Rescue Ranch is perfectly qualified to turn every cent of every dollar donated into great dogs that will help great people live great lives.*

Another text.

Marcus: You're going to do GREAT!

The hysterical laugh she tried to stifle turned the heads of only, oh, sixty or seventy of her closest neighbors.

With an apologetic smile, she returned her attention to the podium, only to realize that the speech was over, and everyone was applauding.

Grabbing her folder, she escaped the ballroom and hustled to the boardroom. She wanted to be ready for Thornhill when he arrived.

Wait.

Should she be ready for him? Or should she come in after he did—act more casual? No, she was desperately sucking up to this guy, and he knew that. She needed to show him all the respect he and his wallet deserved.

But still. Maybe she should at least get a drink of water from the fountain down the hall so she didn't croak when she spoke.

Sweat pooled in the small of her back as she opened the door of the boardroom to make her escape—and smacked right into the overinflated belly of their potential donor.

"Howdy, darlin'!" Thornhill said.

"Oh. I'm so…so sorry," she babbled. "I was going to… Never mind. I'm glad you made it, Mr. Thornhill."

"This is my associate," he said, introducing her to a swarthy young man in a suit that must have been custom-made to fit over his enormous biceps. "This is Butch, my accountant."

"Where's your man?" Thornhill asked, his voice huge in the small room, his friendly expression growing cooler.

A sense of foreboding thickened the air, making it hard to breathe, but Emma reminded herself that was all in her head. She thought about the little pep talk Marcus had given her earlier. She knew this stuff. She could do this.

"Ah…Marcus isn't feeling well this morning, and we decided that I should come ahead and do the presentation without him, rather than ask you to wait until we can both be present."

Thornhill stared at Emma—or rather, he stared at her chest, then shrugged and took a seat next to his friend. "I can't say I'm not disappointed—I like him—but let's hear what you've got to say."

At least he was upfront about his opinion of her. She shook that thought off. It was up to her. "Okay, then. Um, I have a PowerPoint to show you, so if you'll just give me two seconds, I'll get it up and—" She looked at the electronic contraption in the middle of the table. And then at the front of the room next to the screen. And then the back of the room, near the projector. Nothing had a USB slot. "I, uh… Just a minute." After wandering around for a few more moments, she had to acknowledge that she had no idea how to get her information onto the screen.

The hotel management had assured her there would be a laptop available, so she'd left hers upstairs.

She looked at Thornhill, who seemed oblivious and was messing around on his phone. She picked up the house phone and hit the number for the concierge.

"I'm sorry, Ms. Stern, but we don't provide computers for guests," the attendant said in a tone that suggested she was dumber than sand.

That was not what the guy said when they reserved

the room. "Thank you," she said insincerely and hung up. "Mr. Thornhill, I'm sorry. There was some confusion about audiovisual equipment. Give me just another minute, I'll run up to my room and get my laptop."

Thornhill sighed, scratching an eyebrow with a thick pinkie finger—complete with heavy gold ring. He looked up from his phone to Emma's boobs—and then her face. "I don't have time for that. Just give us your spiel. Do you have financial information for me?"

What did that even mean? Like, their actual bank statements and tax returns? The spreadsheet thingy where they tracked everything?

Damn Marcus for not being here to schmooze through this. Their first big donor was slipping through her fingers.

Emma cleared her throat. "Our proposal has information about the ranch and a summary of our expenditures and budget, as well as a wish list with estimates." Opening the folder, she pulled out the hard copy she'd had the presence of mind to have printed out at the business center.

She laid it on the table next to Thornhill, who blinked at it before he pulled it closer and began flipping through as she went into her spiel.

"The Big Chance Rescue Ranch was started by my brother, Adam Collins, and his two friends Marcus Talbott and Jake Williams this year because they recognize the need for trained service dogs to support their fellow veterans in transitioning from military to civilian life."

Thornhill continued flipping pages, and Emma kept talking.

"Many combat veterans have physical disabilities, and many suffer from traumatic brain injury, the signature wound of recent conflicts. It's difficult to gauge how many of our veterans suffer from post-traumatic stress disorder. The Big Chance Rescue Ranch is equipped to train animals to help veterans deal with all those issues. We don't propose to help every single one, but we do plan to make a difference for the vets who come to us. Adam was an MP and a military working dog handler in the army and comes from a family of dog trainers. Our grandfather—"

"What's your financial situation now?" Thornhill asked. "Bottom line."

She found the right page and showed it to him, and he raised his eyebrows. "You do need money. I don't believe you've even got enough to get out of the gate." He glanced at his friend.

Butch glanced at the paperwork and gave a slight shrug.

Thornhill rubbed his chin. "I'm not pouring money into a business that won't use it wisely."

Emma thought fast. There was still Granddad's nursing-home money. "My brother sold a piece of property recently, and there's a respectable amount from that, which can cover some operating costs and improvements for the first few months. We didn't list it on the paperwork because we want to make sure we have things squared away with our accountant for tax purposes."

Now the look Butch gave Thornhill was more of a nod.

Thornhill didn't bother to look at the projected budget page before he pushed the papers toward Butch and slapped his hand onto the table. "I'll have to see the operation," he told her breasts.

Emma stared. Why would he say that? This wasn't going well, and disappointment made it difficult to keep an upbeat tone. "Okay. If you'll look here…" She moved behind him and bent over his shoulder—where he couldn't look at her chest—and flipped to a photo of the ranch. "This is the Big Chance Ranch property…"

He waved a hand and said, "Not this. I'd need to *see* it in person before I wrote a check. Make sure you've got that income from selling the property in your account by then."

Crap. She'd just given away Granddad's living expenses, hadn't she? Once they transferred that money to the non-profit's account, they wouldn't be able to use it for anything else.

She bit the inside of her cheek to keep from crying when she realized they wouldn't be able to afford Golden Gardens for Granddad. He'd have to go somewhere that wasn't as nice—or she'd have to keep him at home, and now wasn't the time to realize she wasn't able to care for him on her own anymore.

Gathering herself, she pointed to the business card tucked into a slot inside the folder and cleared her throat. "Here's contact information for the ranch. If you'd like to visit, just give us a call or drop an email and let us know when to expect you."

Thornhill nodded and rose. "I'll be in touch."

Chapter 17

MARCUS FLINCHED WHEN PATTON HOISTED HIS BULK onto the mattress beside him. It had taken a good twenty minutes to get his shoes and pants off, and another thirty to lower himself to a horizontal position. Every degree of movement released another dagger into his spine, but he'd finally managed to find a measure of at least less *dis*comfort. Having eighty pounds of *assistance* canine disrupt that blessed freedom from agony was a cruel joke.

But then the dog snuggled up, pressing his body into Marcus's side, and he felt a little better. Marcus had heard all the dog propaganda about how having pets was good for the blood pressure, slowed the aging process, yada yada, and he'd seen it work with his friends. Marcus's main arguments in favor of dogs had always been that they could do funny tricks and were useful wingmen for meeting girls. Now he wondered if there wasn't some sort of magical vibe the dog released, because he was actually starting to relax.

Hell, he might even be able to doze off for a few minutes, if the planets lined up. He needed a little rest, because his big adventure—from hotel room to café and back to hotel room—had taxed him more than he wanted to admit, and he had to spend several long, painful hours in a car later that afternoon.

And then he had a terrible thought. He wouldn't be able to drive. There was no way he'd be able to move his legs well enough to use the brakes, much less turn his head to see behind him. Emma would have to drive home. She'd made him a nervous wreck on the way here, and his pain level had only been about a five. Right now it was a twelve. He might not live long enough to get home.

Not for the first time, he missed his pain meds, but immediately reminded himself that he didn't need that shit.

Breathe, he reminded himself. Relax into it. Picture Lake Cumberland on a hot July day, floating on a raft, music from a distant houseboat, birds singing...a pretty girl in a bikini floating next to him. Would Emma wear a bikini? He pictured her in something from an old Elvis movie, covering a fair amount of skin, but so much sexier for the way it enhanced her curves.

How was she doing with Thornhill, he wondered. In spite of her stage fright, he was sure she'd done fine. He looked to the open connection between their rooms, then at his phone, which was on and blank. She should be back soon. And was hopefully done being mad at him for bailing on her. Was that what she was mad about? He'd been in so much pain earlier, he wasn't sure, but now he just knew she'd appear in the doorway smiling because she'd convinced Thornhill to donate enough money to keep the ranch going for a couple of years. Then she'd cross the room slowly, stopping at the end of the bed. She'd look at him lying there in his boxers and nothing else, all helpless and hard as a fucking Louisville Slugger, and she'd lick her lips. She'd lean forward, placing her hands on the end of the mattress and begin to move toward him...crawling like a cat, moving along his body...

Click. Before he had time to yank his brain out of fantasy mode and brace himself for movement, Patton was on his feet and jumping to the floor. "Fuuuuck."

Gritting through a haze of pain, he didn't notice Emma at first, standing in the doorway, hands on hips, glaring at him as though he'd eaten all of her Easter candy.

"What's wrong?" he asked.

"Are you kidding me?" Eyes flashing fire, she threw her hands into the air before planting them firmly back on her hips.

"I—"

"I had to give a nonpresentation in a room with no computer, give our pitch to a man who only wanted to hear from you or my tits, only to have him walk out after giving me some bullshit line about coming to the ranch— and you, Mr. I've Got Food Poisoning, were up here *jerking off*?"

"What?" He followed her gaze to his crotch, where his Emma fantasy-induced erection was only now beginning to flag. He grabbed a pillow and covered his junk, because that growl coming from deep in her chest sounded like a precursor to a gonad-removing binge.

He tried a cocky smile. "You know, babe, I wasn't actually—"

"Don't you dare 'babe' me. I've been down that road already. I don't know why I thought you might be…be…" She pressed her lips together, and he thought she might be fighting tears.

What was going on here? He tried to raise his head from the pillow and was rewarded with a fresh spasm of pain that completely paralyzed him. God *damn* it. He couldn't move a muscle to try to get to her and comfort her. He hated being helpless, and the frustration made the pain that much worse. "Em...what can I do?"

With a shuddering breath, she shook her head and looked at him for a long moment, then away. "Nothing."

Patton, who'd run to the door to greet her, nudged her hand with his nose. She hesitated, then stroked his head, shoulders slumping.

Clearly it hadn't gone well with Thornhill, and it was all his fault. Even worse, he'd lied about his reasons for bailing on her. "I'm sorry. I... My back's giving me trouble. I knew if I stayed down there, it would only get worse."

Her head shot up, and she skewered him with her eyes. "Really? You're going to try that line? How stupid do you think I am?"

Oh shit.

"You know," she said, "Todd came home with some little injuries, too. I tried to be sympathetic, because that's what I thought I was supposed to do, but it turns out I was a naive idiot. I lived with that crap for years. The secrets, the lies."

"I was sleeping," he said, torn between wanting to defend himself and the fact that she'd actually shared something about her marriage. "I must have been dreaming—"

"Oh please," she said, holding up a hand. "It's not my business. I should have made more noise coming in. After all, I knew you were serving me a load of BS when you made your excuses after breakfast."

Okay. There was something going on here, but he didn't think it was about his finally deflated erection. If the air was going to clear, he'd have to start first. "I have to tell you the truth," he said. "I didn't have a stomachache this morning."

"No kidding," she said drily.

He didn't want to give voice to this, because anytime he talked about his physical condition, he believed he was jinxing his recovery, but she needed to know. "My back's maybe a little more messed up than I let on. I have a wonky disk or two and a pinched nerve. Today was kinda rough, but it's not permanent. I'm almost completely healed."

"Is that like saying 'I'll quit tomorrow, I really mean it this time'?"

"Seriously. I go back to the doc in a couple weeks, and he's gonna give me a clean bill of health so I can go back to combat. This thing today…this is just a setback. From sleeping in a cramped chair, from being on my feet all day yesterday, from—"

"You're really going back to the army?"

That was what she heard? "Well, yeah."

She shook her head as though dismissing that fact. "How on earth are you going to get your drugs if your so-called bad back is better?" she asked. "Or are you just going to give up on the pharmacy and go straight for heroin?"

"What?"

"Don't pretend with me, Marcus. I understand, but I'm not going to participate. I won't give you money, I won't lie to my family. I won't clean up after you if the withdrawal gets so bad you can't make it to the bathroom. So just stop."

Did she think this was about *drugs*? She certainly seemed to know a lot about addict behavior. Realization dawned— she'd lived it. This was what she hadn't told anyone about Todd. "Your husband was an addict."

She inhaled, sharply. He tried to sit up, to reach for her, to apologize, but she backed up a step. Then her shoulders slumped, and she said, "Yeah. He was." The admission cost her; the light in her eyes dimmed a fraction. How hard had she worked to keep that a secret?

Marcus had a million questions that he was afraid to ask, so he just waited.

She went to the window and stared out—away from him. "When Todd came back from his first deployment, he had trouble sleeping. Nightmares. The docs gave him something to 'help.' It worked best when he chased it with bourbon."

"Oh shit."

"And then one night he got up and tripped over something on the way to the bathroom and messed up his knee. They gave him Vicodin for that, and he was off to the races. When the doctors wouldn't prescribe him anything else, it went downhill."

Marcus didn't need any more details to know that Todd would have found other sources of drugs. He'd have needed money. There would have been arguments, lies, and a ton of hurt.

Emma turned back to Marcus and took a deep breath. "So I think you'll understand why I want no part of your bullshit stories, okay? I let one addict break my heart and nearly ruin my family. I'm not letting another loser have another shot."

He nodded. "I think we need to have a conversation. Could you grab my phone?"

He wanted his *phone*?

Emma was tempted to give Marcus's phone to him

enema style, but something about his expression convinced her to play along.

"My phone? Please?"

It was only a few inches from his head. Why didn't he just get it himself? Was he so messed up that he couldn't find it?

She stomped across the room, picked up his phone and, with exaggerated care, placed it in his upturned palm.

"Would you like me to dial it for you, too, sir?"

His mouth almost quirked, and she almost... Well, she thought about kicking the bed, but she'd probably hurt her foot. "Actually, if you don't mind calling Jake, that would be helpful."

With a sigh, she took his phone and found Jake's number in his contacts.

"When he answers, ask him what's wrong with me."

She was going to have a headache from how much eye-rolling she was doing.

"Hello."

"Hey, Jake. This is Emma. I'm on Marcus's phone."

"Hi, Emma. How...did it go?"

God, she'd nearly forgotten about the donor debacle already, and she definitely wasn't ready to talk about it. "I'm really not sure. I need to, uh, process the meeting in my head a little, then I'll tell you guys all about it."

"Okay." There was silence on the other end of the phone while he waited for her to say something else. Not one to fill empty space with words, their Jake.

"So, yeah. Anyway, I'm here with Marcus, and he wants me to ask you what's wrong with him."

"He does?"

"Yeah, actually, he's right here." She handed the phone to Marcus.

"Hey, buddy. I need you to tell Emma what's wrong with my back." He pushed the speaker button and handed the phone back to her.

"Okay, Jake," she said. "What's going on here?"

Jake sighed. "We got blown up, remember?"

"Yeah." There had been a bomb, which had killed Adam's dog and given Jake the brain injury he lived with.

"Marcus broke four..." There was a pause while he searched for the word. "Four *parts* of his back."

"*Four vertebra?*" Emma shot a glance at Marcus, who hadn't moved from where he reclined on the bed. He stared through the window now, instead of at her. "*Four?*"

"Those are...better. But the...*damn*...the things between."

"Disks?"

"They're smashing his nerves. His doctor—"

"Thanks, Jake." Marcus picked up the phone. "That's probably enough 411 for now."

"Okay, bye." The call was disconnected.

Emma didn't quite know what to say, because she didn't really know what to think.

"So..." She met his resigned expression. "You lied about having the green apple quickstep because you didn't want to admit your back hurts?"

He pursed his lips for a moment, then said, "Pretty much."

She nodded. "That explains the pain pills." But it didn't change a damned thing, did it? Unless what Adam had told her was accurate—that Marcus hadn't taken any more of those opiates after she'd found him unconscious two weeks ago. She clarified the situation. "You're telling me you're up here lying in bed because your back hurts. Not because you're too wasted on your meds to function."

He shook his head. "After that day you found me... passed out...I realized I had to stop. If I'm going to get a clean bill of health, I need to finish my rehab without drugs."

"Can you do that? Finish your rehab, as you say?"

Marcus rubbed his forehead. "I hope so."

A thought crossed her mind. "Adam thinks you're definitely going back. Have you been lying to him about how badly you're hurt, too?"

He glanced away before answering. "Adam knows I have some hurdles to cross."

The evasion in his eyes ramped up her anger again. "Does he know how many? How high they are? How you can't even function as his spokesman right now?"

Marcus didn't change position, but he suddenly loomed as large as she'd ever seen him when he ground his teeth and said, "Adam doesn't need to know a goddamned thing about my health. Got it?"

Oh.

Marcus wasn't keeping his health issues quiet to protect himself, to protect his vanity or some sort of addiction, he was protecting Adam. Adam, who had come home from that stupid war physically fine but emotionally broken, blaming himself for the explosion that killed their friend, his dog, and wounded Jake so badly. Marcus didn't want to add anything to Adam's burden. Instead, he joked around about being good for nothing besides decoration because he had to. She didn't know what to say. She'd been completely wrong about everything *Marcus*. Her stupid heart thunked around and said *I told you so*.

Then he gave a little laugh and went back into Marcus mode.

"Actually, I was lying up here because my back hurts, but I *was* getting a little buzz on."

Her heart seized. "I *knew* it." Although she didn't see any evidence—or smell any evidence—of anything alcoholic or weed-like, or…

"I was getting a little high imagining you coming through that door wearing nothing but a thong. At least, until you took it all off and climbed on top of poor helpless me."

Okay. So there was one impression of Marcus that still held true. He used sex appeal and shock value to mask his own hurt and misery.

Something about this past week or so… Coming to terms with Granddad's situation, trying to figure out how to help launch Adam's dream, and public speaking were all mixed in with Marcus Talbott, and the way he smelled, and the way he smiled at her, the way he made her feel. It made her reckless.

Maybe it was time for Emma to get out of her self-imposed isolation booth and call his bluff.

Chapter 18

MARCUS WAS SURPRISED WHEN EMMA HELD HIS GAZE, A little smile offering a dare, giving him as good as she'd gotten. One eyebrow rose in challenge.

Other parts of him were about to rise in response.

"Hold that thought. Patton, come," he ordered, and the dog, who'd been lounging comfortably against Emma's legs, padded across the room and stood next to the bed. He'd taken off the big harness and vest the dog wore for work, but left on a smaller, soft harness with a very short leash attached, which Marcus now held while Patton slowly moved away from the bed, pulling his broken-down human to a sit.

"What are you doing?" Emma asked, her mysterious seductress face exchanged for matter-of-fact woman-on-the-job. "You should probably stay in bed for a while, shouldn't you?"

Marcus shook his head, even though his body told him that yes, he should absolutely be lying down right now, with her stretched out above him, except suddenly, the idea terrified him. He gave her some semi-truth. "Lying around makes it that much worse later." *Truth.* "It's getting a lot better, actually." *On most days, not counting this one. Long term? Yes. He would get better.* "The exercise routine I do helps a lot." *Hopefully.* If nothing else, he could pull himself up the stairs with one arm if he needed to, though his pecs were starting to look like petrified double D's.

A flash of disappointment was replaced by incredulity. "You're going to work out right *now*?"

"No, I'm going to take a leak." Because he needed to get away for a minute. He needed to think, without her standing there all tattooed and bejeweled and fragile in spite of her kick-ass exterior.

With Patton's help, he shuffled across the floor, pretending he didn't notice the way she watched him, and that he definitely didn't smell that special Emma-roma that pulled him in her direction like a fricking brain magnet.

Finally he made it all ten steps to the head. "Patton, you stay out here, bud." He shut the door and exhaled, holding himself up with one hand on the back of the door for a long moment and tried to think.

Emma thought Marcus was an addict. Or at least, she *had* thought so. Her husband had been an addict. He wondered if Todd's parents knew—maybe not. Emma seemed protective of his memory. Did she still love the guy? Did it matter?

The woman he'd been fantasizing about for months was out there a few feet away, and it seemed she might want to get with him, and he was in here like a nervous wedding-night virgin. The truth was, he was afraid he wouldn't be able to please her. Hell, he could barely walk. How could he put enough motion in the ocean to keep Emma floating for as long as she deserved?

But hell—he was creative, and he'd always had a way with women, right?

Okay, maybe it was more about being able to convince his piano teacher to let him learn something easier than Rachmaninoff's fifth piano concerto for his sixth-grade recital than getting supermodels to swish naked through his bedroom, but he knew how to work it, and he had become a fairly accomplished lover, if he believed what he'd been told. But this situation was different. This woman was different.

From the outer room, he heard her voice. He couldn't understand the words, but it sounded like she was making a request—room service, maybe?

Maybe he'd misread her meaning a moment ago. He didn't think so, but he'd definitely wait for another clear signal before he made a move. He shook his head at himself. He was in no shape to move anything, or anyone. He readjusted his expectations from nookie to conversation over hotel hamburgers.

Food would be good, he told himself. He hadn't had breakfast that morning, what with his back going goofy on him at the wrong moment, and the anti-inflammatory stuff he'd taken wasn't sitting well. That was all he needed. To have Emma maybe, possibly make a pass at him, only for him to yak all over her feet.

He could delay no more. He'd washed up and brushed his teeth. The good news was, the small amount of rest he'd gotten had helped, and as long as he moved slowly, he wasn't in danger of screaming in pain.

He opened the door and found Emma standing in the middle of the room, her arms full of bedding. She smiled up at him, semi-embarrassed.

"Whatcha doin' there?" he asked.

"I'm making you an easier place to rest," she told him.

"Huh?"

She tossed the two pillows she carried onto the bed, and

dumped the pile of blankets at the foot. "Here." She piled up the pillows against the headboard and covered them with a blanket, making a kind of a package that would hold its shape. Then she folded the other blankets and put them a little farther down. "Come sit."

He got himself down to the mattress, then eased back onto the stack of pillows, and he swung his legs around so that his knees were cushioned by the pile of blankets. "This is better than a recliner," he told her honestly.

There was a knock on the door, and Emma went to answer it, admitting a housekeeper with another stack of pillows and blankets.

"What are you going to do with all that?" he asked. "I'm not sure I could get any more comfy here."

She shot him an amused smile and directed the woman to pile the bedding at the foot of his bed. "It's not all about you. I used my stuff, so they brought me more."

A warm little somethin'-somethin' settled in his chest and wiggled around.

It wasn't that no one had ever done anything nice for him before—hell, everyone he knew had been carrying his ass for the past year or so. But the fact that Emma, who had pretty much hated him up until about five minutes ago, was taking care of him—even if he didn't need it, or deserve it... That was going on the pile of stuff to think about when he had the brainpower.

Behind the housekeeper, a waiter pushed in a cart with several covered dishes.

"You can put that over there," she told him, taking the folder and signing the bill.

Emma closed the door behind the hotel staff and turned

to the food, removing silver lids and inspecting the contents. "You want a bacon cheeseburger or a chicken gyro?"

"What do you want? You pick first."

She scanned the choices. "I'm really not all that hungry." But her eyes lingered on that burger.

"I'll do the chicken. I need to watch my boyish figure."

She snorted but looked at him, long and slow, stroking him with her gaze from head to toe before busying herself with the food. "I think you're probably okay."

"I'm not so sure. Maybe you should inspect me more closely."

"I think you should eat something first," Emma said, nerves getting in the way of doing what she really wanted. She handed Marcus a plate and grabbed her own so she wouldn't follow his suggestion and climb onto the bed with him. His long limbs gleamed with hard muscle in the hazy light filtering though the curtains.

Instead of running her hands over him, she pulled out the chair at the little corner table and forced herself to sit and take a bite of the burger.

They were quiet for a minute, each busy chewing and swallowing.

The silence was...not quite awkward, but definitely fraught with tension. Sexual tension.

In spite of her stupid *I like the idea of you immobile*, which had sent Marcus sprinting—well, limping—for the bathroom, he was definitely flirting with her. She was *so* out of her element.

After a few minutes, Marcus wiped his mouth with a napkin and said, "So when are you going to tell me what happened in your meeting with Thornhill?"

She sighed. She'd almost forgotten about that awful man and the nonpresentation. "First of all, he walked into the room and almost turned around again once he realized you weren't there. He had another guy with him—some guy named Butch who he says is his accountant, but who looks like a collections professional." She took a breath. "Then I couldn't find the laptop the hotel said would be there. I should have gone in earlier, but the keynote address ran over and I—"

"No beating yourself up," Marcus said, waving a finger at her. "I know you can think on your feet."

She was grateful for his confidence in her, even after the fact. "Well, it was good I printed that stuff out, because I had hard copies for him. Except he barely glanced at them. The only time he looked at me was when I bent over to point something out to him and he looked down my shirt."

"Wait. You showed him your boobs? I haven't even seen your boobs yet," Marcus said, then before she could lob a wadded-up napkin at his head, he sobered, shaking his head. "I'm really sorry you had to go in there alone. If I'd known he was going to be inappropriate, I'd have—"

"If I'm not allowed to second-guess myself, then neither are you," she said. "He didn't say or do anything *really* yucky."

"I hate to tell you this, but boob checking-out is kind of automatic in a lot of guys who are too Neanderthal to realize it's rude."

"It is kind of microaggressive, isn't it?"

"It's a get-his-ass-kicked-if-I'd-seen-him-do-it," Marcus

said. "I know you can take care of yourself—you could probably take on half the rednecks in Texas and not break a sweat—but my grandma would have my hide if I saw someone being ungentlemanly and didn't stand up to do something about it."

She tried to tell herself—and the warm fuzzies that were starting to gather—that he was gallant all the time, not just for her.

"Well, anyway," she went on, "he half listened to what I had to say, barely glanced at the proposal, and then said he'd have to see the ranch in person before he did anything."

"That's awesome!" Marcus smiled and slapped the mattress.

"What? He didn't even look at the budget part of the proposal."

"Babe, he's coming out to the ranch. He wouldn't do that if he wasn't pretty damned sure he's going to pony up some cash."

Emma blinked. Considered the bad-karma feelings she'd had during the meeting and realized she had been so busy being nervous and offended that she hadn't listened between the lines. "I hadn't thought about it that way."

"Well dayum, darlin.' This calls for a celebration. Is there any champagne in that minifridge?"

She went over and looked. "Nope. Just a seven-dollar bottle of water. I could call room service, I guess, but that would probably cost as much as Thornhill's going to give us."

"Can you toss me my bag?" Marcus pointed at the duffel on the luggage stand.

Emma handed it over.

He pulled it onto his lap and rooted around for a

moment. "Aha! Here we go." He withdrew his hand clutching a plastic grocery bag and pulled at the knotted handles. He showed her his booty. Dozens of miniature Airheads candies. "What's your pleasure, ma'am?"

"Ooh. I like mystery." She chose a white one and tore it open.

"What time are we supposed to check out?" Marcus asked, shifting awkwardly.

Emma held up her hand while she chewed and swallowed, then said, "I told them we're staying another day."

"Oh, thank God." Marcus sighed, seeming to relax again. "I didn't know how I was going to sit in the car that long."

"Well, now you don't have to. If you're not up to riding—or driving—tomorrow, I'll call Adam and tell him to bring the truck. We'll throw you in the back."

He nodded, appeased. "So what do you want to do now?" He held up the bag of candy. "Want to eat our way into a food coma and binge-watch season four of *Supernatural* with me?"

Was that code for *Netflix and chill*? Emma wondered as she piled her replacement pillows against the headboard next to Marcus and kicked off her shoes. She'd been ready to jump his bones since they climbed into that ridiculous car of his a few days ago, when she thought she hated him. It was just the possibility that he had a drug problem that she hated—not the man she'd painted with the same brush as Todd. Marcus was a whole different kind of guy. One who hoarded candy and loved the Winchester brothers. She might as well call room service and ask for a few dozen condoms now.

Chapter 19

EMMA'S PHONE CHIMED WITH AN INCOMING TEXT, BUT she couldn't seem to force herself to surface from her dream, where she floated in a sea of warmth and arousal. Her body was cocooned in heat and she never wanted to move, except to shift toward the *something* that promised to ease the throbbing between her thighs.

She slowly opened her eyes and realized that she was so secure because she was firmly wedged against Marcus's body, his arm wrapped around her waist and holding her close. Everywhere they touched, her blood thrummed, nerve endings alive and yearning.

How had this happened? The last thing she remembered was eating the final mystery flavor Airhead and watching Sam fight some demon thing that was trying to seduce Dean into giving away... She had no idea.

And now the television screen was black, and the room was dark. Daylight was gone. How had she slept so long? It had only been early afternoon when they started to watch TV.

She was in *bed* with *Marcus*. Somehow they'd both fallen asleep and migrated so that they were intimately snuggled up together.

Was this a good thing? Her body certainly seemed to think so. Her brain couldn't come up with any reasons why not at the moment, and reminded her this had been building from the moment they'd entered the hotel. She knew better than to trust her brain, but it had been so long since she'd relaxed enough to let anyone else hold her close, to make her feel safe, that the tiny little voice telling her to be careful, she'd be sorry about this, got drowned out by the soft sound of Marcus's deep, steady breaths moving strands of her hair.

She looked down at his hand wrapped around her forearm and wondered at how different he was. This was beyond race and gender. He was different from any man she'd ever known.

She barely remembered her father as a kind but distant man. He'd worked too hard, was always gone from home— until he was gone from the earth, killed in the same accident that took her mother. Her granddad, who'd taken her and Adam in, was also good, but almost...cold, as though he were terrified to let in the softer emotions. He was fair and hardworking, and gave Emma everything he thought she needed, but he didn't know what to do with her emotional, parentless self. It wasn't until Granddad began to get confused as dementia set in that he forgot to be a hard-ass and allowed himself to laugh and cry.

Her brother was a worrier. Adam had appointed himself caretaker when they'd moved to Texas and still felt responsible for her, though he'd lightened up considerably since he'd let Lizzie into his heart.

And then there had been Todd. Todd was funny, liked to tease—he had that in common with Marcus, but after Todd came home from Afghanistan, he'd become an angry, lost soul, and Emma had been unable to reach him. Marcus, for all that he'd suffered and experienced, seemed to really enjoy life.

Sweet, funny, irreverent Marcus, who was so *present*. Who wanted to help everyone find their way, like Tanner, the new guy. Adam told her how Marcus hadn't hesitated to invite Tanner in and put him to work. He'd done the same thing with Jake, bringing him home from the hospital and then to find Adam to help him find a place.

And now that he'd focused that intensity on her... Whoa.

Her skin was too tight, and her muscles ached with a need to arch, to curve back into his body. Her breasts were tender, and her sex was electrified. She had to move soon... at least to rock, ever so slightly, to ease that need. Her breathing was shallow, and she tried not to pass out from want...

Her phone buzzed again.

"Are you going to get that?" Marcus's voice in her ear sent a thrill down her spine, which detonated somewhere in the vicinity of her uterus. *Zzzzzzt pow!*

His arm tightened, and he tucked his nose into the curve of her shoulder and inhaled deeply. "You smell like home on a summer morning," he said. *Pow! Pow!*

Hoping she didn't sound too breathless, she said, "I'm not sure you meant that as a compliment, did you? Didn't you grow up in horse country?"

"Naw, babe. Farther south. Right near Lake Cumberland."

"Oh well. Stagnant water's so much better."

He chuckled. "Hardly stagnant. And I was thinking more along the lines of honeysuckle and other flowery stuff."

"Mmm." She reached for her phone and reluctantly removed her hand from his arm to check the message alert. Just a reminder of an upcoming doctor appointment.

When she relaxed back against Marcus, it was more than

clear that he was no more immune to her body's proximity than she was to his. That was definitely an erection nestled right against her butt. A sigh escaped her as he shifted slightly. There were several layers of fabric between their bodies, but she could swear she felt him throb against her, although maybe that was her own response.

His arm around her waist moved and his hand, already splayed against her tummy, stroked ever so slightly. She arched in response.

"Emma, if you don't want something to happen here, you're going to have to get out of this bed, because I don't think I can move."

She smiled. "Is it because your back is still paining you, or because my magic heinie has you so mesmerized?"

He huffed a laugh. "It's all you, babe."

As if to emphasize his words, he anchored her more firmly back against him.

So she pulled away.

For a moment Marcus thought his fantasy was about to go up in smoke, but Emma was only reaching to put her phone on the nightstand, and then she was back against him, in the curve of his body around hers. He'd been lying there in agony for a while now—mostly because her delicious ass was nestled against his cock, but also because his damned spine wasn't quite with the program.

A few episodes into the *Supernatural* marathon, after Emma'd fallen asleep, Marcus had gotten uncomfortable and tried to roll to his side. He'd gotten halfway there—up on his right hip—before his back seized up again. As he lay there gritting his teeth, Emma sighed and rolled to her side, backing up against him.

Maybe it was the support her body offered his as he wrapped his arm around her and relaxed, but it sure felt like the arousal rushing through his body from every point of contact was what made his position more than acceptable.

Of course, she was sleeping, so in spite of the ideas bouncing around about the ways he'd like to make her come, he forced his mind to appreciate that he was curled up in bed with Emma—the woman with the hard shell and marshmallow interior.

He'd dozed for a while, but then something—probably her phone—had awakened him, and he lay still, feeling her breathe, sensing her coming to awareness and enjoying the tiny movements that she probably didn't even realize she made, feeling his own body respond to hers.

Damn. He was so hard right now he thought he might lose it.

He had to touch her. He flexed the fingers covering her belly, enjoying the softness, loving her sigh as he moved his hand over her skin.

Up and over her side, up along her rib cage, the side of her bra, and back down again, over the curve of her hip to her thigh, and back again.

If this was as far as it went, he'd die a happy man, but— no. He really wanted this to go farther, though he wasn't exactly sure how far he was able. With the next pass of his hand over her belly, she arched, enough to encourage him to travel higher. As he brushed over her breast, feeling her nipple against his palm, she sighed, so he slid one finger just under the edge of the elastic fabric, a little more, touching, pressing, and she whimpered.

"This okay?"

"Oh yes, please," she said and they both laughed softly, and then there was no more talk while he made love to Emma with his hands.

He pushed her bra up over her small, perfect breasts and toyed with the nipples, one after another, and bent his head to her neck, where he licked and nibbled and sucked while she writhed, rubbing her ass against him until he was sure he would burst.

He moved his hand down her stomach to the waistband of her pants, flicked open the button, and eased down the zipper. For once, he was glad that she wore her pants so ridiculously loose, because it was no trouble at all to slide his fingers under the edge of her panties and then farther down, until he could feel—oh, *Jesus*.

She was wet.

His cock jumped, throbbing, begging for release. *Not right now. This one's for Emma.* He slid two fingers between her folds and smiled against the side of her neck as her moan vibrated against his lips.

He stroked, listening to her breath stutter, learning what she liked, imagined being clasped in all that hot, wet heat.

She whimpered. *Yes.* This was what she wanted. She leaned back into him, her thighs falling open even as they tensed, her breath hard and choppy, little squeaks coming from her throat as she shuddered against his fingers.

He rocked his hand while she convulsed for what seemed like minutes. When she finally relaxed, he wanted to start all over. He wanted to see her come in every imaginable position and from anything he could think of to get her off, because, damn, his Emma was beautiful, from the rosy blush staining her chest to the creamy-white softness of her neck, to the black enameled toes that curled and uncurled against his sock-covered ones.

"Oh God." She exhaled, turning in his arms, raising wide blue eyes to meet his gaze. "That was... Oh God."

He couldn't help it; his lips quirked up in a self-satisfied grin.

She returned the smile, although hers was a tiny bit sly. "I've got my work cut out for me to top that."

Imagining what she might do to him caused his brain to fritz out for a moment. He came back online as she slid her body over his and nudged him onto his back, right into a massive muscle spasm.

Chapter 20

WHEN MARCUS GROANED, EMMA THOUGHT HE WAS responding favorably to the way she pressed her crotch against his erection, but when he gritted his teeth, gripped her arms, and pushed her away, she realized she was hurting him.

"Oh God!" she squeaked, trying to untangle herself from him and scoot away.

In spite of his grimace and frozen position, he laughed. "I have a way of making you say that a lot."

"What?" She'd moved as far away as the edge of the bed would allow, and was about to roll to her belly and slither backwards onto the floor, but his words confused her.

"Oh God!" he parodied—except he sounded more like a cartoon character on helium than she did—she hoped. He grinned.

That's what she'd cried out when he made her come so hard she was still quaking.

"Really?" she asked, trying to regain her equilibrium. "You're going to hold my…my…unintentional noises against me?"

"Oh, babe," he said. "I'd love to hold your noises any way I could, but never in a way to hurt you." His luscious lips teased, even as lines of pain radiated from the corners of his eyes.

"I'm so sorry," she said. "I shouldn't have… I mean, you're hurt, and we shouldn't have—"

"Babe. Hold on a second." He held up a hand and slowly relaxed against the mattress, sliding one leg higher on the jumble of bedding. "Come here." He held out his arm to her.

Carefully, she found a perfect spot to nestle against his body, his arm around her shoulders, her head in that little dip between his upper chest and shoulder. Tentatively, she slid her thigh over his leg and her hand over his hard abdomen, the rise and fall with his breaths soothing her. She was surprised at how easy it was to be comfortable with him in this position—for her anyway. "Are you okay? With me like this?"

"In full disclosure, you should know that I enjoyed every second of getting you off, and even if I have to go through a week of these muscle spasms, I'd do it again in a heartbeat."

"But you're hurting."

"And I just said—"

"I can't do that, let you hurt yourself because of…you know."

"Sex?" The smile in his voice was unmistakable.

"Yes," she said, knowing he was teasing her while trying to distract her from worrying about him. "How often does this happen?"

"Getting busy with you? About once in a lifetime, so far, but maybe a little more often now," he said.

"Marcus," she started, pushing herself up on one elbow. "You know what I'm asking."

He sighed and shook his head. "Not that often. It's getting better and better all the time."

"And you think you're going to be able to reenlist?"

"I'm still property of Uncle Sam," Marcus corrected. "I'm on the temporarily disability retired list until I go back to see the docs in a few weeks and get cleared to go back to my guys."

A few weeks? Her heart stilled, but she forced herself to breathe through it. "How many is a few?" she asked, hoping she didn't sound as freaked out as she felt.

"Three."

"You think you'll be ready?" *Please, don't be ready*.

"Oh yeah," he said, flexing one perfect bicep and laughing. He tugged her back down into the shelter of his arms. "I've worked too hard not to be fit. As soon as I get that medical clearance, I'm back on the job. God willin' and the creek don't rise."

They'd had more than their share of flooding in Texas over the past year or two, and normally flash floods were a bad thing. This was one time when she might ask God to be willing to drop a little rain.

Marcus refused to let Emma's questions resonate in his mind, since he had no room for doubt. He cursed the stupid muscle spasms that had him laid out right now, because he knew that was why she seemed dubious. But she was wrong. He was strong as an ox. He'd just have to make sure he hit the weights even harder when they got back to the ranch, because he had an appointment with the spine guy. Once he was cleared, he'd go for an evaluation before the medical board.

"You've gone all tense on me," Emma said, running a hand lightly over his stomach. "Are you in a lot of pain?"

He shook his head. "It's not too bad, as long as I don't make any sudden movements."

"Can I get you anything?"

As much as he missed his meds, he wouldn't even ask her for aspirin if he needed it at this point. "Nope. Just having you here is like a little dose of chill."

"Oh, please," she said, rolling her eyes and turning her head back into a more comfortable position.

"Whassamatta? You don't know how fockin' haht you are?" he said in a very bad Jersey Shore accent.

"See, there you go," she said. "You talk out of both sides of your mouth. I'm a 'dose of chill' or 'haht.' I don't think you can have both."

"Baby, I want it all, and I'm going to have it all."

"Yeah, and what does 'it all' consist of in Marcusville?"

"My needs are simple. Food, water, exercise. A job."

"And your job of choice is soldier."

"Much to my father's dismay."

"Really? He's not proud of you?"

"He says he is. But he was pissed off when I flunked out of college. He'd prefer I'd gone to med school like my brother or law school like my sister." The disappointment on his father's face the day Marcus told him he'd enlisted was engraved on his heart.

"He was probably terrified for you," Emma said softly.

"Yeah, I can see that now, but at the time my feelings were hurt. Here I was going off to save the world and my dad was barely speaking to me."

"What about your mom?"

"She cried, but she was cool."

"And did your dad get over being mad?"

He shrugged. "When I left, he said, 'If you're going to do this, you damned well better be bringing home medals.'"

"Have you?" she asked.

He snorted. "Well, I've got this Purple Heart, but I don't think 'getting blown up' was what Daddy had in mind. But still, Mom says he brags about me now. Pine Hollow's a pretty tight little town, and they celebrate their soldiers."

"It's nice you've got deep roots."

"Don't you have 'em in Big Chance?" he asked.

She shrugged. "I guess so, but it took me a long time to dig in and let 'em grow. My parents were both army, and we moved a lot. I *hated* moving to new places and having to make new friends. At least we knew that, no matter how bad it sucked, I only had to tolerate it for a few months, then we'd be on to the next place. They retired in 2001, right before 9–11, and we were going to live in Dallas forever.

"But they died. We got sent here to Big Chance, which was the worst of all the places we'd been. When we were in the military, so were most of the other kids at whatever new school we went to. In Big Chance, everyone's family had been here for generations and everyone knows everyone else. It's not exaggerating to say that we didn't fit in very well."

"But you made friends, obviously."

She shrugged. "I had Lizzie," she said. "And a few other friends. And I always had Granddad's dogs."

"That must have been awesome."

"Yeah. It's hard to stay all angsty about mean girls and horrible, awful, nasty boys when you've got puppies to train."

He heard the smile in her voice and had to ask, "Why aren't you working with dogs now?"

Her expression clouded over. "It just hasn't been possible for a while. Maybe someday."

There was more behind that, but he figured he'd already pushed enough for one day. "Well, you should think about it. Even if you don't have one of your own, Adam can sure use the help with training."

"Mmm. Yeah." Well, that was noncommittal.

As though he understood his species was being discussed, Patton poked his head over the side of the bed and stared at the two of them with big, baleful eyes more suited for a hound dog than a golden retriever.

Emma sighed. "If I don't get up and get this dog his dinner and nighty-night walk, we're going to be leaving a hefty cleaning fee behind when we go tomorrow." She disengaged herself from Marcus's arms and got to her feet. "Do you need anything while I'm up and out?"

"I need you, back here in this bed with me." And he needed her not to have to take care of what he should be doing—minding the dog. "But in the meantime, I'll see if I can't get to the head and back while you're gone."

"I can help you," she said, biting her lip and looking between him and Patton.

No way. "I'm good," he said. "Go on, woman. Tend to my dog."

She snorted and said, "Oh Your Highness, please don't wander too far from the royal bedchamber, else your humble servant will be unable to serve your...needs." And with a wiggle in her delectable ass, she pulled the door shut behind herself and the dog.

It only took him five minutes to get upright. *This one was bad*, he thought for the millionth time as he made his agonizing way to the can. Every step was harder. The ever-present doubt tried to get a toehold, but he had a lot of practice at shoving it out of his consciousness.

He felt a little better after he relieved himself and washed up, brushed his teeth, did all those grooming things that made him appreciate civilization—especially after months in the desert, where water for basic hygiene was frequently hard to come by.

He hobbled back into the room and thought about trying to sit up for a while. They did have to leave tomorrow, and he was going to have to be in the car for hours.

But then he looked at the bed, where the pillows and blankets Emma had arranged for him were calling his name. It had been really comfortable.

Oh, screw it. He could sit upright tomorrow. Tonight, he'd chill. After all, Emma told him not to go too far.

He worked his way into clean shorts and the closest clean shirt—another Big Chance T-shirt—then lowered himself to the mattress and leaned back with only a few major curse words escaping. But then he got all settled, and a whiff of Emma's scent rose from the sheets. He hadn't been kidding about the cool and hot thing. She was a breath of fresh air and a sultry, smoky fantasy, both in one.

It had taken him thirty seconds in that Dairy Queen to fall in lust with her, with her short spiky hair, tattoos, piercings, and attitude—so different from most of the girls he hooked up with, but sooooo sweet—and a long, hot summer to finally get in her good graces. And what fine graces they were.

The fact that he'd had to work so hard to get close? He was beginning to think she'd been working some witchy woman magic on him, because he was a thousand times more attracted to her than he'd been at first, and that had been a powerful lot. He not only wanted her, he wanted to *know* her—the kind of knowledge that only comes from spending a lot of time with someone. He realized he was getting in deep and found himself wondering if she was falling, too. He suspected it'd be hard to tell. She kept her heart locked up pretty tight.

The question was, had Todd Stern taken the key with him when he died?

If Marcus wasn't careful, he'd find himself high and dry with a broken heart. On the other hand, if he was to have any chance at all, he needed to be fit for duty, or she'd drop his ass like those socks he hadn't changed for three months two deployments ago. If there was one thing he knew right now, it was that neither of them would be happy if he got stuck at a lousy desk job. At least if he were back on combat duty, he'd be deployed and she could stay in Big Chance. If he had to move her from base to base? She'd leave his ass in a New York minute.

He was getting waaaay ahead of himself, he reminded himself.

The door lock hummed and Emma pushed into the room, a much-relieved Patton by her side. She released the dog from the leash. "Hey, you." Her forehead creased. "You haven't moved?"

"Yeah, I did. Been there and back. But you told me to stick close to the royal mattress, right?"

Her mouth quirked up. "Something like that."

"Well, here I am."

She hung Patton's leash over the back of the chair and moved toward him. "Good boy, Marcus."

"Oh, are we switching from *Game of Thrones* to *Nanny 911*?"

"Mmm." She kicked off her shoes and unbuttoned her pants, walking out of them as she approached. "More like *Fifty Shades of Me*."

Chapter 21

THE HEAT IN MARCUS'S EYES STEAMED AWAY ANY UNCER-
tainty Emma had been feeling before coming through the
door. He was willing, and she was going to make sure that
he was able.

He lay on his back, one hand between his head and the
pillow, the other resting on his abdomen, which rose and
fell with deep, steady breaths. His long, dark legs shifted
restlessly, and he was filling the front of his shorts very
nicely.

"Here's the deal," she told him. "Every time you move,
your back seizes up, right?"

Confusion replaced lust, but he said, "I guess."

"But interestingly enough, your friend there"—she
waved in the direction of his crotch—"seems to be feeling
the need to stretch his, uh, boundaries."

His eyebrows rose as his gaze traveled over her legs and
lasered in on her cotton panties. "I suppose that's one way
to put it."

"Okay." She pulled off her polo shirt and watched his
eyes shift to her breasts.

Her nipples tightened in response as though he were
licking her through the lace of her bra.

"Okay." Her voice came out breathy, but not weak.
"We're going to play a little game."

"I like games."

"Good. We're going to play 'Marcus doesn't move no matter what.'"

He fake-frowned. "I don't know. That sounds kind of boring."

"Maybe. Or maybe not. Maybe the full name for this game is 'Marcus doesn't move no matter what, but Emma moves a lot, and if Marcus stays perfectly still and promises to tell Emma if he's in pain, she'll make him feel really, really good.'"

His eyes widened and his eyebrows rose. "I'm either going to love—or seriously hate—this game a lot."

He watched her approach, and she shivered with anticipation—along with a tiny bit of fear that he'd move and wind up more hurt than he'd been before this started.

The thing was, he'd made her feel so incredibly sexy that she'd forgotten all the crappy things in her life for just a little while, and she had to return the favor. This wasn't simply about evening the score, however. She *really* wanted to get with this man.

The ever-so-slight kinky flavor of this situation—having complete control over this massive, powerful man—was a definite aphrodisiac.

Slowly, ever so slowly, she moved onto the bed, rising on all fours to approach him. Leaning forward, she balanced on her arms while she straddled him. Although she was careful not to touch, she could swear that streams of electrons moved between his erection and her damp panties, which were plain, old boring white cotton. Why didn't she have pretty black lace?

Next time.

And didn't *that* thought make her ache even more?

She began to settle back onto her heels, gradually making contact, her body clenching with need.

Yes.

Just before she settled her weight on him fully, she rose back up to her knees.

Marcus groaned. "Where are you going?"

"Nowhere. But you're not supposed to move, and I'm worried that if I sit on you, I might make you uncomfortable and you'll have to move."

"Naw, baby. I'll be fine," he said.

"Nope. Too risky."

Was that a whimper? She smiled, though she was inclined to do likewise.

"Now." She put her forefinger on her lips. "Why are you wearing a shirt?"

"Good question. Don't you like it?"

"I think I'd like it better off you."

He tensed in preparation to move.

"No, no, *no*. No moving." She reached over to the nightstand to the little grooming kit she'd seen earlier and pulled out nail scissors.

"What are you going to do?"

"Normally, I wouldn't support damaging company property like this," she told him. "But I happen to know that there are plenty more of these T-shirts where this one came from, and these are extenuating circumstances."

"Oh, definitely."

She snipped through the collar and then the first few inches of the actual shirt. Putting the scissors down, she grabbed each side of the material and tugged. It gave easily, and she ripped through the shirt in no time flat. "Huh. No wonder we got such a good deal on these things. They're made of tissue paper."

"Remind me to send the manufacturer a thank-you note," Marcus said as she slid the sides of the fabric apart and ran her hands all over that gorgeous brown skin, paying special attention to his nipples.

He gasped when she bent to lick one, then the other, before trailing down those amazing abs. The elastic waistband of his shorts provided a bit of a conundrum. If she asked him to lift his backside, that would defeat the purpose of forcing him to remain still.

She glanced at the nail scissors, and Marcus rasped, "Do it. I don't need no stinkin' clothes, anyway."

"No," she decided. "Let's see what else we can do."

Her hands slid over the silky fabric of his shorts from his upper thighs to his hips, before meeting in the middle to finally touch that incredible erection straining upward. She molded the fabric around him, learning his contours, appreciating how much her body wanted to feel that inside of her.

"I want to touch you. Let me touch you," Marcus growled.

"I can't do that right now," she said, though she wanted to beg him to do it anyway.

Instead, she reached for the low waistband of his shorts and pulled it down as far as she could, exposing him and making him into a kind of a presentation for herself.

After a couple of teasing caresses, she finally allowed herself to taste him, loving his shuddering groan as her lips closed around him.

"Emma…Emma, please," Marcus begged.

She released him with a pop, but kept her hand sliding up and down, and asked, "Please what?"

"I'm too close." His thighs were clenching, toes

beginning to curl. "You better—" His warning was cut off as she closed her lips around him again.

His breathing grew ragged, and then he was coming and she was loving every bit of him until he shoved a hand into her hair and begged, "Stop."

She released him and glanced up, surprised by the emotions flitting across his face before he wiggled his eyebrows and said, "I like the way you play games. Maybe we can have a rematch?"

She laughed. "I'm sure we can arrange something."

Emma was relaxed and completely blissed out after the "rematch." She wasn't sure how he'd managed to do all that to her, only moving his tongue and hands, but *wow*. Her body was still buzzing so much that it took her a few seconds to realize that she was lying on her phone, and it was ringing.

"Mrmph," she groaned, digging beneath her right thigh to dislodge it. She scowled at the screen and put her finger over her lips to warn Marcus to be quiet as she hit the answer button. "Hi, Dipwad."

"Hi, Buttface," Adam answered. "How's it going down there?"

"It's pretty great, actually," she said.

Marcus, who was close enough to overhear Adam, shot a glance at Emma's crotch and snickered.

She shook her fist at him and turned away so she couldn't see him and laugh.

"Are you okay?" Adam asked. "You sound kinda funny."

"Yeah," she said, coughing. "Just, you know, tired. Big week."

She went on to give him a brief rundown of the meeting with Thornhill, and he seemed optimistic.

Then, he said, "I've got a Granddad report, if you're ready."

"Sure."

"He likes Golden Gardens. A lot."

Her heart didn't ping quite as painfully as she'd expected, though she had to push herself to say, "That's good."

"Yeah, it's good. And they've got a permanent spot for him now if we want to take it. We've got to decide by tomorrow at noon, because they have a waiting list."

"Oh. I won't be home by then," she said.

Marcus, silent behind her, put his hand on her shoulder and squeezed. She didn't know if he could hear the conversation, but obviously he could tell it was hard for her.

Adam said, "Listen, I know this is hard, and I know you need to see him to be sure about things, but I think we should accept."

Emma thought about it. Adam had been there every day since they'd taken Granddad to Golden Gardens, and he said it was top-notch. She'd checked and double-checked all their accreditations. Yes, she needed to see for herself that Granddad was happy and thriving, but that was for *herself*, she realized, not for Granddad. "Okay."

Adam let out a breath. Had he been that sure she'd argue? Well, normally, she would, she supposed. Something about the man next to her made things seem a little clearer. Maybe that was the aftermath of good sex, but she'd take it.

"How much is it gonna cost?"

He told her and she tried not to choke.

"It'll be okay," he assured her. "His social security and Medicare cover a good chunk, and I've already paid for the first year in advance."

"But what if we need that for the ranch?" she asked, thinking of how Thornhill had wanted to see proof of their financial solvency.

"They gave us a little break for paying up front. Then I talked to Joe Chance, and he set up a deal where we can actually loan the ranch the rest of the money from Mill Creek Farm, and Big Chance Rescue can pay it back. We're totally legal."

Well, huh. Sometimes things just work out.

She discussed a couple more details with Adam, then rang off. She was just turning to Marcus, ready to snuggle back into his arms, when *his* phone rang. It was on the far side of the bed, and she reached for it, so he didn't have to.

Emma wasn't being nosy, she really wasn't, but the danged screen was flashing "Maya" at her, so yeah, she noticed there was a woman calling him.

She was very proud of herself for being dignified and handing it over to him without even raising an eyelash to indicate that she gave a damn that some woman named *Maya* was calling him.

Apparently Marcus didn't look at the screen, however, because he answered, and a few seconds later said, "Wait, who is this?" then moved the phone to see the screen—at which point he winced.

"Yeah. Maya. Hi." He shot Emma a glance, gave a fake smile, then looked away. He listened for a moment and laughed. "Yeah. You do?" Another laugh. "I'm not exactly in the neighborhood at the moment."

Was he getting a *booty* call?

Emma reminded herself she had no hold on Marcus. He probably had other women all over the world. He was with her right now, though, and that was fine, she told herself.

Until he shot Emma a sideways glance and said, "Yeah, that might work. Let me, uh, check my schedule and get back to you."

Emma got out of bed to refill Patton's water dish, casually slipping on her panties and shirt so she could make a hasty exit.

From the bathroom, she heard him finishing up the call. "Yep. That works. I'll talk to you later, then. Yeah, me, too."

Emma put the bowl on the floor and casually looked back at Marcus, who was smiling at her. "Maya's my sister's friend," he told her.

Busted. She shrugged. *Don't say anything else. Do not. Say. Anything else.* "Oh. That's nice of her to call and make plans with you."

A slight hesitation, then, "There's nothing to be jealous about."

She snorted. "I'm not jealous. I know you have a life outside of…the ranch." She almost said *me.* As in, *a life outside of me.*

He gave a half shake of his head. "A life? Not one that doesn't involve a particular inhabitant of Big Chance, Texas, at the moment."

Oh hell. Might as well go all in. She cleared her throat. "How long have you known her?"

That hesitation again, then a sigh. "I've known her forever."

"And she's in love with you." Emma didn't know how she was so sure there was more to them than *his sister's friend,* but she just was.

"What? No." He shook his head. "We barely hooked up once, and it was a big mistake." He winced as he said this, clearly recognizing that admitting to the hookup and then admitting to his current hookup that the earlier hookup was a mistake might not be a good idea.

Oof. She did not like the feeling that hit her gut at this admission. *Stupid. Do not get stuck on this guy. He's leaving.* "Does she know that?"

He laughed. "Yeah. I was a little worried, but now I'm pretty sure she was as freaked out as I was."

She had no idea what that meant, but was done with this conversation. With studied nonchalance, she pointed at the mattress and then herself. "This wasn't exactly our wedding night." She cringed inwardly at even mentioning anything about weddings, or fidelity, or the future.

Marcus was still watching her, his eyes so warm and his body so yummy. He smiled. "So are you going to come back here and lie down with me?"

"I think I should get back to my room. I'm a flouncer, and I don't want to bounce you around all night."

His grin was wicked and chased away a little of the jealousy that she was *not* feeling. "I don't mind."

"I do." She made it to the door without weakening and returning to kiss that smile off his face—and probably kiss a few more things, too. "We've got to hit the road early, and since it looks like I'm driving, I want to get a good night's sleep."

She pulled the adjoining door closed behind her before he could talk her into changing her mind—and it wouldn't have been a tough change to make.

Chapter 22

EMMA HAD BEEN BACK IN BIG CHANCE EXACTLY FORTY-five-and-a-half hours before she saw Marcus again. Which wasn't a big deal, really. She hadn't expected him to call her or text her. He probably knew she was busy getting back to work and going to visit Granddad.

Even though she'd accepted that her grandfather was not coming back to her little cottage, was even guiltily relieved, she still wanted to spend time with him.

Yesterday, she'd taken puppies to visit both Granddad at Golden Gardens, and cranky old Mrs. Chance at the community center.

The good news was that Loretta's pups behaved perfectly while they were out.

The bad news was that when Lizzie came to pick up the pups that morning, the driveway was blocked by a downed tree, the result of a late-summer thunderstorm.

The worse news was that there was a bigger problem at the ranch. That same storm had torn a hole in the roof of the barn—the barn that housed a dozen dogs and all their food and all the equipment needed to train them. Fortunately, no animals were hurt, but a few needed to be moved to drier quarters.

And the roof would eventually need to be replaced. Yet another expense they didn't need.

"It's gonna be fine," Adam had assured her. "We've got Mr. Thornhill, remember?"

She certainly hoped so.

It would have been nice to hear from Marcus, though.

Instead, there was silence, which was only exacerbated by the amount of time she had to spend alone at work. Her in-laws, who were usually right up in her business, had been suspiciously absent since she'd come back from her trip. A simple "How was your trip" and a "That's nice, dear," were all she got before the Sterns bustled off to a meeting at their church. She hadn't felt guilty even once while she'd been with Marcus in Houston, which made her feel even more out of whack now, especially since not only Marcus but also the Sterns seemed to be avoiding her.

If he'd just check in with her, she might not be so stressed out.

As she puttered around the Feed and Seed, putting up new stock, dusting old stuff, and not checking her phone for messages, she overthought things as much as any woman ever had. Had she been too quick to jump into playing sexually dominant fantasy girl the other night? Probably. She'd probably scared the hell out of him, and turned him off to boot—at least, mentally. It had been clear that physically, he was on board.

It wasn't like kinky stuff was in Emma's normal sex repertoire—sexpertoire? Whatever. There wasn't much in her box of tricks at all. She didn't normally climb on top of men and refuse to let them participate in their own grat- ification, so maybe she should have gone for something a little—or a lot—less out there, although compared to some of the stuff she read, it really wasn't that dirty, was it? Not so much that he should completely run away.

She wished she could talk to someone about it. Lizzie

was her best friend, but she was almost family and might tell Adam. Her brother wasn't a huge talker, but after he got over the horror of knowing sexual details about his sister and best friend, he might have occasion to mention something to one of them, and that wouldn't do.

That was just an excuse. She trusted Lizzie to the end of the earth, Emma simply didn't know how to share private stuff, even the nonsexual business. Just like no one else knew the details of what she'd been through with Todd, and no one knew how incredibly lonely she'd been when they'd moved to Big Chance.

Marcus did, though, didn't he? She realized she'd talked about her parents as if it was a story she told every day.

Well, she couldn't tell him anything right now because she hadn't heard from him.

Maybe she'd send an email to some anonymous online Dear Abby kind of person: "Dear Abby, I went all sex-crazed dominatrix during my first (or was it second, considering the time between then and when he'd touched her earlier that day? Or even third, if they considered the elevator?)... Anyway, during an encounter with a new partner, and now he hasn't called me. What gives?"

Maybe he was expecting her to call him. For crying out loud, it was way past 1950 and she totally wasn't afraid to pick up the phone—except she didn't want to seem desperate.

But wait. Marcus *liked* fast. Fast was good. Look at that souped-up car he drove. She'd been behind the wheel and knew it could tear up some asphalt. And he'd trusted her with the keys.

She should totally call him. If only to ask if he was feeling better.

Yep. That's exactly what she should do.

As soon as she finished dusting these bubble packs of one-inch screws.

And waited on this customer, the one who had just caused the bell over the door to ring.

She straightened, tucking her dusting rag into her back pocket, and turned to see Marcus. Standing at the end of the hardware aisle looking delicious as always and—uncertain?—as *never*. Patton, ever the loyal companion, panted happily next to his master, knowing that as soon as he wasn't on duty, he could count on Emma for a biscuit—or three.

"Marcus. Hi."

"Hey." He tucked his hands in the pockets of cargo shorts he wore like no one else could.

He didn't say anything else, so she did. "How are you? What's going on?"

He shrugged. "I was in town. Thought I'd stop in to say 'hi.'"

"I figured you'd forgotten about me." She cringed. Did that sound accusatory?

He looked down, actually scuffed his foot, then met her gaze. "I kind of thought you might need a break from me."

She snorted, then said, "Wait. You're serious?"

His face squinched up in the most incredibly adorable way she never would have imagined, and he said, "Sort of?"

What the what? He was uncertain, insecure, *nervous*? "Why?" If he was being honest, she was going to step out of her comfort zone and ask what she wanted.

"I was such a pain in the ass, I figured you needed a break from me."

The cynical burned-by-life girl who lived in her brain said she should take that excuse and run with it. But the older, wiser, slightly more hopeful person who kept sneaking out said, "That's ridiculous."

"Still."

"Still." She moved closer to him, into his personal space, into his magnetic zone of *yowza*. Simply being this close to him put her hormones on overload. And her urge to talk to him. He'd been open with her. Maybe she needed to take a chance and be open with him. Looking up, but not touching him—she was at work, after all—she said, "I thought we made a bit of a connection there. My feelings are a little hurt that you disappeared on me."

"I'm sorry." He was starting to smile, a spark of his normal devil self sneaking back in.

"Is your back feeling better?"

He really smiled then, doing a little twisty-turny move that he wouldn't have been able to manage just three days ago and putting a little topsy-turvy in her tummy. "Right as rain."

"Great."

"Yeah. And so good, I think I should prove it to you by—"

"Oh, Emma! Do you know where the—" Mrs. Stern bustled around the end of the aisle, a computer tablet in her hand.

Her eyebrows rose when she saw Marcus—and saw how close Emma was standing to him.

It was everything Emma could do to move back from him slowly, and not like she'd just been caught kissing in church. She hadn't even been kissing in the Feed and Seed.

"Oh, hello," Mrs. Stern said, putting a possessive arm

around Emma's waist and looking up at Marcus. "What brings you in?"

––––––––––––––––––––––

Trying to stake my claim on your daughter-in-law. He glanced down at Patton, who shifted closer to Marcus, into support mode. Marcus didn't need the support, but he was glad for the reminder not to get into a pissing match with the mother of a dead rival. "Good to see you, ma'am."

Mrs. Stern smiled. "I understand you and our Emma had quite a hootenanny in Houston."

Marcus coughed and caught Emma's blush from the corner of his eye. "Well, I suppose that's one way to put it."

"It sounds like you made some good contacts for your rescue group."

"We definitely got some interest. There are a lot of organizations out there who provide service animals to vets, but since ours is also a rescue program, and is a vets-helping-vets deal, I think we stood out a bit."

Mrs. Stern noticed Patton and said, "You have a beautiful dog. Is he for PTSD?"

Emma cleared her throat, and Mrs. Stern put a hand to her mouth. "Oh dear. That's an inappropriate question, isn't it? I'm sorry, never mind."

Marcus shrugged. "Technically, if you're working in a business and someone comes in with a service dog, you're allowed to ask what task the dog does for the handler. You're not supposed to ask what's wrong with the handler."

"But wouldn't that 'task' tell you what's wrong?" Mrs. Stern wondered.

"Not necessarily," Marcus told her. "If I say, 'Patton reminds me to take my medicine,' that could be anything from insulin to antipsychotics."

"Now that I think about it, why should I be allowed to ask anything?"

Marcus looked to Emma for that one, and she said, "Hopefully to cut down on the number of jerks who put a vest on their neurotic, undertrained lap dogs and try to pass them off as service animals."

Mrs. Stern nodded. "We should get magnets or door stickers with the rules for everyone in town, since you all will be around so much, so everyone understands."

Emma shrugged. "I don't know—in the 'real world,' people don't know, so we have to be able to handle that question while we're 'in training.'"

"Okay," Mrs. Stern said in a slightly different, perky voice. "You have a beautiful dog. What task does he perform for you?"

"He does do a great job of staying close to me in crowds, which is one thing a PTSD dog can do, but Patton's primarily here to provide physical support." And then, because Marcus felt compelled to make sure she knew that he didn't need the dog, he said, "He'll go to a veteran who needs help standing up and can provide stability for someone who might have balance issues."

"Well, he's certainly a pretty boy. He would have been a good replacement for Piper after he passed," Mrs. Stern said, then patted Emma on the shoulder. "Don't you agree?"

Emma's mouth was in a hard line, as though she were biting back feelings, but she forced a smile. "Maybe."

"Piper was a nice little dog," the woman continued, "but

he was too little and too old to play, and Todd had so much energy. And unfortunately, Piper passed away. After that, Todd was just too sad to start over with another dog."

"I'm sorry to hear about that."

Cue the awkward silence.

Marcus felt, in that moment, that he'd made a horrible mistake coming here. Mrs. Stern couldn't stop talking about her son, and Emma was completely locked down. Seeing Marcus in this place that literally dripped with Todd memorabilia—there was a freaking mobile with little photos of the man hanging from the ceiling—had to be ridiculously awkward for her. Marcus decided he should see Emma in neutral territory from now on.

Except this whole town was steeped in the past.

He wondered if his bank account would support out-of-town dates more than once every six months or so. "Okay, so I guess I should get back to the ranch," Marcus said, though he really wasn't needed there.

"I, um, have that thing for you at my place. I'll walk out with you to get it," Emma said, coming back to life.

"Oh yeah. The thing. Great." Marcus tried to hide his grin.

"Mrs. Stern, I know it's not time for me to take lunch yet, but can I have a ten-minute break?"

"Certainly, dear. It was nice seeing you," she told Marcus and actually seemed sincere.

"Likewise." Marcus hoped he was imagining the evil eye burning into his back as he followed Emma out the front door.

"Sorry about that," Emma said, shoulders falling back to normal level once they'd left the Todd zone and walked around the corner of the building toward her little place out back. "I hope she didn't make you too uncomfortable."

"Not at all," Marcus lied. "You all must miss him very much."

They reached her front porch, and Emma was silent while she unlocked her front door. With a leaden thud in his gut, Marcus noticed her wedding ring was back on her left hand.

He and Patton entered her domain and were immediately surrounded in Emma-ness. Color, and plants, and little crafty-type things all over the place.

Emma went to the counter and stood there, her back to him for a moment, before turning around. She leaned back on the counter and crossed her arms, hugging herself.

"Are you okay?"

She nodded, then shook her head, ending with a shrug, then took a deep breath. "I feel guilty for not missing him as much as she does. I think I should miss him more. Sometimes I go for long stretches where I don't even think about our life together, and then when something comes up that reminds me, I'm like, 'Thank God that's over.'"

He was consumed with a physical need to fix something—or chop wood maybe—because he really wanted to hold Emma as his heart broke for the burdens she carried. But he forced himself to stand still and give her space. "It might seem a little self-serving," he said wryly, "but you don't have to pretend with me. Ever."

She gave a wan smile. "I—I'm afraid that if I start telling the truth, I might never stop." And then, seeming to realize what she'd said, she put her hand over her mouth and bent at the waist.

Shit.

Marcus got to her before she hit the floor, put an arm around her shoulders, and sank into a kitchen chair to hold her on his lap. Patton sniffed her knee, then put his head on her leg, looking to Marcus with concern. "I've got her, buddy," he told the dog.

Silent sobs racked her entire body, and tears soaked the sleeve of his shirt while he rocked her and tried to think of something to say. If he'd learned nothing else from living with his sister, it was that *nothing* was better than *something stupid*. He settled on *nothing*.

After a few minutes, her crying abruptly ceased and she sat up, trying to pull away. "Oh God, I'm sorry. I'm so sorry."

"Nothing to be sorry for." He didn't try to hold on to her, but kept his hands on her back and one thigh.

She was almost off his lap before she stopped and sniffed, reaching for a paper napkin from the holder on the table. She kept her face turned away from him while he rubbed her back and waited. After a shuddering sigh, she said, "Wow. Aren't you glad you stopped by today?"

"Yeah. No. I mean… Hell, I don't know."

She finally turned her puffy, tear-stained face to his. "Really? The great Marcus Talbott is speechless?"

"Emma, in case you haven't noticed, you make me question everything I thought I knew about myself. For almost thirty years, I was all about the smooth, but you've got me all twisted up in knots."

She gave a watery chuckle. "I've got to wash my face. I think my break time is up."

"Hang on." He pulled his phone from his pocket. "What's the number over there?"

"Marcus, no. I can go back—"

"Come on, babe. Don't be a martyr for the cause."

She stared at him for a long moment, but finally nodded and gave him the number.

He entered the digits, waited a moment, and when Mrs. Stern answered, said, "Hey, there. Emma's not feeling well, so she needs a little longer break."

"Oh no. Should I come over? I can get my husband to come in."

"No, ma'am, I think she shouldn't have skipped breakfast today. She just got a little dizzy. I'm going to fix her something to eat, and we'll have her back on the job in no time."

"Well, if you're sure." The woman sounded like she believed him as much as he believed himself, but whatever. She played along.

They said their goodbyes and hung up, then Patton helped him stand so he could help Emma.

"Go wash your face. I'll make lunch," he told her, unfastening Patton's harness and vest.

"You cook?"

"I can manage. Patton will help."

"There's nothing in the fridge," she warned, but went down the hall anyway.

Marcus opened the refrigerator. He could cobble together something from just about anything. Except, perhaps, the nothing in her fridge. She wasn't kidding. A bottle of mustard, a pitcher of red Kool-Aid, and a tub of butter.

Okay, maybe the pantry would be better.

Not much.

But he did find a couple of cans of soup, and there was a half loaf of bread in the freezer.

He got to work.

Chapter 23

Emma looked herself in the eye in the bathroom mirror and said, "You're not a bad person for not missing your husband. You're not a bad person." She did her best to believe this.

Emma had been rationalizing Todd's behavior and keeping it secret since well before he died, telling herself it was so his sweet mother didn't have to face the truth. He was gone. He'd never be back.

Nothing good would come of adding to the Sterns' grief with stories of how messed up their son had been, and how Emma had failed them all.

So why did she feel so weighted down?

She looked at her hand, at the plain gold ring she'd taken off in Houston. She almost hadn't put it back on, but then, not wanting to talk to Mrs. Stern about it, she'd slid it in place before her first shift back at the Feed and Seed. But now she took it off again. She took off the chain she wore around her neck, the one with Todd's ring, unhooked it, and added hers. It was time to let him go. She lowered the rings and watched the chain slip and coil into a pile on the counter.

How long would it take for Mrs. Stern to notice? Probably about five seconds, and then what was Emma going to tell her? She could say she'd been gaining weight, that the ring was cutting off her circulation, or maybe that she'd been doing some work around the house and didn't want to damage it. Or she could tell the truth. She was interested in someone else.

Something banged from the kitchen. Marcus, fixing her lunch. Not pushing her to talk about her little meltdown, not grilling her about Todd, and yet he was being there for her, on her own terms.

How rare was that?

And how could she watch him leave to go back to that damned war, where he would experience terrible things that she wouldn't be able to understand? He would go through things that would alienate them, make them strangers—even enemies. She wouldn't be able to help him, because she wasn't enough. Even Granddad was doing better without her help.

Maybe Marcus wouldn't go back. Maybe the doctors would decide he wasn't fit for combat. They'd give him a desk job, like he'd had while he was recovering. Then he'd be safe. Even if he didn't come back to Big Chance, back to Emma, he'd be safe, and that would be enough, right?

It would have to be.

She caught sight of herself again and said, "Time to go out there and have lunch, and not fall apart. Again."

She wiped away a stray tear streak, gave her eyeliner a freshening, and went back down the hall to a sight so foreign to the gray thoughts in her mind, it took her a moment to comprehend.

There was a man in her kitchen, dancing to nothing she could hear. Marcus jabbed at something with the spatula he held like a sword, then moonwalked the short distance to the refrigerator and opened it as he spun around.

He was so beautiful. And *happy*. Why was he interested in her grumpy, broken-down self?

"Hey." He smiled and pulled out his earphones, dropping the wires over his shoulder.

"Aren't you injured?" she asked, amazed at how easily he moved.

He grinned. "Today's a good day. I'm ready and able to have a dance-off with the King of Pop." He paused.

"Michael Jackson's dead," she pointed out.

"Exactly."

She laughed, which was probably his intention.

"You hungry?"

"I am." But what on God's green earth could he have found to prepare?

"Sit." He gently pushed her into a chair and opened and closed a few more cabinets before finding bowls and plates and filling them before bringing them to the table.

"Ta-da!" With a flourish, he set down a bowl of—

"What is this?"

"Chimato Noodle Soup. And grilled peanut butter and jelly."

"Um…"

"Before you go all puritan on me, try it. It's a can of tomato soup mixed with chicken noodle."

"I get that, but why?"

He shrugged. "It's comfort food in my family. My siblings and I could never agree on what to eat, so whoever was in charge of cooking would mix stuff together. This one was my favorite. And I invented grilled peanut butter and jelly."

"I think that was Elvis," she pointed out gently.

"Mmm…didn't he put banana in there?"

"Maybe, but still."

"Don't harsh my buzz, woman. Eat the sammich."

She laughed and tucked in to the food.

Marcus sat opposite her and did the same. "Do you want something else?" he asked after a couple of minutes. "You've got about four jars of applesauce in there. Is that your comfort food?"

"Ewww," she shuddered. "No. That's what I had to use to hide Granddad's meds in when he was being fractious. Now that he's at Golden Gardens, he lines up with everyone else like it's happy hour when the nurse comes around with her cart. He thought *I* was trying to poison him."

"What about lemon? You want some lemon for your tea? You have some fine vintage plastic squeeze-fruit lemon in the back of the fridge."

She shook her head. "Thank you, but no. I'm fine. I can get up and get stuff out of my own kitchen."

"I know, I'm just trying to look after you."

To avoid bursting back into tears at how sweet he was being, she said, "I'm not going to break. I've had my one allotted breakdown for the decade."

He sighed and put his chin on his hand, looking at her in all seriousness. "You should do it at least once every three years, if not more often. It's dangerous to let steam build up for that long."

"Three."

"Yep."

"And you know this how? It's not like you ever fall apart, Mr. Optimism and Encouragement."

Wow, she was determined to knock down the door hiding his anxieties, wasn't she?

This was where his determination to boost other people bit him in the ass. But this was Emma. Emma wasn't "other people." He couldn't hope that she'd share her crap with him unless he was willing to give her a peek at his own. Which was unfortunate, because that meant he'd have to look at it, too.

His biggest fear, when he woke in the middle of the night and couldn't shut off the movies in his head, was that his back wasn't going to heal. That he wouldn't be able to go back to work and do what he knew how to do. His 3:00 a.m. fear list, however, had broadened to include something else, he realized. Along with the slight possibility he wouldn't be cleared for duty was the fact that he didn't know how to do anything but soldier. He had nothing at all to offer Emma.

And he wanted to offer her the universe.

He couldn't tell her that last part, but he did manage to get out, "I'm afraid this back thing might not get better, and that I won't be able to go back to work."

Her forehead creased in sympathy, but then she shrugged. "If you're okay otherwise, can't you get a desk job?"

He tried not to notice the hope in her eyes when she said that. He understood. He knew he was getting ahead of himself, but on the outside chance she was thinking of nurturing this budding relationship, it would be much better to nurture it with a man with a job. Unfortunately, he'd gouge his own eyes out if he had a permanent desk job.

"I'd rather go back to combat. Paperwork's not my thing any more than school was my thing." He didn't tell her that when he'd had that desk job after he'd gotten out of the hospital, he'd been in constant trouble over stupid mistakes because he didn't pay enough attention to detail. And he simply hated it. So he said, "I'm pretty sure I can get back to the job I want. I've been working hard."

"That's what all the weightlifting's about?"

"That, and I like the way you look at me when I flex."

She snorted and threw her wadded-up napkin at his head. Patton, who'd been dozing on the living room rug, padded after it and returned it to Emma.

"What a good boy," she told the dog, giving him a vigorous ear scratch. "You're an awesome dog."

"You're really good with him," Marcus told her.

Her smile was a little sad as she looked down and pushed the last crust of her grilled PB&J around on her plate.

Finally, she met his eyes. "Piper didn't die of old age like Mrs. Stern thinks."

Oh no.

"Todd was…edgy after he got out of the army. He wasn't working, and everything got on his nerves."

Not surprising. Especially if he was an addict, as Marcus suspected.

Emma fiddled with one of her earrings and went on. "It wasn't anything I couldn't deal with. Usually. He'd just blow up over little sh—stuff, then stomp off and…eventually calm down."

Stomp off and get high, she meant. She shouldn't have had to take that, Marcus thought, but she went on before he could tell her that.

"Granddad fell and had to spend a couple of days in the hospital, so I was there, visiting a lot. Todd was in charge of feeding and walking Piper. Heck. He didn't even have to walk him, just had to let him out in the yard a couple of times a day. Piper was such a good boy. He never had accidents and always let us know when he needed to go out. The barking would be annoying, but once he did his thing, he'd just go back to his spot and sleep until time for the next meal."

Her voice thickened, and Marcus put his hand on her leg to let her know he was there for her. "You don't have to tell me," he said.

"Yeah, I do. I've been pretending to believe his story for far too long. I was visiting Granddad, and I got a text from Todd that Piper was acting funny. When I got home, my little dog was lying in his spot—in a pool of bloody urine. Todd said he didn't know what happened. He said he was taking a nap and heard Piper bark to go out, but ignored him and went back to sleep—which I could totally believe. About that time, Todd was either wasted or hungover most of the time. He said he woke up when he heard a yelp, and got up to find out what was wrong. Piper was in the basement, where he'd peed and pooped all over the place. He said Piper must have needed to go really bad and decided the basement was the best place if he couldn't get outside, and must have fallen."

She trembled under his hand, so he tightened his hold on her. She put her hand over his, traced the veins in the back of it, threaded her fingers through his.

"The thing is, Piper was *terrified* of the basement. He'd have no more gone down there to have an accident than miss a meal. Todd said he picked him up and put him in his spot, but Piper was acting weird, which was when he texted me.

"When I picked up the little guy, I felt his ribs move under my hands. His ribs wouldn't have moved like that unless they were broken. And I don't believe a dog's ribs could break from falling down the stairs, even an old dog. I think what really happened is that he was barking, asking to go out, and got on Todd's nerves. I think Todd *kicked* him down the stairs."

"Oh, baby."

She shook her head, holding up a hand to keep him from pulling her into his arms.

"He died before I got him to the vet. And then I didn't know what to do. I shouldn't have left him home alone with Todd. I knew he was in a bad state of mind. I should have gotten someone to stay with Granddad at the hospital."

"It's not your fault."

She looked out the window, dry-eyed. "I know that. I *know* that," she repeated, as though she still wasn't convinced. "But I…I covered it up. I didn't tell anyone. I didn't even confront Todd. I was so freaked out, so ashamed and scared, and… I just pretended to go along with the story, because I didn't know what would happen if I told. What difference would it have made? I didn't have any proof. Piper was gone. And Todd kept trying to get…better. At least he'd say he was, and I'd believe him, until the next time."

Marcus didn't know what to say to that. He couldn't say that he'd have done any differently in her place.

Her phone buzzed from the kitchen counter. He reached to grab it and handed it to her.

"It's the store. I bet Mrs. Stern is getting overwhelmed. Hello?" She listened for a minute, and frowned. "But don't you want to… Okay. I will. Thank you."

"Everything okay?" he asked after she put the phone down on the table and stared at it for a long moment.

"Yep. I think. I've just been given the rest of the day off."

"Well, that can't be a bad thing, can it?"

"I don't know. I'm not sure what I should do with myself now."

Marcus had some ideas, but decided to start off in the safe zone. "Well, you could help me do these dishes."

Chapter 24

"No, I get to wash," Emma insisted, trying to bump Marcus out of the way with her hip.

"Oh no." He laughed, widening his stance and grabbing the counter to block her. "I hate to dry. Besides, I don't know where to put things."

She dodged under his arm to snatch the scrubber from the edge of the sink, but then he had her trapped. "You got it all out, you can find its way back. My kitchen, my rules."

"Nope." His voice made her freeze in place, as it was rumbling, deep and strong, into her ear.

She tried to focus on the issue at hand. "Come on, you cooked, I'll wash up. If you don't want to dry, we'll let 'em air dry." She shifted back, encountering a solid wall of man—which moved a bit closer and was getting more *solid* by the moment. Her hands closed over the edge of the counter, scrubber completely forgotten.

"I don't know if I've ever had to fight with anyone about *getting* to clean up," he said against her skin, making the little hairs on the back of her neck rise.

"I didn't know I'd ever *want* to fight someone for the chance to do the dishes." She was a little breathless and a lot turned on.

His entire body surrounded hers from behind, and she was enveloped in his heat from shoulder to ankle. Her waist pressed against the edge of the sink, where the running water made bubbles froth up and now spilled over the edge.

"Look what you did," she said, turning off the water. "My shirt's all wet."

"Really? Let me see." Instead of turning her to look, he spread his hands over her belly. "Yep. A little wet here."

Her nipples tightened at his touch. Her entire body softened and grew taut at the same time, yearning for more.

"I should check how far up this goes." His large, warm hands closed over her breasts. He didn't squeeze or stroke, just barely supported the slight weights while her entire body ached for more.

"Nope. Not wet here. Should I check anywhere else?"

"Uh-huh." Her verbal skills fled as he moved down again, over her shirt, to the waistband of her work pants.

"Hmm. Maybe a little bit here."

She felt the button give, and he fumbled for a moment with the zipper before his fingers slid beneath the elastic of her panties and down, right where she needed him. "Oh God." So good. Little electric shocks weakened her knees.

"I got you," he murmured, his other arm around her waist, supporting her while he stroked. His mouth closed over the muscle stretched between her shoulder and neck, sucking lightly, nipping and licking.

"More." She reached behind herself and ran her hand over the front of his pants, nearly coming undone at how hard he was.

There was a tangling of hands while she tried to release him and he pushed at her pants.

"Break," he said with a slight chuckle. "You do you, I've got me."

But he didn't let her turn around. She was still pressed between his body and the sink as she wriggled to drop her pants, feeling deliciously dirty with the bare skin of her butt against his front. She was trapped by her pants around her knees and shivered when he ran his hands over her backside. He pressed down on her in an unspoken message to be still. She complied, listening to him breathe as fabric rustled, plastic crinkled.

And then he was back, his hands on her, one caressing a needy breast, the other between her legs, stroking, sliding, slipping.

His erection nudged the small of her back.

"Gotta get in you," he muttered.

How was this going to work, standing here like this? "I'm too short to do it like this."

"You're perfect for this." He turned her away from the sink to the part of the counter that functioned as a breakfast bar and lifted her as though she were nothing. "Lean forward."

And as she lowered her front to the counter, he parted her dangling thighs and ran a hand down her back, over her ass, between her legs, and guided himself into her from behind.

He felt perfect, hitting all the right places as he thrust into her. She tried to hold on to the counter and push back against him, but he had their movements under control, hands on her hips, pushing into her with smooth, exquisite thrusts.

She needed more, wanted more. She wiggled and whimpered until he finally moved one hand around to touch her while he filled her. He barely had to stroke her. His rhythm provided enough pressure and movement to make her tighten, tighten, squeeze…

"Are you coming? Are you coming, baby? Come for me."

His voice. That musical baritone. It sent her over the edge, and she cried out while heat spread from their joining through the rest of her body in a giant, shuddering rush.

And still he moved, steady and hard, muttering against her neck, "I need you, baby, come for me. Come with me. Come with me forever."

His words sent heat rushing to her core and out through her body again. The orgasm went on as his thrusts grew harder, faster, rougher, and he groaned, "Please…"

Even through the condom she felt him pulse into her as he sagged, bracing himself on his arms so as not to crush her.

They stayed like that for a long time, joined and panting in sync as their respiration slowed.

"Wow," he said, finally removing himself from her body. "We still have to do the dishes."

She laughed, straightening and trying to gather her pants—and her wits.

His words echoed in her mind. *Come with me forever. Please.* He hadn't meant it, but damn her weak heart—hearing him say that triggered so many wants that the only thing she could think of to say was *Anywhere.* She wouldn't say it, because it couldn't be real. Not like that. And she was afraid that if he said it again, she'd agree. The truth was, she was starting to think she'd go anywhere with him.

After they cleaned up and got dressed, Emma was quiet. She seemed to have retreated inside her own head. Marcus didn't exactly blame her. After all, he'd pretty much panted out his feelings for her in the least romantic way possible.

Hopefully she hadn't taken him too seriously—at least, not until he was sure his future was wrapped up in a nice, tidy package.

While Emma was in the bathroom, he drained the cold dishwater from the sink and ran more hot water. He'd added a healthy squirt of dishwashing liquid and was watching the bubbles crest the edge of the sink when she came back. As casually as he could, he picked up the scrubber and went to work on the soup bowls and said, "Tell me more about Todd."

There was a moment of hesitation, then, "I can't believe I told you all that in Houston." She sighed heavily, then nudged Marcus out of the way. "If I have to tell you the rest, *I* get to do dishes."

Marcus huffed a laugh and gave way, knowing it would be easier for her to talk if she had something to do with her hands.

It took one bowl and two spoons before she said, "After Piper died, things deteriorated between us."

He could believe that. It must have nearly killed her to allow him the lie that the dog's death had been an accident.

"Not that they'd been great for a long time, anyway, but…" She took a breath. "He'd been taking all kinds of pills since he left the army. Stuff to sleep, stuff for anxiety, pain… and he was isolating, too—hiding out with the computer, watching videos and playing games all night long.

"He didn't see any of his old friends from high school, said they didn't 'get' it, were all full of shit, stuff like that. And I was such a nervous wreck, I didn't know what to do.

The guy I'd married was gone, and the new guy in his place wouldn't let me into his head. Granddad was starting to get more and more confused, and that scared me. I didn't have anyone to talk to about any of it. His mom and dad were great, but I didn't want to complain to them because they idolized Todd. And then Mrs. Stern's mother passed away, and I couldn't bear to add to their burden.

"A couple of times he'd fall asleep and I wouldn't be able to wake him up. I assume he was taking more meds than he'd been prescribed. I don't know for sure, but when I confronted him about it, he'd say he'd stop. Of course, he didn't ask for a doctor's help, just threw everything away—and then he was even worse, because he didn't sleep for days."

Marcus nodded. He remembered how hard it had been to give up his pain meds, and the other drugs—for anxiety and sleep—could be a million times worse to quit, he'd heard.

"Things would start to get better, but eventually something would set him off. He'd disappear for days at a time. He'd started hanging out at this awful bar on the other side of the county. I'm not even sure they have a legal liquor license. I went looking for him once and found him 'sitting and talking' with a woman in the back seat of someone's car."

"Oh no," Marcus said.

"You know, cheating was the least of my concerns at that point. How sad is that? We were living at the ranch then—staying with Granddad because he was getting forgetful and pretending we were going to start an organic produce business."

She put the last clean dish in the drainer and pulled the plug, but didn't turn around. She wiped the faucet with a cloth, over and over. "So one night, we had an argument. He was supposed to help me fix up the garden, and he'd stayed in bed all day instead; but then he got up to go out. I was so mad, I threatened to lock him out. He went anyway. About five in the morning, two guys I'd never seen before showed up at the door. They had Todd in the back seat of their car, and he was barely conscious. They said he owed them four thousand dollars. I assume for drugs, but I was afraid to ask. It didn't matter. I didn't have the money, but I told them I'd get it for them the next day—anything to get them to go away."

She stared through the kitchen window to a day in the past, the memories tightening the skin over her fine bones, trying to age her. He wanted to reach out, to ease it all away, but the sink was empty now, so she started to scrub it and to talk.

"The next day, I had to take Granddad to the doctor. I got Todd up, told him what happened the night before. He pretended it was all a big joke, that those guys were just teasing me, but I knew they weren't, and I could tell he was scared, even though he told me he'd take care of it.

"When I got back with Granddad, Todd said everything was good, he'd made arrangements, but he wouldn't tell me what. And he seemed to get better. For the next couple of weeks he stayed home at night, even did some stuff around the ranch. It wasn't perfect, but it seemed like maybe he'd been scared straight or something. Until I got the credit card statement."

"Uh-oh."

"Yeah. We'd already racked up a hefty balance, mostly nickel-and-dime purchases Todd made online, but it had been manageable. Except all of a sudden, he was getting cash advances. A couple of hundred bucks the first few times, but then more and more—so that by the end of the month, we had a bill for $20,000."

"Jesus."

"I lost it. Just completely lost it. He fell apart, crying, and finally told me he'd been doing coke and somehow figured it would be a good idea to make up the money he was spending by playing the odds. He had a *bookie*, for God's sake. He bet on everything—basketball, football, *swimming*. Who bets on swimming? And he started with this whole 'I can make it up this weekend, though, just let me get a few thousand more out.'"

It sounded ridiculous—like a bad made-for-TV movie, but the tension in her voice was beyond real.

She threw the sponge down on the counter and turned to face Marcus. She put her hands on her hips and said, "I threw him out. I told him that was it, we were done. I didn't want him to go to his parents—I mean, they were so good to us, and I knew they'd be devastated and would try to help us—so I said if he told his mom and dad about it, I'd have him arrested. I didn't know what I was going to do about the money, but I figured I'd just eat ramen for the next twenty years or so, until I was above water. Adam had already loaned me way more than I deserved.

"Todd begged me to give him another chance. Swore he'd change, all that. But I'd heard it before. And to be honest, I was *mad*. So tired. I told him to get out and stay gone. He asked if he got clean and paid the money back, could he come back, and I said no."

She stared off into the distance, her eyes bleak. "I didn't give him any way out. He said he'd make things right and drove off into a thunderstorm. That's the last time I saw him. A few hours later, the sheriff was at my front door with Todd's dad, telling me that he'd crashed his car."

"They ruled it an accident, but I don't believe it. There weren't any skid marks. I know, because I went out there the next day. It was like he was crossing the bridge, and decided to speed up and make a hard turn over the edge."

"Oh, babe. I'm so sorry."

She blew out a big breath.

"And then later, I got a check. He had life insurance. Twenty thousand dollars."

"You don't think—"

"I don't know. Maybe. I didn't even know he *had* life insurance. It was a policy his parents had taken out when he was younger. But don't you see? If I had given him a little shred of hope...that it could work out, maybe he'd have hung on. Maybe he'd have gotten better."

Marcus was afraid to ask if Todd had gotten better, and lived, whether she'd still be with him.

If, if, if.

The sun, sinking toward the horizon, shot a few rays through the window, glinting off the lone tear that rolled down her cheek.

He wanted to pull her into his arms, to promise that nothing like that would happen to her again, because he was a better man, but was he? Could he promise that if he couldn't go back to the army, he'd be any healthier, any less likely to fall into the same pit?

He just had to make sure that wasn't an issue.

She blew out a breath and looked at Marcus, raising an eyebrow. "Nice, huh?"

He shook his head. "I'm so sorry you had to go through that."

Her phone rang, and she sniffed and cleared her throat before answering.

Marcus finished drying the dishes and put them away while she spoke to whoever it was.

When she hung up, she said, "That was Golden Gardens. Granddad's out of one of his meds, and they don't have his prescriptions transferred to them yet. I need to run some stuff out there."

"Do you want to visit him for a while? I'll run out there with you," Marcus offered, not wanting to leave her after she'd shared so much with him. Wanting—needing—to be someone she could count on.

But she shook her head. "You know what? I'm kind of drained. I think I'll take the stuff out there, say hello, and come back here and go to bed early."

After a long, warm hug and a fairly chaste kiss, Marcus and Patton drove off. He looked back before turning the corner, however, and saw that she was watching him with an expression of longing on her beautiful face.

Chapter 25

"I HEAR A CAR," TANNER ANNOUNCED AS HE AND JAKE joined Marcus and Adam on the front porch.

"I hope to God the weather holds out," Adam muttered when the big, black SUV rolled into view under a sky roiling with dark clouds. "All we need is a big storm to make this go crazy."

"All we need is our *visitor* to make this go crazy," Marcus replied as they watched the car doors open. "Just wait."

The only thing that kept Mr. Thornhill from appearing 100 percent Don Corleone was the fact that he'd arrived in the passenger seat of an Escalade and not the back seat of a chauffeured limo.

Adam glanced at Marcus, eyebrows raised as though to ask if this guy was for real, but Marcus couldn't meet his eyes because he was afraid he might laugh. Especially after Thornhill introduced his accountant, burly, ponytailed Butch.

Thornhill greeted the men like they were all old-school chums, shaking hands and clapping shoulders all around. "Well," he said after a moment, "let's have the grand tour, shall we? I've got to get back to Houston by midnight, or the little woman's likely to get another headache, if you know what I mean." He elbowed Jake, who *didn't* appear to know what he meant, but had the good sense not to ask.

Marcus spoke, basically repeating his spiel from Houston. "Thanks for coming to visit us, Mr. Thornhill.

We're starting small and are a little rough around the edges, but we've got a great business plan and good people. But it's not enough. We're getting homeless dogs—and the occasional veteran—on our doorstep on a regular basis, and while we want to help as many dogs as we can, our goal is to be a veterans helping veterans helping dogs helping veterans organization. Right now, about all we can do is take them in and feed them."

"The dogs, or the veterans?" Thornhill asked, which was kind of a good question, and everyone dutifully chuckled.

"Both, actually." Adam took over. "We're just getting started with dogs, and we don't have many resources in place for the veterans. This is my ranch, and I'm the main dog trainer. I'm transitioning from teaching bomb-sniffing to anxiety sniffing pretty well. But I can only work with a few dogs at a time, and most of the animals that come to us aren't going to be able to be trained to be service animals, or even therapy dogs."

"Why not?"

Adam shrugged. "These guys—the dogs—have been through an awful lot. We got incredibly lucky with D-Day, Patton, and Loretta." He indicated his own big, black dog, the golden retriever with Marcus, and Lizzie's sweet pit bull.

"We've got a few more candidates and a mile-long waiting list of veterans who need their various skills. But that doesn't mean the remaining dogs can't be rehabilitated and rehomed. That's where the veterans helping part comes in. We keep getting calls from guys who want to come here and train a dog for themselves. But a service dog isn't right for every vet. And we can't bring all the vets here to train for an entire year, which is what it takes to really train a dog." He waved around at the ranch: the medium-size ranch house that was already bursting at the gills, and the rickety big barn with the smaller horse shed next to it.

"What's your endgame?" Thornhill asked.

Adam took a deep breath and just threw it out there. "We want to add some housing and see about bringing some guys—and women—in to work with the traumatized and displaced dogs for a few weeks, or even months at a time, to get the dogs back in shape to be adopted by someone, while they're dealing with their own life changes. If they make a dog match in the process, we'll go from there. And if they find out it's not going to work for them? Well, they'll have learned something, and I'm pretty sure anyone could benefit from a few weeks of intensive fetch." He emphasized his words by picking up a Frisbee and winging it across the yard. "Go get it, Loretta."

The pit bull, who'd been sitting quietly, took off like a bullet. She caught the disk before it hit the ground and brought it back, dropping it at Adam's feet.

"Meanwhile, we're getting a lot of questions from community members about training, so we're thinking about adding some doggy boot-camp programs, if we can find the space for them," Marcus added.

"That might help your bottom line with a little bit of stability. Will you be doing all the training?"

Adam shook his head. "My sister's qualified, and we can bring on some more trainers as we need to."

"All right," Thornhill said. "I'd like the grand tour. Meanwhile, I'd like Butch to check out your books. I'm nervous about wasting my hard-earned money on a half-assed operation."

"Tanner and I can handle this," Marcus said, and ushered Butch inside.

The screen door shut behind them at the same moment the first rumbles of thunder rolled over the valley.

And then Marcus heard honking. He turned to see a little blue Mustang pull into the yard. "Who the... Oh hell."

"What's wrong?" Tanner asked.

Marcus sighed. "Nothing. It's a—a friend of my sister's. I forgot she was stopping by." He pushed the door open and called, "Come on! You're going to get wet!"

"Damn," Butch commented, when the long, tall blast from Marcus's past ran toward them, miles of braided extensions waving behind her.

Maya glided into the house, bringing a cloud of perfume with her. "Hi, you hunka-hunka hotness," she greeted Marcus, throwing her arms around him and kissing him soundly on the mouth. "God, you look great!" she cooed, running her hands up and down his biceps.

Marcus tried not to roll his eyes. "Yeah, Maya. So I kind of messed up and got double-booked. Maybe—"

"Oh no you don't," she said, looking up at the sky. "I've driven too far to see you. According to the radar, we've got about an hour before this storm hits."

Marcus sighed and looked at Tanner. He hated to leave the kid alone with this guy. Tanner wasn't comfortable with new people and could be kind of an asshole, but the kid surprised him. "I got this," he said. "You go do...whatever it is you're going to do." His smirk suggested there would be more comments later.

Marcus decided not to try to set the record straight until he had to, and looked at Maya.

She frowned. "I was really hoping we could go out in the fields, but I guess we can set up on the front porch," she mused.

Oh hell no. "Can we do this…somewhere else?"

She glanced at the sky. "You got a hayloft somewhere?"

"No, but we've got an old horse shed," he told her, pointing at the small barn Adam's granddad had used for storage, and which would at some point be turned into a bunkhouse.

"Oh, that looks great!" She gave Marcus a once-over. "The jeans are totally sexy, and the T-shirt can come off. Do you have a pair of cowboy boots?"

Marcus glanced at Tanner, who said, "You can borrow mine if you promise not to get anything, er, nasty on them." The unburned half of his face said there would definitely be more discussion later.

Oh, kid, you have no idea, Marcus thought.

CRASH!

Emma flinched at the enormous peal of thunder that accompanied the brilliant light show flashing through town.

Great. She'd just hung up from hearing Lizzie tell her that Mr. Thornhill was scheduled to arrive at the ranch right about—she checked the clock—now. He was gonna be *so* impressed at the way the rain poured in through the roof of the barn.

And Emma couldn't get there until later in the day because she had to work. Not that Thornhill would care if she showed up or not, but she felt like she should be there. And because Marcus would be there, of course.

Her insides warmed at the thought of him, as they usually did. She hadn't seen him in person since the other day, when she'd spilled her guts about Todd and what she'd been through with him, but they'd called and texted each other about a million times.

She figured if her brother didn't know what was going on, he was surely suspicious. Not that they had to keep things a secret, but still.

Another boom, and the lights inside the Feed and Seed flickered and went out.

Crap.

Emma didn't mind working in the dusky haze so much as she hated the way the air immediately grew thick, hot, and wet. Even though the thunderstorm would cool the heat—from scorching to merely boiling—the humidity would go up and even things out, sending the air back to gross.

How had she gone from romantic and squishy to grumpy and dissatisfied with everything on the planet, including this job she thought she loved but now wanted to walk out on? Something had shifted in the past few days. Finally letting out all of that awfulness about Todd, and her poor sweet puppy, had loosened something inside her.

Maybe it was time to change her circumstances and actually consider Adam's suggestion about taking on private dog clients. She could start with a couple of dogs a week and see how it went.

If she didn't suffocate from lack of air-conditioning first.

The first bead of sweat was rolling between her shoulder blades when the front door jingled and admitted Mr. Stern with a blast of wind and rain.

"Shooee!" he gasped, pulling off his John Deere hat and

shaking excess water from his meager fringe of hair. "It's gonna be a good one."

Emma agreed. "Hurricane season might be harder on Houston, but we sure do get our share of leftover rain."

Mr. Stern nodded. "That was hurricane leftovers that killed Todd, this time three years ago to the day, too."

Emma's eyes shot to the calendar above the cash register. It was the anniversary, and she hadn't even realized it. Guilt wrapped her in a familiar cloak of shame and sorrow.

"Oh hell, honey. I'm sorry. I'm trying like the dickens to get Linda to lighten up a little bit, and here I am spreading the gloom." Mr. Stern put an arm around Emma's shoulders and squeezed her, which made her feel both worse and better.

"How is she today?" Emma asked. The last two years, when this day came around, Mrs. Stern had gone to the cemetery and spent the day crying and talking to Todd. Emma went with her the first year, but last year begged off, having conveniently scheduled a doctor appointment for Granddad that day.

"She's sad, of course," Mr. Stern told Emma now. "That's one of the reasons I stopped by today."

"What can I do?" Emma asked.

Mr. Stern patted Emma on the shoulder and leaned against the counter next to her. "You don't have to do anything, sweetheart. You've been a great support to this family, and we love you, but I need to get her out of this town. It's got too many painful memories for us. We've decided to retire and move to Arizona."

Emma blinked. She'd just been thinking about making some life changes herself, but not immediately. Was this some kind of karmic be-careful-what-you-ask-for event?

"Wait, what?"

Mr. Stern said, "We aren't sure about timing, but wanted you to have a heads-up."

How long would she have a job? Emma wondered. She was about to ask when the front door burst open again, admitting Mr. Wagner from the florist's shop next door. "You got any generators?" he asked. "Walt says the transformer out near the highway got hit. It's gonna be a while before we've got power again."

"There's only one in stock, Hank, so you get to be our last customer of the day," Mr. Stern said. Then he turned to Emma. "Honey, you might as well take the rest of the day off. I'm going to close up after this sale."

"Okay," Emma said and gathered her belongings in a daze. She'd taken four steps into the pouring rain before realizing she didn't have an umbrella. "Oh well," she said to no one, then decided she should haul her butt to the ranch to see if she could help with the Thornhill visit.

Glancing at herself in the rearview mirror, she considered the clumps of hair sticking to her forehead and the mascara that had smudged in a not-sexy way. Ugh. She was a mess.

But it was raining even harder now. If she went slowly and ran the air-conditioning, she might dry by the time she got out there. And maybe the rain would stop by then, too. Then she could run inside to the bathroom and get fixed up again before anyone saw her.

As though to remind her of who was in charge, another flash of lightning lit up the sky in the direction of the ranch.

Chapter 26

By the time Maya had finished with him, Marcus was soaked, and it wasn't just with sweat from the weird positions she'd had him in. The roof of the horse shed was almost as leaky as the barn, and Marcus had lost count of the times a stream of water had poured down on his head as Maya cried, "There! Right there. Don't move."

But finally she was satisfied and said, "Thanks a bunch. I've been through a few guys, and none of them were quite as awesome as you."

Marcus shook his head, anxious for her to be on her way before anyone found out what they'd been doing. "Whatever. When will you get the results?"

She wrinkled her nose. "Couple of weeks, probably. I'll give you a call." She laughed. "Everyone's going to be so surprised—"

"Shh…" He wrapped an arm around her and covered her mouth with his hand, because the rain had stopped and he heard people approaching, feet splashing in puddles.

After he saw that Maya understood she should be quiet, he let her go and stepped away.

Through a space between some boards, Marcus was able to make out the entire group—Adam, Jake, and Thornhill coming from the barn, Tanner and Butch from the house, meeting a few feet away.

"Whose car's this?" Adam asked, looking around.

"Some friend of Marcus's," Tanner said.

"Huh."

"We appreciate your visit, Mr. Thornhill," Adam said.

Thornhill looked at Butch, who gave him a silent nod.

"I'm real impressed here, son," Thornhill said, thwapping Adam on the back. "I think we can get some good work done."

"That's great, sir," Adam said.

In the silence of the horse shed, Marcus did a fist pump. *Yes.* He'd come through.

"Butch'll be in touch with details, but I think we can safely promise to make sure your operating expenses are covered, and then some, for at least a year." He named a sum that made Marcus's eyes bulge. "And to tide you over until we can get you a check, let me give you this." Thornhill reached into his pants pocket and pulled out a checkbook. He scribbled for a moment, then peeled it off and handed it to Adam.

Adam thanked Thornhill and then asked Tanner, "Do you know where Marcus is? I know he'll want to say goodbye…" Adam glanced around.

Tanner said, "He took off somewhere with that woman."

"A woman?"

"Oh yes," Butch confirmed.

"Really?" Adam said. "I thought he and Emma—" He cut himself off and shook his head. "Well, I know Marcus wants to thank you, too."

"He's a good man," Thornhill said. "Shame about his disability."

If anything would make him come out of his hiding place, it might have been to protest the label, but Marcus decided now, before he made the big donation, was the wrong time to call Thornhill out.

Fortunately, it was only a few moments before their guests were leaving, and Adam, Jake, and Tanner were waving goodbye.

"Let's get inside before that rain starts again," Adam said, glancing at the sky.

"Phew," Marcus said, once they'd disappeared inside.

"You know they saw my car. I'm not sure why you think you're keeping this a secret," Maya commented.

"I don't want to talk about why you're here," he told her.

"Does this have anything to do with this 'Emma' your friend mentioned?"

Instead of answering, Marcus said, "Let's get you out of here." He opened the door of the shed and picked up Maya's bag of stuff. "Oh crap, woman! How do you carry this around?" he asked as he staggered under its weight.

"Don't be such a baby." She laughed, clicking the remote for her trunk.

A bolt of lightning flashed through the sky, followed by a low roll of thunder, and his concern for her safety outweighed his desire to avoid explaining her presence. "Maybe you should stick around," he said.

"I'll be fine," she told him. "I'll say goodbye here and make a run for the car." Before he was ready, she threw her arms around his neck. He instinctively put his hands on her waist as she rose on tiptoe to kiss him.

He tried to push her back but was distracted by the rumble of an approaching car... Emma's car.

He had no trouble seeing the look on her face as she took in his position—and that of Maya in his arms.

Emma couldn't run inside and fix her rain-damaged hair and makeup before Marcus saw her. Or before his girlfriend saw her.

She did, however, manage to get her car parked and her body into the ranch house before the rain started again, and before Marcus had another chance to kiss his girlfriend and come after Emma to tell whatever lies he was going to tell.

Damn it, she thought, marching past the open-mouthed trio of soldiers in the living room without saying a word and up the stairs to the bathroom. She slammed the door and turned the brass lock. She looked into the mirror she'd used as a newly orphaned adolescent, as a lonely teenager, as a hopeful newlywed, and then a desperate young wife. This was all she needed today. Lose her job, lose her guy, lose her hope, all in the space of, what, an hour?

She was beyond tears at the moment, beyond anger. *What. The. Hell.*

Thunder and lightning growled and crackled outside, almost as loudly as the mess in Emma's head. When the wind picked up and howled, rattling the windows, she felt a kinship with the storm—angry, and chaotic, and desperate to move.

Why hadn't it occurred to her that Marcus would have other women? Of course he did.

What else had he lied about?

Before she could list the possibilities, there was a knock on the door. "Emma? Em, it's me, Marcus."

Like she wouldn't recognize his voice.

"Let me in? I need to talk to you."

Stupid. She was so stupid. She should have turned around and left when she saw him out there with that woman. Now she was cornered in a trap of her own choosing.

"Em? Come on, baby."

It occurred to her that he really was smooth, because he'd must've used some fast talking to get rid of his side-piece and get up here so fast. Or was she the sidepiece? It didn't matter. She wasn't going to be anyone's anything anymore.

With a deep breath, she unlocked the door, opening it to reveal Marcus. He looked at her with concern.

"You're in my way," she said, proud of herself for sounding so calm, but keeping her eyes focused over his shoulder.

"That was my sister's friend Maya," he began.

Emma held up a hand to cut him off. "It doesn't matter who she is. It's not my business." Maya of the hookup mistake. Of course.

"You're my girl," he told her. "It's every bit your business."

Really? Didn't he remember what he'd said about having had a fling with the woman? How dumb was she supposed to be?

She crossed her arms over her chest and looked everywhere but at him, tapping her toe like she had better things to do than get her heart dragged around in the dirt.

"She's just a friend," he insisted, his voice taking on an edge of desperation.

She'd caught Todd texting another woman once, and she'd believed him when he told her she was just a friend from the army, that his friends were none of her business. That was probably six months before she'd caught him in the back seat with that girl from the bar, maybe? Hard to remember as she again experienced the hot shame that had washed through her when she found out how gullible she'd been. She fought it back. This was *not* her fault. She would *not* own it. "Oh for God's sake," Emma said. "If she's just a friend, what were you doing sneaking her out of the horse shed?"

"I didn't want the guys to see her and ask what we were doing out there," he hissed.

Something about his words, about the way he said them, made Emma meet his eyes, finally. What she saw there was a combination of embarrassment and worry. *Hold tough*, she warned herself. "Why wouldn't you want them to see her? She's pretty hot, not that I go for women who are so…so…tall."

"Neither do I."

"Uh-huh."

Marcus put his hand over his eyes and was silent for a moment, then uncovered his face, looked straight at Emma, and said, "I was, um, modeling for her."

"Oh, for crying out loud," she said automatically. "How dumb do you think I am? You expect me to believe you were… *Wait*. You were *what*?"

Now it was his turn to avoid her eyes. "Modeling. Posing. She's a photographer. She's trying to build her portfolio so she can branch out from doing high-school graduation photos. She just moved to Houston—with her *boyfriend*—and knew I'd work cheap."

"That's ridiculous," Emma said.

"I know. That's why I didn't tell anyone."

"I mean…how did she know you'd model for her? Why would she ask you—other than the obvious, I mean." Emma's wave encompassed his whole perfectly muscled body, illuminated with flashes of lightning from the storm outside.

Marcus's voice got even lower then. "Because in high school, I was her senior pictures poster boy," he mumbled.

She must not have looked convinced, because he said, "Look," and pulled out his phone. He tapped for a few seconds, swiped a few times, and held it out for her to see.

There, in full color, was a younger—but no less buff—version of Marcus, wearing a white V-necked T-shirt, baggy jeans, and sneakers…looking up from under the brim of a bright-blue ball cap embroidered with a white UK.

"Your mom let you get your senior pictures taken in a T-shirt?" was the only thing she could think to say.

He swiped again, and she saw another, in which he wore an unbuttoned dress shirt over the same T-shirt and chain, with a blazer. No hat this time, but a seductive smile and tilt to the head.

"Oh. My. God," she said, starting to laugh. "You. Were. Usher."

"Uh…" He reached for the phone, but she had it now and turned her back so she could swipe again. In the next photo, he had the shirt buttoned, but wore a white fedora. "Gimme that," he said, reaching around her with both arms.

She hunched over, still trying to keep the phone away from him, but dissolved in a puddle of giggles as he tried to retrieve his phone.

"Listen, woman. I was just tryin' to convince you I was really modeling for Maya, not givin' you every last shred of my dignity," he complained, but he'd stopped trying to pry the phone from her hands. Instead, he held her firmly but gently in his big, strong arms, his front to her back. "You still mad?" he asked, doing that rumbling thing he did against the skin of her neck, making her shiver and blowing away her anger.

She swallowed, barely able to remember what she'd been so pissed off about. "I'm…"

He rocked her slightly, pulled her back a little tighter, and said, "I don't want anyone but you, you know that?"

Right there, at that moment, he certainly did. The evidence was pressed against her backside.

"Hey, Talbott? Emma? You up there?" Adam's voice, from downstairs, competed with the storm outside. "You got a minute?"

"Gimme a second, Sar'nt," Marcus called back. He released Emma and said, "We okay?"

She wanted to tell him yes. That whatever they were, she was a part of it. Except when he'd answered Adam by calling him "sar'nt," he'd brought his reality into the middle of the hall.

"Em?" he asked, concern creasing his forehead.

"You can't go back," she said.

"What?"

"You can't—"

"But, babe—"

A huge flash and earsplitting crash drowned out whatever he was going to say, followed by shouts from downstairs.

Adam called again, "Talbott!"

"Duty calls," he said, kissing her quickly. "I love you, understand?"

He was down the stairs and out the door before she could ask him to repeat himself, but then decided she'd misheard, which was good, because she needed to explain that she couldn't be there for him, not if he was going back into the army. She didn't get a chance to tell him, though, because by the time she and Marcus got to the front door, the barn roof had erupted into flames, and all hell was breaking loose.

Chapter 27

It was nearly midnight before Marcus got a chance to catch his breath. He finally dropped into one of the creaky rocking chairs on the porch and sat, elbows on knees, head down.

"I'm tired," Jake said, rubbing at his soot-stained face with his equally filthy forearm.

There was an understatement. Marcus had spent the last couple of hours moving dogs, crates, and the few supplies that had been spared, and he wasn't sure he'd be able to move again.

The events of the night ran through his brain like a film reel on acid. The fire department had arrived just as the last dog was rescued from the smoke and stayed to reduce the barn to a pile of soggy embers and ruined supplies. A couple of sheriff's deputies had come to take a report. The veterinarian, who was first cousins of both the sheriff and the fire chief, heard about the fire and came to confirm that the dogs who'd been exposed wouldn't have any lingering smoke inhalation issues. He took a couple of dogs with him when he left, since he had a little kennel space at the clinic. The deputies left, each taking a dog to foster. The fire chief left with four dogs, since he had a big fenced-in yard and no neighbors to gripe about the noise.

Somewhere in there, Emma left, taking one of Loretta's pups with her. She didn't say anything to Marcus before she went. She just…went. Thinking about her words to him in the upstairs hallway—*You can't go back*—Marcus dragged his phone out of his pocket to send her a text, but changed his mind because he didn't know what to say. He'd dropped the l-bomb and she hadn't even noticed because she was so distracted about his damned job and how she didn't think he should try to go back. He was hurt that she doubted he could do it, but to hear her say it to him like that—it just hurt. He'd be okay, and she'd see that, right?

He'd call her in a few minutes, although she was probably already tucked in, dry and safe in her bed. She'd looked done in when she left.

The remaining residents of the Big Chance Dog Rescue were on the front porch of the house, watching the moon float in a now-cloudless sky. Loretta, Patton, and D-Day lay next to one another at the top of the steps, while the other dogs were in crates. Adam and Lizzie rocked slowly in the swing. Jake had collapsed on the floor, back against the front wall of the house. Tanner was in the other rocking chair.

All were sweaty and filthy and had the thousand-mile stares of soldiers after a long, hard battle.

"What happens now?" Tanner asked.

Adam sighed. "We take showers and go to bed. In the morning, I'll call the insurance guy. He'll remind me that I'm only covered for the bare minimum, and that we had an appointment for later in the week to discuss raising our coverage for things like this."

Lizzie didn't speak, only laid her head on Adam's shoulder and squeezed his hand.

"What are we gonna do about the dogs?" Tanner asked.

Adam scrubbed his hands over his face, then said,

"Thank God we only have a few left who need shelter. They can stay in the horse shed. Everyone who's fostering one promised to bring them in once a week to do training drills. It's not ideal, but I'd rather they have safe homes than train every day. Then I guess we clean up the mess and start building a new barn." He reached into his pocket and pulled out a soggy piece of paper. "Thornhill left five thousand bucks, this ought to get us started." He handed it to Lizzie. "Put this in the bank when you go to work in the morning?"

"Sure." She held it with two fingers and waved it in the air to dry. "Let's hope Mr. Thornhill comes through with the rest of his donation quickly."

Adam went on, "Tanner, I'll make a list, and when you get up tomorrow, I need you to get prices on building materials. The fire chief said one of his brothers—I can't remember which one—does construction, and he'd be willing to make sure we're doing things right."

"What…about me?" Jake asked.

"You're in charge of dogs. They're going to need extra exercise and attention tomorrow, since their runs are trashed and they've got to stay in those crates," Adam said, indicating the dogs on the porch. "See if you can rig up a temporary yard or something.

"Then," Adam went on, "I guess there's cleanup duty."

"I'll get that going." Marcus hoped the moving and lifting would take the edge off the stiffness that was settling in his bones. He had his medical board appointment next week, so it was time to put up or shut up.

"I call first shower," Lizzie said, rising and heading for the door.

Even though it would mean there was no hope of hot

water, Marcus graciously offered to go last. He figured that way no one would see him looking like a ninety-year-old man when he tried to stand up.

Emma snatched up her phone as soon as it rang, half disappointed and half relieved when she saw it wasn't Marcus. She wanted to talk to him, to hear his voice, but she was afraid he might repeat what he'd said earlier.

She also knew she needed to have a conversation with him, and now was not the time.

"Are you still up?" Lizzie asked as soon as Emma answered.

"Yep." She was exhausted in the aftermath of all of that adrenaline during the fire, but still wired. "What are you doing?"

"Letting the shower warm up before I use up all the hot water. You kinda disappeared on us. I wanted to make sure you're okay."

"I…I had some things I had to do here," she said, which was sort of true.

"Like what?" Lizzie's voice suggested there was nothing more important than hanging around her brother and his friends and participating in the postmortem barn discussion.

And okay, yeah. As a board member, Emma probably should be involved in any discussions. Just maybe not tonight.

"Well, I needed to get Garth settled in, for one thing." The pit bull pup raised his head from Emma's lap and gave her an adoring smile. Then he made a rude—and stinky—noise and shut his eyes.

Lizzie snorted. "Garth settles in just fine anywhere he can."

"He is a good little guy," Emma agreed. "But I have to do a couple of loads of laundry before work tomorrow, and I—"

"Does this have anything to do with Marcus's mysterious visitor and the argument you had with him right before the fire started?"

"It's irrelevant," she said.

"I don't think so," Lizzie persisted. "I've seen you two mooning after each other since he came to town—"

"I have *not* been mooning," Emma protested.

"—and I want you to know I think it's great that you've gotten together—"

"We are *not* together."

"—because Marcus is a great guy. He's got this too-smooth-for-butter vibe he puts out, but underneath it, he's got the biggest, most loyal heart I've ever met."

Emma didn't have an argument for that. It was true. Marcus was dedicated to the people he cared for. Especially his fellow soldiers. She admired that about him, she really did. She just couldn't bear the thought of losing him when he went back to the army. She had to end it now, before she got any more twisted up in him.

Garth raised his head again and licked Emma's hand as though trying to soothe her.

"Well, I think you're a great couple. We should go on a double date as soon as the dust settles."

Emma sighed. "There's really no point. He's going back to active duty soon, and he's going to be deployed."

"Well…" Lizzie started, obviously trying to come up with another argument in favor of Marcus and Emma—what would that make them? Memma? Ercus? It didn't matter, because it wasn't going to happen.

"Listen, thanks for calling. I'm sorry I didn't stick around to talk about next steps, but I—I needed some space."

"Okay. I'm sorry to push. I just want everyone to be happy."

"The curse of the single girl whose best friend is in a blissful relationship," Emma said.

"One of us will probably be by the Feed and Seed tomorrow to start ordering things to rebuild the barn. Are you working?"

"I'm scheduled every minute we're open this week," Emma said, which was weird, since she wasn't even sure how long she'd have a job. What was she going to do? If she didn't have a job, she'd have plenty of time to visit Granddad at Golden Gardens. She wouldn't have any distracting men in her life, either. She had to just cut it off now before her heart was in any more jeopardy.

Thank God for Mr. Thornhill and his deep pockets, Emma thought after she rang off with Lizzie. His contribution would keep them afloat for the next few months, barring any more unexpected financial drama.

Her phone buzzed again, and this time it was Marcus. She had to do this now, before she lost her resolve.

"Hey," she said, heart thumping painfully in her chest.

"Hey yourself," he said. "You okay?"

Wow, she really was a basket case if that's what everyone always started off with. "Yes, are you?"

"I'm all right. Tired. I wish you hadn't left without saying goodbye."

"Yeah, I checked with Adam and he said things were under control, so I figured it was okay."

"I'm not bustin' your chops, babe, just checkin' in." His voice was hoarse and a little slurry, which she now recognized was a sign he was tired—not wasted.

"Listen, I need to—" she started.

At the same time, he said, "We didn't get to finish—"

When he paused, she kept going. "I don't think we should see each other anymore."

Silence.

"Are you still there?" she asked.

"Yeah." He cleared his throat. "You gonna tell me why?"

Because I love you. Because I can't love another man who's going to go back and let that fucking war ruin him. Because I won't be enough for you if you come back.

"Is it because of what I said before the fire? Because I told you I—"

Oh no you don't. "What did you say earlier? I don't remember," she lied. She couldn't hear him say that. "It doesn't matter. I've been thinking about this for a few days."

His soft chuckle reached out to her even through the airwaves, unsettling her, making her want to touch him. "Babe, we've only been together a few days."

"Whatever. I just don't think it's a good idea for us to be involved. You're leaving to go back to the army soon, but I'm sure you'll still have a relationship with Adam and the ranch, and I don't want things to be weird between us down the road—"

"You're worried about something that might happen in the future? What if we stay together when I go back? I know it's not fun having a boyfriend who's deployed, but lots of people manage, and we're smart—"

"I don't want to be with another soldier!" she snapped, trying to keep the tears from her voice. "I can't go through that again."

"Ah." He was quiet again, and she wanted to ask again if he was still there, but then he said, "I can't promise you I'll live forever. And I know I had a problem with pills when we met, and that's scary, considering what you went through with Todd, but you know not every soldier comes home a messed-up drug addict, right?"

"Yes," she said, her voice small, so she forced herself to speak up. "I do know that. And I know you're okay right now. But you might not be okay later, and I can't be here for that." She was too weak.

"Ah, Emma." He sighed.

And her stupid heart wasn't done. "Maybe you can get a desk job with the army. Something to keep you safe."

"I don't know how to do anything but be a soldier," he said. "I'm an Army Ranger, and if I can't be part of my team, I don't have a reason to exist."

Chapter 28

MARCUS TOOK ANOTHER SLUG OF COFFEE AND TRIED TO focus on the conversation in the ranch-house kitchen.

"We just need to get those footers in, and we can start hammering shit." Adam grinned, pouring himself a fresh cup. "The concrete guys will be here day after tomorrow. It'll be good to have a day off to relax and work with the dogs a little." He leaned against the counter, all chill, as though part of his world hadn't burned to the ground last week.

Well, that was good, right? If Marcus believed in anything, it was that optimism was a cure for almost everything. Even that Emma might thaw and answer one of the very casual, nonstalkery ex-lover texts he'd sent since she'd given him the heave-ho.

He wasn't sure how he would overcome her objections to a relationship with him, but he had that Ranger stick-to-itiveness, and if there was a chance, he'd take it.

Adam pointed at Marcus. "Don't you have something to do this afternoon?"

Marcus tried to swallow the bite in his mouth so he could answer, but Lizzie's homemade hemp and chia seed waffle wasn't going down easily. She'd promised it would cure whatever ailed him. It was curing him of any latent desire to be a granola-crunching hippie, that was for sure. He held up a hand, but finally choked down enough to answer. "Yeah."

Adam smirked, opened the pantry door, and magically

produced a beautiful, gorgeous rectangular package of silver, which he handed to Marcus. "Chase that down with this."

"You're a man among men," Marcus gasped, tearing into the package and sliding out the—"Oh, man. Blueberry. My favorite." He ate about half the first Pop-Tart without breathing, then added, "I go to the spine guy and then the medical evaluation board."

"You good?" Adam's forehead wrinkled. "I didn't know it was so soon."

"Yeah. I'm good," Marcus said, hoping it was true. He was…sort of good. Mostly okay, anyway.

The week had passed in a blur of sweat and aching muscles with Adam, Jake, Tanner, and Marcus—mostly Adam, Jake, and Tanner, with Marcus standing around with his thumb up his ass, riding out a muscle spasm—getting the site for the new barn cleared and a new foundation laid. "I wish you didn't have to spend all that money on a new barn," Marcus said.

"We were going to have to put up a new one soon, anyway," Adam said. "There was no way to retrofit the old one with sprinklers, and it was stupid as hell of us to keep dogs in there without that kind of safety system."

Marcus tried to get Adam to give himself a break. "Hey, your granddad ran his kennels without sprinklers for years, and nothing bad ever happened. And you had plans to put them in with the new roof. What were you supposed to do in the meantime? Hang a hose from the ceiling and stand in there twenty-four seven, just in case? The dogs are all fine, and now you'll have a better, cleaner setup."

Adam shook his head at Marcus. "You do have the power of positive thinking down to an art, don't you?"

He sure as hell hoped so. He was managing to get up and down without Patton's help. He hadn't given his inflamed body much of a chance to settle down this week, what with trying to help with the cleanup efforts, but he felt confident that his appointment tomorrow would be just fine. The spine guy would check him out, send a clean bill of health to the medical board. Then he could stop slacking around here. He'd tell Emma how rosy the future could be, she'd fall into his arms…

"So," Adam said. "About my sister."

Marcus inhaled a bite of pastry and coughed while Adam pounded him on the back and laughed.

When he could breathe again, Marcus said, "I didn't know you knew."

"I kind of thought something happened while you were in Houston. Watching you chase her up the stairs the other day was another big clue."

"I, uh…"

"I think you're good for her," Adam said. "She's been moping around here about Todd for way too long. I think they had a tough time there before he died."

You don't know the half of it, Marcus thought. He said, "I like her a lot." Another understatement.

"You'll do right by her, no? She needs someone to put her first."

"We're, uh…not quite there at the moment," he hedged, not willing to lie to his best friend, but admitting that she'd tried to dump him was a pathway to defeat. "I'll do my best." As he wolfed down the last bite of Pop-Tart, he wadded up the wrapper to toss across the kitchen to the trash. He missed and rose—slowly—to retrieve it.

Adam's phone rang, and he answered it, saying, "Hello... wait, who is this?"

Marcus reached the shiny ball and crouched to pick it up as Adam said, "What the... No. No, I did not approve that. Who the—"

Marcus looked up to see Adam turn white and slump into the wall.

"What the hell?" Marcus shot up, disregarding the pain, and grabbed Adam's arm while the dogs crowded in around the two men.

"Yes. I... Okay. Thank you." Adam hung up and stared into space.

"Sar'nt, what is it?" Marcus asked, hoping that addressing Adam by his rank might help him pull it together.

Finally, Adam nodded that he was okay, and Marcus let him go, backing up but still watchful.

"Sar'nt?" Marcus repeated.

Adam cleared his throat. "Someone cleaned us out at the bank."

"Cleaned us out? Like stole the ranch's money?"

Adam nodded. "And every cent I had invested from the sale of the Mill Creek property. Moved it."

"Well, tell them to get it back!" Marcus said.

Adam shook his head. "They said it's been moved to some offshore account."

"How did that happen without your approval?" Marcus demanded.

"Someone impersonated me. Went in and changed my contact information, had all the passwords, account numbers, everything. That was the bank manager, wanting to know what he could do to get my business back."

"Who would do that? You don't think Tanner... Naw."

Adam shook his head. "I don't think so, either."

Realization dawned. "Thornhill."

Adam nodded. "I've got to go into town and talk to the bank's fraud guy and a few dozen law-enforcement agencies, but it's probably long gone."

Marcus felt the Pop-Tart try to make its way back out of his stomach. This was on him. He'd brought that bastard here, then left his "accountant" alone with Tanner while he went and played harebrained games with Maya. "It was that Butch dude. I bet he got Tanner to show him everything we had."

A gasp made both men turn their heads to the kitchen door, where Tanner stood, the unburned side of his face blank with shock.

Adam put his coffee cup down. "It's not your fault," he said, but Tanner was gone, the front door slamming behind him.

Marcus cursed as he reached for Patton and shuffled after, swearing loud and long. This wasn't Tanner's problem. It was Marcus who'd invited Thornhill to visit. Marcus who'd left that accountant alone with Tanner and the money.

Marcus who'd done nothing but cause trouble since he'd arrived at the Big Chance Rescue Ranch.

"The FBI thinks Thornhill is really Douglas Schaller, a con man they've been tracking for a while. He's played this game with charities and nonprofits all over the country," Adam told Emma, who stood behind the counter of the Feed and

Seed with her hand over her mouth, disbelieving what she was hearing.

"But why would he think we had money in the first place?" she asked. "Especially since we were out trying to get donations when he met us?" She tried to suppress the memory of kissing Marcus in celebration, but as with every other memory of the man, it wouldn't leave her alone.

"We think he saw the story about Mill Creek Farm online. Knew we had something."

"And he gave you that check the other day. What was that about?" Emma asked.

"False sense of security?" Adam shrugged. "He might have been trying to launder it. They're looking for him in connection with a bunch of things, including drugs. His buddy Butch has a little problem with gambling and prostitutes, so he leaves a trail wherever he goes. If they can find him, there's a slim chance we can get some of whatever money they've got. Us and all of their other victims."

"What about the ranch? What are we going to do?" Emma asked, realizing how unfair it was to always look to her big brother to fix everything.

He hesitated, then said, "I'm not sure yet. If we can't get some money, I'm going to have to shut it down."

Shock froze Emma's brain for a moment, but then she said, "No. You can't. We'll pull together and make this okay." She couldn't fix this, but she could cut expenses to the bone in order to contribute, she decided. "I'll make arrangements to get Granddad back home," she said. *Make them give back the money you already paid.* "I don't know how it'll work, but maybe we can all take shifts with him, and I'll get a job in Fredericksburg at the tire factory.

Maggie Reynolds's older brother works there and he'll get me on, I'm pretty sure—"

"Wait." Adam held up a hand. "The tire factory?"

Emma sighed. Adam didn't need this right now, but she told him anyway. "The Sterns are retiring and moving to Arizona."

Adam looked around, up at the portraits of Todd hanging from every surface and crooked his mouth in a half smile in spite of the grim circumstances of their meeting. "What'll happen to the shrine?"

In spite of herself, she laughed. "Shhh…"

"What, is the ghost of Todd going to hear me?"

"No, but the Sterns might come in."

"Well, Todd would have thought it was funny," Adam told her. "I can picture his face, walking in here and seeing all of this."

Maybe his *before* face, Emma thought. But not the one he wore after he came home from the army. *That* Todd hadn't found humor in anything.

Adam's expression softened and he looked at her. "I'm sorry. I know this is an important place for you."

Important to leave. Since learning that she'd be losing her job, she'd felt a surprising lightness, in spite of the fear, and in spite of the weight in her heart that came from missing Marcus.

Getting out of the Feed and Seed might be the best thing to happen to her in years, she thought.

"I may need to move back to the ranch," she told Adam. "Not sure what they're going to do with the house out back."

"Oh," Adam said, looking skeptical.

"I can throw a tent in the yard," she said, figuring he

was already reconfiguring room assignments—although Marcus's room would be empty soon. "I don't have to deal with it right now. Right now we have to figure out what to do to keep the ranch afloat."

"I'm not long on ideas at the moment," Adam admitted.

"What about a bake sale?" she suggested, half joking.

"It might come to that, but I don't think there's enough sugar in Chance County to make all those cookies," Adam told her.

"Then we'll run to Fredericksburg for more," she promised.

Adam's phone rang, and he held up a finger to her while he answered. "Yeah. Good. You made sure he understands it's not his fault, right?" He sighed. "Well, then, he'll just have to stick around until he works through it." He listened for a moment, laughed, and then said goodbye before he hung up and shoved his phone back in his pocket.

"What's wrong?" Emma asked.

"Tanner got his panties in a wad because Butch stole all that information on his watch. Thought he was going to take a runner there for a while, but Marcus seems to have talked him down."

"That's good," Emma said.

"Yeah, I don't know what we'll do without Talbott around here. He's got a way with people, you know?"

Yeah. Emma knew. But the reminder that Marcus was leaving soon shoved something into her throat, making it hard to breathe and impossible to answer.

"I was kinda surprised when I realized you'd hooked up with him," Adam told her. "I didn't think you'd ever get involved with another military guy."

"Neither did I," she managed to get out, assuming he knew it was already over.

"I'm sorry about how tough it was with Todd there at the end. I don't know everything that happened, but I wish I could have been here to help."

She shook her head. "No. That wouldn't have helped. He would have hated for you to see what he'd become."

"Will you tell me?" he asked. "You've never talked about it, you know that?"

"It's not pretty," Emma said, shame searing her insides. "He had PTSD, I guess. He was depressed and not dealing with things. He was taking a bunch of meds, which got out of control."

And I didn't do anything to stop it. She didn't say that, though. Instead, she ended with, "It went downhill from there. You know what happened at the end."

"I'm really sorry I wasn't here."

But if he had been, he wouldn't have been in Afghanistan with his K-9, protecting Marcus and Jake. Even though their last mission had gone wrong, he'd been there with his dog every other time, keeping them safe, making sure they were going to be coming home.

He wouldn't be there when Marcus went back this time.

Adam cleared his throat. "Anyway, I think you and Marcus are lucky to have each other."

Oh. He didn't know. "We're not. Together."

Adam looked surprised.

She shrugged, knowing she'd make him feel bad about his own PTSD if she explained how she couldn't face living with more herself. "We had a good time, but it's not a thing, not really."

She figured if she told herself that enough, she'd start to believe it. That way, she wouldn't sit here in this godforsaken town, praying that her man would come back to her, only to lose him all over again when she wasn't enough to help him deal with his demons. Because even if he'd made it out relatively intact the first time, there was no way he'd be so lucky again. Especially if he had to come back to her and her bad luck.

Chapter 29

PERMANENT, IRREPARABLE DAMAGE. THE WORDS ECHOED in Marcus's head on repeat, like an earworm from an over-played pop song. He flipped through radio stations, trying to find something—anything—that would purge the doctor's words from his mind.

Over the next sixty minutes he learned how to make a traditional Lithuanian chicken casserole, everything that was wrong with the Houston Astros' back office, that the top song on the American country music charts for that date in 1983 was "Islands in the Stream" by Dolly Parton and Kenny Rogers. But he hadn't been able to forget, not even for a second, that he was a dead man walking. Or a permanently disabled one, anyway. In other words, completely useless.

If only he could turn back time, he could skip the doctor appointment, skip the damned MRI that showed *continued degradation of disks with increased fragmentation and spondyl-*some-bullshit-or-other, all of which meant he was screwed.

No time machine was going to fix that, unless it sent him back to before he enlisted, before that damned bomb went off, but then no way could he have missed that, missed being able to drag an unconscious Jake from the fire, missed being there for his men. He wouldn't have missed that, as terrible as it was, for anything.

If he did it differently, he wouldn't have met Emma. Beautiful Emma who didn't deserve another man who couldn't take care of himself. He'd thought he'd come back with good news and convince her to give him another chance.

The doctor suggested surgery, and for a few minutes, he had hope…if he stayed on the TDRL list a couple more years, and rehab—again—maybe…

"Will the operation fix me up, then?"

"Well…" The hesitation in the doctor's expression told Marcus all he needed to know, but he listened to the rest anyway. "I can't promise that you can start taking bull-riding lessons. Most people do improve enough to live pain-free with fairly decent mobility—though there is a risk that the grafts won't fuse properly, in which case we'd need to take further actions. But I can tell you this. If you don't do something to stop the progression, you *will* suffer perma-nent, irreparable damage. You *will* have constant pain and possibly be unable to walk within the next five years."

If the nerves that controlled his muscles stopped work-ing, it wouldn't matter how hard he worked out, he'd be unable to walk. He could live with the pain. He'd been living with it, hadn't he?

He looked at the white paper bag on the seat next to him. "While you decide what you want to do, here are some more pain meds," the doctor had said. Marcus had been too stunned at the news to tell him he didn't want the pills.

But now that he had them, now that he knew he couldn't go back to the war, what was the harm in taking a couple?

Emma.

The fear and hurt he'd seen when she'd thought he was using was enough for him to throw the bag so it bounced off the passenger window and disappeared into the detritus in the footwell.

What now? He had an appointment with the medical evaluation board tomorrow, who would decide the next steps. He didn't have to hear the words to know that he wouldn't be approved for return to duty.

It was all he'd wanted since getting hurt, all he'd worked for, and it was gone with the flick of an X-ray light box.

He was going to have to spend the night in a shitty motel so he could be up bright and early tomorrow for a hearing that was only a formality at this point. When the medical evaluation board brass went over his case, they'd refer him to a physical evaluation board, and sometime in God only knew how many months, he'd get an assignment for retraining into his dream—or rather, nightmare—job, that of desk jockey.

He growled and shoved a tape into the eight-track deck. Usually a little classic Motown eased his savage beast, but today it just reminded him of Emma and their drive to Houston.

Damn. He hit the steering wheel with the heel of his hand, which only served to send him careening over the center lane and made his hand throb. As he regained control and waved an apology to the oncoming semi, he gave a half second of thought about just doing it. Driving off a bridge. Into a tree, or oncoming traffic. And imagined Emma coming to identify his corpse. His family shaking their heads over the waste of his life. He shuddered and reduced his speed to near safe levels. No way.

Was that how it had been for Todd? Had he been so fucked up about how messed up his life was that he stopped thinking about what effect his loss would have on everyone else and only focused on ending his own pain? Maybe he thought they'd be better off without him. Was the fear of getting better, of admitting his weakness and needing help so strong that it outweighed the fear of death?

Permanent, irreparable damage. That was a sure thing. Pain-free with decent mobility—that was possible. With rehab. Lots and lots of rehab. He wasn't afraid of hard work. But to go through all of that and not be whole…

But hopefully employable, he realized. Too damaged to carry a rifle through the desert, but not too damaged to work. He'd have the surgery, because it would give him a chance. He'd take that damned desk job and make it his bitch. He'd do it because if he had a career, he had a chance with Emma.

He had to try. Before he packed it in for the night, he sent her a text.

> Hey, just wanted to say hi. A little nervous about my meeting in the morning. I wish—

Nah. That was stupid. He didn't need to be pathetic. He went to hit the erase arrow, and hit the send arrow instead.

Great.

Well, she probably wasn't reading his messages anyway. She hadn't answered any in over a week.

He'd get a good night's sleep, he decided, and go before the board in the morning with a fresh attitude and be willing to take whatever they dished out. Even if it was a desk job in Alaska.

Then he'd send Emma another message.

Chapter 30

EMMA CAREFULLY WIPED THE TOP OF THE LAST CAN OF furniture wax and replaced it on the top shelf. She then stepped off the stool, looking up to make sure she had the cans and jars all lined up neatly.

Since learning that the ranch was in trouble, she'd rearranged everything in the shop and cleaned it from top to bottom twice.

Todd's high-school graduation picture smiled down at her from the wall above the spray paint, his reckless smile pointing out that she was wasting her time.

Well, damn it, my new boyfriend—the one I don't want because I'm afraid I'll lose him, that one?—seems to have disappeared on me. What else am I supposed to be doing? she mentally asked him.

Anything but this, he seemed to be telling her.

"If I knew what to do, I'd be doing it!" she told him, out loud this time.

"What?"

Emma jumped and nearly smacked Mrs. Stern with the dustcloth she held. "Oh, I didn't hear you come in!" she said, embarrassed to be caught talking to herself.

"Obviously," Mrs. Stern said, smiling. Then she looked up at Todd's portrait and said, "I talk to him sometimes, too."

Emma suppressed a snort, but Mrs. Stern seemed to intuit her thoughts.

"I know. He wasn't exactly easy to be around those last few years."

"I... He..." Emma didn't know how to respond. She'd never, not once, discussed Todd's issues with his mother.

Mrs. Stern sighed. "I'm so sorry I didn't step in to help."

"But..."

"I'll admit, it took me a while to realize that he was struggling."

Emma nodded. She'd done her best to help Todd hide his problems from his parents. At first it was because she was sure things would get better. And he was really good at pulling himself together when he needed to, especially for his mom and dad, which gave her hope that he *would* get better.

Mrs. Stern went on. "It seemed like he needed time to readjust to civilian life, so we gave it to him. Then we realized he was depressed and tried to talk to him about that, but he said he was getting help, that he just needed a little time. Not to go to you about it, because you were having your own issues with your grandfather and your worries about Adam."

Realization dawned. "He told me the same thing. Not to bother you because of your mom's health."

His mom sighed. "He isolated us from each other. Here we were, the people who loved him the most, working together every day, and we both thought we were helping each other by keeping his secrets."

"When we could have been helping him." Emma's failures were like a tropical depression, making the air thick and hard to breathe. "I stayed in denial for too long. Way too long."

"We all did. Him most of all." Mrs. Stern grabbed a

tissue from the box on the counter and wiped her eyes. "Remember how much he loved to have parties? He always wanted everyone to be happy."

"He was really upbeat, wasn't he?" Emma asked. "Before..."

She smiled, nodded. "He was. I prefer to remember the boy who grew up here. That's who I talk to."

Emma realized that was the Todd she had just been remembering, too. With a thump of longing, she felt her eyes begin to burn, but she couldn't bear to shed any more tears. She had to find a way to move on.

Both women were silent for a long time, lost in their own memories.

"We couldn't have saved him," Mrs. Stern finally said.

Emma didn't think she'd ever completely believe that. Part of her remembered that last day, when she'd sent him away, and that she hadn't wanted to save him. "If only I'd come to you. I should have—"

"No." Mrs. Stern put a finger over Emma's lips. "He drove us apart, pushed us away. I've given this a lot of thought and prayer, and spent a lot of money on therapy. I think he was so lost in his misery that he wanted us to hate him.

"We can never know what happened to him, what he did or saw that changed him so much, but he made the decision to stay that way. Not you. He got in that car and drove off that bridge. You are not to blame yourself over this anymore. Understand?"

Emma nodded.

"Really?"

She gave a partial smile. "I'll try."

"Good." Mrs. Stern stood and took a deep breath.

"Now. What were you arguing about with Todd when I came in?"

Emma laughed. "I don't remember," she started to lie. Then, recognizing that the time for holding on to her truth was long gone, she said, "The ranch is in trouble. We thought we had someone lined up who wanted to donate a lot of money to us, but it turns out that he was a fraud and actually managed to steal every cent Adam had in the bank."

"Oh dear. Do the police know?"

"The police, the FBI, the IRS, Secret Service, heck, I thought everyone knew about it."

"Everyone except me, apparently," Mrs. Stern said drily. "Story of my life." She glared up at a mid-deployment photo of Todd in camouflage, holding a rifle, in front of a blown-up building, then refocused on Emma. "What can I do to help?"

"Don't sell the Feed and Seed until I find another job." Emma hadn't realized that was what she needed until it was out there. She'd been so consumed with fear of the future and grief over losing Marcus that she had barely thought about talking to the Sterns about her situation.

"We thought you'd take it over!" Mrs. Stern said.

"The store?"

Her mother-in-law nodded.

"God, no!" Emma blurted out. "I mean, thank you. Wow. That's…very generous. But I'm not sure…" She glanced up at a graduation photo of Todd from after basic training.

"I'm taking the photos with me when we move," Mrs. Stern told her gently. "They should have come down a long time ago, but people seem to like seeing him there—to remember who he was. Of course, you can keep copies of any that you want, but I don't imagine your new fella's too thrilled with your late husband staring down at him every time he comes in."

"My new…" Mrs. Stern meant Marcus, of course. "No. That's not…not happening."

"Really? You looked like you like him a lot when I saw you together the other day."

"I do," Emma admitted. "I did. But he…he's a soldier."

"Well, yes. That's how he wound up with your brother, right?"

"Yes. And he wants to stay in the army. He's going back to fight."

"Oh dear." Mrs. Stern was quiet a long time. "Life—love—is about taking chances and leaps of faith. Marcus is different than Todd. I can't promise that everything will be okay. But if you really love him, you should give him a chance. You're different now, too. I think you can love someone without losing yourself in the process."

"I don't know about that," Emma said.

"Well, only you can make that decision. All I'm suggesting is that you hear him out."

As Emma rearranged a shelf of nuts and bolts, she thought about that. She didn't think it was a good idea, but she had been kind of a jerk since she'd given him the heave-ho. Maybe she should answer a couple of his texts.

Chapter 31

"Sergeant Talbott, we're going to recommend you be medically retired with a seventy-five percent disability rating," the officer told Marcus the next afternoon.

It took a few minutes for the words to sink in.

Hell, he wasn't even sure how he'd wound up in front of this woman so fast. After the doctor's words yesterday, he knew this morning's evaluation would probably go badly, but then there was supposed to be paperwork. From what he'd heard, it usually it took weeks—hell, months—to get through this process. Lucky Marcus, there was a perfect storm of information transfer and personnel, and here he was. Apparently being put out to pasture.

"But I don't want to retire," he said. "Can't you send me for retraining?"

"You do understand you're being given the opportunity to leave the army with significant support and benefits, don't you?"

"I hear what you're saying, but it doesn't make any sense," he said honestly. "Can't you just put me back on the TDRL for a while longer? I can have that surgery the doc suggested, then we can see—"

She shook her head. "Even if that surgery's successful, there's no more 'temporary' to your 'disability.'"

"But the doc said there's a chance—"

"Sergeant Talbott, our decision is final," Captain

Sitting-Next-to-the-First-Executioner added. "Of course, you can ask for a formal hearing, but I have to tell you… I've been doing this job for a long time, and the decision won't change."

Marcus left the base and drove, though he wasn't really sure where he was going.

He stopped for gas and dug his phone out of the glove box, knocking a pile of paper and God only knew what onto the floor on that side.

Damned phone was dead. He plugged it and scrounged for some change, hoping that there was an actual pay phone somewhere nearby. There was, and he called a couple of military disability lawyers he found listed on a flyer at the base. At first he couldn't make them understand what he wanted. "Our clients generally want us to help them get the army to give them more disability benefits, not less," he was told by the first guy. "I'm not sure I'd know how to represent you."

The second was worse. She laughed until he hung up on her.

He should at least file the paperwork for the hearing, right? It would take months, most likely, for his case to be reviewed. Months in which he would still technically be a soldier.

And do what, he wondered? Sit around on Adam's front porch in a rocking chair, mooning after a woman he didn't deserve?

Great idea. Especially since he felt certain there would be no point. The army wasn't known for changing its mind once it was made up. He was done.

He was halfway through his second tank of gas before he made a decision. He pulled into a rest area and unplugged his phone from the charger and powered it up. He ignored the missed calls and text notifications and pressed 1 on speed dial.

While he waited for his call to connect, he wiped his suddenly sweaty hands on his thighs.

"Hello?"

"Hey, Mama."

"Demarcus! How are you, honey? Is everything okay? You never call in the middle of the week. Let me get your daddy on the other line."

"Mom, I want to talk to you first—" But she was already hollering.

There was a click, and then he heard the gruff "Marcus. What's wrong?"

"I—" He wanted to tell them everything was fine, he was just checking in because he thought maybe he'd drop in for a visit, but his voice wouldn't work right. When he finally spoke, he sounded squeaky and strange. "Mom, Dad, I—I'm not a soldier anymore." That was the last coherent thing he said for a long time, but his mom and dad listened and told him they loved him, and that he should come on home.

It took a while before he was ready to drive again, but he finally got his old Camaro back on the road. He was going to Kentucky, but needed to clear out his shit from the ranch first.

"Come on, Garth," Emma pleaded as the puppy sniffed a dead leaf, jumped away, then returned to pounce on it. "It's dead. Pee on it, and let's go, huh?"

Garth ignored her, growling at a blade of grass that offended him.

She should have eased her way back into dog training with one of the older dogs from the ranch, not a half-grown puppy with a mind of his own.

"This is what you do, though," she reminded herself.

Probably if she'd slept more than an hour last night, she'd be able to dig deep enough to find some patience, but she'd spent the whole night tossing and turning, worrying about Marcus.

Lizzie told her he'd gone to see his doctor yesterday to find out if they thought his back was well enough to go back to work. Then today, he had something called a medical evaluation board to get his clearance to return to duty.

Just before the evening news last night, she'd received a text. She'd promised herself she wouldn't answer his messages, but that one last night had seemed…off. She debated, but finally decided the least she could do was text him back.

She'd sent a good-luck message early this morning, and he hadn't responded immediately like he usually did.

Emma walked Garth and took him to work with her, where she spent a very long day trying to distract herself from the fact that Marcus still hadn't answered her by practicing canine good citizen behaviors with the pup—who had a way to go before he'd be a good citizen.

Now she was done with work, had fed and walked Garth…again…and still nothing from Marcus. She learned—through a completely casual phone call to her brother about flea and tick treatments—that Marcus should have been home by lunchtime, but no one had heard from him since the previous morning.

Except her. She'd had a cut-off text before bed.

A thrumming disquiet had been building in her gut since that message last night, and it began to gain strength as the day progressed.

Where was he? What had they told him? Had they embraced him and yanked him immediately back into service? Not likely. She was pretty sure he'd at least get a chance to phone home first anyway.

More likely he was celebrating his impending triumphant return to the battlefield in some dive bar, telling fish stories and shooting tequila.

Unless something had gone wrong. The list of things that could have gone wrong stretched into the setting sun.

She was done at work, finished with her dinner, and she had nothing to do but get in her car and drive to the ranch.

"Come on, Garth. Let's go for a ride." The gangly adolescent dog galloped around her as she got her keys and remembered doing this a couple of weeks ago because the same man wasn't answering his phone.

Everything was quiet when Marcus finally pulled the Camaro up next to the horse shed. Lizzie's vehicle was there alongside Tanner's little subcompact, but Adam's truck was gone, so maybe they'd all gone to town together or something. He could hope.

He cut the motor and sorted the convenience-store food trash from the paperwork on the passenger side. He found a bandanna with Patton's name embroidered on it and stuffed it into his pocket. Something rattled, so he fished around on the floor, finding the prescription pain pills. He shoved the bottle in his pocket and made his way to the front door. Pushing it open, he was met with a soft woof.

"Patton." He managed to kneel and buried his hands in the dog's fur, giving him a good scratch and tussle. "I missed you today." He'd left the dog at home because taking a service animal to a medical board appointment had seemed like a bad idea, but given the way things had turned out, maybe he should have had him there. Maybe he'd have gotten a higher disability rating and a higher future paycheck.

He couldn't believe he was thinking like that. He hated guys who talked about how many body parts they'd have to blow off to get a lifetime of government support. That was *not* why he'd enlisted.

"What's going on, buddy?" he asked the dog, getting to his feet with a groan. Seemed like since his body got the news that it was useless, it had decided not to bother cooperating. "Where is everybody, huh?"

Could he hope to get in and out without having to talk to anyone?

"Hey."

Apparently not.

Tanner walked into the room, crunching a slice of apple while he cut another misshapen slice with a knife. "How did it go?"

"Not good."

Tanner stopped mid-apple-kill and lowered the knife. The unscarred side of his mouth compressed in sympathy. "No go?"

Marcus shook his head. "Nope. Not even a desk job.

I'm in the process of becoming completely medically retired."

"Cool," Tanner said, restarting his apple massacre. "You can stay here with us and *Emma*," he said, drawing out her name like he was about to add "*k-i-s-s-i-n-g*."

Marcus shook his head. "I'm leaving for Kentucky in a couple of hours."

"What?" Apple forgotten, Tanner reeled as though he'd been stabbed.

"I'm gonna move back in with my folks for a while." *Until I'm about fifty or sixty*.

"What are you going to do in *Kentucky*?" He said it as if Kentucky was the eighth level of hell.

"Dude. You're from East Nowhere, Louisiana."

"Yeah, but at least we've got the Tigers."

Marcus gave a half smile. "I'm not sure what I'll do," he said in answer to Tanner's earlier question. "My dad's church needs a youth minister, so I'll probably fill in there for a while."

"You're shitting me," Tanner said, laughing, then stopped mid-guffaw when he realized Marcus was serious. "Sorry, man. But you're, like, the coolest guy I know. No way can you keep that car if you're going to be a *youth* minister. I don't see you breaking up fights between the stoners and the mean girls at Bible study every week."

Neither did Marcus, frankly. But if that's what it took to earn his keep, that's what he'd do. A thought occurred to him. "Hey, about my car."

"Yeah?"

"I'm flying to Kentucky. Can you give me a ride to Austin and bring it back here? I was gonna leave it at the airport and figure out what to do with it later, but if you bring it here, maybe…I dunno. Maybe you guys can auction it off to raise money."

Tanner blinked his good eye. "No shit?"

Marcus shrugged. He didn't know why he loved that car so much anyway. It was just a damned tin can, and a man without a life had no need for fancy wheels. "I'm gonna go grab some stuff from my room, then maybe we can take off, huh?"

"Sure."

Marcus didn't have much, so it only took a few minutes to empty the drawers of the little dresser into his duffel, then gather a few toiletries and a couple of books from the top, and then it was as if he'd never been there.

Patton had walked upstairs with him, so Marcus sat on the edge of the bed to give the dog one last good petting session. "I'm gonna miss you." He was afraid he'd miss more than the dog's easygoing nature and soft fur. Having to navigate the last two days without his service animal made him realize how much he'd come to rely on the dog. And if his body really, truly wasn't going to get much better, he'd be wishing he could have Patton at home. But that's not what Marcus had taken the dog on for. Patton deserved to go to someone who had a life to live, so he could make the Big Chance Dog Rescue proud.

Marcus's phone buzzed, and he checked to see a text from the airline confirming his tickets. He'd missed a few messages over the past twenty-four—including one from Emma.

He almost didn't open it. The idea of always having a message pending from her appealed to him.

But that was just crazy-ass bullshit. If he'd learned any-thing over the past day, it was that he had to get his head out of the clouds and live in the real world. He'd never have the body he'd had before that bomb went off. He'd never be a soldier again. And he'd never again hold Emma close through the long, dark night.

She wouldn't go through life with a broken-down hope-less veteran.

> **Emma:** Hey, how's it going? I wanted to
> wish you good luck at your appointment this
> morning.

The others had also sent messages like that, but this one had a…a feel to it. What had she meant by that? She'd been having a change of heart? Then maybe—

Patton sneezed, and Marcus reentered reality and hit Delete. She was wishing him luck because she was nice.

He rose, lifted his gear, and said, "Come on, Patton. Let's go find my ride." Patton rose, ears up, tail wagging. A step sounded in the hallway, and Marcus looked around.

Emma stood in the doorway, silhouetted by the hall light. "I'm glad you're home."

Chapter 32

"THANKS FOR STOPPING BY," HE SAID IN A POLITE—BUT flat—voice, as if he were speaking to a stranger. He moved toward her, but paused in the doorway with eyebrows raised.

She stepped back. He nodded his thanks and moved past her into the hall, turning his back to her.

"Sooo…" she began, trying to figure out how to ask what happened. All she'd gotten out of Tanner was a grimace and a negative head shake when he pointed toward the stairs.

Marcus ignored the conversational volley and started down the stairs, leaning heavily on the handrail.

She'd been relieved when she pulled up and saw his car outside—he was home. And even more so when she'd seen him sitting on the bed, petting the dog, all in one piece.

But this—this freeze-out—scared her as much as any other paranoid scenario she'd come up with.

Following, she asked, "What happened? How did your meeting go?"

He stopped at the bottom of the stairs and turned, meeting her eyes levelly when she was on the bottom step. The lack of emotion chilled her. "Not the way I wanted it to."

The relief Emma thought she might have felt didn't come when she understood that he wouldn't be going back to combat.

"What are they going to reassign you for?" she asked,

hoping that if she kept talking to him, he'd turn back into himself.

His mouth quirked, but there was no pleasure there. "Nothing."

"What does that mean?"

"I mean I'm being medically retired. I'm out."

Well, at least that was more than three words.

He glanced into the living room. "You ready?" he asked Tanner, who rose from the couch, sliding his phone into his pocket and releasing Garth from a quivering sit-stay. The pup galloped over to leap on Patton, grabbing a mouthful of furry ear. Patton batted the puppy in the head, and they began to tussle. No one bothered to correct either of them.

"I'll go warm up the car," Tanner said, sliding past Emma and Marcus to the front door, clearly trying to give them a minute alone.

"It's still warm," Marcus said and followed him through the door.

Emma was on his heels, a desperate need to reach him pushing her. "Marcus, wait. Where are you going?" She hated the pleading note in her voice. She'd ended things with him, and here she was dogging him like the codependent wife of a drug addict.

He sighed and stopped, turning to face her, but didn't quite meet her eyes.

"Are you okay?" she asked, though it was clear he wasn't.

"I'm fine," he told her, and then, as though he were reciting a long-memorized speech, he said, "I'm flying home to Kentucky to stay with my parents while I wait for my paperwork to come through, and I'll probably help my dad at church until I find something else to do. I'll be fine."

This was not right. He was not fine now, and she worried that he wouldn't be fine later. It was just like with Todd, and she wasn't going to let it happen again.

"You can't go," she said, feeling desperate. "I don't want you to go."

He flinched.

She rushed on. "I mean—I know I seemed like a jerk to tell you I didn't want you to go back to fight in the war, but that's because I care about you, and I'm scared, and we don't want to lose you," she said, waving to encompass the entire ranch. "*I* don't want to lose you."

His brow creased in, his lips parted, and she thought maybe she was getting through, so she pressed on, grabbing his free hand in both of hers, stopping short of dropping to her knees, but begging nonetheless. "Please stay. Let me help you figure it out."

He shook his head, pulling free. "This isn't your party. You aren't supposed to save me. You don't have any more to do with this than you're responsible for how Todd lost his way."

"But don't you see that we need you? I need you. When I'm with you…I believe in myself."

His expression didn't soften a bit when he looked into her eyes. She didn't recognize the man who said, "You don't need me. You're strong. You've got it all in you. I'm not…I'm not part of that. Sorry, baby, but this is about me, not you."

What did that mean? He wasn't part of what? Her life? She wanted to unpack that, to figure it out and get it to make sense, but Tanner had rolled up and Marcus was shoving his bag into the trunk.

He looked down at Patton, who managed to gaze back with concern and quiver with excitement at the open car doors.

"Take care of my buddy, will you? Make sure he gets to someone who can use him."

Emma put a hand on the side of Patton's head and pressed the other side against her leg as if she was going to keep him from hearing this crap. "What? No. He's your dog," she said. "You need him."

"No he's not. He never was." He didn't even look at Patton when he opened the car door and got in. He reached into his pocket. When he pulled out a piece of blue fabric, his change fell out, but he ignored it as Patton trotted over to sit next to the open door while Marcus tied his "Don't pet me, I'm a Big Chance Rescue Ranch Service Dog" bandanna around his neck. "There. Go." He pushed the dog away, but Patton wouldn't go, not understanding why he wasn't invited on another trip.

Emma automatically stepped closer and grabbed his collar. "Come on." When they started to step back, something else rattled from Marcus's pocket to the ground.

She bent to pick it up.

It was a prescription bottle.

Oxycodone/acetaminophen.

Stricken, she looked at Marcus, who took it from her hand so casually that it could have been a bottle of soda.

Marcus's heart stopped when those damned pills fell from his pocket. He hadn't taken a single one, yet he felt as low as if he'd been caught shooting heroin.

The stricken look in Emma's eyes made it a hundred times worse. He wanted to protest, to explain that he was going to flush them, and he'd simply forgotten they were there.

"Marcus?" she asked. "What's…" Her voice trailed off as though she knew *what* and didn't need to ask more.

He saw his escape. "Yeah, the doc gave 'em to me. I figure there's no reason not to take 'em if I feel like it."

"Oh, Marcus—"

He shook his head and mustered his old screw-the-devil smile. "I'm fine, sugar. Don't worry about me."

"You don't have to do this," she said.

He just shrugged. Then he turned to Tanner and said, "Let's roll," because he couldn't bear to see the way Emma crumpled in on herself. He hated himself in that moment, but knew she'd be better when he was gone.

He stared straight ahead, ignoring the only woman he'd ever considered loving forever.

"Let's go," he told Tanner.

"Dude. I'm not sure—"

"Please," he added softly, because his throat was raw and tight.

Tanner shrugged, but started down the driveway.

When Emma yelled, "Damn it, Marcus, you told me you love me!" the kid slowed down, but at Marcus's slight head shake, sighed and continued on.

When they reached the mailbox, he heard the barking. In the side-view mirror, Patton galloped after them.

"Come on, Tanner," Marcus said. "I'm gonna miss my flight." He forced himself to look away from the backward view of the driveway for the Big Chance Ranch, but not before he caught one last glimpse of Emma, chasing after Patton and falling to her knees, arms around the dog.

Chapter 33

Mid-November

THE TAPE HOLDING THE *GOING OUT OF BUSINESS* SIGN TO the window gave way to condensation again. When the plastic placard flopped over, Patton leapt at it, pulling it off the rest of the way.

"No. Leave it. Down," Emma commanded, and Patton, ears so flat to his head you'd think she'd corrected him for stealing the pumpkin pie, let go and slunk to his haunches, resentfully stretching out until he was all the way down.

Emma tore off another strip of tape and tried to find a dry spot to stick it. This cold drizzle was a pain in the neck. "Patton, stay," she reminded, as the dog tried to army-crawl across the floor. "What, do you think you can move, even if you're still technically down? What am I going to do with you?"

Patton whimpered and put his head on his paws.

"Oh, for crying out loud." She was having enough trouble focusing on the work she needed to do without a canine miscreant pouting around the Feed and Seed.

"He looks so miserable." Mrs. Stern laughed, adding another box of odds and ends to the Clearance table.

"I know." Emma sighed. "He makes me feel guilty for making him behave."

"Todd was like that, always giving me the big eyes when

I caught him with his hand in the cookie jar. I always wound up trying not to let him see me laugh."

"Oh jeez," Emma said. "It's probably a good thing we never had kids, I'd have been a complete pushover." She only realized she shouldn't have said that when her mother-in-law didn't respond. Emma could, technically, still be a mother at some point, but Mrs. Stern's only son wasn't going to be the father, and she was never going to be a grandma.

"I'm sorry," Emma said, dropping the *Going Out of Business* sign and putting her arms around the other woman. "That was a dumb thing to say."

Mrs. Stern hugged her back, then waved her away. "Don't feel bad. Remember? We're not feeling bad about Todd any more than we have to."

"Right. Sorry." The truth was, she hadn't been feeling bad about Todd as much lately. At least, no worse than she felt about anything else—like Marcus, and what was or wasn't going on with him.

As though he could sense the turn of her thoughts, Patton moaned.

"Oh my God," Mrs. Stern said, looking down at the dog. "What on earth is wrong with your world? Not enough kibble with your bits?"

"I know he's probably not getting enough exercise," Emma said. "With this crummy weather, I can't seem to bring myself to take him for long walks, and my house—" She cut herself off, not wanting to complain about the cottage and its lack of square footage. She'd be looking for something new soon enough, and chances were good it would be much smaller—and more expensive—than what she had now.

"There's not enough room for a big dog there, I know," Mrs. Stern said.

"I tried to leave him at the ranch after..." She couldn't even say his name—not only because it hurt her heart, but when Patton heard anyone say, "Marcus," he leapt to his feet and barked crazily. "But he drove everyone out there crazy, pacing and crying. At least with me he eats and sort of acts like his old self."

"No word from...he whose name shall not be mentioned?"

Emma sort of smiled and went back to putting 50 percent off stickers on paint cans. "Not on my end. I guess Tanner talks to him, so we know he's alive."

"That's good, right?"

"I guess so. Tanner says Marcus is taking online college classes, so that's definitely good. He's planning to do something." Over the past month or so, since their long talk about Todd, it had gotten easier to talk to Mrs. Stern about Marcus, even while it was harder to think about him while she was alone. She thought it should be getting easier by now, but it wasn't, especially during the long nights, when Emma's thoughts turned darker than the moonless sky.

All of the things she should have done differently, could have said to make him stay ran through her mind, over and over, as she saw him take that bottle of pills from her and shove it back into his pocket. Tanner told her Marcus had made him stop at the sheriff's station on their way through town, and he had seen the pills get dropped into the mailbox that had been converted to an "unused medicine" waste box, but she worried about him. Imagined him going home, being in pain, giving in to the need for chemical relief. She didn't want him to hurt. If he needed the drugs, then he should have them. He was a big boy, and his family was there for him. There wasn't anything she could do to make his life easier, better, or less painful.

And then after she finished worrying about Marcus, she worried about the ranch. About how they were going to keep running without any money to rebuild the barn. The horse shed, which was supposed to become a bunkhouse, was now a temporary kennel. There was nowhere indoors to train dogs now that the weather was so often cold and wet.

Emma's tentative plans to begin training private clients was on hold until she had somewhere to work with dogs. And somewhere to earn a living, with the Sterns planning to close the Feed and Seed by the end of the year.

"Earth to Emma."

She looked down and realized she'd put four stickers on the same can. "I'm sorry. I was off in space, I guess."

"That's okay. I know Mr. Sad Fur over there's not the only one missing his person. I really hate to see you going through this…again."

"It's not the same," Emma was quick to protest, but Mrs. Stern waved a finger at her.

"Grieving is grieving. I saw a spark in you relit when he was around. I even thought maybe there'd be some little babies around for me to spoil."

"Whoa." Emma had only imagined that in her wildest fantasies. Knowing Todd's mom was imagining Emma having children with Marcus threw her for a loop and made her a little dizzy.

Mrs. Stern was on a roll now. "I know you were only together for a very short time, but I'm pissed as hell another man is letting his own self-pity smother your joy. I've got half a mind to jump on a plane to Kentucky and grab him by the ear."

Emma really did laugh then, imagining little Linda Stern holding Marcus by the ear, giving him a load of what for.

The front door bell jingled, and a gust of wet wind fluttered the sign on the front window. It held, fortunately, and Patton only looked at Emma before sulkily giving up on the idea of going after the sign or Mr. Stern, who was followed by Joe Chance, Big Chance's mayor and almost everyone's lawyer.

"Oh good, you've got the papers," Mrs. Stern said, wiping her hands on her slacks and giving Joe a hug.

"Emma, I need a couple of signatures from you, and then I can file everything."

Emma was confused. "Is this about getting Granddad back from Golden Gardens? I thought we'd decided we had a few months to find more money to keep him there."

Joe looked at Mr. Stern. "She doesn't know?"

Mr. Stern looked at his wife. "You didn't tell her?"

"Oh dear. I guess I didn't, did I?"

"Tell me what?" Emma was getting nervous, with everyone staring at her. Patton, sensing her distress, overrode her "stay" order and rose to press his body into her side.

"Well," Mrs. Stern said, "when you said you didn't want to run the Feed and Seed, we didn't know what to do with it. There's really no point in trying to sell the business, not with the Home Depot opening up out near the highway, and it just seemed to make sense."

"What makes sense?" Nothing, as far as Emma could tell.

Mr. Stern shook his head in mock frustration. "The Feed and Seed, kiddo. We're giving it to you."

Confusion was supplanted by a giant, impending freakout. "But I—"

Mrs. Stern smacked her husband on the arm. "You big dummy, you're scaring her. We're not giving you the Feed and Seed. We're giving you the building. It makes more sense to sell it to you for a dollar. Then you can use it for your dog-training classes and bring the ranch dogs here when they need somewhere indoors to work."

Well. That wasn't what she'd expected.

"You're giving me the building?"

"Selling it. For a dollar."

"I don't know what to think. Or do." She tugged at an earring, fighting tears.

"You could find a dollar," Joe suggested.

"Two," Mr. Stern said. "One for this place, one for the house. If you want it."

"Do I want it? Of course I want it. Mr. Stern, Mrs. Stern, I...I don't know what to say."

"Say thank you," Mrs. Stern suggested. "And for God's sake. When are you going to call me Linda?"

"I don't think I can. I try, honest. L...l... See? It won't come out."

Mrs. Stern laughed. "Well, it's just as well that you didn't have children with Todd. I can't imagine being called 'Mrs. Grandma.'"

"I don't know what the future holds, but if there are babies in it, you'll get to be whatever you want to be to them."

Marcus peered at the computer screen, trying to force himself to read the case study required for his online marketing class. After a long talk with his parents and a fishing excursion with one of his dad's friends, who just happened to be a career counselor, he'd agreed to take a couple of "exploratory" classes to see if anything tripped his trigger.

So far his trigger was firmly in the untripped zone, but at least it was a distraction from thinking about the decision he *had* made.

"Do you need anything else from the pharmacy, baby?"

He eyed the three shopping bags full of surgical dressings, over-the-counter pain relievers, and sudoku books next to the window and smiled. "No, Mama, thank you. I think I'm all set."

"I'm just afraid we'll get you home after your operation and run out of something." She entered the room and reached into the first bag, shuffling items around. "Are you sure we have enough of those elastic wraps?"

"I'm sure the visiting nurse will bring anything we forgot when she comes that first day, and if not, there's a twenty-four-hour Walgreens five minutes away."

"I know I'm being ridiculous," Mom said, hands on hips and frowning. "But I worry."

"I know you're being wonderful, and I appreciate it." He rose to wrap his arms around her. "Everything's gonna be fine," he assured her as she left to buy something or other she was afraid they'd run out of over the next week.

When the front door shut behind her, Marcus returned his attention to the computer, but was interrupted by his phone. He thought about ignoring it. He'd answered no calls and very few texts since he'd come home to Kentucky, preferring to shoot a brief "Hey, I'm fine" text in response to Adam, Jake, and Tanner's voicemail messages.

But today when he saw Adam's name pop up on caller ID, he picked up. Something about needing to make sure he'd said the things he'd left unsaid, in case this was his last chance.

"Hey," he greeted.

"Whoa. Didn't expect a live person," Adam said. "How's it hanging?"

"A little to the left, low as always," Marcus said. "How're things at the ranch?" Of course, he knew. Things were tight. They were trying to keep the ranch running on next to nothing.

"Not too bad," Adam said. "We got a whole building donated to us this week, so that helps a lot."

"Like, somebody dropped a barn off in your front yard?"

His friend's laugh warmed something inside Marcus. "Not quite. But we have room to hold classes in town. It helps. And we've got two dogs right now that we think will make it through the program. We can probably graduate them in six months or so."

Marcus swallowed a lump and said, "Who do you have Patton matched up with?"

"Ah…no one," Adam said.

"What? Why not?"

"He's just, you know, having some quirky behavior."

No, he didn't know. Patton was a perfect dog. "Explain."

Adam sighed. "He got pretty depressed after you left. Jake tried to keep him happy, but he quit eating for a while until Emma took him home with her."

The sound of her name pinged around Marcus's heart

like an arrow, and he wanted to ask for all the details, but didn't dare.

Adam went on. "He's better now. At least he's eating, but he's acting like a six-month-old puppy—giving her a really hard time."

Was it shallow of him to be pleased that Patton wasn't going to another veteran? Yes, yes it was. He was also glad that Emma had him. He'd managed to not ask Tanner about her in any of their emails, hoping he'd forget she existed. It hadn't worked. "Well, I'm sure she'll get him whipped back into shape."

"Yeah, she will." Then Adam said, "Listen, I promised myself to leave you alone, but we could really use your help back here. Any chance you can come back to work with us?"

Marcus blinked. "Doing what? Watching the grass to make sure it grows up instead of down?"

Adam huffed a laugh. "Well, that would be good, too."

Yeah. No one screwed up quite like Demarcus Talbott. "I don't think so."

"Why not? You're good at wrangling people. It's what you did. Jake might have been the ranking officer, but you were the motivator, the organizer, the one the younger guys went to when they had troubles, right? We need you here to help manage the vets who are coming to us for help. We need your people skills when we go to fund-raisers. Jake can't do it. I've got my hands full with dogs. Come back, man. Help us out."

Marcus tried not to let Adam's words spark desire in his heart, he really did.

"That's really nice to hear, Adam," he said.

"It's not nice, it's true. Will you at least think about it?"

Marcus sighed. "I can't—"

"Wait. What about this. There's a convention in Chicago between Christmas and the new year. Like that one you went to in Houston. Really weird time of year, but it's got some sort of New Year, New Start theme. Anyway, you're not too far away. It's a bit too far for any of us to drive, but if you could—that would be great."

He was tempted to say yes. It was on the tip of his tongue. He so badly wanted to do something to help his friends. But he couldn't. "I'm having surgery tomorrow."

"Whoa. That…that thing the doc recommended?"

"Yeah. Even if it works, I'll be laid up for a pretty long time afterward. I don't think I'll be moving by then." That wasn't strictly true. The doctors told him if he had the surgery a few days after Thanksgiving, he'd be up and around by Christmas. But he wasn't sure he'd be running any marathons, or even walking with less pain.

"Oh hell. Well…I'm glad I called, then. I… Will you let us know how it goes? Or ask your mom to call me?"

Marcus felt bad for all the times Adam had tried to call him, the times he'd let the call go to voicemail. He missed his friends with a fierce pain and regretted shutting them out. "Yeah, you know what? I'll make sure to call you myself as soon as I'm allowed to have my phone. You can give me all the Big Chance news, aight?"

Adam seemed to understand what Marcus was saying, because he said, "Good. That's great." Then he went on, "Listen, I promised myself I'd stay out of it, but I have to tell you. Emma—" He broke off, and Marcus could have sworn he was getting choked up.

Shit. Marcus dropped his head into his palm. Please

don't say she's holed up alone with fifteen cats. Or worse, dating some loser who's not good enough for her.

"She's doing great."

Double shit. His head came up. "That's…good to hear."

"Yeah. I think hanging out with you did her some good. At first, I thought she was bummed out about you leaving, like maybe she had a broken heart or some crazy shit, but then all of a sudden she was working her ass off, fixing up the Feed and Seed. The Sterns gave it to her, and she's running public dog-training classes there. She's even starting to make videos. Tanner's out there right now helping her."

"That's…great," Marcus repeated.

After a few more assurances that he'd call as soon as he could after his operation, he rang off and sat, staring through the kitchen window, for a long time.

And he tried not to think about going back to Big Chance. He really did.

When his phone rang again, he didn't even look before picking up. "Hello."

"Marcus, it's Maya. Have I got news for you."

Chapter 34

"WHO THE HELL NAMES A DOG 'BUTTONS'?" GRANDDAD asked. "That's the kind a name you give a cat or a psycho clown or something."

"Cut," sighed Tanner, turning off the recording with a scowl.

"Granddad, why don't you come outside with me and tell me if you think I need new tires on the truck."

"I know what you're tryin' to do," Granddad grumbled, "but I'm not going to buy you new tires for that heap of tin. You've got a job. You can pay for them yourself."

"Well, then you can tell me how much you think I should spend." Adam helped Granddad up and ushered him out, shooting Emma a *You owe me* grin.

Yeah, it had been her idea to invite Granddad for a day out to see what they'd done with the Feed and Seed, thinking a little outside stimulation might be nice, and besides, she missed her former partner in crime. Thirty minutes into the visit, it was clearer than ever that she had to find a way to help keep his rent paid at Golden Gardens.

"You ready to go again?" Tanner asked. He was turning out to be really great with electronic media. The four short dog-training videos they'd put up had gotten nice reviews—for both Emma's delivery and Tanner's videography and editing.

"Okay, let's do it."

"Take Four," Tanner said, starting to record again.

"Hi, everyone. I'm Emma Stern, and these are my dogs Patton and Garth."

At the mention of his name, Garth stood up, seeming to grin at the camera. Patton ignored it, intent on licking his butt. "This week's 'Patton's Pen Pals' question is from Sarah G., in Middlesex, Wyoming. She wants to know why her dog Buttons won't stop barking at the mailman."

Emma looked down. "What do you think, Patton? How do you feel about the mailman? With Christmas right around the corner, we're all going to have lots of chances to practice new behaviors."

On cue, the bell rang as Jake, dressed in a mail carrier's uniform, pushed open the front door of the Feed and Seed.

Patton was interested now and leapt to his feet, barking furiously at the uniform while Emma held on to his leash for dear life. Jake turned and left, and Emma went on to explain about the various reasons dogs bark, and how to desensitize an animal that was reacting to a specific stimulus, like a mailman.

"Patton likes everyone," Emma said. "Except the mail carrier. We found him tied to the mailbox at the Big Chance Rescue Ranch, so maybe he associates that uniform with his abuse, or maybe he's just hoping to keep the mailman from bringing so many bills."

"Or maybe he wants the summbich to bring his master back." Granddad was back.

"Cut," Tanner called.

"That dog's depressed," Granddad announced. "He misses that fella you was carryin' on with. You just aren't cutting it for him."

Emma wanted to argue, to say that even if she might not

have enough on the ball to keep a guy safe and happy, she certainly could manage a dog, but the truth was… "You're right. He misses Marcus."

"You miss him, too," Granddad said. "I think you oughta go get him back here."

She smiled, though her heart felt like it was breaking all over again. "He doesn't want to be here, or I would."

"Well, that's just—"

"Sorry," Adam interrupted, lugging a big cardboard box through the door, followed by Jake with another. "But the actual mailman brought something."

Tanner crossed the room with something akin to anticipation, and Emma wondered if he knew what was in the boxes. Adam sat his on a chair and tore off the tape. He peered in and pulled out an envelope.

"What's it say?" Jake asked, leaning in while Adam opened and scanned the letter.

"I'll be damned."

"What?" Emma was interested now, too, and tried to see over the men's shoulders.

"'Dear Big Chance Ranch, I wanted to personally thank you for allowing me to shoot my portfolio images at the ranch. My project was originally intended to be an abstract study of light and shape using the human body, but while I was shooting Marcus in your horse shed, I took quite a few photos of him with Patton.'"

"Huh?" Adam looked up at the rest of the crew. "What did I miss?"

Emma sighed. "That day Thornhill was at the ranch, Marcus's sister's friend Maya was there. She's a photographer, and he was modeling for her."

Adam's mouth quirked up. "How did I not have a chance to give him shit about this?" He looked at Jake. "Williams, did you know about this?"

Jake shook his head and held his hands palms up, all innocence. "I forget a lot."

"So anyway…" Emma prompted, and Adam went back to reading.

"'I showed the photos to my mentor, who felt that my images brought life to the concept of the bond between veteran and support dog and suggested I expand on the theme, which I'm thrilled to announce has been contracted to become a real, actual book by a real, actual publisher.'"

"Holy shit," Jake said.

"'I've spent the past several weeks shooting veterans with their service dogs all over the country, and while it's going to take months to finish the text that goes with the images, we've produced a calendar to generate buzz until the book's done. Sales have been brisk around college campuses in the Midwest, and as Marcus requested, I'm enclosing the profits in a check made out to the Big Chance Ranch Dog Rescue.'"

Adam fumbled with the envelope and pulled out a check. He blinked and handed it to Emma.

"How many zeroes is that?" Jake asked, squinting at it.

"Enough to keep us in business for a few more months, that's for sure," Adam said. "I'll be damned."

Granddad had pulled one of the calendars from the box and flipped it open. "What the hell does anyone want to look at this for?" he asked.

The August photo was of Marcus, naked from the waist up, Patton on his hind legs, front paws in Marcus's hands, and they appeared to be waltzing. And laughing like that moment was the best time in the universe, ever, and nothing bad could ever intrude.

"And lookit here."

There were two more interesting months. September was a portrait of Tanner, burned face in vivid relief and squinched up with laughter as D-Day licked him from chin to forehead. And October was Jake, apparently sleeping on the front porch with two of Loretta's pups sprawled across him.

"Forget a lot, huh?" Adam asked Jake.

"Well…"

"She came back out a few weeks ago," Tanner explained, "and talked us into doing this. Thought it would be a great surprise for you."

"It's a big surprise, all right," Adam agreed.

"What else does she say?" someone asked.

Adam scanned the letter, then said, "A bunch of stuff about cutting us in on royalties from the book, stuff like that. Pretty cool."

"How is that Black fella anyway?" Granddad asked. Even on days when his mind was in the present, his filter was not.

"Marcus, Granddad," Emma snapped. "He's not that 'Black fella.'"

"Well, he ain't Mexican."

"Granddad, it's getting late," Adam said. "Why don't I run you home."

"Fine. But Little Miss Broken Heart there might want to get off her high horse and go find that…*fella* before it's too late."

"I think it already is," she muttered, walking to the other side of the room, where Tanner's camera sat, red light still recording everything she'd said. "Damn it, Tanner," she cursed. "You better delete everything on there except the important bits."

"Don't worry," Tanner assured her. "I will."

Why didn't that make her feel better?

"I think that went very well, don't you?" Mom asked as she slid into the back seat of the family's "Sunday" car, a perfectly maintained 1988 Buick Electra woody station wagon. She reached over the seat and squeezed Dad's shoulder. "Beautiful sermon, honey."

"I can't wait for dinner," Grandma said. "Demarcus Talbott, you better not tell me you're not eating your grandmama's dumplin's on this day."

"No, ma'am." He pulled the seat belt over his lap and buckled it, praying harder than he had at any point in the past hour that he wouldn't throw up as the car lurched up and landed hard.

"Damn those parking stops," Dad grumbled, frowning in concentration as he pressed the gas, eliciting a horrific screech of undercarriage dragging across concrete, followed by another painful jolt when the back tires cleared the barrier. "I don't know why we have to have them in my parking lot anyway."

So maybe the car was perfectly maintained everywhere but the undercarriage, which was somehow surviving Dad's failure to yield every weekend.

"Don't take the Lord's name in vain on His day," Mom reminded deaf ears. "And those stops have been in place since 2005. I don't know why you can't remember they're there."

"Or get a Land Rover," Marcus suggested.

"I like that idea," Dad said, nodding.

"Oh no you don't." Grandma snorted. "Hell's gonna freeze clear over before I climb into one of those mud jumpers in my Sunday finest."

"Even more reason to get one," Dad murmured from the side of his mouth.

"I heard that, you ungrateful son of a gun. You're not getting the pick of the dumplings after all, neither one of you."

"I don't need those carbs anyway," Marcus said, putting a hand on his *almost* still-flat stomach. "If I don't get out and get moving, you're gonna have to wire my jaw shut or I'll be buyin' a whole new wardrobe." He was only half-exaggerating. The three weeks since his surgery had been spent moving from bed to couch to physical therapy and back again, Mom and Grandma hovering over him, feeding him the whole time.

"You could start with some new slacks," Grandma pointed out. "Only thing besides shorts you own are those army pants."

Marcus looked down at the dress pants he'd had to borrow from his dad to wear to church. They were about six sizes too big, but Mom had somehow managed to use duct tape and safety pins to form pleats so they didn't balloon into MC Hammer pants when he moved.

"I sold fourteen of your calendars to the ladies in the choir," Grandma announced.

"No kidding?" Marcus was impressed. There were only seven people in the choir.

"I don't kid on Sunday," Grandma said primly.

"No, but she drinks and smokes," Dad muttered.

Marcus suspected Dad would find a way to keep him riding in the front seat for many Sundays to come, if only so he had someone close who appreciated his Grandma snark. Emma would appreciate it, too, though she'd never crack a smile. He imagined she'd be folded right into the middle of the back seat between Mom and Grandma and indoctrinated into the family.

Now why did he have to think of that today? Or ever? Had she seen the calendars? What did she think? If she thought his high school Usher photos were ridiculous, she'd bust a gut over these.

"The guys at the ranch will certainly appreciate your help, Grandma." Marcus made a mental note to shoot Tanner a text to share with Adam and Jake. They'd get a kick out of how enthusiastic Grandma and Mom were about their calendar fund-raising efforts.

"The women's Bible study asked about sponsoring a dog. Do you think they'd be allowed to name it if they came up with enough money to support one's training?"

"Ah…I'm not sure how that works," Marcus hedged. What he wasn't sure about was how excited some veteran would be to get a dog with a name like Azubah or Meshach, because the ladies certainly wouldn't be satisfied with something easy like Zeke.

"Now who do you think that is?" Mom said, leaning up between the seats to peer at the car parked next to the curb in front of their house.

Oh no. Marcus recognized the little blue Mustang seconds before Mom saw Maya leaning against it, golden braids in stylish disarray, smiling as they pulled into the driveway.

"Who do you think paid for that hair?" Grandma asked

while they waited for the garage door to go up. "Because you know *she's* not making that kind of money in art school."

"I doubt it's her mama," Mom said, giving in to the temptation to gossip. "She doesn't have a pot to piss in, now that Reggie's going to that private school in Lexington."

"Well, I hope she knows better than to let some sugar daddy pay for her hair. She's too smart to let some man use her like that. And I don't think that boy needs a fancy private school anyway," Grandma said. "He needs a good whuppin,' you ask me."

"We didn't," Dad said as he finally, mercifully, put the Buick in Park and Marcus was free to escape.

His exodus from the family truckster wasn't fast or painless, but better than even a few days ago. He wasn't positive, but felt like he might be on the mend. As long as he remembered to carry that stupid cane.

He missed Patton. Which made him miss Emma. Again.

"Maya!" Grandma called, as though she hadn't just been shredding the woman's reputation from behind automatic windows. "You better be here for Sunday dinner."

"Oh, gee, Mrs. Jones, I wish I could, but I just dropped by to talk to Marcus for a minute. Thank you for the invitation, though."

"Well, you tell your mama I said 'hello' and 'Merry Christmas,' you hear?"

"Yes, ma'am." Maya walked up the driveway to meet Marcus, pulling her bright-red wool coat tighter around herself and tucking in the coordinating scarf.

How cold was it in Texas right now? Did Emma have a pretty winter coat? It didn't matter. She'd be beautiful in a beat-up Carhartt.

"You want to come in?" Marcus asked.

"No, I just stopped by because I need your help."

"Ahhh… I don't think I'm ready to show off my scars for your camera right now," he said, waving his hands to ward her off.

She laughed. "No, I need you to go to this veterans' services thing with me in Chicago the week after Christmas."

"Oh, I can't do that," he said automatically. "Adam already asked."

"What if they could get one of the dogs up here? That would be great. It would be really nice to have someone who's actually in the calendar show up. I think we'd sell a lot more. We could work together and promote the ranch and my calendar and book at the same time."

"You can call and find out, you know," Marcus told her.

"Yeah, I guess so." Was that the icy wind or a blush making Maya's normally tawny skin so bright? "Well, anyway, I really hope you'll change your mind."

As he said goodbye and wished Maya a happy Christmas, Marcus tried to quiet the little jerk in his head that wanted him to go to the conference and pimp service-dog stuff if only to have a little connection to the life he'd left behind. He could do it, he figured, if he was careful and used his stupid cane.

Still. It was best if he stayed away. He'd only shred his own heart a little more if he got involved again.

"Fifteen minutes 'til dinner," Mom said as Marcus shuffled through the kitchen.

Just enough time to check his email. Usually Tanner sent a newsletter on Sundays.

Opening his email, he saw there was, indeed something

from Tanner. With trepidation, he clicked the link to the video.

He watched it. After it ended, he stared at the blank screen for few very long minutes.

"You comin'?" Dad said.

"Yeah," Marcus answered, but didn't get up.

"What's wrong?"

"Nothing. But…how do you feel about driving me to Chicago the day after Christmas?"

Chapter 35

"Good boy. You've done this before," Emma reminded Patton, clutching his harness for dear life. Patton looked up at her. "Yeah, I know, I'm really talking to myself," she said, searching the tables and booths for her number. "Oh, here we are."

Patton did remarkably well while Emma laid out the flyers from the Big Chance Rescue Ranch and fielded questions from interested exhibitors passing by.

They'd just made the announcement that doors to the public were opening when Patton rose to his feet, ear pricked, sniffing the air, waving his head back and forth.

"That's kettle corn you smell," she told him. "If you're good, maybe we'll get some later."

Patton gave her a dubious look, sniffed again—in a direction away from the kettle corn booth—and lay back down, but didn't rest his head on his paws and go to sleep as he normally did.

The conference was fairly well attended, considering this was the first year for this event and it was scheduled at such a weird time of year, and Emma found herself chatting with a lot of people. Of course, a dog was a conversation starter wherever she went.

She'd been working hard to get Patton back to where he'd been when Marcus had him, but she still didn't entirely trust him, so she kept his hands-free leash draped over her shoulder the whole time she was selling calendars and promoting the ranch.

"There's a guy and some lady over there with calendars, too," a woman told her.

"Really? Well, there are a lot of dog-training groups," Emma said, nodding.

"I think they're from the same one as you."

Really? Emma looked in the general direction the woman was waving, but the crowd had grown and she didn't recognize anyone. Except, wait a minute…who was that big guy talking to the representative from the wheelchair basketball organization? Could it possibly be—

"Hi, can I get a calendar?"

Emma waited on the customer, but when she turned back in the direction the woman had indicated, didn't see anyone and decided she was mistaken. Patton, however, was starting to pace.

"Okay, do you need a break? I'll ask someone to watch our stuff in a minute." If she had a minute. Patton was practically dancing.

———————

"I can't believe we sold out!" Maya squealed and jumped to hug Marcus. He managed to get a hand up, and she stopped herself before she undid all of Doc Watterson's hard work. "Sorry, I keep forgetting."

"That's okay, I don't." They'd finally fallen back into the easy friendship they'd had before their quasi-hookup, and Marcus found he was enjoying himself almost as much as the time he'd gone to Houston with Emma—well, it didn't suck as badly as he'd expected, anyway.

It would be nicer if he knew there was a clean, firm mattress a few floors away where he could land after this long day. Why had he thought it would be a good idea to drive home tonight? Even though he'd been sitting most of the time, he was exhausted—though he'd never admit as much to Maya or his dad.

"Hey, have you seen the reverend lately?" Marcus asked.

Maya shook her head. "Not since he went to get kettle corn."

Huh.

Marcus clutched his cane in his left hand and the edge of the table in the other, pushing himself to a slow stand so he could gaze around the dwindling crowd. Nope. No Dad. He shrugged. "He can't get far. I've got his keys."

"He left you the keys to Woody?" Maya raised her brows, clearly impressed.

"Yeah. I've passed some sort of manhood test, and I am now allowed to hold the keys to the world's longest-lived family truckster." Not that he ever hoped Dad would let him drive it—which was fine, because he never wanted to drive it.

"Do you have any more of those calendars?" a young woman asked Marcus.

"Nope, sorry. We sold out. If you go to this website, though, you can order one," he told her, handing her a flyer for the Big Chance Ranch.

"That's okay. I'll go back and get one from that other lady."

"Okay, thanks for stopping by," Marcus said automatically

before the words processed through. The other lady probably had completely different calendars, but still… "Wait!
What other lady?"

"The one over by the kettle corn. With the big golden
retriever."

The answer was like being punched with a fistful of
sparklers—painful but pretty, and something he wanted
to look at, too. Why hadn't he considered that Adam might
have found someone else to go after he declined? Did he
assume he was their last choice? Or that they should have
told him they were sending someone else?

The realization that his current life was now truly separate from his army life killed those sparklers with a hiss of
steam and smoke. He didn't like this feeling. He felt suddenly, terribly alone.

"Hey, Maya, I'm going to stretch my legs a little and see
if Dad's over there." He waved in the direction the woman
had pointed.

There was no way Emma was here, but he knew if he
didn't confirm that for himself, he'd be awake all night
trying to talk himself out of texting her—even though
he'd become an old pro at avoiding the urge to send
middle-of-the-night (or morning, or afternoon) messages
to Emma.

Reaching the end of a row of booths, he stopped, trying
to decide between left and right. He was about to go left,
toward the food booths, when a familiar voice boomed
across the room and smacked him in the face. He turned
so quickly, he nearly fell, but he still had a little hyper-
alertness in reserve and was able to quickly find the source
of that obnoxious bullshit generator. *Yep.* There he was. The

asshole himself, Dale Thornhill. Looked like he had a new fish on the line, because he was talking a blue streak to a couple who stood in front of a booth displaying home adaptation modifications.

Marcus wouldn't have imagined that sonofabitch could be trying the same con again, to another big-hearted pair of veterans' advocates, but there he was.

"There you are!"

Marcus might have jumped a mile when his dad put a hand on his elbow, but caught his breath and said, "Dad, I need you to call 911, right now."

"Why? Are you okay? There's an aid station right over there—"

"No. Listen. That con artist I told you about. Thornhill."

"Yeah?"

"He's here. I'm going to try to get over there before he sees me, but I need you to call the police and tell them there's a wanted felon here, and you think he might be dangerous."

Dad's eyes widened, and he tried to see where Marcus was looking. "Where?"

"Shh, Dad, just act like you're calling Mom." He started to walk away, because he thought if he could get within touching distance, he could grab Thornhill and hold on to him until security arrived. He wasn't going to be able to pin him to the mat in a choke hold, but he could still hang on pretty damned tight.

As he started in that direction, however, several things happened in a micromoment.

Dad ignored Marcus's instructions and marched past him, intent on taking matters into his own pulpit-soft hands, calling out, "Hey! You! Slime Bucket!"

Thornhill turned his head toward the yelling. He froze for an instant, eyes locked with Marcus's.

And over Thornhill's shoulder, a few dozen yards away, was a woman with a dog. A short White woman with tattoos and piercings, the leash of a golden retriever in one hand and the lobe of her ear between her other thumb and forefinger.

And then all hell broke loose.

Thornhill immediately began to walk casually in the other direction, toward Emma. Patton, who must have recognized Marcus's scent through the crowd, gave a joyful bark and leapt forward, nearly toppling Emma in the process.

"Patton, no!" Emma cried.

"Thornhill! Stop!" Marcus hollered and pointed. "Stop, thief! Stop that man!"

Dad was almost to Thornhill when a burly kid in with a bright-orange jar-head haircut and a USMC sweatshirt grabbed Dad, who swung around to grab at the marine. Emma started to run after Patton, but then recognized Thornhill and stopped just in time for Thornhill to mow her down. Fortunately, that also caused him to trip and land almost upside down, his face and one shoulder pressed into the ground and most of his immense torso crushing Emma.

Patton, who'd been so focused on Marcus a moment ago, must have heard Emma cry out, because he turned, leapt onto Thornhill, and started trying to pull him off his human, immense jaws around the jerk's shoulder, causing him to cry out in pain.

It was all over as quickly as it started. By the time Marcus made his way to them, Thornhill had rolled off Emma. She was sitting in the middle of his back, holding on to Patton's collar while Thornhill cursed and spat.

The marine must have realized his mistake—could it have been the clerical collar that clued him in? Divine intervention? At any rate, the kid reached to help Emma stand. He then yanked Thornhill to his feet and turned him over to a pair of police officers.

Marcus stood there like a useless lump of clay. Hell, even his dad moved faster than he had.

Before he had a chance to even say hello to Emma, he was being interviewed by a detective, and by the time he finished explaining the situation, she'd disappeared and he could barely stand to look for her.

Before he could go home, he wanted—needed—to speak to Emma. He looked around, but she and Patton were both missing. Maya had left an hour ago—because she needed to catch a plane and hadn't seen anything anyway—so he couldn't ask her where Emma had gone. *Damn.*

He felt the bottom drop out of an already empty well.

"Come on, son, we've got to get you into bed." Dad took Marcus's arm and tried to help him walk toward the lobby of the convention center. "I got us a room for the night so we don't have to drive home."

That was a good thing. No way could he have managed five hundred miles in Woody—ten hours, in Dad drive time—the way he felt now. On the other hand, the distance to the hotel lobby looked to be almost as far and was probably going to take him almost as long to travel.

"All right, Dad, let's do this." Leaning heavily on his dad and his cane, he began the slow, arduous journey.

He hadn't gone ten yards, however when he heard a woman's voice. *The* woman's voice.

"For crying out loud. What are you doing, staggering

along like Granddad when you've got a perfectly good service animal more than willing to take you wherever you want to go?"

Marcus grinned, his well suddenly less empty.

Chapter 36

In spite of Marcus's broad smile, Emma was nervous. They hadn't spoken in weeks, and their last interaction had been—ugly.

She yanked her tote bag up to secure it on her shoulder while he greeted Patton and took over the harness.

"Hey," he finally said in that velvety chocolate voice she so desperately wanted to roll around in.

"Hey," she said back.

"Leave your ear alone."

She jerked her hand down, shoving it in her pocket, then pulling it back out and finally putting it, awkwardly, on her hip, which made his smile grow.

They must have been standing there staring at each other like a couple of sick cows, because the man with Marcus cleared his throat pointedly.

"Oh. Yeah. So, Emma, this is my father, Reverend Talbott. Dad, this is Emma."

"Nice to finally meet you, Emma," Reverend Talbott said, taking her hand in a nice, firm grip. "I've heard a lot about you. You're even more beautiful in person."

As Emma all but swooned, Marcus practically whined, "Da-a-ad, really?"

Reverend Talbott laughed, and Emma saw exactly where Marcus had gotten it. She bet the ladies at his father's church didn't miss many services. "I'm going to go on over to the hotel and have myself a cocktail," he said. "You all have a nice talk."

The convention staff was busily tearing down booths and tables, and Emma didn't know what to say anyway, so she and Marcus were both quiet until they got to the lobby.

"Do you want to go sit—" she started, as he said, "Do you mind if we sit—"

So they sat. Cue more awkwardness.

"It's really good to see you," he said.

"You too. You look…you look like you're doing great?" She tried not to phrase it as a question, but that's how it came out anyway. "I mean…how are you?"

He shrugged. "I'm a mess. They think the surgery was a success, but it can take months for the bones to completely heal. So far I'm…a little better than I was before, but I'll know more once I'm allowed to work out with weights."

"That's good, then," she decided. "But how…are you? The last time I saw you, you were—"

"I'm sober," he said, holding up his hands. "Nothing but Tylenol since the fifth day."

She smiled at his quick self-defense, then admitted, "I wasn't even asking about that. You had a definite 'abandon all hope' vibe the last time I saw you."

He sighed, burying his hands in Patton's fur. Patton also sighed, completely blissed out to be back in Marcus's arms. Emma could relate. Not that she was back anywhere, except in his presence—but that was some pretty powerful stuff, she realized.

"I don't really know what to do with myself," he admitted. "I've got the attention span of a gnat. It's even worse than when I was a little kid, I think. I'm taking some classes online to try to figure it out, but…" He shook his head.

Emma took a deep breath. She had to ask. She might get shot down, but she'd kick herself for the rest of her life if she didn't ask. In one big breath, she said, "Why don't you come home to Big Chance?"

He looked at her, long and searching, his eyes running over her face, practically stroking her with his gaze. "Home? To Big Chance?"

"Yeah. To, you know, us. We need you. The ranch needs you." She squirmed uncomfortably, because that wasn't exactly what she'd meant to say. In a rush, she threw it all out there. "I want you to come back with me, for me. I want you there. You're not the only person who fell in love back there, you know. But even if that's not in the cards—even if you don't want to find out where this thing between us—if it's still between us—can go, you've got a place at the ranch. You can deal with people in a way Adam never could, and Jake never will. And Tanner won't. Or me. Not people. I don't people well."

He laughed at that. "You do okay," he assured her.

"Anyway. Adam needs you, and even if you don't want to be with me, I won't be weird. I mean, I'm weird. I'll always be like, you know, me. But I won't take it out on you."

"Hold on," Marcus said, pulling her earring hand into his palm, holding it snugly, interlacing his fingers with hers. "You may be right about not being able to people well. You're telling me how it won't be weird if we're not together, but you're not really selling me here. Tell me how amazing it will be when we are together."

"Oh." That stopped her. She was so busy building a

defense to keep herself from falling apart that she hadn't dared imagine what would happen if he said he wanted to come back with her. *With her*. "I, um… I think we could be pretty amazing together. We are pretty amazing together, aren't we? We captured a wanted criminal this afternoon, and you already know the sex is good…"

"I never thought I'd get an invitation that included good sex and wanted criminals in the same sentence," Marcus told her.

"I'm sorry… I told you the weirdness is probably permanent."

"I like weird, but I prefer quirky and independent and able to take down wanted criminals in a single fall."

"That was pretty amazing, wasn't it?" she asked, finally letting herself relax enough to smile and to feel hope. It filled her heart, then the space around it, then her entire body, until suddenly the whole enormous room was full of it, and she wanted to run up and down the street like George Bailey from *It's a Wonderful Life*, proclaiming how great the world was.

"I'm scared," Marcus said then, bringing her back down to earth. "I'm afraid my recovery will take a bad turn or stall out. That I'll never find a spot where I fit. I thought I'd stay in the army until I couldn't pass the physical, at which point I'd fade away into the night or something. Sit on the porch in a rocking chair making up stories for the grandkids. That didn't work out, and now I feel like if I'm not pulling my weight, I don't have a place."

"You do your share," Emma said. "Just being who you are is something. You're the cool head when everyone else is freaking out. You're the take-charge and adopt-a-stray guy. You made me believe in me again."

"Wait," he said, holding up a hand. "Can you say, 'You complete me'?"

"Show me the money," she countered.

"Okay, I'm in," he said, nodding. "If you promise we can watch *Jerry McGuire* every year on Valentine's Day."

"Whatever you need," she said, and meant it.

He leaned in then, put their joined hands on Patton's head, his other arm around her shoulders, and pulled her in for a kiss that lasted a long, long time.

Chapter 37

"WHAT ARE YOU DOING IN HERE?" EMMA, ARMS OVER-flowing with Big Chance Ranch welcome bags, paused on her way to the front porch. Garth, who trotted next to her, halted, and she gave him a quick "Good boy."

Marcus was sitting in the computer room, intently one-finger typing instead of greeting the new recruits. "I thought you were already outside," she said.

"Yeah, I know. I'm on my way. I want to fix something first."

"What could you possibly need to fix?" As she entered the room, he hit a button and the word-processing screen was replaced by a screen saver image of Loretta and her puppies. "What are you hiding?" she asked, more surprised than offended.

"Nothing," he said, then sighed, enlarged the Word document again, and leaned back in the chair so she could look.

She put down her bags and rested her hands on Marcus's shoulders while she read what he was doing.

Welcome to the first boot-camp platoon at Big Chance Rescue Ranch.

We look forward to getting to know you over the next few weeks as you get to know our dogs…

"You're writing your speech?"

"No. More like…getting my thoughts together."

"Don't tell me you're *nervous*?" She started to laugh until she realized that he *was*. Nudging Patton out of the way, she pushed the desk chair around so she could see him as she knelt in front of him. Garth happily flopped down next to the older dog, taking one big ear between his teeth and tugging. Patton whapped the puppy with a giant paw, then glanced up to make sure he wasn't in trouble.

"Garth, leave it. Get in your spot," Emma commanded, pointing to the floor, a few feet from Patton. Garth pouted, but slid away and lay down, head on paws.

She turned back to Marcus. Putting a hand on each of his knees, she looked into his brown eyes until she was sure she had his full attention. "You got this."

He nodded, but a quick sideways glance betrayed his confident smile. "I know." Then he shook his head. "I don't know, babe. You read the files on these people, right?"

Yes, she had. When a veteran applied for a service dog and a stay at the Big Chance Ranch, they had to fill out an extensive application, which included details of why they needed a dog. Every board member read everything before they decided who would get an invitation.

Their first four recruits included two women and two men. Both women had experienced sexual assault—one at the hands of the enemy, the other raped by one of her fellow marines. One of the men was a double amputee—one leg and one arm—who'd been blown up by an IED. The other had been a medic who'd seen God only knew what. All four suffered PTSD.

"I don't know how to talk to these people," Marcus admitted now. "I'm not a shrink. I can't take care of them."

Emma blinked. She knew Marcus wasn't as carefree and confident as he wanted the world to believe, but she'd never seen him this uncertain. Even when he'd thought his own world was crumbling a few months ago, he'd gone into the situation with guns blazing.

She thought about her own life and her own experience with veterans—Todd, Adam, and now Marcus, and thought she knew what to say. "You don't have any trouble talking to Adam, Jake, or Tanner," she said.

"Yeah, but those guys… I mean, I served with Adam and Jake. Tanner…he just kind of slid in there. Those guys—" He waved toward the front of the house, where four families waited to have their veteran welcomed into the Big Chance family.

"Those guys are soldiers, too. Er…soldiers, a marine, and a sailor. Just don't get *that* part wrong."

The side of his mouth quirked up.

"Seriously. I think…everyone comes here wanting to feel human again. That was a common theme in almost every interview we did. So maybe the key is integrating where they came from with where they're going. Remind them they know how to be soldiers. I mean…you probably don't want to play drill sergeant, but the routine, that stuff will help…and the rest will work its way in. It's not your job to fix anyone." At that last part, she raised her eyebrows.

Marcus laughed softly, getting her point. "Come here and kiss me," he said, crooking a finger at her.

She stretched forward, sliding her arms around his neck as he encircled her waist. His back was still pretty stiff, and he couldn't quite bend toward her enough for a kiss. He huffed out a breath with frustration, and she rose, sliding onto his lap until she was looking down at him. Then she pressed her lips to his, sighing with pleasure when his tongue barely touched her bottom lip before retreating. "Better?"

"Much better," he said, running a big hand over her backside. "Have I told you lately that I love you?" he asked.

"Not in the last hour or so."

He grinned. "I can show you how much, in case you forgot."

"Ahem." Tanner's faux voice-clearing was followed by "Excuse me."

"What do you want?" Marcus didn't look away from Emma.

"There's a whole bunch of people out there waiting for you to tell them what to do. You think you want to take care of that?"

"I don't know," Marcus said, but his smile told Emma that he did know, and that he was ready. Emma slid off his lap and rose, signaling Patton to get ready to do his job.

"Okay. I'll send them away. Tell Adam to take those dogs back to the pound. Call Jake's parents and tell 'em to come get him."

"Send you home to your mama?" Marcus asked.

"Oh hell no," Tanner said. "Not that."

"I guess I'll have to show up for work, then." Marcus took Patton's harness handle. When he saw the dog brace himself, he got to his feet, and as a well-rehearsed unit, they began to walk to the door.

Tanner helped Emma gather the goody bags. "These things are heavy. What else did you buy?" Tanner asked her, opening one to look inside.

"Nothing that wasn't on the 'requisition,'" she told him,

rolling her eyes. Tanner took his job as financial gatekeeper very seriously. "Two T-shirts each, a water bottle, and the official first draft of *Big Chance Ranch Guide to Guide Dogs*."

"Still too much, I say," Tanner grumbled.

"Listen, sport," Emma said, "We got half of our money back from Thornhill right before he was indicted, and the FBI guy thinks we can get some more. We're not in terrible shape. We can afford this."

"For now," Tanner said.

"Do I have to put you two in time-out?" Marcus asked.

"Are you looking for an excuse to procrastinate?" Emma asked, taking Marcus's free arm and snuggling into him— right where she belonged. He gave her a quick kiss that almost turned into a long kiss, then looked deep into her eyes and said, "I think I'm ready for whatever comes next."

Together, they went outside, where the first guests stood waiting. Marcus took a deep breath, and said, "Welcome to the Big Chance Rescue Ranch."

Acknowledgments

Now for the tricky part…trying to thank everyone who helped me get Marcus, Emma, Patton, and Garth's story onto the page.

As always, Tom has been my rock—steady and strong while I flap around trying to write, holding the fort while I disappear into my own head for long stretches of time. I love you to the moon and back times eleventeen. Karen, Sam, and Dan have been great listeners, whether I'm griping or brainstorming. I'm so proud of all of you as you do this adulting thing. Thanks, Mom, for reading early versions of my work and making sure I get out for a non-home-cooked meal to vent over once a week or so.

Everyone at Sourcebooks—you guys are amazing. Cat, Rachel, Sarah, Diane…everyone else who had a hand in turning a pile of random thoughts into a halfway decent story deserve way more credit than they're getting. From the amazing covers to the publicity support and all the behind-the-scenes stuff I know nothing about, y'all are starting to make me believe I can actually pull this off. My Sourcebooks author sibs have been an incredible source of support, and I thank you for your friendship.

To Harper Miller, whose thoughtful comments helped this clumsy author navigate some of the intricacies of writing Black characters. I have a long way to go, but I hope if we all keep trying, we'll get there.

Nicole Resciniti, you are the best agent in the world. You nurtured this project from the very beginning and have been there for our many ups and downs, all while giving birth a couple of times and herding the cats that make up the Seymour Agency with style and grace. I have this vision of you with a baby on each hip, a laptop balanced on your knee, and a phone tucked in there somewhere, directing traffic like the lady boss you are. To my Seymour Agency Sibs, you're the best.

I want to mention Tracey Kinney—dog rescuer extraordinaire. Thanks for letting me invade your home for an afternoon and giving me a glimpse into your life. I'm so impressed with your pack (and your Christmas photo). Keep up the good work!

To Sarah and Xiaoxian at UC—you've cheered me on and helped me more than you can ever know. To the Malik lab at Cincinnati Children's: Devin, Archie, Dylan, Sarah, Katye, Scarlett, and Sydney—thanks for welcoming me with such open arms and giving my brain a reason to come back out of the clouds on a daily basis.

And to you, my readers! I can't believe I get to make stuff up and that there are people who want to read it. People who aren't related to me, even! Thank you, thank you, thank you. Keep comin' back, ya hear?

About the Author

When Teri Anne Stanley isn't working as a professional science geek, she's usually writing, though sometimes you'll find her trying to convince her rescue dogs that "sit" doesn't mean on the couch. She's definitely *not* cooking or cleaning.

In her endless spare time, she's the human half of a therapy dog team, an amateur genealogist, and a compulsive crafter. Along with a variety of offspring and dogs, she and Mr. Stanley enjoy boating and relaxing at their estate, located between Sugartit and Rabbit Hash, Kentucky.

Visit her at teriannestanley.com.

Read on for a glimpse at where
Big Chance Dog Rescue all began in
Big Chance Cowboy

Prologue

Afghanistan, nine months ago

"Hey, Collins, are we clear?"

Marcus Talbott's voice crackled into Adam's earpiece, barely suppressed tension thickening the soldier's Kentucky drawl.

Tank snuffled next to Adam, tugging at his lead. "Hold back," Adam murmured into his mic. The dog hadn't alerted to explosives but continued to weave his head back and forth, every now and then pausing when he caught a hint of something that troubled his world-class nose. He didn't stop for long in any one spot however.

Adam forced himself to breathe in and out for a count of five and tried to let Tank take his time. Adrenaline and exhaustion fought for dominance in his blood, and it was only long hours of training and experience that kept Adam from urging Tank to give the all clear so the team they were assigned to could do their thing. Everyone was tired and ready to end this. Four other highly trained soldiers crouched close by, weapons ready to blast their target the moment Yasim Mansour showed his evil, drug-dealing, bomb-building self.

It would have been safer to make sure the run-down shack was clear of innocents, then blow the bastard up from a distance, but that wasn't an option. Mansour had important information about the next link in the chain of terror.

"If he's in there, he'll be in the back bedroom," First Lieutenant Jake Williams whispered through the airwaves. The kid was still wet behind his West Pointy ears but smart as hell. He knew everything there was to know about their insurgent of the moment, so Mansour would be exactly where Jake said he'd be.

It was up to Adam and Tank to make sure the path to the bad guy wasn't booby-trapped. And Tank, the chillest IED-detecting dog Adam had worked with, wasn't ready to stop searching. Tank raised his head, ears pricked, then sniffed at a shadow. He looked back at Adam as if to ask if he should keep going. Adam nodded, mentally promising Tank half of his own dinner tonight for working overtime on this mission.

"Come on, Sar'nt," Talbott urged.

Adam held up a hand that he hoped the team could see through the dim, dusty twilight, asking for patience. He and Tank had been assigned to this unit for a couple of months now, and the team knew how he worked with his dog, had accepted the pair as one of their own. Some of the younger guys treated Adam like a respected elder, but others, especially Talbott, added Adam to their own special brotherhood, which was probably why the lunkhead was screwing with him now.

"I've got a date with some pictures of your sister," Talbott continued. "So, you know…"

Adam sent another hand signal, one used for offering opinions to bad drivers and other assholes around the world. Tank was tired, damn it. So was he, and in no mood for Talbott's normally tension-defusing banter. Talbott chuckled in Adam's earpiece, about to continue, but then Jake spoke. "There's a light on in the back bedroom now. I can see two people. We need to get moving before they vaporize through a vent." These guys had more escape routes than a meerkat colony. "Can you give us an all clear?"

Adam considered the dog. Tank stared back at him, patient and trusting. He'd done his job, and it was time for Adam to do his part and make the final call.

Once again, Adam raised his hand, this time with the go signal. He clicked his mic and murmured, "Stay on the right." He summoned Tank to his side and waited for the team to silently enter the house and gather behind him. Adam and Tank would take point until they reached the end of the hallway, then Talbott would sweep around and kick in the door.

The door.

Why was there a door? Most of the rooms in these houses had curtains, if anything. It niggled at Adam, but everything made his hair stand on end these days, even someone knocking on the side of the damned latrine. There was a door because the bedroom wasn't really a bedroom. It was a command center for one of the biggest scumbags in the Middle East.

Talbott, no longer joking, jaw set, moved silently toward Adam and Tank. He was followed by Emilio Garcia, Max Zimmerman, and finally Jake, the young lieutenant.

The operation began like clockwork. The soldiers moved past each other in near-perfect silence, the only noise the sound of their own adrenaline-amplified heartbeats.

And then it all went to hell.

———————————————

Later—days later—when the brass debriefed him, Adam said Tank suddenly started to freak out, barking and fighting the leash, and tried to run to the front of the line of soldiers. The dog knocked Talbott against a shelf on the wall. If that was what triggered the bomb or if it was the men in the room beyond, no one would ever know. The ensuing explosion blew every damned one of them into the street, and not a single man could remember exactly what happened.

Not Adam or Max Zimmerman, who each had a mild concussion and a few bumps and bruises. Not Marcus Talbott, with a cracked pelvis, knee, vertebra—if it was bone, Talbott's was broken. Not Jake Williams, who was in an induced coma following surgery to relieve pressure in his brain. And not Emilio Garcia, because he was on life support in Germany.

Why hadn't the dog alerted to the danger? Tank wasn't talking. He was lying under four feet of desert sand, his collar hanging from a post.

Chapter 1

Present day, just past the middle of nowhere, Texas

HOUSTON WAS THREE HOURS AND A COUPLE OF BROKEN dreams behind her when Lizzie Vanhook crossed the Chance County line, right about the same time the Check Tire Pressure light in her dashboard blinked on.

Crap. She'd been in the homestretch. There was something symbolic about an uninterrupted beeline home, to the place she planned to find her center of gravity. Maybe start doing yoga. Eat all organic. Drink herbal tea and learn to play the pan flute.

"Get over yourself," she said to the boxes and suitcases in the back end of the SUV. She'd do that getting over herself thing just as soon as she checked this tire at the truck stop.

Flipping the turn signal, she pulled into Big America Fuel and stopped near the sign for *Free Air*. She stepped out onto the cracked gray asphalt and bent to search for the pressure gauge her dad always insisted she keep in the pocket of the door but came up empty.

It's here somewhere. Lizzie would admit to giving a major eye roll for each Dad-and-the-art-of-vehicle-maintenance lesson her father had put her through, but she was secretly grateful. She was surprised Dad hadn't sent her text updates about the traffic report in Houston before she left this morning. There wasn't much going on in Big Chance, so he watched Lizzie's news on the internet and always called to warn her of congestion on the way to work. Her throat tightened when she acknowledged the reason he hadn't sent her a text today was because he was at the clinic in Fredericksburg getting his treatment. He and Mom might claim this prostate cancer was "just a little inconvenience," but Lizzie was glad she'd be home to confirm he was as fabulous as he claimed to be.

She abandoned the driver's side and went to the passenger door, hesitating when she noticed the dog leaning against the nearby air pump. The *big* dog. It was missing some significant patches of hair, and the rest was black and matted. Its *big*, shiny teeth were bared in what she hoped was a friendly smile. Its football-player-forearm-sized tail thumped the ground, raising a cloud of sunbaked, Central Texas dust. Lizzie sneezed. The dog stopped wagging and raised an ear in her direction.

"Good boy," she told it, hoping that was the right thing to say. It was one thing to misunderstand the intentions of a tiny fuzzball of a dog and need a few stitches. Ignoring a warning from something this size could be lethal. It had to weigh at least a hundred pounds.

She kept the beast in her peripheral vision while she bent to search for the tire gauge. *Ah ha!*

"Y'all need some help?"

"No!" Lizzie straightened and turned, the pressure gauge clenched in her raised fist.

"Whoa there!" A sun-bronzed elderly man, about half Lizzie's size, held his hands in front of him in a gesture of peace.

"I'm sorry," she said, relaxing slightly. "The dog—" She gestured, but the thing was gone.

"Didn't mean to scare you, darlin'," the old man said, tilting his *Big America* ball cap back. "We're a little slow today, so I thought I'd check on you." He indicated the vacant parking lot.

"It's fine," she said. She should remember she was back on her own turf, where it was way more likely that a stranger at a gas station really *did* want to help you out rather than distract you and rob you blind. "It's been a long drive, and I'm a little overcaffeinated."

"No problem. You local?"

"Yes," Lizzie said. Even though she'd been gone for years, it was about to be true again.

The attendant squinted at the tool she carried. "You got a leaky tire?"

"I don't know." She stooped to unscrew the cap of the first valve. "The little light went on while I was driving." *Nope.* That one wasn't low. She put the cap back on and continued her way around the car while her new friend followed, chatting about Big Chance. He wondered about the likelihood the Chance County High School quarterback would get a scholarship offer. Lizzie had no idea; she hadn't been keeping up. He speculated on the probability that the Feed and Seed might close, now that there was a new Home Depot over in Fredericksburg. She expected she'd hear about it from her mom and dad if the local place was closing and wondered if her friend Emma still worked there.

It had been ages since Lizzie had spoken to Emma, and a wave of guilt washed over her. After swearing to always be BFF's, Lizzie left for Texas A&M and only looked back on

Christmas and Easter. She'd gone to Austin for Emma and Todd's last-minute before-he-deployed wedding but hadn't been able to come home for Todd's funeral.

Finally, the last valve was checked, and she screwed the cap back on. She reached through the open window and dropped the tire gauge on the passenger seat while she said "Everybody's full. Must be a false alarm." She wrinkled her nose as she caught a whiff of the interior of her car. *Sheesh.* The service station probably sold air fresheners; maybe she should invest in one. Compared to the breezy, wide open spaces of home, her car smelled like an inside-out dead deer. She wanted to get home, though, so she decided to deal with it later.

"Well, everything's got enough air," she told the attendant. "I don't know why the light went on."

"Those sensors are a waste of time, if you ask me. You don't have nitrogen in there, like those fancy places put in, do you?" he asked, then launched into a diatribe about modern technology.

One of the things she'd not missed about Chance County was the tendency of the residents to ramble as long as possible when given the opportunity. "Well, thanks again," she told the man. "I've got to run."

It wasn't until she was backing out onto the main road that she realized the awful smell inside her vehicle wasn't just long-drive funk. There was something—something big and black and furry—sitting in the middle of her back seat, panting and grinning in her rearview mirror.

"Ack!" She hit the brakes, then jammed her SUV into forward and pulled into the parking lot again. She opened the door to jump out, barely remembering to put the SUV into park before it dragged her under. She finally whipped open the back door and glared at the scruffy passenger. "Out. You. Out."

She looked around frantically for the old man who'd been chatting her up, but he was nowhere to be seen.

The dog panted and tilted its head at her.

"Out. I mean it."

It wasn't wearing a collar, not that she'd reach in to grab him anyway, in case he mistook her hand for a Milk-Bone.

"Come on, puppy. Seriously. Get out."

The dog sighed and lay down, taking up every inch of her back seat.

She was afraid to leave the thing alone in her car, so she pulled her phone from her pocket and stood next to the back end. She Googled the number for the Big America station and waited for the call to connect.

"Y'ello," said the gravelly voice she'd been chatting with a moment ago.

"Sir, this is Lizzie Vanhook. From the air pump just now."

"Sure, darlin'. What can I do you for?"

"I'm right outside."

"I see ya."

She looked up, and sure enough, he was waving to her through the glass.

"There's a big dog in the back of my car."

"Oh, yeah," the man said. "He showed up here a week or so ago. Kind of invaded, so we've been calling him D-Day. Real sweet little guy."

She eyed the sweet *little* guy. *Uh-huh.* "Could you come help me get him out of my car?"

Laughter. "I don't think you can get that boy to do anything he don't want to do."

"But he's in my car."

A sigh. "Well, I've been threatening to call the animal control officer for a few days now, but I kept hoping his family would come looking for him."

"Don't you think the shelter would be the first place they'd go?"

With a snort, the man said, "There's only room for a coupla dogs over there. Don't even take cats. They'd probably have to fast-track that one to the gas chamber, seein' as how he's so big and would eat a month's worth of food at one meal. Besides, he's ugly as sin, with all them bald spots."

Right on cue, D-Day sat up and stuck his nose through the open window, giving Lizzie's arm a nudge and turning liquid coal eyes up to gaze at her. Reluctantly, she stroked his surprisingly silky head. And then she gave his ears a scratch. *So soft.*

D-Day licked Lizzie's hand. What the heck was she going to do with this guy? Mom and Dad weren't too crazy about dogs. Lizzie loved dogs, but Dean, her loser ex, had been unwilling to get a dog of their own. As a matter of fact, one of their biggest fights was the weekend she'd volunteered to babysit a friend's perfectly mannered labradoodle. Then, when Lizzie called her mom for support, she'd gotten an "I don't blame him. Dogs are a pain in the neck."

"I can't take this dog with me." Lizzie sounded defeated even to her own ears, which contradicted her plans for an optimistic return to Big Chance and a fresh start.

The attendant said, "I'll give the shelter a call. Shame, though. I think he's still a pup."

Those big black eyes stared up at her. D-Day needed a fresh start, too.

Lizzie decided that Mom would tolerate a canine house guest if Lizzie promised he was moving on. "Never mind," she said. "Thanks anyway."

Who did she still know in town who might take a dog? The Collins family came to mind right off the bat. Adam Collins specifically. *Oh no.* She wasn't going to start thinking about him, now that she was moving home. Not. At. All. And really, she wouldn't be running into him. It had been years since he'd joined the army, and his main goal in life, other than becoming a military policeman so he could work with dogs, had been to get—and stay—as far from Big Chance as possible.

She got back in the car, rolled down all the windows, and turned the fan to full blast.

"Listen," she told the dog, who leaned over the seat and licked her ear. "I'll bring you with me. But we're stopping to get you a bath at the car wash on the way through town right before we go to the vet. Then I'll find you a new home as soon as possible."

The dog barked.

"No. No dogs for Lizzie. I mean it."

"Beer, bologna, and white bread. That's all you're gettin'?" The middle-aged grocery clerk—her name tag said *Juanita*—glared at Adam as though he'd personally offended her. "How's a big boy like you gonna survive on that?"

Adam fought the urge to wipe away the cold sweat that

had broken out along his hairline in spite of the frigid air-conditioning inside the Big Chance Shop-n-Save. He'd about reached his out-in-public time limit. *Don't snap her head off. Just smile politely.* She was simply being friendly, in that judge-everything way people had in Big Chance. "Well, ma'am," he found himself explaining, "it's just me, and..."

"Hmmph." She crossed her ample arms instead of scanning his food items.

Come on, he silently begged. *You don't really want to see me go into full frontal meltdown, do you?* He looked around for a self-checkout, but the store apparently hadn't been upgraded since he'd left for the army, and it was old then.

The clerk—Juanita—peered at him now, eyes squinched up to inspect him. "You're that Collins boy, aren't you?"

I used to be. "Yes, ma'am," he said.

"I heard you was back. Holed up out there like some kinda hermit on your granddad's ranch. You know he used to come in here and talk about you like you was the second coming of Patton."

He was momentarily stunned that Granddad had spoken of him at all, much less with pride. For Granddad, the greatest praise he'd ever offered Adam was "Well, you didn't fuck that up too much, I guess." Maybe it was just as well that his grandfather had lost most of his grip on reality these days, because he wouldn't even be able to say that much about him anymore.

Adam told Juanita, "Thank you. That's nice to hear."

She shook her head. "So sorry for how he's gotten to be. He was a good man in his day."

Granddad was something, all right. "Yes, ma'am. Thank you."

"Your sister's doing a good job with him, though."

"Yes, she is." Unfortunately for her. The war Emma had fought at home, while Adam was deployed, was as bad as anything he'd suffered overseas, and she wasn't free yet. If only he'd known how bad things were here, he could have… what? Gotten out sooner? Not reenlisted—twice? He didn't know if he could do things differently, because until that last mission, finding IEDs with his dog had been the one thing he was good at.

Now here he was, sweating through his clothes in the grocery store, wanting nothing more than to get back to hiding out in the place he'd avoided for the last twelve years, at least until he could move on again.

Juanita still hadn't scanned his loaf of bread or his lunch meat. Or—*please, God*—the beer. The country music playing on the intercom seemed to get louder, even through the buzzing noise, which Adam knew didn't exist anywhere but in his head. The sound, always present at a low hum when he was in town, intensified. He inhaled on a count of ten and exhaled.

"Sooo…" He waved at the supplies, hoping to get checked out and into his truck before his vision narrowed any further.

"You still in the army?"

"No, ma'am."

"You were in a long time."

"Yes, ma'am." Hell, he'd planned to stay in the military until they pried his dog's leash from his cold, dead hand, but that wasn't how it had worked out.

She nodded. "You need some meat. Homer!" she barked over her shoulder at the elderly man standing a few feet away.

Adam flinched at the volume. Nothing compared to an IED or gunfire but jarring in its own way.

"Yep?" Homer moved a step closer, tilting his head in Juanita's direction.

"Go get some a' them pork chops, and bring me a couple big Idaho bakers. Oh, and a bag of that salad mix!"

Homer nodded and shuffled off.

"Ma'am, I don't need—"

"Yes, you do. You can't keep that fine body strong on nitrates and Wonder Bread."

Adam snorted. He wasn't having any trouble staying in shape out on the ranch. There was enough work to be done that he could sweat from morning until night for a year and not finish all the hammering and scraping and scrubbing.

"Am I right?" She raised her eyebrows. "You need to keep up your strength."

Homer thunked Juanita's order down on the counter.

She pushed the twelve-pack toward Homer and said, "Take this beer back to the cooler and bring me a gallon of that sweet tea."

"Really, I—" Adam reached for his beer, but the old man was already staggering away under its weight.

Juanita shook her finger at him. "No ifs, ands, or buts. You get some good food in you." She stopped then, her eyes wide and sympathetic. "Unless…you don't have anyone to cook it for you, do you?"

He assumed she meant a woman. But instead of mustering some righteous feminist indignation on behalf of his sister and all the women he'd ever met, he just felt tired. It was good that he lived alone—no one besides himself to make miserable. "I do know how to cook, Miss Juanita. I don't do it much, though."

Juanita snorted. "That's ridiculous. What do you eat for breakfast? You're not buying any oatmeal or even Pop-Tarts." She held up a hand. "Don't tell me you eat at that cesspool diner at the truck stop out on 15."

"No, ma'am." He'd tried it once, in the middle of the night, figuring that would be a safe time, fewer people. Something about the vacant, litter-strewn parking lot reminded him a little too much of his time in the desert, though, so he hadn't been back.

"Well, that's good, anyway," Juanita said. "But you better not be going to that superstore over in Fredericksburg, either. They got radiation in their eggs, you know."

"Really?" Adam didn't mind a little radioactivity. It was a failure to find the right balance of desperation and anti-anxiety meds that had him stuck buying food in Big Chance instead of going farther away, where no one knew his name or cared what he bought to eat.

Juanita smiled and slapped the counter. "You know what? You gotta get offa that property. Bein' alone ain't healthy. You come on to town some Saturday night. There's movies in the high school gym, bingo at the Catholic church, and there's gonna be a big shindig on the Fourth of July in the square. There'll be a band and dancing and food trucks and everything. There's all kinds of unmarried women there, just dying for a big strong man to take care of. Some of them girls are divorced, but don't let that stop you from givin' 'em a chance. They probably know how to cook, too."

"I've got a lot of work to do out there at the ranch. It

keeps me pretty busy." And away from town with its memories. Although, if he did wander through the town square one night, he wouldn't run into anyone he'd thought about over the long nights in the desert. Last he'd heard, *anyone* was seriously dating some land developer mogul-type and living the big life in Houston.

Homer returned with the jug of tea, plunking it on the counter next to the paper-wrapped bundle from the butcher and several plastic containers, one containing something green that he leaned to look at—beans?—and one full of coleslaw.

Juanita nodded. "That's better."

"Can I keep my bologna and bread?" Adam asked. Maybe he could get out of here with his bachelorhood intact if he hurried.

"Fine. But you better not come back in here and buy more of that crap."

The chances he'd be back soon were getting slimmer by the minute, and a grab-and-go convenience store diet was looking better.

He gathered his bags and stepped into the already oppressive early summer afternoon. His white pickup truck sat alone in the parking lot, and only a few cars passed by. Big Chance was still more or less alive—there was someone down near the vet's office—but most people had the sense to stay in their air-conditioning today. A plastic grocery bag blew from between two buildings and did the twenty-first century tumbleweed thing down Main Street toward him. He put out his foot and caught it on the toe of his boot. He bent over and pulled the plastic free, wadding it up and shoving it in his pocket while keeping an eye on the street. A quiet neighborhood wasn't any less likely to wield danger than a busy market place, but it was easier to avoid distractions.

Except for the activity two blocks away, where a woman struggled with what was probably a dog but looked more like an elephant calf. It wasn't stupid, whatever it was, and it barked in protest. *Smelled one veterinarian's office, smelled them all*, it seemed to be saying, and no one ever saw the vet just for the treats and pats on the head. Adam suppressed a pang of longing—dogs had been a big part of his life for as long as he could remember, but the smarter, more experienced part of him was glad he didn't have the responsibility and problems anymore. The woman shook her head at the dog, a move that seemed familiar. He couldn't see her face, but when she tripped over the dog, who had stopped to sit in the middle of the sidewalk, there was something about the way she tossed her hair as she laughed that took him back.

Back to memories of the night before he went to boot camp, when he'd kissed a girl in the dark summer night. Kissed her and touched her and *wanted* her like he'd never known was possible. He'd never had any doubts about joining the military, wasn't afraid of basic training, knew how to handle himself, but that night, holding Lizzie Vanhook in the moonlight, he'd felt a trickle of regret and longing for what he was leaving behind.

A car door slammed nearby, jerking him back to his own space. With a hot prickle of anxiety, Adam shook his head and turned toward his truck. Time to make tracks back to the ranch and get back to work. He'd promised his sister he'd stop and visit Granddad this afternoon, but he'd been in the presence of humanity for long enough.

He glanced back down the street, but the woman with the dog was gone. Just as well. Lizzie would never have settled for the likes of him, and now he was even less respectable than when he'd been the kid with dog crap on his cowboy boots, who thought this little redneck town was the worst place in the world. He'd had no idea how much worse the outside world could get. As of now, Big Chance was just one more reminder that the kid he'd been hadn't turned into the man he'd expected.